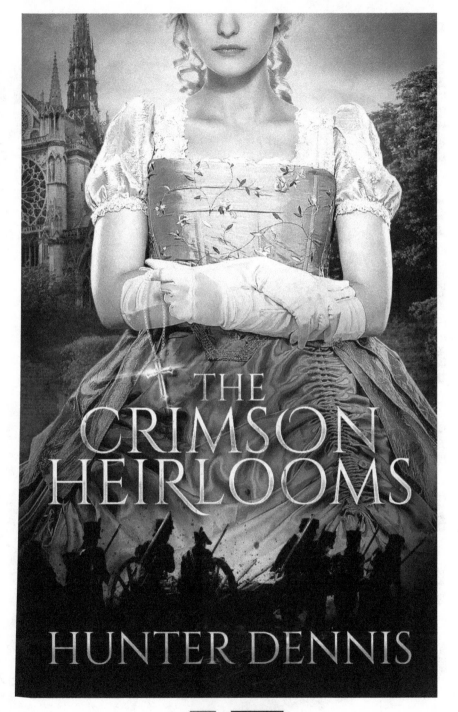

THE CRIMSON HEIRLOOMS

HUNTER DENNIS

A-R-B

BOOKS

thousand oaks, ca

Dedicated to Daniel Rabourdin

"*Le professeur a réussi au moment où son élève devient original.*"

Maps, Illustrations and Photographs

Table of Contents

Please supplement your read with the pronunciation and definition guide located on page 431.

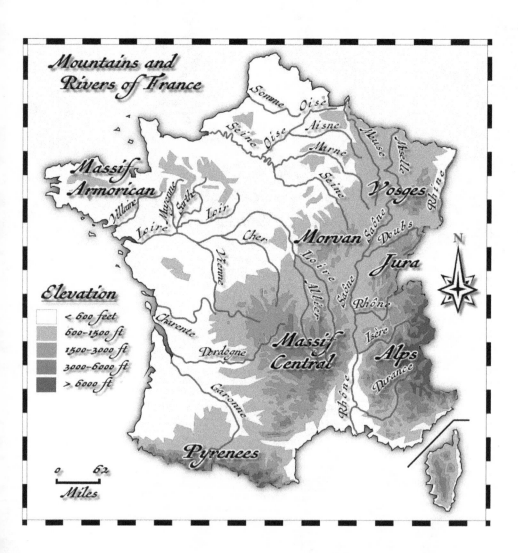

Prologue

Crimson Heirloom was a legal term coined in 1832 by the highest court of France, the *Cour d'Assises Spéciale*.

There were precisely two.

The first was a priceless necklace named the *Cross of Nantes*. It had a storied history closely tied to the fortunes of its creator - the Traversier family of Nantes. It was stolen in 1754, miraculously reappearing twenty years later, then was lost again in 1805 - although *hidden* would be more accurate.

Soon after, a rumor abounded that if the Cross were found, a provision of will entitled the possessor to unconditional ownership of the mighty Traversier Mercantile Trust. When journalists discovered this fantastic tale was actually true, a legend was born. The Cross of Nantes became part of the national folklore of France. It was a mysterious lost treasure, a pendant fit for a king – whose owner would be worthy of it, being christened merchant royalty upon bestowal of the trust.

Those who had actually seen the Cross wrote and spoke of it as if nothing - no story, no price, no fortune - could ever compete with the beauty of the thing itself. It was made of Olmec jadeite, and diamonds of the rarest crimson hue. When light touched the necklace, Antares bowed its head to truer stars of scarlet.

Not a year went by without false headlines proclaiming the rediscovery of the Cross, or a group being formed to search for it based on some new clue or evidence. The mystery proved to be so intriguing that these stories never grew old - a new Cross story always made the front page of the newspapers.

As decades passed, the Cross entered the realm of myth - in spite of its existence, and the promise of the Traversier Trust, being very real.

The second Crimson Heirloom was less tangible, if not utterly mysterious or even the product of madness. It was legally defined –by no less than the highest court of France - as, *"the words of the devil's song, as he danced across the blood-drenched hills of the Vendée Militaire."* This definition was not ironic or metaphorical – it was literal and serious as a sword thrust.

It was the court's ruling that a specific individual, upon pain of death, search for these two Crimson Heirlooms for a period of no less than five years. It seemed absurd that such a thing could be possible in the modern age, but stranger things have certainly happened.

Such facts might be remembered only as trivia to amuse at dinner, except for one thing: The Cross of Nantes, and the words of the devil's song, were both found.

The Time of the Heirlooms

1776

Xavier

Nantes
1776

Saint-
Clément

Faubourg Saint-Clément

E-r-d-r-e

University of
Brittany

Faubourg du Marchys

Nantes
Cathedral

Faubourg de Richebourg

(Cathédrale Saint-
Pierre-et-Saint-Paul)

Centre-Ville

0   1000

feet

Couerfroid
Townhome

Château des
ducs de Bretagne

Manoir de
Jean V

Château
Meilleur

Port au Vin

Isle Feydeau

Prairie de la Madelaine

N

Isle Gloriette

Loire

Chapter One

The night was in early June. But the city of Nantes was veined with rivers and it was a cold Summer, so it was therefore dank, mildewed and chilly. At four hours before midnight, a thick fog rendered it dark when it would have otherwise been light. But the moisture gave added edge to sound and Xavier's large coach, called a *german*, clattered merrily down the cobblestones of Rue Saint-Nicolas as it made its way to the Cœurfroid townhome and the first Summer ball.

The man who stared out the window of the german was slim, his face was long, and his chin squared off from the jaw. His trimmed beard and shoulder-length hair were streaked dark blonde. He was the handsome heir of the Traversier of Nantes - and society judged him far more on the fortunes of his family than his countenance.

Although not customary, Xavier had no choice but to go to the ball alone. He didn't have any friends to speak of, and his mother no longer attended social events. He was snubbed by those in his appropriate social circle - yet here he was. Xavier was in a good mood, even excited. He seldom felt this way. There was usually little to celebrate and, even if there was, he usually kept his emotions under tight rein. But tonight, Xavier had gloriously let his guard down; in his opinion, deservedly so.

The honor of being invited to a dance on a Summer's evening was not normally associated with hard work, planning and perseverance, but for Xavier it had taken all three. He felt as if a turning point had been reached. He was joining society, and all he could think of were the wonders that such a thing entailed. There were smiles and laughter in that embrace, even love and friendship. Conversation, connection, and perhaps a wife and family awaited him. To some, these things came easily. Nothing, however, had come easy for Xavier.

It was an odd fact, considering that Xavier was a Traversier, one of the oldest and most successful families in Nantes. But Traversier was now a ghost of its former self, and only Xavier and Madame - his mother, Philippine - were left to roam the labyrinthine halls of the Château Meilleur. Things did not have to be so difficult, but there was a madness surrounding his house, one that had affected Xavier throughout his life. The root cause was simple: his father had died, though no one knew how, where, or exactly when.

Madame thought – knew - in her bones, that this was not true. She was sure, as if the fact was the rising sun, that Monsieur - his father, Priam Paul - was alive and would return shortly. His mother believed it, so Xavier believed it. When he was eleven, his mother began to wear black - although she admitted nothing. The subject of his father simply became taboo. Two years later, still wearing her mourning, Madame stopped leaving the house. Xavier had come to realize she was broken in some ways. It was strange to think of her in such a way. She appeared to him as nothing but strong; a towering presence, even imperious and cruel.

Their relationship assumed its tone at Xavier's birth. A woman of means never cared for her own infants. The elite were above the act of breastfeeding, changing soiled diapers, or being tormented by screeching in the night – much less being forced to care for a creature with such poor odds of survival. The newborn Xavier was therefore farmed out to the Martins, a middle-class family living in the west of Nantes near the Port au Vin. They did not shower him with love or affection, but he lacked for nothing material and was duly taught what should have been conveyed to him. As was custom, the Martins, to this day, still received favors and presents from the Traversiers, as if they were distant relatives.

At the age of three, Xavier returned home. His father left on his last voyage a short time thereafter, and Xavier had little memory of him.

Xavier's waking life was filled with learning, and an unending parade of tutors. He had little contact with his mother, but when he did she was invariably dismissive. The servants, sensing this, were not particularly kind to him, either.

His worst run in with Madame happened when he was nine. Incautiously, he had run the length of the upstairs hallway and accidentally shouldered a Baroque giltwood console table. An alabaster jardinière had fallen on the rug, thankfully unharmed. Madame appeared and carefully returned the vase to the table. She turned to face him, calmly bent down – and quickly slapped his face. "Simply because you lack any sense of color, art, taste or style does not give you the right to destroy items that you are incapable of assessing. Do you see the painting above you?"

Truth be told, the paintings of the house did not overly interest Xavier. But he dutifully looked up and saw a painting of a man.

"That," she said, "is a Lundberg. A portrait of your father. When he returns from the Americas, you will be a great disappointment." And with that, she turned and gracefully floated from view.

Madame was right. There was something intrinsically wrong with him. He was deeply flawed, and could not fix his inadequacies despite his superior education.

Xavier only looked forward to his tutors in subjects in which he did excel. Occasionally, the teachers relaxed their guards and let loose a smile, compliment or warm thought. There was no one else with whom he had regular contact. Madame had no friends, and they were obligated to spend time around other people less than ten times a year. The Traversiers were not religious, and never had been, and Xavier lacked the comfort of the church and its regular gatherings.

At the age of ten, he was shuffled off again, this time to the University School of Nantes, part of the old medieval *Studium Generale* of the Archduchy of Brittany.

It should have been a hard and difficult time for him. There was a strict hierarchy amongst the boys, based on age and the social standing of their families. Xavier was a Traversier, but Traversier was not currently part of the social circles of Nantes. Worse, they were supposedly princes, at the top of a ladder they no longer deigned to climb. He was, at first, a target for other boys. But Xavier was not easy prey. He perhaps could have been, given his upbringing. But nature was always clay and kiln together, and Xavier's nature saved him. He did not consider himself better or worse than any of the other boys, nor did he seek to become more by making others less. He was respectful, but without being overly friendly or approval-seeking. He did not create confrontation, but did not shy from it either. Xavier was not popular, being neither overly vivacious, kind, humorous or generous, but he was respected. He had to be respected, because disrespect brought confrontation, and confronting Xavier brought no laurels. Xavier fought until he had victory, regardless of cost, in whatever arena he was confronted. He did not relish in the fight, and would easily shake a hand if pardon was truly sought. He made a much better friend than enemy, and it was not hard to be his friend.

As the months and years passed, Xavier's universe expanded with every person he met, every book he read. When he was twelve, one destroyed his universe, and then rebuilt it whole again. The novel was called *Emile, or On Education*, and it was written by Jean-Jacques Rousseau.

> *Hold childhood in reverence, and do not be in any hurry to judge it for good or ill. Leave exceptional cases to show themselves, let their qualities be tested and confirmed, before special methods are adopted. Give nature time to work before you take over her business, lest you interfere with her dealings. You assert that you know the value of time and are afraid to waste it. You fail to perceive that it is a greater waste of time to use it ill than to do nothing, and that a child ill taught is further from virtue than a child who has learnt nothing at all. You are afraid to see him spending his early years doing nothing. What! is it nothing to be happy, nothing to run and jump all day? He will never be so busy again all his life long. Plato, in his Republic, which is considered so stern, teaches the children only through festivals, games, songs, and amusements. It seems as if he had accomplished his purpose when he had taught them to be happy; and Seneca, speaking of the Roman lads in olden days, says, "They were always on their feet, they were never taught anything which kept them sitting." Were they any the worse for it in manhood? Do not be afraid, therefore, of this so-called idleness. What would you think of a man who refused to sleep lest he should waste part of his life? You would say, "He is mad; he is not enjoying his life, he is robbing himself of part of it; to avoid sleep he is hastening his death." Remember that these two cases are alike, and that childhood is the sleep of reason.*

In Xavier's world, no one had ever expressed tenderness for children - except for this man. Rousseau was a cry for kindness, to hold youth in reverence, and not belittle children for being less than adults. It was the first time Xavier realized the nature of his being might have value. He read more Rousseau, he read nearly all of Rousseau.

His words were bold, "Man is born free, and everywhere he is in chains." And Man was good, it was the chains that turned him evil. Rousseau changed Xavier. This new Xavier looked at the world as if it were diabolically imperfect, and he had been infernally mistreated. He himself, however, was good, righteous and above the flaws of his environment. His own poor behaviors became, in his mind, qualities that did not emanate from himself. They were instead imposed upon him by the oppressing world. He glorified his own soul, and the struggle against the troubles besetting it. His new philosophy was a juvenile attempt at strength and independence, but not a true one.

When Xavier was thirteen, Madame brought him home without explanation, and he took the coach to his classes - all the way across the city.

That lasted a year.

Then he was pulled completely out of school forever.

His mother did not discuss it. It was as if school, and its termination, had simply never happened. Xavier did not bring up the issue - he knew better.

Xavier did not remember much from those times. He often daydreamed, except there were no images in his mind during those states - just a vacuity of consciousness.

One incident, however, stood out in his memory, an odd moment that happened the next Fall. He had awoken from one of his dreamless daydreams, and found himself in front of the two-hundred-year-old Venetian mirror in the upstairs hallway. The frame was in the shape of a Greek temple, ornately-sculpted, gilded gesso plaster, complete with cherubs, caryatids and columns. To Xavier, it resembled a crude fireplace, with a mirror in place of flames. Despite the best efforts of its ancient craftsmen, there was not a straight line to be found in the whole affair. The glass of the mirror had flaws, and sometimes the images could be unsettling. When Xavier was fully conscious, and found himself staring at the mirror, his reflection was transparent, and slowly becoming more so as he looked on.

It was plain to see that he was fading away.

The startling, hallucinatory image did not overly surprise him. He felt hollow, empty - nearly gone. Why would he look any different than he felt? His life was dreamlike and hazy, even without the mirror's reminder.

One day, a family of cousins, the Grimpeurs, came to visit. There was Madame; cold, Monsieur; bored, and haughty, young Mademoiselle; Zara, his second cousin, and his own age. After they were ushered into the manor, Philippine was summoned. Xavier crept to the top of the stairs, and peered down at them.

Madame came into the foyer. She was obviously surprised at their visit: her small talk and pleasantries were strained and nervous. Soon the adults disappeared further into the manor and Zara was left alone, standing erect and graceful. Xavier came down the stairs. As he did, she must have sensed his presence, and yet she did not stir or look at him.

"Good morning, Mademoiselle."

Her head came to swivel in his direction, and her eyes met his. She was expressionless.

"What brings you to the Château Meilleur?" he said.

She did not reply, and her expression did not change. Only when he spoke the words *Château Meilleur*, did the corner of her upper lip momentarily twist toward her ear.

Xavier stared at her until she looked away. He continued to stare, until she looked awkward and uncomfortable. He continued even then, until she looked scared and indecisive. Xavier wasn't particularly angry or irritated, just aware that he was somehow being confronted. Now aware of victory, he left and went to his room.

Philippine threw open the door soon after. "You will no longer be marrying Mademoiselle Grimpeur upon your majority."

Xavier said nothing. Madame stood with her hands clasped. After a moment, she gracefully turned, and, with a soft swish of her raven skirts, exited his room without shutting the door.

Xavier had no idea he was to marry Zara. It was uncomfortable knowing there were hidden destinies in his future. He wondered what else was in store for him.

Xavier soon discovered the opiate of his bed during the daylight hours. His heart was numb, but the gears and wheels of his mind still churned, however slowly. One day the machine produced a thought. Xavier had an important choice, his mind had discovered. He could allow himself to fade away and disappear, until the flawed, medieval mirror did not register his appearance at all, or he could attempt to halt the change. It was a simple decision: to move or not to move - to live or to die.

After a quiet debate in his head, a decision was made. Xavier chose the fight. He chose action and movement. He chose the struggle.

It was an adult attempt at strength and independence. But he made his choice in utter darkness, as he stared into the contempt of nothingness. When a choice for life was made under such circumstances, it solidified hard and sharp. It became a living thing - deadly, merciless - an armored bull elephant with claws and fangs, cornered and fighting for survival, forgetting or unknowing that it was more dangerous than any enemy it could possibly face.

The elephant forced Xavier out of bed, and into the family library. It was a strategic retreat to the old sanctuary of books. The Meilleur library was far more impressive than the one at university. It encompassed two huge rooms, each three stories high, forming a *T,* and composing an entire wing of the older house. Xavier, febrile, rifled through the shelves for another Rousseau, another author to inspire him. The hunt took Xavier to the highest levels - the third story, actually the highest shelves of the third story, only accessed by a ladder on a catwalk. It was there he found the curious, uniform, unmarked volumes, all written by hand with quill and ink. He opened a volume to a page somewhere in the middle, and the first words he read destroyed his world, and those thereafter remade it whole again.

> *I asked myself whether I was done, if this was the very*
> *moment when life beat me into submission. I asked myself*
> *the question directly and succinctly - "Priam Paul Traver-*

*sier, are you done with the struggle? Are you done, Mon-
sieur?" When confronted so directly with such a sentiment,
one can only scream* no, *as loud as one can, into the howling
wind of failure.*

This shelf of books had to be his father's memoirs. He had never really known his father and yet here he was, speaking to him from beyond the grave, giving him the very ground upon which his heart could stand. After reading more, and understanding the man better, he knew his father had to be dead. Such a man who could write those words never gave up, never left business unfinished. Priam Paul was in the fight or he was dead, it was that simple.

He devoured the memoirs. They took him all over the world, to Africa, to America, through crushing defeats and mountainous victories. Through it all, Priam Paul exhibited an iron will, a refusal to accept the finality of failure. If Rousseau was a comforting hand on a crying child, Priam Paul was a fist-grab of shirt, jerking the child to his feet and pushing him back into a schoolyard fray. Priam Paul's writings were an utter refutation of the impact of feelings. Emotions were ignored - suppressed, extirpated - in order to secure victory and complete the race. Every decision, at every step, was consciously made to move closer to his goals.

He also discovered that his father was a Freemason. Xavier did not know precisely what that was, but from the writings it appeared to be a secret society. His father sometimes used code when he wrote about the meetings, making his thoughts completely indecipherable. Even when he wasn't writing in code, he always used nicknames for fellow members. All of them soon began to take on personalities. *Jackrabbit, Softrock, Tornsail, Glibtongue, Flaxcloth* and *Gorilla* all became beloved characters, whoever they were in reality. The meetings were always guarded, always secret, and followed a strict protocol. There were notes on the extensive, formal rites and the ponderous language of their ceremony. Their discussion was alive with philosophy, the authors of which Xavier later tracked down in the library and read. He began to understand who the Freemasons were, and why they existed.

Although his father was a member, Xavier couldn't tell if he was a true believer. He probably wasn't. Most likely, Priam Paul simply thought the Freemasons were the future.

Nantes, then and now, had only one god, who was Mammon. Her sacraments were commerce and trade. Her holy hosts were gold, salt and slaves. There was nothing the men of Nantes would not do for money, and everything done for money was excused, or even glorified. But Priam Paul, even being a proper son of Nantes, had looked to the horizon and seen the Freemasons ascendant. It was perhaps a safe bet. The Freemasons were composed of the intellectual cream of Nantes society. They were politicians, nobles, merchants, and clergy – a social circle unto themselves.

Xavier realized that if he became a Freemason, he could enter society another way, one that didn't include Philippine. The Freemasons were the key to his prison, and his father's membership could be his entrée.

The search for the real identities of the men in the memoirs began. Priam Paul was meticulous in his desire to hide their identities, but the writings were substantial - and no one could be perfectly meticulous throughout a shelf of volumes.

There was a man whom Priam Paul despised, nicknamed *Gorilla*. Xavier wasn't sure why he hated Gorilla. The man was described as physically imposing, and was well-mannered, generous and successful with a lovely wife and children. He was a merchant of preserved foodstuffs from the Loire valley, warehousing everything but wine. That fact alone narrowed his true identity to one of a dozen people. But then he found a better clue:

> *Gorilla is not a risk-taker. His margins are thin, but his business is so extensive that he is immune to downturns. In a way, this is admirable, but he is not a Traversier, and does not understand.*
>
> *Traversier is a house of risk-takers. We are the heavy-lifters, the men with vision. At our height, we could buy and sell Gorilla and everything he owns ten times over. I want to be a Traversier, I do not want to be Gorilla. It grates my teeth that he is always giving me advice.*

Perhaps Priam Paul discussed Gorilla somewhere else in the memoirs, in an incident taking place outside of the meetings and accidentally used his real name. If so, Xavier was looking for a man who was gratingly paternalistic, who gave Priam Paul advice in a way that greatly annoyed him.

The hunt began. Every event in the memoirs that took place outside of the Freemasons was examined. Now there were real names aplenty - and Xavier found his man:

> *Monsieur Cœurfroid began a conversation with me on the docks. His tone was utterly condescending, as if he was my father and I needed his advice. His teeth-grinding sermons always seem to revolve around the same issue: riverine trade. Yes, old documents give Traversier the right to trade. But to exercise those rights now would be to go against the guilds, and the ones who perform the trade now. Additionally, it would inevitably take bribes and favors to*

get the imprimatur from authorities to make the ancient rights current once more.

Neither is Riverine trade qualitatively similar to ocean-going trade. It is a safe bet, brings in very little income, and is simply not worth the trouble. It would save Cœurfroid money if I was shipping his goods, that is all.

Monsieur Cœurfroid was properly Maurice Adam Cœurfroid. He was older than Xavier by nearly twenty years. Maurice was married, and had four daughters and three sons, the oldest of which was nearly Xavier's age. The Cœurfroid business was food. The rich harvests of the Loire valley were preserved in various ways, and shipped throughout Europe from Cœurfroid warehouses. Whether one ate smoked ham in Paris, or soup made from tomato powder in Kiel, there was a chance it bore the Cœurfroid family stamp.

It had to be him.

Xavier decided to send Cœurfroid a letter. He agonized over it, before he finally realized receiving a letter from a fairly strong connection was of no import to a normal person of means, who would simply take it at face value. He then wrote a formal, yet friendly, short version, simply asking for a meeting at Monsieur's convenience, as if he would know of Xavier already. Cœurfroid wrote back promptly with a time and date for a rendezvous - as if he knew of Xavier already.

And so, Xavier clattered his family coach to the white stone townhouse of Monsieur Cœurfroid in the Centre-Ville of Nantes.

He was overly prepared for the meeting.

Upon his arrival, he was ushered inside the foyer. It was as well-decorated, but was far smaller, than that of the Château Meilleur. He was not ushered into a sitting room or library to wait for Monsieur's convenience, rather Cœurfroid came to greet him himself. He was a big-boned man, with short legs and long arms – but was still inches taller than Xavier. If his legs were the right size for his body, he would be forced to stoop through doorways. He was crudely and broadly featured, with dark blonde hair and mustache. His stocky build was such that his clothing did not seem to fit, although it did, and was very fine and stylish. To Xavier's great surprise, he was greeted like a long-lost brother. He was embraced and kissed and tears came into the great man's eyes. He shook his head and apologized, as if their meeting should have been long ago, and at his behest, and not that of Xavier.

And soon they were ensconced in the thick bergères of Cœurfroid's study, wearing silk smoking jackets, with good cognac and Spanish cigars, rather than the snuff partaken by the nobles. The conversation regarding the cognac and cigars was quite long, perhaps purposefully so. The cognac was *Hors d'âge* Charentais. The cigars were Cuban Oscuro cheroots - sweet, complex and heavy. To

Xavier, they paired well with the dry Cognac. He was pleased when Cœurfroid echoed his sentiments - he was not usually perceptive about such things.

The conversation drifted to business. Cœurfroid told him that the wheat of Picardy, and the area around Nantes, was considered to be the worst in France by the bakers of Paris, and it was a godsend to be absent from the city's dietary responsibilities. Paris was provisioned by farmland present in a series of wide, concentric rings around the city called crowns. A good harvest meant the police culled grain only from the first crown to feed Paris, or perhaps the first and second. Even in times of poor harvests Nantes was unaffected, being outside the outermost crown. But in times of famine, all bets were off, so to speak, and police would control food distribution in all parts of the country, and even bring in grain from international sources. But those times were infrequent. Without much oversight from authorities, the harvests around Nantes could be sold as one wished. One could deal successfully in food in Nantes, and export as one wished to make the largest profit – to Paris or otherwise. Business was good in Brittany.

After a moment of comfort and silence, it was time. Cœurfroid closed his eyes, and leaned back in his chair. "Monsieur Traversier," he said lazily. In truth, his words were meant to be a starter's pistol. Xavier understood.

"Are you familiar with the Bouchon loom?" asked Xavier carefully.

"No," was the quick reply.

"A Bouchon loom uses a roll of perforated paper, called a Bouchon roll, to program the pattern of the fabric."

"Program?"

"Yes, that is their word - as in, an order of events. In the weaver's case, the order of colored thread. You see, in this particular loom, a thread is woven into fabric depending on whether the perforations in the paper allow it to be used. The Bouchon roll determines the fabric's design, because it determines which threads the loom will use at any given point in time."

Cœurfroid grunted and nodded.

Xavier continued, "I have come to find that every man has something akin to a Bouchon roll, a program determining their actions."

Cœurfroid cleared his throat and fidgeted. "Explain your metaphor further please," he said.

"The loom is the man. The fabric is the chosen actions of a man's life. The Bouchon roll is the mind's programming, to use the weaver's language. The Bouchon roll is a man's emotional driving forces, his beliefs, his character, his views on the world based on his history and education. The interior program that determines his actions."

Cœurfroid grunted and nodded.

"Religion is part of a man's Bouchon roll, or lack thereof. Culture. His personal drives for love, money, status."

"It is complex, this Bouchon roll," Cœurfroid said quickly, putting a subtle emphasis on *complex*.

Xavier felt a rising panic. His line of reasoning might be far too oblique. But it was too late now. He squelched his feelings and continued, "To add further complexity, I have come to find that man is island and clan together. There are things that drive us as alienated beings, but we also change as we commit to a certain group, or tribe, if you will, and are thereby defined forthwith."

Cœurfroid grunted and nodded.

"I believe every pattern of our species is always represented by at least one individual, always. But one must also concede that, in any given time, huge swathes of the population tend to be from only a few patterns, giving rise to differences in thought depending on the era and its influences."

Cœurfroid grunted and nodded.

"I have come to find that the most important factor in the study of humanity is that of the predominate Bouchon patterns, if you will. A study of the similarity in Bouchon rolls in a particular age leads to a deeper understanding of history."

Cœurfroid slowly nodded, "Let us call it the Bouchon Pattern uniformly from now on. That seems fair to the ears." He paused and took three puffs on his cigar. "So – there is nothing new under the sun. But men of different times, for whatever reason, decide to dust off certain Bouchon patterns and put them in the loom en masse– determining the fabric of the age, yes?" He took another puff, and continued, "Your model is overwrought, I think, but not inaccurate. Why is its explanation important now?"

"My father was a Freemason," Xavier offered quietly.

"Did he cut stone? Design cathedrals, your father?"

"No."

"Why then was he a Freemason?"

"The Freemasons were indeed stone workers in their genesis, the high Middle Ages. They taught their craft only to a select few. Their unique skills enabled them to move freely throughout Europe, or, should I say, gave them the power to insist upon it. They raised themselves above the law. They were indeed masons, and they were indeed free."

"Interesting. My question stands, however."

"I will let it stand for the nonce, and continue. The Freemasons were free, but no one else was. In fact, I would imagine it was impossible for most to understand the very concept of freedom. Our world was defined by the church. Man serves God, man is enslaved to sin. In worldly terms, every man's destiny was predetermined, they were born into a class and occupation. The idea of man being able to determine his own destiny was utterly foreign, so much so that the concept was unable to be contemplated, much less understood. The Masons had to keep their ideas secret, for their own protection."

"So, something changed? In the Bouchon Pattern." Again, his tone was neutral. Xavier could not tell what he was thinking.

"The very world changed, Monsieur. Freedom became a word that educated people understood. The Freemasons saw a similarity between themselves and the intelligentsia. They realized they were less about stone, and more about ideas. It was time to open the ranks to like-minded thinkers, not necessarily those capable of building churches."

"When was this?"

"For certain? No one knows. Fifty, sixty years ago, in Britain, probably Scotland. It grew quickly. Here, it started amongst the nobles."

"The nobles?"

"It doesn't make much sense, does it? Why would the people who benefit the most from the current system want to change it? But there it is -- our nobles were enraptured with all of it. From them, it spread to the clergy, and finally to us. It even came here, to Nantes, where silver and gold are altar and throne, and high-minded ideas wear no crown."

"And what are these ideas of which you speak? When did they start? Who promulgated this?"

Xavier leaned forward, "As you quoted, there is nothing new under the sun, but the modern age embraces old patterns, when told by new voices and espoused under new names. When the time is ripe, the age finds its voice and its idea. It dusts off an old Bouchon pattern, calls it something new, and puts it in the loom. In the Sixteenth Century, we were rife for a reawakening. The church was corrupt - and all-powerful. Technology advanced, man had more time, money and leisure - but, more importantly, more opportunity. We rediscovered the Greek and Roman philosophers, who in the majority believed their own gods to be flights of fancy, and were determined to forge intellectual bedrock without them. And amongst their writers was every nuance of thought one could possibly conceive. Radical old ideas emerged under new names, different Bouchon patterns were taken from storage and placed in the loom. As time passed, the old Catholic patterns found themselves more frequently on the shelf."

Now Cœurfroid leaned forward, "Go on."

"It happened all at once."

"When?"

"It started in 1513, and by 1532, it was done. Everything that came after was postscript."

"Not 1641?" said Cœurfroid. His tone was leading, but Xavier was not going to be led. He did not believe he was wrong. But now he, a teenager, had to convince a man old enough to be his father that this was so.

"1641 refers us to Descartes, and the publication of *Meditations on First Philosophy*. It was a hallmark year, indeed. But the ideas of Descartes were seeds," Xavier said carefully, "And, if thrown on stone, forever seeds remain. But they were not thrown on stone, rather on fertile soil. Let us talk of the soil."

Cœurfroid leaned back again, "The soil then."

"The soil was individualism over collectivism, and humanism over religion. The old ways were formally undone by three men, who represented the most powerful forces of mankind: the lust for power, the drive to spirituality, and the desire for ease and pleasure. They came in that order, and perhaps that fact, in and of itself, speaks volumes regarding the nature of mankind."

"Three men. Firstly?"

"Machiavelli, in 1513."

"*The Prince?* In pamphlets, perhaps. Not widely distributed. He wasn't published until 1532."

Cœurfroid was better educated than he let on. But his true opinions were still a mystery. Xavier continued, "Machiavelli implied, by accident or design, that the pursuit of power, and let us include wealth here, could be the ultimate end, a life's pursuit, and all other aspects of identity could be subservient to it, thereby eviscerating traditional morality and religion."

"A new Bouchon pattern - or a resurrection of one, according to you. And your second perpetrator?"

"Martin Luther, 1517."

"Luther despised Greek and Roman philosophy. He saw their moral baseline as you do, as anti-religious, and therefore discarded them."

"Indeed, indeed. But I would argue that, in a tremendous irony, he was their greatest proponent."

Cœurfroid said nothing.

Xavier could not tell whether it was a good sign or bad, but continued, "Martin Luther's ultimate lesson, whether he wished it to be so or not, was that an individual has the moral and intellectual authority to invent, discard or accept any moral or religious teaching he wishes. An individual now has the moral authority of God."

"Quite a potent assertion of individualism. And thirdly, your man of pleasure?"

"Rabelais, 1532. He wrote comedies, but he was deadly serious about his philosophy."

"And what did he espouse?"

"I know a passage by heart."

"Why? Do you agree with him?"

"No. I simply know it by heart."

"Then proceed, Monsieur, by all means."

Xavier spoke softly, "Because men that are free, well-born, well-bred, and conversant in honest companies, have naturally an instinct and spur that prompteth them unto virtuous actions, and withdraws them from vice, which is called honor. Those same men, when by base subjection and constraint they are brought under and kept down, turn aside from that noble disposition, by which they formerly were inclined to virtue, to shake off and break that bond of servitude, wherein they are so tyrannously enslaved; for it is agreeable with the nature of man to long after things forbidden, and to desire what is denied us."

Cœurfroid had closed his eyes to listen. He slowly opened them. "*Fais ce que voudras.* Do as thou wilt. Because the nature of an educated man is honorable and good."

"And any constraint on good men turns them to evil."

"Our Rousseau is not so original as we thought."

"In Rousseau's defense, he is more democratic. He believes all men are naturally good, not just the educated."

"So those are your three? Your soil, so to speak."

"Yes. And to put an even finer point on it, I will say this: those three men unraveled culture, religion, and political structure in the minds of the intelligentsia. As society reached its apex under the Catholic order, it was burned to ash in the minds of all those who truly mattered."

"A sharp, fine point indeed, Monsieur Traversier."

"An intellectual phoenix had to rise from those ashes, Monsieur. That phoenix was the Enlightenment. The Enlightenment changed the world. It made all of thinking Europe into Freemasons."

"The Enlightenment, then. And Descartes, of course."

"We do not start with Descartes."

"Oh? Then with whom?"

"Francis Bacon, let us say 1597. All knowledge should be based on inductive reasoning, and nothing else. The supernatural is dead. The mind, as informed by the senses, reigns supreme. Now Descartes, 1641. Our ability to reason determines all. Man is reasonable, the problems and mysteries of man can be solved as readily as a mathematical equation. The study of man can be a science. Then Locke, 1660 - we are born a blank slate, our Bouchon pattern is derived from our experience only, there are no absolute universal truths. The same year, Spinoza - there is no God. The Bible must be replaced by a scientifically-derived man-made religion. Montesquieu, 1738. The purpose of government is not despotism; indeed, it is the preservation of individual freedom, and government should be structured to handicap its own base desire for power. Hume, 1739. Our feelings, our instincts, not our reason, determine our behavior - man is simply an animal. Diderot, 1746 - reason and feeling are equal. Reason creates virtue and tempers feeling. And then, overarching all - and expressed by many: the populace, now responsible to itself, must be properly unified and trained in virtue, to use the Roman term, in order to be good citizens."

"The General Will."

"Yes, Rousseau would say the General Will."

A moment of silence, as if Cœurfroid expected something further. He finally cleared his throat, "And what more of Rousseau? And Voltaire, for that matter?"

"Voltaire is a satirical polemicist. As such, he only criticizes what has already been torn down by others. He chews intellectual food, so those who have no teeth can eat. This makes him famous and popular, and no one would doubt his intellect. I simply call him a Crusader, and not a Christ. Rousseau has a wider range as a writer, and is more talented. I enjoy what he has to say about youth and children. He inspired me, and changed my life. That is his forte - he inspires. Of the modern, living philosophers, I would say Kant is the greatest mind. He argues that morality is a function of reason, which is interesting and might even be true. I enjoy what Beccaria has to say about the abolition of torture and the death penalty - why should the state be given such power over the individual?"

Cœurfroid nodded, "Why indeed." Another moment of silence spread out like wine on a tablecloth.

Xavier felt challenged. He leaned forward, "You are a Freemason, Monsieur Cœurfroid."

"Did your father tell you that?"

"How would he have done such a thing, having passed away when I was a child?"

Cœurfroid took a deep drag from his cheroot, picked a fleck of tobacco from his tongue, and took a small sip of Cognac.

Xavier lost all sense of trepidation, "I wish to be a Freemason as well."

"How old are you?"

"I am exactly halfway between my sixteenth and seventeenth birthdays."

"Fascinating," he said, and took another pull from the cigar. "You do not often directly quote your sources, rather you explain what their introduction into the Bouchon pattern truly wove. The consequences of thought, as it translated into action. A shocking and indicative approach, especially from one so young."

Xavier did not feel particularly young. No one who has fought for their survival ever felt young afterward.

Xavier did not reply. He said what he had to say. Instead, he leaned back in his chair, took a mouth of smoke and a swallow of cognac, for it was done, for good or ill. The flag had been hoisted.

Minutes passed. Oddly, Xavier felt at peace. He sipped his cognac and smoked his cigar. When Cœurfroid spoke again, he was almost surprised.

"Describe the beliefs, the Bouchon pattern, of the Freemasons - using one word only."

"Freedom," said Xavier, without having to think.

But something odd happened. Xavier had said the word with absolute conviction, but immediately felt like a liar. Did freedom mean anything to him? Or was all of this only a means to an end? There were other things that meant much more to him, but he could not think of a specific word for what he truly longed for. What is it called when you enter your own abode, and you are greeted with love, and gladness that you are now home? That was what Xavier truly wanted, however it was described.

Cœurfroid caught the conviction, but not the afterthought. He nodded, and spoke, "I will bring you to a meeting, blindfolded. You will serve or not serve, at the whim of the masters."

Xavier nodded, and they continued to smoke and drink in relaxed silence.

Cœurfroid was as good as his word. Xavier found himself at a meeting, and, rather than waiting blindfolded in the antechamber, he was introduced and allowed to participate. He was questioned extensively by the brethren. Xavier's feeling was that Cœurfroid had described him to the other members as some sort of juvenile phenomenon. Xavier knew his philosophers backwards and forwards, he even knew some of the rites from his father's writings. His time front-and-center was absolutely triumphant, in the beginning.

Then they began asking him questions about what was happening *now*.

"What are your thoughts on the Flour War?" said a voice. Xavier did not answer before the next voice.

"What do you think of Malesherbes advocating the calling of the Estates-General to end the debt crisis?" said another.

Xavier almost sniggered. The last Estates-General was in 1614. No one would ever suggest an Estates-General, and the king would never call it. He thought for a second that the questions were jokes played upon him.

"Do you think Turgot is justified in using such force in suppressing the riots?" added a third.

Xavier, in the resulting humiliating silence, realized it was no joke - and he had no answers. Although he was Achilles when it came to the contents of his library, he was the same man's heel in regard to current events. Within minutes, he went from prodigy to embarrassment.

Before his coach ride back to the Meilleur, he walked Cœurfroid to his home. "Monsieur Cœurfroid, nothing like that will ever happen again. I will be an expert in current affairs as soon as humanly possible."

Cœurfroid nodded, "The next meeting is on Tuesday."

Before the week had passed, Xavier knew the names of every government official in the decision-making process, however lowly or obscure. Not only was he thoroughly aware of everything going on in France, he was well-versed in international affairs, especially those of Great Britain. His level of knowledge enabled him to add history and context to current events, to see past the surface, to discern motivations and identify political ruse. A month after that, he could have been consul to the King.

He was a Freemason on his seventeenth birthday. The next oldest of the Nantes brethren was twenty-eight.

Xavier

When Cœurfroid invited Xavier to the ball, he did so naturally. Xavier considered the invite to be his greatest achievement. His first action was to take the ugly, medieval mirror off the wall and bring it to Monsieur Écureuil, the family's antique dealer. To fetch a high price, it would have to be brought to Paris. Xavier opted for a quick sale for two thousand livres. He took the money and invested in dance and etiquette teachers, new outfits for himself and the footmen, and cosmetic repairs for the family's primary coach. In none of this did he consult Madame. Oddly, she said nothing. A painting from the attic suddenly appeared where the mirror used to be, and that was that.

And so it was that the newly-painted and lacquered coach, with its new leather and burnished brass, made its way to the Centre-Ville of Nantes, and the stone townhouse of Monsieur Cœurfroid. Xavier was immaculate, the footmen were glorious, and the coach was a wonder.

The carriage turned onto Cœurfroid's street, the Haute Grande Rue. A line of coaches waited to disgorge passengers, and a bevy of footmen and valets waited to accommodate them. Across the street, a large crowd of onlookers had gathered to watch the spectacle.

Xavier heard a muffled voice from the driver's bench, "Do you wish to enter the line, or walk from here, Monsieur?"

"The line, please." Xavier wanted nothing more than to exit the coach precisely where he should, enter as he should, and join the society of Nantes inside, as he now should.

It was not a long wait. Soon the carriage door was opened, and Xavier descended to the pavement. Well-dressed men and women waited in line to be announced. He caught whiffs of wig powder, makeup, rosewater perfume and citrus *Eau de Cologne*. The crowd was expectant and merry. Occasionally, someone smiled at Xavier when their eyes met, and it warmed his heart.

Inside waited the absolute cream of Nantes society. The mayor, Pierre de la Ville de Chambarde, would be in attendance, along with other nobles of Brittany who were politically friendly - which was most of them. The new bishop of Nantes, Jean-Augustin Frétat de Sarra, and other wealthy, politically-liberal clergy would be in attendance, most dressed in silk jackets and *culotte* leggings, like dukes of Versailles - even the pretense of clerical vestments sacrificed for style. Then there were the bourgeois: merchants, traders, ship captains, slavers, financiers, and, last but not least, the wealthy and powerful taxmen, the Farmer-Generals. They were not political allies and most had purchased titles, but it was prudent to have them on one's side.

Xavier finally entered the foyer. It must have been lit with a thousand candles, from no less than four chandeliers and innumerable sconces and holders. A valet crossed to him, his white gloves holding a silver tray. "Your card, Monsieur," he said. Xavier obliged him. "One moment, Monsieur," and the valet disappeared.

A different valet appeared a moment later, "This way, Monsieur."

Xavier followed him into the crowded, well-lit ballroom. A herald at the entry tapped his cane on the floor, "Monsieur François-Xavier Érinyes Traversier, of the Traversier of Nantes."

Xavier saw the faces of nearly every partygoer turn, then look away – nearly in unison.

The feeling here was quite different than the queue.

Twenty couples danced in the center of the parquet floor. In the bordering crowd, a few here and there were happy and boisterous, but most were not. They were rather unselfconsciously self-conscious. They stood in bolts, one or two talking, the rest looking around without expression, casually surveying the others in the crowd. Fans snapped and fluttered in measured beats. In the back of his mind, Xavier remembered being told that every rhythm of the fan meant something different, that a woman could speak with her fan. Alas, she could not speak to Xavier, for he did not know the dialect. He realized there were dozens of social dynamics going on in this room, and he was totally ignorant of most of them. It was only his impression after a moment's glance, but, increasingly, Xavier's impressions were more and more accurate as he got older. He could rely on his intuition - and it duly informed him that he was woefully underprepared for the night's business. He truly knew nothing of Nantes society. His dancing and etiquette lessons were only grammar for a language he did not speak.

A waving arm saved him from darker thoughts. It was Cœurfroid.

The ballroom was two stories high. An expansive parlor adjoined it, separated by marble columns, only one-story high with a balcony overlooking the dance floor above it. A hallway ran down the length of this room and emptied into the ballroom, separated by more pillars and Chinese silk screens. Cœurfroid lounged halfway down the hallway with a knot of men Xavier recognized as fellow Masons. He crossed to the hall, formally greeted them, and took his place in the circle. Inevitably, conversation eventually boiled down to philosophy or politics. Tonight, it was politics.

"What do you think of the events in the Colonies?" one asked of him.

"The Declaration of Independence?"

"Exactly so."

Xavier began calmly, but in a purposefully interesting and intense voice, "In the first paragraph, the Americans utterly reject any affiliation with the British and their system, but, more importantly, do not cite classical ethics, or even Christianity, as the basis of their moral imperative. As their authority, they cite Rousseau's Nature God and his Law of Nature. Rousseau's philosophy is the American faith and moral compass. The Declaration of Independence is a complete repudiation of Christianity, not just the British monarchy. It is, profoundly, a document of Socialism and Freemasonry."

A round of nods and knowing sounds.

A movement caught Xavier's eye. Staring from the shadows in the opening behind the men, he saw a little girl. She was perhaps six or seven, thin as sticks, dusky and tow-haired with bright green eyes. She was wearing makeup, gloves, jewelry, shoes, and a dress - all very obviously made for a woman twice her height. She held a fan in her hand, somewhat awkwardly because of the loose rings on her gloved fingers. Xavier knew this crafty little person must have had to evade a small army of relatives and servants to be here. He averted his eyes, so as not to draw attention to her.

Xavier continued, "The Declaration begins boldly, 'We hold these truths to be self-evident, that all men are created equal, that they are endowed by their Creator with certain unalienable Rights, that among these are Life, Liberty and the pursuit of Happiness.' Pure Rousseau! In contrast, our good priests would have us believe we're here to repent and find faith - our life, liberty and happiness so utterly secondary to these goals they are beneath mention. No, this American Creator is clearly the God of Rousseau, not the Bible. The rest of the document is also clear; it is not God who will free the Americans, they will free themselves and serve their own interests - those that they alone will determine. Man's law defines man's liberty. Man's law is grounded in the power of the state. A government of Rousseau's natural, free men will ensure the liberty of all citizens. America has proclaimed itself as the first Rousseauian Socialist revolutionary government."

Cœurfroid nodded, "They have taken what we believe, and put it into action."

"Precisely. America is an experiment. Our beliefs have left the printed page, and are now being tested in the world. The events happening in the Thirteen Colonies are the most important in history, led by the most brilliant assemblage of minds that mankind has ever seen. Franklin, Adams and Jefferson alone could move mountains with their intellect."

"Are they Freemasons?" asked Cœurfroid.

"Franklin and Jefferson, but not Adams," replied Xavier.

Chapelle, a lawyer, shook his head, "So far they have won as many battles as they have lost. But I think their long-term prospects are slim. They will never beat the British, once they bring their full force to bear upon them. This Declaration is nothing but fool's laughter."

Jérôme Charles Olivier, an ocean shipper of mainly salt and wine, gave Xavier a piercing stare, "Then what does this bode, if anything?"

"We will eventually aid the Americans, because France must avenge herself on Britain. In that, all of France is in accord - from King to kitchen, we howl for revenge. We will die to the last man, and purchase his musket with our last coin. They cannot win against such determination, unless they possess it themselves - and they do not." Xavier saw another round of nods. "Britain *will* lose – to *us*. America will succeed and flourish, and be the shining example of our beliefs –

us, the Freemasons. The coming of Socialist America dooms the monarchy of France and, perhaps, all the monarchies of the world. And the French king himself will ensure America wins its independence, because the humbling of Britain is a national imperative."

"You seem very sure of this," said Jérôme.

"Mark my words in this moment, if you please. But for now, I must bid you all *adieu*. I cite my status as bachelor, as excuse and impetus for the parting. Good evening for now, gentlemen." And with that, Xavier tipped his hat and walked away. He heard them talking, when he was supposed to be out of earshot.

"He's brilliant, that one. If anyone can save the fortunes of Traversier, it is him," said Cœurfroid.

Xavier's heart burst with pride.

Now he wanted to meet as many people as possible. He especially wanted to dance. He longed for love, he longed for the laughter of a woman to fill the dark halls of the Meilleur. There were plenty of young ladies here, and they were all magnificent, all dressed and prepared as if this ball was the most important event in the whole world. It certainly was for Xavier.

The nearby sinfonietta started a minuet. He realized he knew the song, and which dance it required. Looking around for a partner, he saw a group of young women - staring at him and laughing, then quickly looking away. He then turned and, with calculated nonchalance, moved out of their eyesight, and surreptitiously crossed behind a marble pillar, where he could listen without being seen.

"I heard they are now in the antique business," said a voice dripping with sarcasm and honeyed vitriol. All of them twittered in laughter, in agreement rather than humor. Xavier thought he recognized the voice - a third cousin, Quennel Tonnelier.

"There are but two of them left in that whole house," said a bored young lady.

"And an army of servants paid with nothing but debt." A third voice, filled with soft hate.

"What else could they pay them with?" Another.

"They are not who they used to be." The Soft Hater again.

"But they still think they are. Truthfully, he doesn't belong here anymore." His cousin's voice, regretfully.

"Does he not? Traversier blood runs through all the old families. I believe every single one of us are related to them, to some degree or another." Xavier wished he knew that kinder voice, but he did not.

A different girl then replied. This one was angry. This voice he recognized, although he had not seen her for years, and at their last meeting, she had not spoken.

Zara.

"Our families have surpassed their roots. Nantes belongs to us now. The Traversier are upper middle-class, at best - and only for now. There are other families, hosting other events, they should now attend. He does not belong here. The Traversier are no longer part of *haute société*. Once they are forced to sell the Château Meilleur, they will be but a memory. And whoever buys the Meilleur will be the new First Family of Nantes."

Xavier felt his emotions rise. He might have won some kind of victory over Zara long ago, but she had won something more substantial here - and there was nothing he could do. He had lost a Florentine conflict to a Valencian Borgia - outmaneuvered in the shadows, where people whisper in daggers.

He turned and moved toward the front of the house. His ears were burning, his temples were pounding, his chest hurt. He felt sick to his stomach. He was absolutely enraged. He felt ashamed and belittled, his honor and pride stolen in an unforeseen attack. He had to leave as soon as possible. He headed quickly for the foyer.

His mind whirled. The first woman, Quennel, had said they were in the antique business, a not-so-subtle slight that meant they pawned their valuables to survive. Xavier had sold only one thing. What else must have been sold to start such a rumor?

But they had also spoken of the Meilleur. The first construction of the Château Meilleur had been completed over two centuries ago. There were only two true heirlooms of his house. The first was the Cross of Nantes, and it was lost. The other was the Château Meilleur. They would starve before parting with it. Their situation couldn't possibly be so dire.

But what if it is, and I am the last to know? he thought.

He looked around again as he walked, and saw that other groups, who now spied him, were talking behind their fans, or in low tones. He imagined their conversations as identical to the one he had just overheard.

There was a reason why Madam did not attend social events.

Traversier was a dying lion. The vultures circled, certain they would turn into similar great beasts once their beaks tore the hide of the expiring king. That was it, he realized - that was the first impression he had when he looked across the ballroom. They looked down on him, and were pleased to do so, and looked forward to someday devouring what was left of his house.

Xavier finally made it outside and nodded to his footman, who ran off to summon the coach.

A little piccolo of a voice came from behind him, "Your ideas are intriguing, Monsieur."

Xavier knew who it was before he turned. It was the tiny, twiggy blonde with the big green eyes. "I don't believe we have met," he said, trying to be appropriate through his mood.

With an acute sense of drama, the little girl put a hand to her chest, "I am Jeannine Cœurfroid."

"*Bonsoir*, Jeannine Cœurfroid. I am Xavier Traversier."

"Will you not kiss my hand?" she said, and raised five gloved fingers.

Xavier kissed her hand. She narrowed her eyes, "You kissed your own thumb, Monsieur!"

"If a woman is wearing gloves, a man kisses his own hand."

"Why, that is ridiculous!"

"A man would never smudge a lady's satin at a ball, Mademoiselle."

Chéri looked away, and thought about this for a long, dramatic moment. She finally turned, "I forgive you, Monsieur."

Xavier forced a smile.

She nodded, and said nothing more. Xavier's coach pulled up, and the door was opened. "This is my coach." said Xavier, "It was a pleasure to make your acquaintance, Mademoiselle."

"Likewise, Monsieur. We will meet again," she said cryptically. It only made him think that this innocent girl, and the crueler, older ones inside, were probably all destined to be *Mesdames*.

Xavier boarded the coach and the cabin door was shut. Xavier's thoughts went immediately to the words he had overheard. He cursed himself for having no control over the desires that brought him here. The rejection still stung.

No, that was the wrong word.

Rejection was no sting, it was a sword blow. It cut one from shoulder to groin and spilled your guts on the floor.

Boiled to its bones, the problem was that Xavier was stained with the sinking status and honor of his family. The young women had even implied that Traversier was headed for ruin.

And what if they're right?

For better or for worse, Madame was broken in strange ways. She appeared in her mannerisms as nothing but strong. Nonetheless, she had shown an inability to properly assess or deal with change - especially regarding his father. She was also as tight-lipped as a parish priest. It was entirely possible that the family was living on borrowed time without his knowledge.

Perhaps that was the root of all her issues - at least her issues with Xavier. He had frequently tried to understand her on a deeper level, and had found it difficult. She wasn't precisely a dying Empress. She wasn't a queen who found herself imprisoned. She was more a former, celebrated Empress, famous and beloved, but one who suddenly found that everyone around her was slowly forgetting her, slowly believing she was of no account - as if she was becoming a ghost with form, only risible and ridiculous rather than mysterious or frightening. Her young son was the only one capable of remedying her condition – but he was not so young that he could not be cursed and reviled for his impotence in the construction of her cure. But, admittedly, apart from his Masonic brethren, she was all he had.

Families were the strangest creations of nature. Xavier understood this. It was odd to think that his mother would fight and die for him. But, however cruel she had been, there was a bond.

The coach pulled into the circular drive, and stopped below the front door. Footmen opened the carriage door and Xavier exited. The entrance doors were opened for him, and he entered to see several of the staff waiting for him. He stopped in front of his head servant, Monsieur Miette, the maître d'hôtel, "Monsieur Miette, have my mother woken from slumber and dressed."

"I'm sorry, Monsieur?"

"Have my mother woken from slumber and dressed."

"It is quite late, Monsieur."

"I'm aware of the hour. I have much to do this night, and no time to argue. Wake Philippine, and have her maids dress her."

"Monsieur, you do not wake Madame – she wakes you."

"After we speak, within minutes, she will be at my leisure. Do you understand?"

"No, Monsieur."

"Your employment is terminated."

Miette's face twisted, then he calmed. "If that is so, I need my severance pay, Monsieur."

Xavier quickly counted out fifty livres of coin, then looked up at Miette. There was something about the smug look on his face. Xavier threw the coins to scatter across the floor.

Miette's nostrils flared, "How dare you! I served your father."

"You have exactly one minute to pick up your pay and leave my house."

"Before what?"

"Before I beat you with my cane, until the police come to restrain me."

Miette began picking up the coins. Xavier turned to another servant. "Wake and dress my mother."

"Yes, Monsieur." All of the servants began to scatter.

"Wait." They stopped. "I need all of the house account books brought to the library. I also wish our accountant fetched, Monsieur Colonne. Tell him to bring all of the family business accounts with him."

"At this hour, Monsieur?" said a young maid.

"Yes. And tell him if he does not come, I will come tonight to him. And I will not be pleased."

"I-we should-footmen fetched... to go to him, I think," she stuttered.

"Yes, tell a footman to take the coach to deliver my message."

"The footmen do not listen to maids."

Xavier was quickly losing what little patience he had left. "Tell the footmen that I am passing my orders through you. And if they don't like it, I will be along presently to reiterate them, and follow my commands with a glove across someone's *damné* face. Now go!"

The maid ran off in a quiet terror.

Xavier sighed. It was going to be a long night. He suddenly intuited that success in life might very well depend on the ability to think clearly with no sleep, and to focus for long periods on mind-numbing tasks. If that was so, tonight was practice for a long journey that would not be pleasant or easy.

He took a candle and moved into the library. He sat at a table, and lit the other candles resting upon it. But the library was too large, and only his desk was illuminated – a lonely island in an inky void.

A valet, Monsieur Fidèle, entered the room with a thick, leather file box tied with a rawhide cord. "Here are the house accounts, Monsieur. Madame is on her way. The footmen have left with your message."

"Excellent, thank you."

The valet bowed and disappeared.

Xavier opened the accounts and quickly separated them into piles. Each pile was carefully perused. The first pass revealed no obvious cases of embezzlement, or even poor bookkeeping. It was very obvious, however, that the Traversier family spared very little expense. They still lived the life of fleet-owning Nantes royalty, just with no fleet. Income was sporadic, and only came when the coffers were empty. A single, large sum would then suddenly appear, listed only as *Écureuil*. The girls at the ball were then precisely correct. The Traversier were antique dealers, who sold artifacts from their own collection and bought nothing. It would last until the Meilleur was empty, then the Meilleur itself would be sold.

Madame, his mother, Philippine Traversier, appeared in the doorway, braced by a pair of servants holding candles. She was dressed in a white silk *robe à la Françâis*, as if going to a ball herself, complete with jewelry, makeup and wig. She had a smug, proud look, her chin cocked arrogantly as she stared at Xavier with knowing eyes.

He was utterly perplexed. It must have taken her at least two hours to dress. Had he been so involved in the accounts that such time had passed? Why had she done this at all? And for what reason would her expression be so inexplicable? But he could not dwell on it. "Madame," he said, "I am now taking over the household accounts and the family business. You will no longer be involved in either."

She smiled, "Indeed you are, Monsieur Traversier."

And they stared at one another. Xavier had nothing more to say, except goodnight, but he did not utter it. Finally, she spoke again, "It is said the mothers of Sparta would tell their sons 'Return bearing your shield, or return being born upon it.' But I will not say this to you. I would rather repeat what someone said regarding them: 'All Greeks know what is right, but only the Spartans will do it."

Then Xavier realized why his mother was thus arrayed. She knew what he was about to say, and she was proud. Her words were meant to inspire him, to light him on fire. But Xavier knew his journey required more than just fire. Fire burns hot, then it burns out. His journey required the energy of a river - inexorable, deep, powerful and consistent in its resolve over incredible distances. He spoke to her again, "I will give you a quote of my own, Mother. The Spartan way was created by Lycurgus, the lawgiver. When King Agesilaus was asked what the greatest benefit Lycurgus conferred on his countrymen, he replied 'Contempt of pleasure.' Do you understand my meaning?"

"Yes, Monsieur, I understand."

"Good. Many things will be sold tomorrow that we do not need, and most of the staff will be discharged from their duties."

She looked as if she wished to say something.

"Yes?" he offered.

"Do not sell anything that celebrates or records the history of our family."

"No, of course not. But understand that we are not returning to a budget within our means. We are returning to an even smaller budget to create surplus. We have no more credit, and we still pay off debt from my father's last voyage. Surplus is our only chance to save for the next journey."

"To which destination do we go?"

"I go to Africa, then to Saint-Domingue."

"In what? With what?"

"Hence the need for surplus."

"It will take years."

"It will."

"We cannot sell heirlooms to purchase a fleet."

"No, indeed."

She said nothing for a long time. "Xavier," she finally uttered, "do you ever wonder why I keep that portrait of me, the Nattier?" Xavier shook his head. He knew nothing of it, and could not care less. She continued, "It is because it reminds me of who I am now. *Ego sum umbra, olim magnus. Lignum in umbra mortis - nisi illud occidit scutum lux.*" She said it in poorly-worded Latin, presumably to keep its meaning from the servants. *I am a shadow of past greatness. A tree dies in shadow - or it kills what shields the light.* Her metaphors were awkward: she compared herself to a shadow, then to a tree that suffered from shadow. But Xavier understood.

Her eyes flared, "Return this family to greatness. I don't care what we must endure. I don't care what you force others to endure. I don't care what you must do. Only do it."

That was precisely what he thought she meant.

She turned, and strode from the room.

Xavier shifted his attention back to the books. He had little time. The business accountant would be here soon. Xavier would learn everything he could before dawn - and then the accountant's employment would be suspended until things improved. He would take over. He would manage.

Xavier suddenly realized that tonight was the first time his mother had not worn black - indeed, she had worn white. But why this night?

Then he understood.

He was now exactly who she wanted him to be.

There had been another Florentine war in the shadows, one that spanned his entire life - and a Queen Sacrifice had led to a checkmate. In the very moment Xavier declared his manhood, supposedly securing his independence, Madame had won.

But in the end, it did not matter. The river was indiscernible, opaque even a foot below its surface, and - in its depths, at its heart - as mercilessly cold as newly melted ice.

The river knew what it had to do.

Xavier

Fifty-Six Years Later

1832

Jake

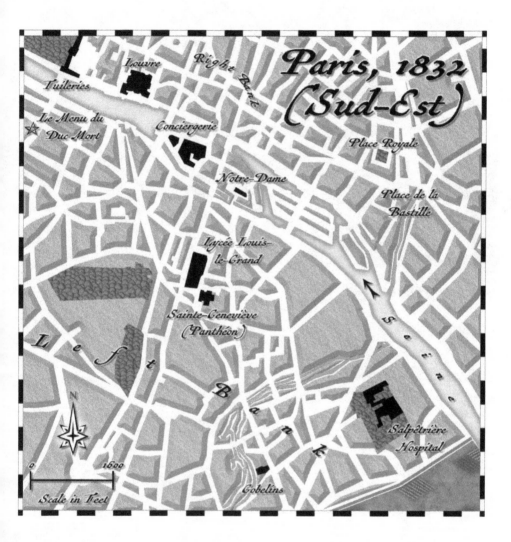

Paris, 1832
(Sud-Est)

Tuileries

Louvre

Right Bank

Le Menu du
Duc Mort

Conciergerie

Place Royale

Notre-Dame

Place de la
Bastille

Lycée Louis-
le-Grand

Sainte-Geneviève
(Panthéon)

Le f t

B a n k

Seine

N

Salpêtrière
Hospital

0   1600

Scale in Feet

Gobelins

Chapter Two

Jacob Esau Loring, Jake to his friends, was an American student in Paris. He was eighteen years-old and could be dead before night's end tomorrow. He was the leader of a revolutionary cell composed of fellow students at the elite school of Louis-le-Grand, located in the heart of the Latin Quarter of the left-bank.

Jake fumbled at the latch of the casement window, in the dormitory room he shared with his roommate Franck. He tried to open it quietly, but it was impossible. Although Louis-le-Grand was undoubtedly the best school in the world for young men aged eleven to eighteen, it was built in 1563, and, most likely, he tugged at the original latch.

"*To hell with it*," he said in English, and threw open the window, mindless of the ensuing noise.

"Jake! Be careful! Are you mad?" Franck spat from the darkness.

"So no one gets warm at night? It's June, Franck. A thousand windows are being thrown open as we speak."

Jake leaned out the window. There was no sill, and a look downward offered a four-story drop to the cobblestone courtyard below, encircled on four sides by the school. All of the student dormitories overlooked one of seven internal court-yards, most likely to prevent precisely this sort of maneuver. But Jake was a crafty, industrious Yankee and he would not be caged so easily. He had escaped a hundred times, or what seemed like a hundred times, and tonight would be no different.

He looked up and saw the eaves of the roof, or rather darkness where it blotted out the ochre clouds, dimly lit by the lights of the city. He brought out his rope, widened the lasso, and threw it as hard as he could at the top of the attic window. It didn't catch, so he pulled the rope back in to try again.

"Jake."

"What?"

"This is quite serious, isn't it? What we are doing."

"Yes, it is. Serious, but worthy."

"I know it's worthy." Franck said, rather downcast.

Jake turned to him, "This is the adventure of our lifetime. We've found ourselves at the center of the universe, at the perfect time and at the right age, to restore the rights of man. Our actions will resonate through history. Think of it."

The rope finally caught on Jake's third try - the fewest tries ever. Jake grabbed the rope with both hands and tugged. "Be back soon," he said, as he began to climb.

"Jake!" said Franck in a loud whisper. Jake stopped and turned to look at him. Franck grinned, "*Pour les droits de l'homme!*"

For the rights of man.

Jake smiled back, "*Pour les droits de l'homme, mon ami!*" and, with that, began to climb. He reached the lead and slate roof and went flat. Moving on all fours and distributing his weight, he maneuvered behind the attic window which angled up sharply from the roof. He pulled the rope up, carefully coiling it for the return trip.

He let his eyes adjust before making his way to the peak of the roof. He turned, straightened, and looked around. Louis-le-Grand was near the top of the south hills leading to the huge church of Sainte-Geneviève - called the Panthéon when leftists were in charge. In the opposite direction, the lights of Paris stretched out beneath the school like a bowl of yellow stars. He turned, straightened, and carefully walked down the length of the roof. It was a slow journey of hundreds of feet.

Jake heard Franck attempt a bird call. As usual, it was quite wretched. Jake smiled.

He had met Franck in their first year, at the tender age of eleven. Franck was a loner, but was similar in temperament to most of the other students. Jake was more extroverted, but considered to be a bit of a loose cannon. Franck had a knack for numbers, was methodical, precise and always received high marks. Jake hated math, loved poetry and history, but usually did well in most subjects due to an amazing intuitive intelligence. They naturally hated each other.

The pot came to a boil over chess. Both excelled. Franck read chessology books, and catalogued the moves of every game. Jake barely knew the rules.

Word was whispered to both of the other's prowess and conflict became inevitable. They played three games back-to-back, surrounded by half their class. Jake won all three games. A month later, Franck asked Jake for a rematch - and Jake lost just as speedily as he had won before.

They became inseparable. The students who found Jake intimidating and foreign could now connect with him through Franck. The ones who found Franck to be staid and boring warmed to him through Jake. The pair of them became a popular fixture of their class.

But when Jake first began his escapes from the school, Franck was not the sort to accompany him. Alone, Jake drowned himself in experience. His father always sent him money, and he had absolutely no use for it except to finance his nocturnal itineraries. He went to every play of the theaters of the Boulevard du Crime in the Marais, whether written by Scribe, Dumas, de Musset, or anyone else. He saw Rossini's opera *Guillaume Tell* and Meyerbeer's *Robert le Diable,* and even *La Sylphide*, a grand ballet, at the beautiful Le Peletier theater. He read every scandalous news pamphlet he could get his hands on. He even saw a midnight duel at the Place Royale, where a man was cut deeply on the arm. He went to the wine taverns, and, apart from enabling his wish to become stumbling drunk for the first time, they weren't exactly what he expected. They were places for the people of the neighborhood - men, women and children - to socialize after work, and the wine flowed with the gossip. Right about the time Jake arrived, the taverns devolved into places of drunken arguments and violence. His visits - to them, at least - became infrequent. He sometimes entertained thoughts about employing a lady of the night, curious as all young men are, but he was far too romantic to carry through with such a thing.

Jake discovered his regular haunt quite by accident. One night, while walking the border between the Latin Quarter and Saint-Germain-des-Prés, he saw an establishment that looked somewhat like a café, named *Le Menu du Duc Mort*, which was curious in and of itself. The tables seemed much larger than in a normal café and, rather than a coffee counter, doors led to a large, well-appointed kitchen. Although it served food, it was plainly not an inn or public house.

Jake saw a thin, balding, young man cleaning tables. "*Bon soir*, Monsieur," Jake had called out, "What manner of establishment is this place?"

"Why, it is a *restaurant*, Monsieur."

"And what is a restaurant?"

"You truly do not know?"

"I do not."

"Then sit down, and I will tell you."

Jake sat. The man gave him wine and bread, and an interesting yarn. During the revolution, it went, the aristocrats fled the country - or their heads fled their shoulders. Their cooks and *chefs de cuisine* were suddenly unemployed. They came up with an amazing idea: why not continue creating food fit for kings, only now for normal citizens? An entire culture was suddenly born on the right-bank, near the theaters. This man, the head chef and owner, went by the nickname of *Fatiguer,* and was thanklessly trying the same thing on the left-bank. He had studied under Marie-Antoine Carême, the man who invented *grande cuisine*, this new "high art" of cooking. Poor Fatiguer had been given his name because he could never sleep after the bustle of dinner service. He would dismiss his staff for the night, work on new recipes, serve stragglers himself, and was always tired the next day. But, because he could not sleep, his restaurant was always available during Jake's late-night outings.

Fatiguer's dishes were exquisite. On Jake's first visit he had a black truffle *camembert* so delicious it had literally brought tears to his eyes. Jake had no idea food could create such emotion. Soon he met the other men and women who joined the late-night haunt at *Dumort*, as it was known, and he began to look forward to the conversation as much as the food.

Jake was a product of his education at Louis-le-Grand. He was therefore a member of what was then called the Left-Wing. The words that casually issued from his mouth were both anti-government and revolutionary.

He was noticed.

One night, Jake was sitting at a table, talking and laughing with three locals he knew only as Arouet, Daumard and François-Marie. Suddenly, another man, a stranger, sat at their table uninvited. Jake's three friends stood up and left the restaurant without so much as a word. Jake was dumbstruck.

The intruder was tall, and of average build. He was well-dressed in a black suit under an exquisite ermine cloak and top hat. His features were large and crude. He had blue eyes, and light brown hair streaked with grey.

Jake regained his speech, "Who are you?"

"Who I am is not important. What I am, however, is."

"Then what are you, Monsieur?"

"Address me as Citizen, if you please." That meant he was an anti-monar-chist.

"Very well, Citizen."

"What I am is a *bourgeois*. Do you know this term?"

"Vaguely, Citizen."

"A *bourgeois* is a new class of man. Advancements of the modern age have produced opportunities in industry, trade and finance. Those who have taken this new path are called *bourgeois*."

"I see."

"Our new class has a new religion. Gold and respectability have taken the place of Christ and salvation. We are not faithful or adherent, but we are scrupulously honest and forthright. We believe in hard, smart work, governed by order, rules and law. We call ourselves men of reason, and our time was the Age of Enlightenment."

"Yes, of course. I have studied-"

"Studied!" he snorted, "That is a point in and of itself. In intellectually lazy times, it is hard to understand an age obsessed with thought. But once, long ago, the world was besotted with the promise of ideas. Ideas moved men and nations, philosophy trumped custom and memory. Ideas glued people together in new ways, and then drew their blood - in old ways, but for new reasons."

Jake was spellbound. He had never heard anyone talk quite like this.

The man calmed, "But what of you? A student from Louis-le-Grand, are you not?"

"I am."

"Voltaire, Diderot, Desmoulin, Robespierre, Saint-Just. Do you know of these men?" he asked.

"They are graduates of Louis-le-Grand. Extraordinary and famous ones, at that."

"Why extraordinary?"

"Because they changed the world."

"How?"

Jake was starting to enjoy this mysterious conversation in spite of himself. "The first two invented the concept of the modern age. The second three brought it about. Two philosophers, three revolutionaries."

"What is the concept of the modern age?"

Jake thought about it for a moment. "Rousseau, with perhaps a little bit of the Roman classics mixed in. As if Rousseau met Cicero, and they agreed with each other."

"Go on."

Jake organized his thoughts, "God may have created the universe, but he is now gone from us. Death is but the great sleep. We have only here and now."

The man nodded.

Jake continued, "Man is basically good, and all men are equal. Because man is good, man deserves freedom and happiness."

"If man is basically good, why is there so much evil?"

"Evil is the product of oppression and slavery. Freed from oppression, man reverts to nature and goodness. I believe that man, in his natural state, is capable of creating a wondrous and fair society."

The man nodded, "I believe, like Rousseau, that youth is sacred. For youth is humanity in its natural state. Care and education of the young is paramount. The new youth, of which you are a part, will change the world. The question is, into what? Into what state do we mold our world?"

Jake took a sip of wine, and pursed his lips, "The state must be strong, and its law paramount, for its duty is sacred."

"What is the duty of the state?"

"To protect and secure individual freedom. It is the duty of all citizens to be civic-minded and virtuous: to uphold the state and its values - with their lives, if necessary."

The man smiled, "Rousseau meets Cicero indeed."

Jake, for some reason, was very proud that his conversation was satisfactory to this man, and he didn't even know his name.

"I wonder, if these men changed the world, these graduates of Louis-le-Grand, why does France now have a King?"

"France has a king because of many reasons, mostly because of the world's combined force of arms."

"And why, at one point, did we not?"

"Why did we not have a king?" Jake thought about it, "I suppose because men invented a different way of life, and fought to bring it about."

"Why can we not do this now?"

"But we can!" blurted Jake. The man, who Jake soon knew by the alias of Citizen Bouche, had smiled. He had come to recruit Jake - and Jake had recruited himself.

Monsieur Bouche was a high-ranking member of *The Society of the Rights of Man*, or just *The Society*, a group forming the current wellspring of rebellion. For the last fifty years, secret societies had been the backbone of rebel movements. In the decades preceding the True Revolution, it was the Freemasons. Now it was *The Society*. As an act of self-preservation, the King had outlawed all secret groups. If more than twenty people were associated by secret membership, they could be arrested for doing nothing else. All cells of *The Society* were therefore composed of exactly twenty people.

After indoctrination and some rudimentary training, Jake was tasked to create a military cell by recruiting students from the school, a splinter group he was told to name *Student Soldiers for the Constitution*. Jake had a hard time keeping the membership below twenty, finally gave up, and ended up with nearly double. As pupils attending Louis-le-Grand, they were of higher status within the movement than their ages would indicate. As a security precaution, Jake had only met one man from *The Society*, who was Citizen Bouche. He had a suspicion that his three former friends - Arouet, Daumard and François-Marie - were also members, but he never saw them again.

Jake found his life's purpose through his secret identity. To be a revolutionary was to feel as if one were in love, spiritually enraptured, and an artist at work on a masterpiece - all at the same time. He had often thought about why it felt so true and so right. Perhaps it was because he wanted to change the world, and he wanted to do the right thing. Neither course is easily plotted, but now he believed he was assuredly doing both.

But there was one other thing, he came to realize. Jake had an emptiness, a canyon of darkness, of which he never spoke. It was caused by a tragedy too painful to think about – which precluded healing, or moving past it. The revolutionary cause seemed to fill the emptiness, or at least put a board over the chasm.

He was part of something that started before he was born - the True Revolution began in 1789, around the time Jake's father was born. The rebels actually overthrew King Louis, and had off his head. Napoleon took power, dismissed the revolution completely, and proclaimed himself Emperor. Jake was only an infant when the world finally managed to subdue him, humbling and restraining France as a criminal nation. It had been chaos ever since. Another King Louis was placed back on a rebuilt throne – and Jake was a child when this new Louis passed away and King Charles succeeded him in 1824. But two years ago, in 1830, there was a second revolution. King Charles was overthrown and replaced with King Louis-Philippe. Unfortunately, at that time, Jake hadn't yet found a way to escape the school. He thought he had lost his opportunity to be a part of history, his one chance at a great destiny gone.

Paris had other ideas. The city, indeed the world, roiled in the throes of a cholera epidemic. Whispers that the plague was the product of a government plot were widely believed throughout the wine taverns. Jake heard nonsensical tales of government agents dressed in black, creeping around the city at night, poisoning wells and violating casks of wine and brandy. Cholera then claimed the lives of two well-placed ministers: Périer; doyen of the rich and powerful, and, less than a week ago, Lamarque; beloved of the poor. Both were keeping the wolves at bay, and King Louis-Philippe lost what little support he had with their deaths. More and more, the revolution of 1830 seemed a fraud - just a pacification of the mob's energy and a return to the status quo.

Then the letter was delivered to Jake at the school - five characters on an otherwise blank sheet: *0001 G*, advising him of a meeting that night, at one minute after midnight in the Gobelins quarter of Paris.

Jake realized he hadn't missed anything. Paris was boiling over. It was time again for radical action. Soon the air would ring out with gunfire, and voices singing the *Marseillaise* and the *Ça Ira*.

Jake came to a T-shaped intersection, where the roof angled-off nearly straight north and south along the Rue Saint-Jacques.

And Rue Saint-Jacques was no street inside Louis-le-Grand: it was Paris, a pendulum of starvation and wealth, a city gravid with ideas, art and philosophy. Violent, rude, drunk - ancient, its buildings raised when men fought in chainmail and plate: a chaos maze of tall, shaky, medieval warrens barely separated by narrow cobblestone streets. Its main roads were laid by the Romans before Christ met his cross. Its name was taken from even more ancient inhabitants: the Parisii Gauls. And this city was no virgin, either. She had been burned, looted and plundered - time and time again, changing hands like a coin to the bearer of the longest sword. No single person knew all its streets and buildings - much less its sewers and secret passages. It was full of dark places and ideas, full of hidden history - the foibles of man etched upon it like the rings of a tree. Yet this city was a beacon to intellectuals and theologians, not to mention artists and craftsmen. The modern age was invented here – along with all other ages after the fall of Rome. The western world was the child of mother Paris, truth be told, like it or not. All of modern European history - right or left, east or west - started here.

Jake neared his destination. He came to the roof of another raised window, coming up from the attic like a stone wave. He felt along the base of the wave, and found his second rope, hidden there long ago. He secured it to the top of the jutting window, and threw it over the side. He climbed down to the end of the rope, which was purposefully short so it could not be seen from passers-by on the sidewalk. A bone-rattling jump landed him on the cobblestones of Paris.

He was free.

***

At the very same time Jake was exiting Louis-le-Grand, a private carriage entered the city by the old toll gate of Barrière d'Enfer.

Only one man sat inside. Since he had entered France, he had used an alias - usually, but not always, Monsieur Tyran. His ancient travelling papers indicated he was a French citizen, had left the country long ago, and his true name was Jacques Bonhomme Cale. The name meant next to nothing, for when Monsieur Tyran was called by his true name he was of little account. But the name of Monsieur Tyran was to be known in France very soon, and to a cabal of powerful men, who would soon wish to know his true identity. Their agents, who would search the rolls of the admitted at ports such as Nantes, would scan over the name of Jacques Bonhomme Cale without a second thought, and be no more aware of anything.

Monsieur Tyran had many reasons to be in Paris, but every single one of them - without exception - revolved around Jacob Esau Loring, Jake to his friends. Tyran was easily twice Jake's age, they were not related, they had never seen each other, nor would they recognize the other. Monsieur Tyran, however, knew Jake's name, how and why he came to be a student at Louis-le-Grand, and the origin of his family. Indeed, Monsieur Tyran was convinced that Jake was the key to his own salvation. Monsieur Tyran could not tell anyone the true nature of his obsession, at least for the foreseeable future, because the airing of the truth might eliminate its chance of success. Rather, Monsieur Tyran had half-truths and outright lies ready for the telling, to completely obfuscate what he was really after and what he truly wanted.

For now, it was simple. He knew Jake had a cheap cross around his neck. It was a flat, simple thing, stamped with numbers and letters – and the year 1805, the same year that a priceless heirloom named the Cross of Nantes went missing. It was no coincidence. Jake was star-crossed, doomed by the heavens, and Monsieur Tyran was to bring him word of his dark destiny.

Monsieur Tyran, at the end of a long journey across ocean and dusty road, was soon to make the fateful decision to go to his hôtel in the Marais, and not go directly to Louis-le-Grand. On the surface, his decision made absolute and perfect sense; it being of a late hour.

On the morrow, he was to miss Jake by less than half an hour, and this proved to be a costly mistake for both men.

***

For Jake, it was less than a two-mile walk to the staunchly-Republican Gobelins neighborhood to the southeast. The route involved nearly all major streets - narrow but well-lit, and well-patrolled by the ultra-competent Paris Night Watch police. Apart from almost being run over by a huge carriage - no mean threat - the trip had been quick and uneventful. In less than an hour, he found himself alone at a table, in a dimly-lit wine tavern on Rue du Fer named *Tribus Coloribus*. The smoke from cheap, native-grown Franche-Comté tobacco burned his eyes and made him nauseous. The dirty wood and plaster walls were decorated with military memorabilia - but nothing was from before 1789 or after 1815. A tricolor flag, damaged from battle, hung over the bar. It was late, and most of the patrons had stumbled home. A few were left, an unusual handful of men and women, frightening and strange in the flickering lamplight. They were all of different classes and stations, but all of them were furtive and suspicious-looking, as if plotting separate coach robberies. Jake thought it was a foul and secretive place.

Citizen Bouche entered.

He emanated power and energy. He stopped two steps into the room, looked around, and then removed his gloves, ever so slowly. It was as if he waited for his authority to fill the place, poured out by the power of his presence.

He sat without removing his hat or cloak. He nodded a curt *no* to the bartender, flipped a gold louis on the table for his trouble, and only then looked Jake in the eye. "It is tomorrow."

"After Lamarque's funeral?"

"And during. Understand something: as of this moment, we can only rely on five-thousand comrades."

Jake nodded. "How many muskets do we have?"

"More than enough. And once it starts, plans have been made to raid armories and magazines. Muskets are not the issue."

"Then there are no problems."

"Don't be so sure. There are twenty-thousand Parisian National Guard inside the city, and some additional forty-thousand army regulars within a day's march."

"So, we are outnumbered twenty to one."

"Within twenty-four hours, yes. We five-thousand can only be the spark, Citizen Loring. Our spark must ignite the city. Paris must take to the streets, like the times of old."

"What is the plan?"

"Regardless of the response, we hold as long as possible. There will be no orders to stand down or retreat."

"I understand."

"The funeral will be a showcase of political theater, something akin to what Jacque-Louis David would have designed during the first revolution."

"The True Revolution."

"Exactly. As you know, the liberation movements in Poland, and the Italian and German states, have experienced temporary setbacks. Some of our comrades have come here as political refugees."

"Do they still want to fight?"

"They do. We have completely infiltrated all three communities, and they will be there in force tomorrow."

My God, this is really happening, thought Jake. It wasn't a joke, a fantasy or an idea - they were taking to the streets.

"Does my cell have any specific orders for the morrow, Citizen?"

"Indeed, it does. First, the funeral. There will be a procession accompanying the funeral cortege to the Place Vendôme. You will make your way as close to the carriage as possible. At the signal, you will rush the carriage, and take command of it. The idea is that soldiers will have a harder time firing at youth. We postpone open war until it suits us."

"What is the signal?"

"There will be shouts of '*Down with Louis-Philippe, long live the Republic.*' In that exact syntax: 'Down with Louis-Philippe, long live the Republic."

"Where are we taking the carriage?"

"Place de la Bastille. The people need to be reminded of what they are fighting for. There will be a round of speeches, and another signal. A unique flag will be raised, a red flag with a black border. The words *Liberty or Death* will be stitched upon it. Upon the unfurling of this flag, you are to fight your way through any policing government troops, and move to your next assignment. Are you familiar with Quinze-Vingts, or Saint-Antoine?"

"No, I am not," Jake whispered.

"Go there tonight and reconnoiter. Your cell will build a roadblock to completely seal off Rue de Charenton twenty paces north of the Petite Rue de

Reuilly. Saint-Antoine is a neighborhood of deep revolutionary sentiment. Once the inhabitants realize we have taken control, they will come to us for direction, as sheep come to the shepherd. Hopefully, by midnight, we will have the numbers to storm the Tuileries Palace, and take control of the government. If that happens, we can demobilize the National Guard, or subsume it." Bouche leaned in closer and whispered, "Do not alienate the citizens of Saint-Antoine. Your primary purpose is to excite and recruit them. That is our true purpose behind the effort: to enable the neighborhood to rise."

"We are not using their furniture for our roadblocks."

"No, indeed. Not unless they donate it to you." Citizen Bouche looked around in the darkness, and saw all attention was elsewhere. "When I hand these to you, put them away quickly. Are you ready?"

"Yes."

A bulging coin pouch was noiselessly placed on the table top. "One hundred francs for supplies, sundries or bribes." Jake tried to put it away as carefully.

Citizen Bouche handed him a cockade, a circular knot of emerald ribbons. Jake slipped the cockade into his breast pocket. Bouche continued, "A green cockade means you hold the rank of Junior Commander. Green and white denotes Senior Commander, green and gold cockades are worn only by Generals. You will take orders from the latter two. Your men will wear tricolor cockades, or the red and blue of Paris. Now listen, this is important: the refugees will wear tricolor cockades, or they will wear blue. If they wear blue, they have no command. Your assignment-"

"At the barricade."

"Yes, at the barricade. Your assignment at the barricade requires more men than you have. It is imperative that you find blue cockades at the cortege, and enlist them into your unit. Once you do this, you will give them a tricolor cockade." Bouche placed a cloth bag on the table, presumably full of cockades, and Jake pushed it down into a side pocket.

Next came a bayonet in a scabbard. Jake slipped it under his arm inside his jacket. A large, odd-looking pistol followed. "That is a Lefaucheux twenty-round double-barreled revolver. It uses self-contained metal cartridges."

Jake slipped the large pistol into his jacket pocket, "I've never seen one of these before."

"There are but a handful in the world. Technology advances. We are the future, we must use the tools of the destined. Unfortunately, science has not provided us with longer-range weapons of such modernity. Your men will be using .69 caliber Charleville '77's, but what they lack in technology they make up for in storied history. They are absolutely lethal, and reliable as sunrise."

But notoriously inaccurate, thought Jake. Luckily, the enemy would be using the same weapon.

The man placed a box of metal cartridges on the table, and Jake quickly slid it into his other pocket. Lastly came a scrap of paper. "This is your barricade location, and the address where the carts will be."

"Carts?"

"Holding muskets, powder and shot. It is where you will be issued arms, ammunition and a flag. You will bring a flag staff of some kind for the purpose."

"The cart will be guarded."

"Yes, it is a command center of sorts. You will return to the cart for more ammunition, and send your messengers there to drop off communication."

"Yes, I understand."

"Memorize your barricade placement and the cart address, then burn the paper and be on your way."

"Will I see you tomorrow?"

"Probably not. It doesn't matter. You are now an officer of the revolutionary government, with the authority and autonomy to fulfill your orders."

"We will take and hold the intersection. No one will get past us."

"But more importantly, excite and recruit. If something happens and you are unable to fulfill your assignment, you need to tell a Senior Commander, as soon as humanly possible. Your assignment is very, very important."

"I understand."

The man stood, and offered his hand. "Good luck, Citizen. Thank you for fighting for the future of my country."

Jake took his hand, "Thank you for fighting for mine."

The man smiled, and left.

Jake looked around the tavern. He noticed a difference in the stares of the other patrons. They were respectful, intimidated - even subordinate. Jake felt like a man, in charge of his purpose and destiny. The look on his face changed as well. He took on the part of the revolutionary commander: hard, strong, impassioned and determined.

He left the tavern, and headed to the right-bank to scout.

The Time of the Heirlooms

1776

Jérémie

Chapter 3

Jérémie D'Uts Bouvillon was a commoner of France. He was a peasant, a farmer and a good Catholic. Jérémie had never traveled further than fifteen miles from the small village of Saint-Recipas, in the province of Orléanais. He knew his fields, which officer of the Throne would advance him his salary, and where he should bring his harvest. He knew where to buy the things he needed for when he had the coin, or where to trade for them when he did not. He knew the town and he knew the inside of his church. That was all he knew.

Jérémie, and his little town, had been left behind. In this, they were not alone. A little over a century ago, a scheming Cardinal had created a way to centralize power around the King. A palace was built, a city in edifice named Versailles, where all the nobles could live with the King himself. They vied for royal favor through trivial tasks, popularity contests, and courtly wit. Soon after, the nobles of Saint-Recipas left their ancestral homes, and headed to the beige Olympus. The peasants quickly became forgotten, and were recorded only as numbers on a balance sheet, to be taken to Versailles by accountants, and then perhaps glanced at, or perhaps not.

Agricultural storage and preservation techniques had improved - indeed, been revolutionized. Blight and disease control measures were being adopted. Crops were introduced that were more appropriate to certain climates of the country. The peasants of Saint-Recipas had no idea this had happened. They were backwards and oppressed, and their lords did not know, and did not care to know, and certainly would not have cared to tell them if they did. The ancient right to create more arable land by cutting down trees, or draining swamps and such, had been abolished. Forests were kept pristine so lords could hunt in them. Peasants were not allowed to hunt. God help the peasant who was seen killing doves eating his newly-planted grain. The lords kept such birds at their châteaux, even if they were close to their peasant's fields. If the birds did not eat all the seed, deer nibbled on the shoots and greens soon after, and were even more prized and protected than the doves.

There were perhaps a few hundred souls working the land around the small town of Saint-Recipas. There was a nice, old church and a poor, emaciated *Abbé* named Father Eliphas. He was growing old, but seemed wise and solicitous of their welfare. There was a host of magnificent châteaux dotting the area that one dared not approach too closely. Mostly the nearby forests were the hunting preserves of nobles, and one dared not approach them too closely either. Although the poor farmers knew who the châteaux belonged to, and who their lords were, they were simply called *les Seigneurs*. *Les Seigneurs* charged them rent if they did not own the land, and taxed them if they did. The land they plowed with oxen, or their own backs, was given to them through ancient and archaic laws of inheritance. Most farmers had a multitude of small plots dotted over miles. They would work one of the little patches, and then take their oxen to the next one, if they had oxen.

They never saw the lords, or nobles, except from a distance, and certainly never spoke to them. Instead, they dealt with overseers, commoners like themselves, but roughly-mannered, and usually from the city. The overseers did not help the farmers, or listen to complaints. They simply collected. If there wasn't enough to collect, they evicted and replaced. One dared not fight them. To fight them meant being arrested by the efficient and competent Royal Police, charged, tried, broken on the wheel, and finally executed. After such a miserable end, one's family was still duly evicted. Vagabonds, either evicted farmers or migrant laborers, seemed to be everywhere. They were a plague on the roads, eating from the fields, and sometimes even stealing livestock. They ended up criminals and beggars in Paris and other cities. If they committed crimes, the cold judicial system thinned their ranks through torture and execution. If they remained law-abiding, the cold Winters still culled the herd. But regardless, come Autumn, their ranks were brought back to full strength by the merciless course of evictions.

That was not the only hobgoblin affecting Jérémie and those like him. There were other men who called themselves farmers - but they farmed men and money, not the land. They were independent tax collectors, called the Farmer-Generals, who made their living collecting for those who claimed the right to receive. Taxes had risen steadily over the last sixty years to a full two-thirds more, mostly to pay the war debts. If the Farmer-Generals did not get what they wanted, they could be equally rapacious - and their hunger was insatiable. If a peasant owned their land, they had to pay a land tax called the *Taille*. The lords were exempt from this tax because they were lords. The *Taillon* tax paid for military expenditures but did not cover the debt incurred by the previous wars. There was a newer tax called the *Vingtième*, which was simply one-twentieth of everything. All of the peasants were legally forced to buy salt, in a tyranny that masqueraded as a tax, by a law called the *Gabelle*. The price for salt was arbitrarily set by the Farmer-Generals. In Orléanais, the price was thirty times higher than it was in Brittany, where salt was collected and the citizens were exempt. The salt was of poor quality, but they had no choice regarding the amount they had to buy or at what price. There were also the *Droits Féodaux*, a long list of petty duties for every possible event or activity in a peasant's life. There was a duty to be paid in order to inherit land, to marry, to use the watermill or even the roads, to be exempt from doing mandatory chores for the local lord, and for a host of other things. The King, who loved his people, had done away with many of these duties, but some still remained. The *Dîme* took one-tenth of everything and gave it to the church. Since the *Abbé* was as hungry as the peasants, Jérémie had no idea where the goods generated by this tax were actually going. On top of everything, the peasant owed his labor to France. At any time, he could be called up in the *corvée,* and forced to work on the roads and bridges, or to repair walls or government buildings. This labor was performed without pay, and one could be called up for service in the middle of the harvest. The peasant also owed his life to the King. He could be forced to join the army through the *levée*. At least in this the peasant was paid, given uniforms, and necessary tools and weapons to ensure some chance of success.

The police controlled every aspect of the harvest. They knew every acre of arable land in the country, and what was being grown upon it. France could barely feed herself - it was a royal imperative to ensure that grain was sown where it could be grown and the harvest went where it was supposed to go. The police ensured that there was no hoarding, and that the price restrictions were obeyed. Jérémie grew wheat, but could not eat his harvest, only sell it at fixed price that he received in advance. He could not afford to buy back and eat what he grew, so he usually bought simpler fair for his family or ate his own small harvests of vegetables, barley, and rye. The provisioning of France - especially Paris - was extremely organized, but what the country really needed was less mouths or more land, and she had lost nearly all her colonies in the star-crossed war of 1754.

It would have also helped if the mouths of Paris were not so discerning. From the lowliest craftsmen to the richest noble, Paris ate nothing but high-quality white bread. Sometimes there were riots in Paris when the flour had to be made of rye - not when there wasn't enough bread.

Besides the authority of nobles, police and taxmen, there was the parish council, composed of Jérémie's neighbors, and of course Father Eliphas, the *Abbé*. Any knowledge of the world was limited to the King's Messages and the news that Father Eliphas would deliver after mass.

Two years ago, a new king had ascended to the throne. What Jérémie wasn't told was that the new king inherited a country that was nearly bankrupt, and the central government was at its wit's end as to how to solve the problem. Jérémie knew the Winters were long and the harvests were poor. He did not know they were poor nearly everywhere in the country, and there had been widespread riots - so far ranging that the troubles were called the Flour War. He knew from Father Eliphas that the King had dismissed two head ministers in two years. He did not know that they were both forced from office by the nobles, because they attempted to tax them and revoke their privileges on behalf of the King. He had heard the name of Malesherbes, who was a minister of France. He did not know that Malesherbes was the first to suggest the calling of the Estates General to break the deadlock, or even what the Estates General entailed.

Jérémie was incredibly strong of body and will. He could eat little, work all day and still maintain his strength. He did not tend to fat, as others did who had this ability. He was the last of his family, the rest dying of disease, perhaps born of hardship, or poor diet. He inherited their fields, a host of small patches of land. One of them was near some chestnut trees. Chestnuts were considered beneath human consumption, but a tree could still feed a starving family through a harsh Winter if the need arose. He also had a small two-story house made of stone a half-mile outside the village. He slept downstairs. The flood-proof second story was for the most important things he owned: baskets filled with seed for the next planting.

He married a young woman named Sitis. She was small and dark and beautiful. He never would have been able to marry her, except her father died, and her fortunes had suddenly changed.

Jérémie loved her more than anything in life. Every day with her was a new wonder. Jérémie and Sitis loved their four children together, as one heart. The three eldest were his daughters Jemima, Ketsia and Kéren. Ketsia and Kéren were like their mother, but somehow Jemima was fair as a Summer morning. With her blonde hair and blue eyes, she looked like the Queen - so much so that a noblewoman once stopped her coach and gave her a green silk ribbon for her hair. She was inordinately proud of it, but let her sisters wear it more than she did. His youngest was his only son, named Hervé, and he was the spitting image of his father. Life was difficult, but Jérémie paid such things no mind. There was no work too strenuous, no task too difficult, no meal too small. He was thankful to be alive, and he loved his life. His was a heart soothed through nothing more than the sound of the wind through the trees.

Taxes were high, however, and harvests continued to be poor. Strangely, the Winters were always bitterly cold these days, and lasted far longer than they should have. Jérémie, through no fault of his own, found himself in a position where he had enough seed to plant his fields in the Spring, but no coin, and nothing else left to eat. They thought they would still have the chestnuts.

But that Winter, vagabonds were a locust plague. Jérémie fought them everywhere he could. He was strong and agile and could give them a thrashing regardless of their number, even if they picked up sticks and rocks. The whole village fought them, as best they could according to ability and courage. It was a war for survival: whether they won or not, only the chestnuts really mattered. Soon they were all gone, except for those on the highest branches.

Lack of food brought starvation. Starvation, even if not fatal, could bring sickness and disease. Jérémie remembered why he was the last of his family, and the thought brought great consternation to him.

One day after mass, Jérémie went to the parish council and requested guidance and help. There were only two choices before him, he explained. The first was to turn his remaining seed grain into bread, and have no future harvest. The second choice was to starve, plant the seeds, and hope they all somehow survived. The parish council was empathetic: Saint-Recipas suffered communally under the same conditions. The Royal Police also knew of their situation; being the oversight agency in charge of the harvest. Other agents of the Throne and Altar had been alerted to the dire situation of the village as well, and help was hopefully on the way. The council had no idea what to expect. Things were difficult everywhere.

Unsatisfied, Jérémie went to see the *Abbé*, Father Eliphas. The *Abbé* had a strange habit. He would leave a visitor in the doorway, go fetch an apple, then return to usher the visitor inside his quarters. While he talked, he would take a bite of apple, then hand it to his company. After they took a bite, he would beckon for it back. He would take another bite, then hand it over to his guest once again. Once the apple was completely eaten, the meeting was ended.

Jérémie took a bite of apple, and handed it back. He explained to the *Abbé* that he needed God's intervention. Surely God did not want this for his family.

"It is not for you to say what God wants, Jérémie," Father Eliphas gently replied.

Jérémie requested clarification.

The *Abbé* obliged, "There are two things one must keep in mind. The first is the nature of man. The greatest gift the Lord bestowed upon us was free will. But free will allows us to create suffering for our brothers. Truthfully, even when there is enough to eat, we still somehow manage to torment ourselves. Secondly, we know God allows the devil to exist, therefore temptation and evil are part of our lives. One is left with only one conclusion: our worldly happiness is not important. God desires us to repent our sins, to return to him in love, and has designed a world to help us do this. God uses suffering to force us to confront our own selfishness, to beg his help in our quest for personal redemption. Suffering is a tool to find Christ, and he endured suffering himself, as a man, to achieve our redemption. If even our God died in terrible agony, by design of the Father, can we ask for an end to such a thing? Suffering is a gift from God."

"Is God then evil, to want us to suffer?"

The *Abbé* smiled, "Every impulse for good in us comes from God. Sometimes we understand the greater purpose behind our pain, sometimes we do not. It does not matter. Our quest, only and always, lies within ourselves. With our will and God's will in tandem, we enter grace."

"Why would God make me so happy, only to murder my family from want of food?"

"When a baby is hungry, he cries to beckon. His mother hears and comes. But an infant has lived only a short time. And the time it takes for the mother to hear the baby cry, until she places her teat in his mouth, is significant, at least to the babe. Does the babe then curse the mother? When the babe lays in its own *merde*, does he curse his father for not changing his rags in that very instant? Such a thing would only be said in jest, for we are babes for just short years, and we easily forget the petty trials of our infancy, do we not?"

"Yes, *Abbé*."

"We are on this earth but an eyeblink. Nothing here belongs to us, only to God. You will suffer, and you will die. Your only hope is to pray for the Lord's help in finding peace, the simple joy that emanates from serenity. Serenity only comes from grace – the meaning of Christ and his suffering."

This was not helping. "That is my purpose then?"

"Your purpose is to repent. Suffering is a gift to aid you in your purpose. Death is not a tragedy, it too is a gift. It frees us to be with our Creator for eternity. In heaven, you will forget the pain of your infancy here on earth. Give your suffering to God, understand that death is a release, know your true nature as a heavenly soul - but enjoy and appreciate the majesty of God's creation, while on this short trip to the material world."

"But can you help me, Father?"

The *Abbé* was quiet for a moment, then spoke softly and intensely, "Yes. I can tell you what to do. It is a simple task to explain, but one that is difficult to accomplish."

Jérémie found himself becoming excited. There was a chance, a small one, that the *Abbé* was about to tell him something that could actually be helpful. Perhaps he knew the location of hidden wild crops, or buried seed - a chestnut tree just inside a royal preserve that no one dared to harvest.

Something. Anything.

The *Abbé* finally spoke, "You must doubt your every intention with absolute humility, as if you are tempted in every thought by the devil himself. Do not have faith in anything of this earth, especially man and our own ideas. Wish for nothing but the grace of the Cross. Learn from your suffering, and give your pain to God. Pray for Him to help you change, for you cannot change your own nature without His help."

For Jérémie, the room became small. He looked at the *Abbé*, and saw nothing but an old man. He finished the apple and left.

Jérémie decided, with his wife, to survive on charity and chestnuts, and keep the grain for Spring. They prayed and prayed and prayed.

To everyone's astonishment, their prayers were answered. From both the King and the Church came cart after cart loaded with rye flour. Unloaded in the village center, all was doled out in a fair and organized manner by the Royal Police. There were no dry eyes. Everyone cheered their King and God until their throats were hoarse. Jérémie managed to walk out of eyesight of his neighbors before he collapsed to his knees. He burst into sobs, "Lord God, Heavenly King, Almighty God and Father, I pledge myself to you. Use me in any way you wish, Lord. I am yours. Your will be done, forever and ever."

Jérémie hurried back with his family's share of the charity. His wife and children were weak with hunger, so he baked their bread himself. He ate none of it. Rather, he put them to sleep with full stomachs, then went out to look for chestnuts. He found a few - enough for his meager needs.

Over the next few days, he watched the blood return to his family's cheeks. Tears of gratitude would streak his face on his lonely walks foraging for chestnuts. He would only see Father Eliphas, who had turned down the rye as well, giving his share to the community in favor of his apple tree, and the few remaining chestnuts he shared with Jérémie.

One Monday, he did not see Father Eliphas. On Tuesday, a panting youth, Onfroi Dessein, delivered a note from Father Eliphas, and then ran off again without another word. Jérémie could not read, and decided that, in his straights, the message contained nothing that could not wait a few more days. He was surprised that the *Abbé* didn't know he couldn't read. To Jérémie, it implied there were other things Father Eliphas did not know. The thought worried him.

On Wednesday, he returned home from his scrounging, opened his front door, and saw three of his children dead on the floor. The fourth was dead as well, only on her knees as Sitis garroted her from behind with the green silk ribbon. Sitis was shaking, as if having a seizure. Her eyes were alive and burning, orange and contorted. Ominous redness and swelling were upon her joints. She looked up, saw Jérémie, and began to speak in an earnest tone, as if she had an important message to convey to him. Despite her effort, only disjointed words and gibberish escaped her lips.

Jérémie stumbled out of his home, his mind unhinged, and ran to the village. He saw no living soul on his way to the church. He burst into Father Eliphas's house, only to find it empty. He ran into the seemingly-deserted village shouting his name.

Finally, a girl, Edmée Marquer, ran out and beckoned him. He went inside her home, and saw the Father tending to the Marquer family. All of them had the seizures and the red, swollen limbs. Jérémie, terrified, ran from the house as fast as he could. Father Eliphas followed after him. He could not keep up, but shouted so Jérémie could hear, "It is Saint Anthony's Fire, a disease from the rye. It changes the mind, akin to drunkenness, only far worse. The limbs enflame and become gangrenous. It is on the rye, Jérémie! The rye!"

Jérémie ran, but there was nowhere to go. He finally went home, having convinced himself that this was all a dream - none of it could have happened, it was simply too horrible to be a part of life.

When he arrived home, he found his four children dead. Sitis had hanged herself, surrounded by the family rosaries and other Christian artifacts to ward against evil. Jérémie was destroyed in that moment. It is not often that mountains were leveled, but they were indeed and always have been.

There was no cure for Saint Anthony's Fire. It reared its head from time to time throughout history, killing high and low. Nearly all of those affected perished from gangrene while in the throes of full-blown hallucinations. Even the ones who survived usually did so after losing limbs. It was a frightening and terrible disease that was not fully understood. Extreme waking nightmares leading to terrible acts were rare, but certainly occurred.

The *Abbé* and Jérémie's surviving neighbors tried to console him, but to no avail. A change had come over Jérémie, a darkness. Jérémie was always considered to be a handsome man, but now his pale complexion, dark hair and black eyes did not lend themselves to the change. He assumed the countenance of a walking corpse. He was a ghost, a dead man who walked and spoke. Wherever he went, he scared children and adults looked away. But no one blamed him. In the gut-wrenching pain of the present, it is hard to accept an inscrutable plan, however divine in origin.

One day, Jérémie disappeared from Saint-Recipas, and was never seen again. His former neighbors did not know it, but Jérémie never again used his real name, nor did he ever say, from that moment, where he was from, or who he had once loved - whether they were of heaven, or of earth.

Several times, the broken man tried to throw himself from high places to end his life. He was stopped at every attempt, as if by an invisible hand. He drifted further away, down the Loire like human flotsam - a vagabond drifter, forgotten, lost and broken. He had become what he had once despised and fought against.

The river finally brought Jérémie to the city of Tours. He crept in at night like a ghoul, and found himself in the ancient ruins of the gigantic Romanesque basilica of Saint Martin. He steeled himself, and climbed to the very top of what was called the Charlemagne tower, though the tower was much, much older than even the ancient king himself. He stood at the edge, at least fifty feet from the rubble on the ground. But, again, he could not force himself past the edge. He sat down, right where he stood, and buried his head into his hands.

After a long while, he looked out over the fair, storied city. From his lofty perch he could see it all: the spires of its churches, the bridges over the Loire, the handsome trees and buildings on its banks. There were huge Lebanese cedars by the river, like those mentioned in the Bible, planted and nursed by monks long ago.

Jérémie sighed and spoke to God, quietly and without rancor, "I do not understand. Why is my life so important that you would have me keep it? It is you who convinced me it is not. What destiny do you have for me that is so important that I must bear this pain?" There was no answer from God, only the sounds of the waking city, and the breathtaking view.

Jérémie stayed in Tours. Somehow, he knew it was in his purpose to be there.

1832

Jake

Chapter 4

"Jake!" said a distant voice, barely carrying over the din of hundreds of rowdy Parisians. The currents of the human flood pushed Jake east on the narrow Rue Saint-Honoré, shadowed by modern townhomes of stone, and ancient medieval buildings of wood and plaster. Jake heard his voice screamed again, now from a different direction. Looking around, he saw no friendly or familiar faces. Jokers in the crowd were echoing the call in annoying tones. Jake had no idea where anyone was, and felt lost and alone in the tight, slow-moving crowd.

The good people of Paris had stayed locked in their homes. Amongst those who followed Lamarque's funeral cortege were revolutionaries, a few who loved and respected the man too much to stay home, and the vile king rat referred to as *the mob*, reeking of cheap wine and sweat. In the past, they were called *Sans-Culotte* because they wore work trousers instead of leggings. Sometimes they were the *Poissard*, because they spoke the language of the fishmonger; a grotesque, sing-song slang using contemptuous rhymes. Amongst them sauntered a good share of women who were, if anything, even more foul and intimidating than the men. They were certainly louder, their sneered leers of missing teeth vomiting profane *Poissard* rhymes, ready threats, and insults.

Jake decided the Poissard needed to learn some respect before it ate his young troop for a late *déjeuner*. Jake, despite being an American, had never used a gun in his life. Now was to be the first time. He took out his pistol and fired once into the air. The sound was impossibly loud, leagues stronger than what

Jake imagined a sound could achieve. His ears rang, the inside of his head hurt. His hands, arms, and face were covered with tiny bits of still-burning powder, and there was a pall of choking black smoke.

When Jake's mind landed back in his body, he noticed the blast had cleared a good space around him and quieted most of the nearby voices into scared, wide eyes. A few older men, walking past to his left, were yelling some sort of chastisement, but Jake still couldn't hear anything. He screamed into the crowd, "Student Soldiers! Student Soldiers to me!"

His voice sounded muted to his own ears, but soon Jake saw his fellow students converge on him. Thirty-two students had left Louis-le-Grand that morning in double-file line, looking to all the world as if they were going on a rare escorted outing. If all thirty-two weren't here now, there seemed to be enough. He breathed a sigh of relief when Pascal, bathed in sweat, moved toward him carrying a fifteen-foot pole. Pascal had been sent to fetch the flag staff. He had found one, and must have come back at a run. "Is this sufficient?" he gasped between breaths.

"Yes, hold it steady." Jake said as he tied a Louis-le-Grand pennant to the staff, "Hold it high. Stick close to me."

Franck walked up with a smile on his face. "Utter madness this."

Jake shook his head, "I'm glad someone's enjoying themselves." Jake looked around, and saw the rest of his command struggling through the crowd. Three of the smaller boys were being jostled a bit too enthusiastically near the rear. Jake had enough sense to look around for soldiers this time, then lit off another round just over the heads of the tallest bully. Jake was disappointed to see his fellow students start the most from the sound. But the rowdy men of the mob were pacified, and stared stupidly at him.

"Do you thwart the revolution?" Jake screamed. "Let them through!"

They did, and the students made their way to Jake, who found himself staring into the scared faces of his command, "All right. Buck up, now. We have to force our way to the carriage now. Realize that we are the power behind the mob. We are the leaders of the revolution. This energy, this chaos, serves us, and our cause." At that moment Jake saw a dark, balding man in his thirties wearing a blue cockade. "Hey! You!" The man didn't look up, but just quickened his pace. "Grab him." Jake said to his command, and they did. The man looked frightened and pulled up sharply, but then saw their cockades and visibly relaxed. "Find out what language he speaks, make sure he knows he's one of us now. He needs a proper cockade. Who has the extras?"

Franck stepped forward, "Raymond, take the bag from me. Those who speak Italian, German, or Polish, don't wait for orders. Start rounding up the blue cockades."

Good, good, thought Jake. The more people helping him move the herd of cats through the sandstorm, the better.

A young, well-dressed man, wearing a green and white cockade, made his way against the direction of the mob and came toward Jake, "Hey, you there," he shouted.

"Yes, Commander."

"Did you hear the gunfire?"

"I did, Citizen. Two shots."

"Do you know who is responsible?"

"I have no idea, Commander."

"*Dis tout!* Very well. Keep a sharp eye out. If it's one of us, tell them to stop straightaway. We don't want anything to escalate until it suits us, yes?"

"Yes, Citizen."

Jake watched the Senior Commander move upstream, further into the crowd. Franck smiled at him, "Crafty bastard."

"Let's keep moving. How close are we anyway? I can't see a thing."

Through the crowd, Jake caught sight of a stumbling drunk urinating against the side of a windowless stone building. The passing mob cheered, booed and joked. Suddenly he was attacked by two men wearing blue cockades and savagely beaten. A few in the passing crowd tried to intervene, but then more blue cockades piled in. Jake was bewildered, but then realized the wall belonged to the small-but-soaring dome of Our Mother of the Assumption - and the Polish-Catholic mission. They were nearly at Rue Cambon, a few blocks from Place Vendôme at best. The carriage bearing the body of Lamarque might already be inside the square. Perhaps some poor revolutionary screamed the signal, and had been arrested, all because the students responsible for hijacking the cart were nowhere to be seen.

First things first.

"Franck, where is Gutek?"

Franck shouted, "Gutek! Gutek!" and voices all around repeated the call, some of them belonging to nearby drunks. Gutek, née August Jeziorkowski, stepped forward; a serious, tow-haired, fellow student from a noble Polish family, "I'm here, Jake."

Jake pointed toward the fracas, "Tell your countrymen they have better things to do, and we have cockades for them. Then catch up quickly."

"That is feasible." Gutek nodded, and went his way.

Jake turned to the rest. "With me, as fast as you can."

Jake moved forward. He thought about taking out his pistol and brandishing it to impress the crowd, but thought better of it. Instead, he took out his bayonet, but without removing the blade from its scabbard. As he patted shoulders with it, the long, thin knife encased in leather seemed to do the trick, "Make way! Make way for the soldiers of the Republic. We are on the Nation's business for the people of France!"

Cheers went up, and suddenly the way was clear. The Poissards slapped them on the back as they passed. As the crowd parted, the street opened up into a large cobblestone courtyard fronting the church where it met Rue Cambon. Jake saw at least fifty Parisian National Guard in their blue and red tunics. It stood to reason, Jake thought grimly, that at the exact moment he announced himself as a rebel, and his men moved as one, that he would see the King's men out in force. Jake kept moving, but his eyes stayed on the soldiers. Luckily, they didn't seem too interested in the passing river of humanity. The noise was such that the brutal fight just around the corner hadn't reached their ears. Soon Jake passed the courtyard, and the soldiers disappeared from view. Jake heard Franck, and others, taking up the cry to make way again. Looking around, he noticed the doors to every business and home were shut to the mob, as if the buildings themselves were hiding from the tide. A horrible female voice sing-songed over the din, in harsh *Poissard* rhyme:

> *"King's guards are dumb,*
> *His soldiers play,*
> *While the rebel students,*
> *Find their way."*

Laughter and cheers rang out. Jake heard Franck behind him, "*Sang du Christ*! With friends like these, who needs enemies?"

Jake didn't reply, but hurried forward. The next intersection was the wide avenue of Rue de Castiglione, which turned into Place Vendôme when one turned left. They completed the turn - and moved from a stream to a lake. The funeral cortege was before him, surrounded by thousands. The Place Vendôme was a cobblestone rectangle of perhaps a hundred yards by one-hundred-fifty yards, pierced by streets to the north and south, and ringed by handsome stone hôtels. A gigantic bronze obelisk commemorating Napoleon's victory at Austerlitz squatted in the center. The huge obelisk, too tall and thick for the square by far, was nearly obscene in its suggestive gigantism and detracted from an otherwise elegant address. Regardless, the presence of the obelisk was why the cortege had diverted to Place Vendôme. Lamarque had served under Napoleon, and the moments under the ponderous obelisk honored his achievements. The hôtels surrounding it were urban châteaux - palaces and ministry buildings of Paris limestone, all appropriately imposing, all adding to the spectacle. The crowd filled the entire space between them like a liquid.

Jake kept moving through the crowd, tapping people on the shoulder with his bayonet, until he abruptly came face-to-face with a stone-faced soldier in blue and realized he had reached the front of the crowd. Soldiers of the regular army, not the Paris guard, formed a human barricade between the masses and the carriage in the shape of a square. The soldiers were immaculate, each of them wearing a black sash. They were expressionless and uniform - both in garb and statue-like attention.

Jake's fate, and those of his fellow students, would rest on their reaction when they rushed the carriage. Considering Lamarque's politics, there was a chance the soldiers were of Republican sentiment.

One could only hope.

The carriage itself, properly called a catafalque, was grand indeed. It was black with silver trim, and adorned with sashes of red, white, and blue. Instead of a cabin behind the driver's bench, there was a proper funeral bier where the white and gold coffin rested in display, surrounded by white roses and calla lilies. Six black horses of uniform height pulled the carriage. All sported ostrich plumes from their pewter and black leather tack.

Jake saw a knot of older men and uniformed officers by the obelisk, taking turns to speak. Their words, uttered perpendicular to Jake, were drowned out by the unruly crowd.

One of the officers blew a whistle, and the soldiers moved in unison. Heels snapped together. Muskets slapped into hands, then were shouldered. A second whistle was heard, and the horses pulled the carriage forward. It turned, and moved toward Jake in unison with the men. Jake cursed, and realized that they were now headed back to the intersection of Rue Saint Honoré. Jake turned in order to proceed the cortege. Franck, confused, walked backwards staring at him, as did most of his men.

Soon they reached Castiglione. The crowd had no idea what to do; some went east, some west. Jake realized he had to make a choice before any of them knew what direction the carriage was actually turning. Jake knew the cortege, at some point, would head south. But right here, at this street, it could turn either way. If they chose the wrong direction, they could be wildly out of position and miss the signal.

Then Jake heard a chorus of screams: "Down with Louis-Philippe, long live the Republic!" shouted once, then twice – then three times. It was a dozen voices at least, raised in unison, to shout the same slogan at the same time. It was, unmistakably, the signal of *The Society*.

Franck turned, "Jake?"

Jake nodded *yes,* then shouted at the top of his lungs, "With me!" and then spun, turned, and sprinted past the soldier.

He found himself looking up at six huge horses. The front two neighed, and one reared up on two legs. Jake lunged to the right to get out of their way. With a shock of impact to his shoulders and neck, he hit the legs of fellow student Pierre d'Évreux, also running at top speed for the carriage. After realizing he was prone on the dirty stones of the square, Jake dazedly raised himself to a sit. Pierre, on the ground as well, looked at him uncomprehendingly.

Jake was lifted to his feet by two pairs of arms. He could not help but to move in the direction of the carriage, and found himself climbing up onto the driver's bench. *Where is the driver?* was a dim thought running through his head as he was squished next to Zacharie, squashed in his turn against five other students sitting on the same bench. He turned at the sound of voices, and saw the entire bier platform was packed with students and men from the crowd. An incredible din nearly drowned out their excited voices. The crowd was surging forward, all of them screaming at once at the sudden action.

Everyone nearby seemed to be shouting at him, shouting his name, asking what to do. *Who has the reins?* He did, they were resting on the pewter bar in front of him. He pulled them to the left, and absolutely nothing happened. He pulled harder, his hands going over his left shoulder. Nothing happened. He stood up, and screamed as loud as he could, "People of Paris! To the Bastille! To the Bastille!"

Another deafening roar went up from the crowd. With a jolt, the carriage began to move, and Jake was sent hard into his seat, his neck snapping the back of his head into the top of the bier platform. He leaned forward and held his head. It hurt terribly, as only a sharp blow on the skull can hurt. Jake heard a voice.

"Are you well? Jake, are you alright?"

It was Zacharie. Jake sat up, and nodded at him. He looked around, and saw men from the crowd were now riding postilion on all six horses. Others in the crowd were pulling them by their harness. Men and women were everywhere around them, jumping, falling, gesticulating and screaming. The crowd was moving up and down so violently that it truly resembled a rowdy, wavy sea. Jake, awestruck, knew he would never forget the sight. He couldn't see any soldiers. Either they had been swallowed by the crowd, or had quickly vacated. Jake hoped it was the latter. If he was an officer of the funeral escort, he would have prepared for such a moment as this, considering how chaotic the city had been for the past few days.

Suddenly, ten-thousand lips rose in song:

"Arise, children of the Fatherland,
The day of glory has arrived!
Against us tyranny's
Bloody banner is raised,
Do you hear, in the countryside,
The roar of those ferocious soldiers?
They're coming right into your arms
To cut the throats of your sons, your women!
To arms, citizens,
Form your battalions,
Let's march, let's march!

Let the blood of those of impure race
Soak our fields!"

It was the *Marseillaise*, the old battle hymn of the True Revolution. Jake had imagined this moment, leading the insurrection, as his soldiers sang this very song. He was nearly in shock, all pain forgotten, as he realized it was actually happening.

Suddenly a hand grabbed him from below and shook him violently. Jake looked down and saw Franck, laughing, standing on the driver's running board, "Jake, this is brilliant!"

"Are we going the right direction?"

"Yes! Yes! And I think the crowd is going to propel us forward the entire way!"

"Do you want to sit?"

"Is there room?"

"We'll make room!" Jake grabbed Franck and pulled him onto the bench, and into the laps of everyone seated. Franck laughed as he righted himself, and then everyone on the bench was squished tight indeed.

The narrow Rue Saint-Honoré curved to the south, and joined Rue de Rivoli. Rue de Rivoli turned into Rue Saint-Antoine. Rue Saint-Antoine flowed directly into the Place de la Bastille. They were three miles away at the outside, and they could be there in less than two hours. Anything could happen. It was a hot day. Perhaps the crowd would lose energy and thin. Perhaps headaches from too much wine would pound drunken temples. Perhaps the soldiers would disperse the crowd. But maybe, just maybe, this revolution would overthrow the King, and re-establish the rights of man.

In any case, they had fulfilled the first part of their orders. And, gloriously, it seemed as if they were the only rebel leaders in Paris - and the newborn revolution of 1832 obeyed their every command. Jake laughed in abandon and joined in the song.

***

The Place de la Bastille was a paved lake, fed by no less than ten roads that poured traffic into the square. It was expansive, several times as large as the Place Vendôme. At one point, it held an infamous keep, the Bastille, that was stormed in the early days of the Revolution and subsequently demolished to the last stone. Napoleon, wishing to channel revolutionary ardor to his purpose, decided to make a monument to his own prowess where the castle once stood. But as his decision neared its apex, the treasury approached its nadir, and bankruptcy forced his hand. No real monument was ever built. A huge plaster elephant stood where a similar-looking, but far more magnificent, future bronze was to be installed. Over the decades, the pachyderm discolored to a gangrenous black from ash, filth and mold, and its hollow mass became cancerous with rat nests. Refuse and more rat nests surrounded it. It smelled of garbage and urine, when not of defecation, and continuously buzzed with flies. Its head had decayed, its tusks had fallen off, and it was unrecognizable as one of God's creatures. Now it was just an evil-looking, formless mass - like some sort of demonic behemoth haunting a graveyard.

Place de la Bastille was as packed as the Place Vendôme had been, maybe more, and Jake was at the very center of it all. From his perch on the funeral catafalque, he saw an older man striding toward him - thin as a rail, wearing a gold and green cockade and surrounded by burly, armed men. Jake stood.

"Citizen Loring?" he asked, upon reaching Jake.

"Yes, General."

"The first part of your assignment is complete. Ready for the second."

"Yes, General."

The General gave Jake no time to react. He and his men pulled themselves up to the bench and bier of the carriage. Jake and the other students jumped from it as if the carriage were aflame, and found themselves together on the north side of it.

Jake turned to them, "We've been relieved."

"Yes. Evidently so," Franck smirked.

Jake gave him a look, and continued, "Rue de Charenton meets Place de la Bastille. Let us move slowly in that direction." No one moved. Jake rolled his eyes, "Follow me."

Jake put on his revolutionary face, and moved through the crowd. The crowd, transfixed on the drama happening on the catafalque carriage, could see him and gave way. He pushed through slowly but surely, sheathed bayonet in hand.

The General's voice boomed from the top of the carriage in a feral, furious tenor, "Citizens! We are here to celebrate a man who fought for France against the foreign and domestic enemies of the revolution. He fought in the Pyrenees against rebellious Monarchists. He led our armies against the Vendée when they rose up yet again in 1815. This hero fought side-by-side with Napoleon in Spain, and in the German states. But there is something you may not know. He used his fortunes to transform his lands with cutting-edge machines and modern agricultural techniques. He joined the government, and was an outspoken critic of oppression, and the monarchy itself. He was a friend of the common people, and a defender of liberty. That is why you are here. It is why we are all here! Long live the Revolution! Long live the Republic! Down with the King!"

It was uncloaked sedition. Jake could see the crowd getting more and more agitated. There was nothing subtle about it. Fists bunched at sides, bodies shifted back and forth on the toes of feet. People now began to smile when they saw Jake's cockade. Some nodded, or wished him luck. Jake only moved faster, his every thought regarding what was about to happen next.

The General continued, but his words were becoming difficult to hear over the rising rumble of the crowd. "We find the funeral cortege of Lamarque stopped in the Place de la Bastille, under the former shadow of the monarchist prison. Do you not remember that shameful pile of bricks was pulled down by the people of Paris and Saint-Antoine? Do you not remember the time when the King feared his people, and not the other way around?"

Suddenly, a different kind of rumble, an exclamation of surprise and recognition, went through the crowd. Jake turned to see what was going on. He quickly observed that another man had ascended the carriage. He was equally as old as the General, perhaps older, but still muscled and thick. He had a florid red face, and a red wig to match. Some in the crowd murmured in recognition, but Jake couldn't hear what they were saying.

"Franck, who is that?"

"I don't know. Where's his cockade? Is he even with us?"

"I'm not sure."

And then the florid man spoke, and his voice carried louder and further than that of the General. Jake heard him clear as a pealing bell, "Do you know who I am, Citizens? Do you know my name?" He was answered only by furious whispers. He spoke again, "I am Citizen Gilbert du Motier. But I am more well-known by an old title. I am also called the Marquis de Lafayette."

Jake's jaw dropped in astonishment, "He fought side-by-side with George Washington."

Franck shook his head in wonderment, "He wrote the *Declaration of the Rights of Man and the Citizen* with Thomas Jefferson. His revolutionary credentials exceed those of anyone present, even Lamarque."

Indeed, there was no larger hero of France now living. Monarchists thought he had betrayed their class, some others disagreed with him, or disliked his politics, but all knew him as a brave, capable man driven solely by his values and ideology. Jake, like everyone around him, was thunderstruck into silence.

But not Franck, who nearly giggled, "He's going to proclaim a provisional government right now. This is it. France is about to catch fire. The Revolution begins with his next words."

Then Lafayette spoke, "Go home, Frenchmen. Let Lamarque rest in peace. The very word revolution has changed because of what we have done. It used to mean a slow righting to a natural order, as a planet is observed to move in regular pattern. But no more. Because of us, the essence of the word has changed forever. Now revolution denotes violent, rapid change. It is an overthrow of order. It is chaos and blood. It is a beast that eats itself, until it is put down like a rabid dog."

Jake found himself locking eyes with Franck. Without speaking, both of them turned to observe their compatriots. It was the same look on all faces; a pensive searching of conscience. Franck believed Lafayette had the power to light the fire. Jake now realized he could also put it out.

Lafayette spoke again, "Yes, we have a king. I threw the tricolor around his shoulders myself. But we also have a constitution. We have a way to move forward without gunfire or guillotine. We have order, representation and internal peace. At least until the death of Lamarque, we had peace. But I ask you, did Lamarque lead a rebellion against the Throne? Or did he seek election to office? He was an official, my friends, working from within for change and progress. To honor him, let us have a true revolution, as the word was previously defined. Let us continue a slow righting to a natural order. Let France glide as a celestial body, to elegantly and gracefully slip into position. Let us not spill the blood of France unless we must! Have we not killed enough of our brothers? French bones are buried from Moscow to Gibraltar; from India to Guyana. We have burned our own cities, and butchered our own sons. How many of you have seen war? How many of you have seen the horror of civil war? And how many of you now work to advance our nation in a better way, one that preserves life and liberty? Would you trade our slow, but inexorable, progress for a revolution that will claim the lives of your neighbors? Would you desert your civility, and your hope, and exchange it for the blood of France? I say no! No, my brothers! Not this day! Not this day!"

Lafayette turned to speak in another direction. Out of respect, the crowd around Jake only softly whispered. Even the revolutionary general, who stood with him on the carriage, dared not interrupt such a man.

Franck shook his head, "Amazing. He must be seventy-five years-old."

"He comes from a different era," Jake replied.

"We'll never see his like again, will we?"

"No, I don't think so." Lafayette was living proof of why the word *noble* used to mean someone of high moral principles.

Just then, a roar went up from the crowd. This time, it truly was a roar - animal, savage and bloodthirsty. Jake looked up to see an army of fists raised in the air. Beyond them was a tall, pale ghost of a man on horseback, carrying a huge, fifteen-foot-long flag on a twenty-foot pole. It was a red flag, bordered in black, with the words *Liberty or Death* stitched upon it. The sound of the crowd buffeted Jake. The noise was a battle scream, echoed by the buildings, reverberating in every direction.

When Lafayette was Jake's age, he was one year away from being a Major General in the Continental army. Now he spoke of slow change and evolution. There are tasks for water, and there are tasks for fire. There was a time for Lafayette's soothing words, and a time for the red and black flag that presaged death and battle.

Jake realized there was no more time for intellectual hand-wringing, argument, introspection or self-examination. He was on one side, and someone else was on the other. This was his time, this was his Revolution. He turned to his men, and shouted with a ferocity he did not know he possessed, "That's the signal! Move out!"

Some looked scared, others looked unconvinced, but nearly all were dragged in Jake's direction, as if the force of his voice had chained them all together. Jake saw other columns of cockaded men as they also forced their way toward Rue de Charenton.

Gunfire rang out up ahead. Shouts and screams followed, more gunfire, then more shouts. The difference between civilian and combatant became more apparent. The crowd streamed away from the intersection - Jake and his fellow revolutionaries moved toward it.

Jake reached Charenton. Now half the people were wearing cockades; every combination of red, white, blue, green and gold abounded. There were students from other schools, local youths, workers, toughs and refugees. Off to the side, Jake saw a knot of roughed-up, unarmed Paris National Guard in torn uniforms, bent over one of their comrades laid upon the ground. He was perhaps thirty, a handsome, dark-haired man with a mustache. His tunic was open, exposing a white shirt hopelessly soaked in blood. The man looked more irritated than anything else, although the expressions on his fellow soldiers' faces were far direr.

The panorama was wholly surreal.

In Jake's thoughts and fantasies, soldiers were always faceless animated statues, or lifelike mannequins. They didn't show emotion, they weren't unique, they didn't look irritated when they were shot.

And then they were past. He heard a fellow student, Cyril, laugh gaily at the sight of the dying soldier, then cheers and jeers from others. Jake found it shocking that they had such a reaction. Jake could have turned around and said something, but he needed a few seconds to gather himself.

They walked quickly, still surrounded by quite a crowd, although the rebel columns had moved in several directions after entering Rue de Charenton. Some of the store and tavern owners had their doors cracked to sell mugs of watered-down wine to thirsty passers-by. Jake turned, walked backwards, and counted his troop. There were exactly twenty students. He didn't know whether he'd lost the rest to cowardice, ideology or geography, but he'd misplaced over a third of his command. But there were easily thirty of the recruited refugees. To his best estimate, Jake commanded over fifty men.

The memorized address of *The Society's* waiting supply carts was less than a thousand feet away and closing. Within minutes, they would be armed, and therefore traitors and rebels according to any legal standard. The Throne would have to use force to dislodge them from the streets of Paris. Tens of thousands of troops might be arrayed against them. Even if Jake survived, he still might be maimed or captured. There were few crimes as serious as armed sedition. The punishment was usually death.

Jake only felt pressured and anxious. Somehow all of this didn't seem as exciting as it once did.

1778

Xavier

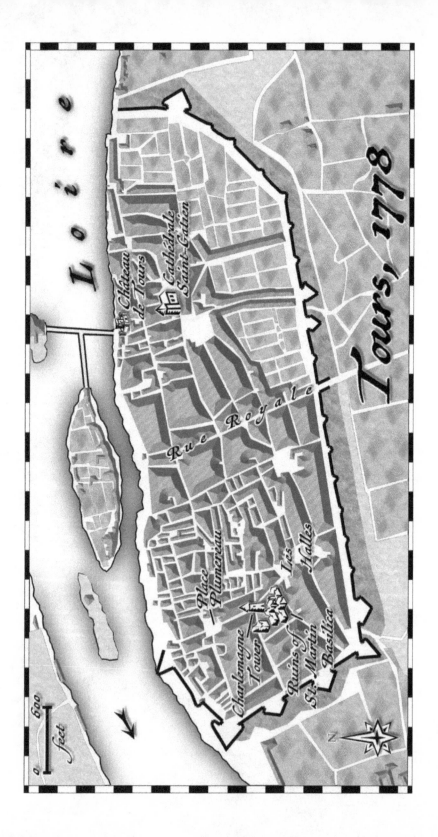

Tours, 1778

Loire

Château de Tours

Cathédrale Saint-Gatien

Rue Royale

Place Plumereau

Charlemagne Tower

Iles

Halles

Ruins of St. Martin Basilica

N

0   600
Feet

Chapter 5

Xavier opened his eyes. As his senses slowly returned, his first thought was that he was dying of thirst - right before every part of his body began to hurt. A sharp pain went through his head like an icepick. He thought he screamed, but only a low moan escaped his lips. After the pain subsided, he opened his eyes again. He was looking up at a ceiling of Gothic arches made of white Tuffeau limestone, which meant he was somewhere in the Loire valley. He was warm - uncomfortably hot, actually. He was covered in blankets. He couldn't move a muscle. He remembered absolutely nothing.

What on earth happened to me?

Xavier searched his memory. An image coalesced in his mind, of him sitting on a library catwalk and reading his father's memoirs. Astonishingly, he remembered the words with near exactitude:

> *France is a centralized and ferociously well-ordered state. It is a nation subject to a King. The perception of the duties of the King has changed over the years. Nowadays, people look at the King as a father, the personification of national greatness responsible for providing safety and sustenance to all citizens. The King, and the ordered, centralized apparatus of state, have done precisely this, to the best of their ability, and their lavish lifestyles are now rewards*

*for their beneficence. Opportunity has been virtually oblit-
erated in favor of giving every subject a participative role
that is determined at birth. Not only does the state regulate
activity, but other stifling regulatory agencies have centuries of tradition, such as guilds. No one need think too much
about the future - it was mapped out for all before they were
born. I think that is why we are a nation consumed with the
present. We enjoy the now - because we must. We enjoy performing the actions of now in a special and particular manner - for there is nothing else for us. We enjoy the senses of
now and the details of now - it is the spirit of* joie de vivre.
But Traversier looks to the future. To hell with joie de vivre,
I say faim de plus! *We circumvent the idiocy of the central-
ized state, and seek opportunity. We resent being held back,
and told what we can and cannot do. We demand that our
own natural abilities, spirit and persistence determine our
height of accomplishment - not our birth, and not our king.*

How could he remember his father's word with such clarity, and nothing else? He remembered being deep in thought regarding those words, reading them over and over, and amending their ideas in his mind. His father's words were well and good, but, in the end, France was an ordered state, and one had to obey the laws. Business regulations came from everywhere: Throne, police, the Parlements of nobles, the guilds and regional authorities. One could not simply become a cooper and make barrels. One had to be an apprentice to a guild master cooper, then advance up the ranks as a journeyman, and, finally, to become a master himself. If one did not have the opportunity to know a master cooper, one was not able to become a cooper at all.

Within days of the disastrous Summer ball, Xavier began pouring over his family's licenses and contracts, looking for any kind of loophole that would allow him to engage in some kind of business he could afford to begin.

He focused on the two most promising documents. The first was a license for "Genèse de Gaul Traversier, and his direct descendants of every proper stripe" to engage in "trade over oceans of no nationality, and domestic riverine", dated 1513, from the Marquis d'Auray, Queen Anne's treasurer, when she was Archduchess of an independent Brittany. Brittany had an uneven, and sometimes bellicose, relationship with France. When they peacefully merged in 1532, King Francis the First of France was eager to make the transition smooth. He duly honored and modernized the torts of the Archduchy, leading to the second document. In it, the Archbishop of Reims, the Royal Archivist, "for now, and for all of time until the second coming of our Lord," legalizes and endorses the license of 1513, "and whatever business, craft or trade be necessary for their fulfill-ment."

That was it. That was the loophole.

Xavier was undoubtedly the true and proper heir of Traversier. He was therefore licensed to engage in ocean and riverine trade. More importantly, he was entitled to engage in any and all activities surrounding, abetting, enabling or secondary to that trade - by royal edict. If any business or activity helped fulfill the requirements of oceanic or riverine trade, he could legally engage in it. The only problem with starting these ventures would be angry competitors, used to their monopoly and protections - throwing rocks in his windows, smash-ing his machines, or burning down his factories in the night. Xavier would have to go about this in a careful and diligent manner.

He did.

He arranged a meeting with the Mayor, the Vicomte de Chambarde, citing his friendship with Maurice Cœurfroid, and his status as the Traversier heir. Soon Xavier found his coach - which had undergone remodeling yet again - clat-tering through the city. The Mayor's offices were in the old castle of the Arch-dukes, which dominated the southeast corner of the city. Its towers were gigantic obelisks of stone, a hundred feet high, thick and wide - nearly keeps in their own right. They were connected by equally impressive walls, and there was a draw-bridge over a deep moat. Inside the castle walls, the bailey - the grounds - were considerably higher than the surrounding land, nearly as high as the towers them-selves. The space was filled with stone buildings set against the walls, some built for defense, and others for administration and living. The Mayor's offices were in the tall Mannerist keep against the north wall. Xavier arrived, gave a *pour-boire* of a thick coin purse to the attendants, and gave strict instructions for the placement of his carriage.

And in he went. Formalities and informalities were observed. The Mayor was young, in his thirties. To Xavier, he seemed well-mannered, well-educated and somewhat intelligent, albeit narrow-minded. He was good-looking, but not overly so. He was tall and thin, but, again, not overly so. He was dressed in brilliant blue silk, high heels, a powdered white wig and wore tasteful makeup.

Xavier finally thought the time was right, "I would like you to see some-thing. Could you indulge me, Monsieur?"

The Mayor laughed nervously. "You wish me to travel?"

"Only to your window, Monsieur Mayor," said Xavier as he gestured.

The Mayor cautiously moved to the window. "I see a coach."

"Look carefully."

"It is a well-made coach, older in design, with modern accoutrements and custom design work."

"Closer."

"A closer look? Yes, well… the horses are very fine. I… I'm afraid I am at a loss."

Xavier handed him a telescoping glass. It was a sailor's tool - the Meilleur held several. The Mayor took it and looked again. "Perhaps the door," offered Xavier.

The Mayor laughed, "Is that-? Why yes, it has my family crest upon the door!"

"Indeed, it does."

"How did that come about?"

"Your crest is upon the coach because the coach is yours, Monsieur."

"Mine?"

"Indeed."

"Are you bribing me, Monsieur Traversier?"

"No, I do not engage in any unlawful activity, nor will I ever. It is simply a gift. It is a gift to celebrate the return of the Traversier family to Nantes, awarded to her Mayor."

"I see," said the Mayor, pleased.

"May I present several documents to you?"

"Of course, Monsieur."

And Xavier duly presented his licenses to the Mayor, and explained that he now wished to lawfully engage in businesses relating to his future maritime enterprises. In Xavier's mind, this was the riskiest part of the entire venture. He did not currently engage in any trade at all, so technically there were no trades he could engage in to support what did not exist.

The Mayor was at a loss, but his mind went in a different direction. The gift of coach and horses was a staggering investment. If Xavier's paperwork was in order, what exactly did he really want?

It was simple. Xavier wished the Mayor's legal blessing, in writing, of his current and completely legal enterprises - and a formal introduction to the Prelate of Police of Nantes.

And the Mayor's future friendship.

Done.

Xavier now had in his possession a modern document eliminating an ancient loophole. It was worth ten times the coach.

The Prelate of Police sent an unenthusiastic introduction letter less than a week later. Xavier made an appointment to see him.

The Prelate of Police was Monsieur Jacques Berlière, a man without title, but the grandson of the Marquis de Landerneau. He was stern, officious, clever, good-looking and tall. He seemed resentful at having to meet Xavier, but had no choice, being politically outmaneuvered. Xavier proceeded as if they were old friends. He showed Berlière his licenses and paperwork, and allowed the Mayor's renewal of his entitlements to play protagonist, front and center.

Xavier proceeded apace, but gave himself time to figure out the man. He liked him. Berlière was an honest and diligent sort who cared about his duties and his responsibilities.

"Monsieur Berlière, it is important that you understand something."

Berlière sighed, "I am listening."

"I am an honest man, thinking in long-term fashion regarding the building of a business. I wish nothing more than to adhere completely to the letter and the spirit of the law."

"Then I must ask you, Monsieur, what you are doing here? Honest men do not spend time in police stations if they do not have to."

"I am about to engage in the rope-making and sail-making businesses. Perhaps others, but those for now."

"Outside of the chartered businesses and guilds? You are about to make a lot of people angry."

"That is why I am here, Monsieur."

"Rest assured, Monsieur Traversier, that lawbreaking will not be tolerated in the city."

"I wish to stop it before it begins."

Berlière did not look happy. "I see."

"I think it would be beneficial if police were to meet with my competitors, and warn them."

Berlière's face turned hard. "Be more specific."

"I was perfectly specific. That is all I want. I want my competitors to know that I am protected. I want to compete with them through the marketplace. I want the ship captains of Nantes to buy my merchandise instead of theirs, because of the quality and price of my goods in comparison. I want you to ensure that this can happen. I want your good attention to your lawful duties. I want law and order. I want a fair chance. Monsieur Berlière."

Berlière considered him. Xavier had something very potent moving in his favor - he was telling the absolute truth. Xavier wanted to bury the guilds, destroy his competition - but only by being better and cheaper. Berlière finally spoke, "You break my budget, and waste the time of my officers."

"No, no indeed. You will bill me for the extra time of your officers. They will do this outside their normal duties, for their customary salary plus one half, which I will gladly pay. In addition, simply as a token of respect and for my gratitude, I would like to make a gift to this station."

"To the station, you say?"

"Yes."

"Of what?"

"Two mantel clocks. One for the squadron room, and one here in your office."

"Monsieur Traversier, you must understand something. I will never break the law for you."

"Monsieur Berlière, you must understand something as well. I am law-abiding. I need the law to be incorruptible, so I can rely upon it. As a lawful businessman, I want the police on my side, and protecting my interests." Berlière said nothing, so Xavier continued, "If you addressed your ranks, and told them everything we have discussed here, would there be anything to hide?"

"What would I say to them?"

Xavier considered this, then spoke hypothetically, "I spoke with a local businessman named Monsieur Traversier. He is worried that competing businesses may want to break the law in order to thwart him. He wishes us to make it clear to his competitors that this will not stand. To be clear, there has been no law-breaking as of yet. Monsieur has generously offered to pay us for the extra duty, and has donated two clocks to the station. Who would like to volunteer?"

Berlière raised his hands in a gesture of surrender, and smiled. "I will say exactly that, at the next morrow meet with my officers."

"Thank you for your time."

And that was that - but only part of Xavier's plan.

He had created a timeline for the next ten years of action, carefully considered and mapped. He had fired his accountant, and nearly all of the servants, and those who stayed had additional duties relating to the business. The Meilleur was denuded of artifacts, only heirlooms, items of historical value, and true masterpieces remained. Both carriages were gone, and all of the horses but one, a gelding named Clop that Xavier cared for himself. The household diet was meager, and they had no budget for clothes. The Meilleur was freezing cold, and her grounds were being torn up and built upon. Xavier could not hire workers fast enough. He forced himself to hire only those he could count on, who would do their jobs when no one was looking over their shoulder.

Apart from hiring, everything else revolved around flax and hemp. Neither crop was difficult to grow; in fact, they could fit within the wheat harvest and were good for the soil. But after harvest, both plants needed additional processing in order to be used. Flax processing was especially arduous. The plant was pulled whole from the roots, to preserve the longest fibers. The seeds were threshed and winnowed away, then the plant was soaked in tanks or pools, in a process called retting. This would separate out the individual fibers. Months later, the plants were dried and combed for the long fibers. The short fibers, seeds and other parts were used for linseed oil, tow and a pulp called shive used to make paper. The work was intensive, and the peasants performed it themselves – but only for extra money and when they had time. As a result, flax and hemp fiber, not to mention linen, were difficult to acquire without contacts.

Xavier had thought long and hard about this problem, and came up with an idea - he would simply process the plants himself. Whenever he could, he traveled to the lands north of Nantes and told the farmers directly that he would buy any amount, of any quality, of leaf-to-root hemp and flax plants. The individual farmers could not process all of the flax they were able to plant and harvest. Now they could plant all of their land, process what they could, and sell the rest to Xavier. He would buy it on the cheap, because it was raw material, but it would also be a windfall for the farmers, who were used to selling small amounts of the final, refined product after a tremendously time-consuming process. Xavier would acquire his material for next to nothing and process it in bulk, with his employees working in stages like a new world sugar plantation.

Once the fibers were extracted, Xavier would make rope and sails. The trick with rope was that in order for the strands to be twisted and spun together on special hooks, an enclosed space had to be built that was slightly longer than the rope's final length. Short rope was cheap and easy to come by. Xavier had his eyes on the longest lengths of maritime rope, which were quite thick, and tapped out at some impressive three-hundred-and-fifty yards. Currently, Nantes had to import such lengths. Xavier could easily offer a cheaper price and corner the market, and perhaps force captains to buy the rest of their lengths from him as well.

The best flax fibers, however, would be used for making sails. Currently, sails were shipped to Nantes from linen-producing industrial towns such as Lyon, Flanders, or - even worse - foreign centers such as Holland, Switzerland and Spain. Sails required looms of high quality, with several skilled workers per loom. Xavier knew he could undercut prices by saving on transportation costs. He could also use the looms to create linen fabric, not just canvass.

Xavier outlaid a small fortune, and soon had the best and newest looms in Nantes. His sails would be of the absolute highest quality, saving captains money and aggravation. With sails of such quality, and no transportation costs, he could easily charge more for the sails than what they fetched at the Lyon factories – and Xavier's canvas would still be cheaper than Lyon's once they finally arrived in Nantes. Xavier would offer discounts if the captains bought their sails and their rope from him together. Papermaking from the shive by-product would come later - but would certainly occur - so he began to warehouse it. Xavier simply didn't have time to research the process in order to figure out a niche and a plan. He sold tow - it was cheap and made little, but why have any part of the process go to waste?

But that was a long time ago, Xavier realized as he laid in agony. In fact, months and months had passed. His rope and sail-making businesses flourished. He had even hired many of the people he had put out of work, some of them for more pay than they had previously generated for themselves.

His mother was constantly nagging him about moving the operations off the grounds of the Meilleur. He was trying, but it was hard to move or replace a three-hundred-and-seventy-yard-long building – much less the host of other operations surrounding it.

Then something else had happened, Xavier now remembered.

War.

France had finally recognized the American Colonies, and Britain had declared war. His sail looms and rope hooks were running twenty-four hours a day to keep up with the demand. The extra money was unanticipated, and he decided to put it to work.

I purchased a river barge.

It was an old, decrepit, leaking thing called *Le Roi Midas*. He was trying to expand his business and generate more funds by shipping cargo up the Loire. Nantes was placed as far inland as ocean-going ships could sail. Cargo then went by barge further east, where the Loire and its tributaries became increasingly more treacherous and shallow. Barges were pulled upstream by oxen run by local contractor teams. To help them, Xavier attached a mast to his barge that could be lowered and raised with pulleys to fit under bridges. Xavier had generated some merriment with this innovation. Shipping prices were determined by the guilds and central authorities, why would anyone care to go faster or make it better? The guild bargemen didn't even bother to cover their cargo from the rain.

But Xavier was not regulated.

He would barge faster, cheaper and better - and undercut them all. Cœurfroid had been ecstatic that Xavier had moved into riverine transport. Xavier gave him a fair deal on cargo, extraordinarily generous compared to the guild prices, and Xavier had personally taken a shipment of Cœurfroid foodstuffs and his own flaxseed oil to… somewhere. He remembered.

Tours. I am in Tours.

He had delivered his cargo to Cœurfroid's agents at the city's *Halle*, the central market. He had been prepared by his father's writings for a unique feature of business in France: all of the measurements were different - everywhere. Sometimes they had the same names but different values, sometimes the names and values were different, but from region to region one had to know the unique system of measurements, and speak in the local language of weights and measures or be lost. To some, it might seem ridiculous, but to Xavier it only smelled of opportunity. If Xavier and his future merchants navigated the shoals of measurements effectively, it would put them ahead of their competition. Different kinds of measurements in every town simply meant another hurdle Xavier could jump - and some of his competitors could not.

It was more difficult to have positive feelings regarding the *traites* and the *octroi*. The *traites* were internal customs duties. If you moved goods from one province to another, it was as expensive as moving them from one country to another. The *octroi* was a city tax, levied on all goods sold within the limits of a given town. Tours had a relatively humane *octroi* compared to places like Paris.

It was as if the government was sucking the blood from its cows, instead of milking them. If the country needed funds so badly, it did not make sense to consistently lower the total amount received by strangling commerce. Xavier was left with almost nothing, but almost nothing was more than exactly nothing - it was a small step forward.

After the Halle, he had gone to the local Freemason lodge for a meeting. He had given a speech and met several important contacts.

Then what? What had put him in this bed?

A young Priest came into his vision, "Good afternoon, Monsieur."

Xavier tried hard to speak, "Where am I?"

"You are in the Cathedral of Saint-Gatien."

"Cathedral?"

"In one of the outbuildings. In the Presbytère. You were brought here. You were found in the street. You were attacked, Monsieur."

The clue was enough to jog Xavier's memory. He could never sleep after a meeting, and asked where an interesting amble could be found. Place Plumereau was suggested, a bustling medieval square filled with cafés. On the way to Plumereau, he became distracted when he thought he was being followed. He found himself in an alley, near the ruins of the colossal Roman basilica.

He remembered seeing a man lying in a doorway.

He was barefoot and dressed in tattered peasant rags. A nearby *réverbère* lantern flickered light over his face, and his jet-black eyes stared up at Xavier like those of a corpse. Xavier slowed until he found himself standing stock-still and looking down at him. The man was older than he looked, probably nearer middle-age, but the living corpse was granted an ironic gift of youthfulness, and there was power in the man's limbs. Judging by the hardships indicated by the state of his clothes, by all rights he should have been utterly emaciated. Perhaps Xavier was in a strange frame of mind after the Freemason meeting. For whatever reason, he found himself speaking to him, "What has brought you to this doorway, Monsieur?"

The Man did not blink. Suddenly, as if life bubbled up from thick mud, he finally spoke in an even voice, "Go to hell."

Xavier continued looking down at the man, as if the same forces that compelled Xavier to speak to him would now make the man answer his question.

And after a moment, he did, "I have nothing. I am nothing. I wish nothing. From you, or from anyone else. What I had, no one can return. There are your answers, Monsieur, to every question you could ever ask. Now go, and leave me be."

Xavier nodded. He took out a gold Louis and, rather than dropping it, or demanding that he take it, placed it on the ground next to him.

Xavier walked away, absolutely bewildered by his act. Every last sous he could save, he did. Yet he had given the man gold.

Gold!

Why in God's name had he done such a thing? But, just then, his thoughts were interrupted by masked ambushers. They had come out of nowhere. Their first attack had driven him to the stones. They used thick, short rope wrapped in rawhide, to viciously torture and hurt with each impact, but not break bones or kill. Xavier moaned and gasped like a child with every blow, powerless to hide his pain. In a moment of clarity, he managed to bring up his forearms to cover his face. Scars could be hidden and bones could mend, but his teeth had to remain in his head. As the blows rained down, Xavier distinctly remembered seeing glimpses of the black-eyed corpse-man - who had shifted, if only to get a better angle on the melee. His expression was still without emotion. The gold Louis next to him duly glinted in the lanternlight. He had not bothered to pick it up.

When the men were done beating him, their leader searched him quickly and took everything he had, even his Freemason apron and his shoes. He looked Xavier in the eye and spoke, "Xavier Traversier, do not return to Tours. Do not have your barges return to Tours. Do you understand?"

He knew my name. This was no accident.

Xavier could only nod. It was evidently not good enough. The man slapped him, spoke his name again, and calmly repeated the question. Xavier forced himself to reply as loud as he could, telling the man that he understood. He heard the words barely croak from his mouth. The man motioned to the others, and they quickly disappeared. Xavier remembered nothing more. The men who attacked him were just *Sans-Culotte*, poor townspeople paid to do the unsavory work of another, wealthier villain. But Xavier did not forgive either party. Such things were not supposed to happen in the cities of France. It was a ridiculous breach of order. The French police were efficient and competent. They needed to deal with this immediately.

Xavier cursed himself for not anticipating this. He had become lax in the safety of Nantes. Now he was trapped in a priest's bed by shackles of agony.

"I am Father Almo. What is your name?" said the priest.

"Xavier Traversier."

"Where do you live? Can we summon your family?"

"I am from Nantes."

"Ah, I see."

"How long have I...?"

"You are lucky to be alive at all."

"How long?"

"Two nights and a day. You have slipped in and out of consciousness, from the pain and the exertion of healing."

"I wish to send a letter. Help me."

"Yes, of course." Father was prepared. He moved to a desk with a quill and ink. "When you are ready, Monsieur."

"Address the letter to Monsieur Antoine Thibault Greffier. I am unsure of his address." He was the Grandmaster of Tours.

The Father chuckled, "Does Monsieur Greffier know you?"

"Yes."

The Father sobered quickly, "Very well then. He is known in Tours. Getting a letter to him will not be difficult."

"Please write that I am the victim of a crime, and to send the appropriate authorities." If there was a Freemason detective, he would be on his way as soon as the letter was delivered.

"I can summon the police if you wish, Monsieur."

"No. Just send the letter. And get me some water. Please."

Father finished the letter, and helped him drink the rest of a bowl of water. Xavier thanked him, and he left.

The men had robbed him. The funds he was carrying were mostly destined for Maurice Cœurfroid, and were payment for the goods he had transported. He would pay Cœurfroid the money regardless, and say nothing of what transpired, of course. Between the barge and the goods, the trip down the Loire was going to be extraordinarily expensive. This might set him back a year, even with the benefits from the war.

Xavier, to his surprise, wept. He was nineteen, and far too old for tears, but his body hurt everywhere, and the added sting of disappointment had peaked his emotion. He had tried so hard, and sacrificed so much, for so long. And just when everything seemed to be coming together, when the carriage was finally at speed, so to speak, unforeseen barriers had broken the horses' legs. No matter how powerful one became, the world found more powerful enemies. How long could he go on like this? He was doing the work of five men. He was a servant - several servants - an accountant, a sailor, a merchant, and had spent time behind his own looms, and spinning rope on his own hooks. He didn't sleep, he barely ate, and now he was broken from foot to pate. It hurt. Everything hurt. He never thought a body could betray one with so much diabolical agony. What was the point, the objective, of his nerves? What benefit did he receive from this extraordinary amount of pain? He took in several deep breaths and willed himself to calm. He addressed himself.

Is this the moment when life finally beat you? Is this the moment you give up? Do you quit?

They were almost his father's words. Now he spoke them to himself and found the same answer. Faced with such direct self-questioning, the answer could only be a resounding *no*. He spoke to himself once again. This time, his own words.

My reason and intellect are more powerful than my emotions. In all things, I assess what course of action provides the most benefit. Tears are useless. They do not provide benefit, nor do they aid the process of thought.

Xavier found himself feeling better.

I am a Spartan who does what needs to be done while others do nothing.

I am a Freemason. I am a Traversier of Nantes.

I am a citizen of the greatest nation on earth. France is the inheritor of Rome, the seat of Charlemagne. Modern Europe is our invention. We stopped the Muslims outside this very city, and saved Christendom.

I am a man of Nantes. A man of the rivers.

No.

I am the river.

If the river is wide and deep, even nations of men cannot dam it or change its course. They exist with the river at its whim, and pray it does not overflow its banks.

Xavier was no longer crying. He was calm. He was back.

Disadvantages, challenges and disappointments - whether new or old - were simply factors in a continuing calculation. What was important, in this moment, was that the negative forces within his own soul had been beaten. Xavier had won the fight within himself. He was neither ahead nor behind. He was a series of calculations and actions, designed for the greatest benefit, in a continuing struggle that would last over decades.

The Father left, but Xavier didn't wait for his return. In any case, he felt like a bit of a hypocrite accepting his help and ministrations.

Xavier dressed alone. Every movement hurt. By the time his hat made it to the top of his head, he was exhausted. He grabbed his cane, pausing for a moment to control his breathing. He vaguely remembered that his hat, his cane, and his shoes had all been stolen - yet here they were.

A policeman entered, "Good afternoon, Monsieur Traversier. I am Detective Chouette."

Xavier was surprised to see him so soon. He was a mason - Xavier recognized him from the lodge. "How much do you know about what happened, Detective?"

"Everything, I believe."

Xavier forced himself to walk.

The Detective frowned, "Are you sure you are quite all right? I must confess, the last time I saw you, I did not think you would survive the night."

Odd.

"You've been here already? Before I sent the letter?" As he spoke, Xavier moved through the door, into a hallway.

"Yes, I was here the night of the incident. As soon as they found the apron."

Ah, that made sense.

The Detective followed him, "The Father told me you have blood in your urine. Such a thing is very serious, Monsieur Traversier."

"There was a man in the street. He witnessed the entire incident. He was barefoot, in tattered rags. But you can identify him plainly, just by his eyes. They are black, Monsieur *le Détective*, jet-black without color of any kind."

"Yes, that is quite an accurate description."

"You have found this man?"

"He is quite an interesting character. I would have judged him villainous, were he not so courageous and forthright."

"I am surprised you had such an easy time with him. Perhaps I can corroborate his story, if need be."

"That really won't be necessary."

"What do you need from me, Monsieur?"

"In terms of what?"

Xavier found himself getting impatient. He was hurting, and the obtuseness of the detective wasn't helping. But the man was a brother, and losing his patience would avail him nothing. He answered calmly, "What do you need from me in order to catch these perpetrators, and hopefully retrieve the remainder of my effects. I do not anticipate getting anything back, but one never knows."

"Ah, this explains much."

"What do you mean?"

"The Father hasn't told you anything."

"No, nothing. I thought no one had heard of my case until my letter was delivered."

"Then I will not keep you in suspense. We caught them all."

"Excellent. But I believe they were simply agents for a stronger, more insidious party."

"Yes, they were. We caught him too. We have retrieved all of your effects, and all of your money."

"Detective, I had over a thousand livre just in paper *actions au porteur*."

"Yes, you had exactly two-thousand-three-hundred and twenty-three livres, in paper *actions* and coin."

Xavier was completely taken by surprise. Something akin to a gasped chuckle escaped his lips. But immediately afterward, he was nearly overwhelmed with emotion. He realized he had won the fight with himself, even before receiving this news. Not only had he persevered in the face of total failure, he had not actually been defeated at all. He smiled, and shook his head,

The Detective continued, "Your friend, the one with the black eyes, he followed your five attackers."

"Where did they go?"

"To the stones, Monsieur. He waylaid them, one on five."

Such a thing could not be possible. "They were armed, in a fashion."

"Indeed, they were. But he took them by surprise, and had a plan. He was a bit lucky as well, I'd wager. Perhaps more than a bit."

But the man's actions didn't make any sense. He had simply watched, as Xavier was mercilessly beaten. But that conundrum was to be unraveled later. Xavier turned back to the Detective, "Tell me about the mastermind, the one who hired them."

"His name is Marc Marie-Florent Avenir. He is perhaps thirty. He started with nothing and now owns a small fleet of barges. He became a guild bargeman, and perhaps did this to you on the orders of the masters. I suppose they saw you as a young buck after their does, so to speak."

"How many? Barges."

"Nine."

"He has done well for himself."

"Indeed, he has. In fact, if you were not who you are, there are those amongst the police of Tours who might not have searched for the one who hired your assailants with such diligence. His thugs would be punished, of course. At some point, Avenir would be spoken to, warned about what he can and cannot do. But you are who you are, Monsieur, and you know who you know. Marc Marie-Florent Avenir is in jail. And his advocates beat on our doors, to no avail."

Xavier smelled opportunity. To a smart man, opportunity trumps vengeance - always.

"It would be a shame to disgrace a son of Tours," Xavier said, softly and evenly.

The Detective looked up at Xavier, in surprise. The surprise quickly disappeared, and turned into a piercing, re-evaluating stare.

"How did you come to identify him?" Xavier said quietly.

"The five men who assaulted you were questioned for hours. They were in pain from their beating, they had not slept, they had not eaten. With patience, one doesn't even need to raise one's voice. And, once one of them cracks, it is easy to break the rest."

"You have records of their testimony?"

"The King's justice system is a carriage pulled by paper horses, Monsieur. We have volumes of accurate and collaborated records of every possible type regarding this incident."

"It would be a shame to disgrace a son of Tours," offered Xavier once again - but differently. It was subtle, but the slight tonal differentiations of the sentence carried a message, an offer.

"Yes, it would be," the Detective offered wistfully, "It ultimately does not serve Tours, nor France, to have such a one as he in jail."

***

Xavier, the Detective, and two tall policemen in civilian clothing waited in the carriage, on loan from Monsieur Greffier, which was fine and large indeed.

The door was soon opened, and Marc Marie-Florent Avenir climbed up, and stopped. He looked at all the occupants of the coach, hoping his observations would give him answers. Xavier, in turn, evaluated him. Avenir was dark, of medium build. He was not handsome, but had broad, masculine features that many women found irresistible nonetheless. He had a tough, brawling demeanor, but seemed intelligent, or at least crafty. He had turned zero barges into nine. Something was working inside of him. He had spent the night sleeping on straw, in a cell reserved for poor criminals who had committed the worst sort of crimes. His station and purse had availed him nothing, and he was not allowed to speak with his advocates. Considering everything, his appearance was remarkably adequate.

The Detective, as agreed previously, spoke first, "Sit down, Monsieur Avenir."

He sat, "Detective."

"Do not speak, unless you are spoken to."

Avenir nodded. He appeared calm, in control and compliant. He had intelligence and survival instinct.

Good.

Xavier was impressed.

The Detective hit the roof of the coach with his cane, and the driver whipped the horses into a slow trot. Xavier looked out the window. Time was on his side, silence only reinforced everything he was about to do. He actually needed time, his plan involved timing. He knew also that looking out the window would give the man an opportunity to appraise him. Xavier had no bruises on his face, and none that were not covered by clothing or gloves. He looked pristine. He also knew he was handsome and well-built. He was a Traversier. There are ways one carries oneself that cannot be taught. Such things must be in the soil of one's birth.

Xavier finally spoke, slowly and carefully, "Life is composed of choices. But choices are only meaningful if we commit utterly to them. There is no such thing as half a choice, because everything in life ultimately depends on action. Even to transmit thought requires action - that of speaking or writing. Our choices must always translate into action, or else they are meaningless. And there is either an action performed, or there is no action. There is no half-action. Perhaps there is ineffectual action, but that avails us nothing. And then we are back to the reconsideration of our choices, are we not?"

"Yes, Monsieur."

"A wise man once said the King's justice system is a carriage that runs on paper horses. If that is so, I wish you to imagine the paper horse that has brought you to this coach. Perhaps, in your mind, it is a fire-breathing nightmare. If so, you have spotted it true."

Avenir did not reply. Xavier let him stew in his own angst, then continued, "Your first choice is to ignore the implications of your actions. You will spend coin and time to defend yourself in court, and your outlay of coin and time will be considerable, for you already perhaps understand the forces that are arrayed against you. Most likely, even with considerable expenditure, you will lose your fight. You will lose a percentage of your business, with one-hundred percent being an option, and perhaps even your freedom, or your life. It will be an ignoble end, and your talents will be lost to France."

Xavier turned and looked at the man. He used every ounce of guile he could muster to give him a hard and piercing stare, "You became overconfident. Breaking the law endangered your business, far more than it helped it. But your present demeanor gives me hope. If you were lost and useless forever, you would not act in this manner. You would be imperious and demanding, or what passes for imperious and demanding on the streets of Tours, and your manner would be a choice, in and of itself. Do you understand where I am driving?"

"I think, Monsieur," Avenir said very carefully, "I am open to other choices."

"Your entire business belongs to me. You are a salaried executive for the Traversier Trust, in charge of riverine transportation on the Loire, under the license of my family - not the guild. Whatever muscle you employ will be used to protect our operations, but only from thugs and criminals arrayed against us. There will be no more offensive operations in this manner, the manner that has brought you inside this coach. You will find, if you have not already, that order is the greatest ally of business. The primary purpose of law and government is to ensure the smooth flow of goods and specie. The secondary purpose is the maintenance of power, but that becomes impossible if its primary purpose is neglected. Once the beast of law and government is harnessed for one's business, it is the most devastating weapon of all. If I become your benefactor, you will fall under the aegis of this protection. As you grow my business, you will be amply rewarded. As the rest of the business grows, I will aid you, in expanding your fleet. If you cheat me, or endanger my operations through illegal actions, you will be arrested for the crimes you have already committed against me, and tried." Avenir nodded gravely, and Xavier continued, "A letter will arrive for you later today, with the name and address of a local legal advocate. If you agree to this second choice, you will appear at the given address at four hours after noon, with all necessary titles and paperwork to make this transfer official and proper."

"I need assurance that I will not be prosecuted after signing over my business."

"You have my word, the word of a Traversier of Nantes. Accept it, or do not. But I will say this: I will make you rich, and I will make you respected. I will deal with you honestly, and I will deal with our hired men fairly. It is the Traversier way."

"My men. The five."

The Detective spoke, "Commoners who commit such crimes are given the sentence of death by torture. You will watch them die when the time comes."

"By the wounds of Christ," Avenir said softly, "I knew these men well."

"You are a commoner like us, are you not, Monsieur Avenir?" replied Xavier. "Perhaps there is a lesson here, one that needs to be injected more forcibly into your mind."

The carriage stopped. Xavier had played this perfectly. They were in front of Avenir's townhouse at the perfect moment in the conversation - the end of it. "It seems we are at your stop, Monsieur."

One of the policemen opened the door and stepped out. Avenir exited the coach. The policeman reentered, shut the door, and the coach moved away. The detective shook his head, "You are formidable, Monsieur Traversier. I am glad we are not enemies."

"No, we are the opposite. We are brothers. Not only that, I am in your debt and you have my gratitude. I am a man of manners: I always repay my debts, and I always show my gratitude. I am at your disposal." Xavier smiled at the detective, who didn't look convinced, "Do you perchance know any local legal advocates, one who can help us with this matter? Preferably a brother."

The Detective shook his head in wonderment.

***

The man slept under the loose hay of the stable loft. It had cost him, this bed. He had been working all day, mucking out the stalls, brushing horses, buffing leather and moving bales. The amount of work was meaningless. What mattered is that he had eaten his fill, and had a warm place to lay his head. The best way to sleep under hay or straw was to have a blanket or sheet between one and the hay. The man had nothing, and it wasn't as warm as it could be, but it was the warmest bed he'd had in weeks, and he slept soundly – until he was abruptly awakened by noise. Looking down, he saw the stable doors open. It was the police again. Another man entered, a gentleman. The police handed him a lantern, and shut the door after him. The gentleman crossed beneath his eyesight, and began climbing up into the loft.

Xavier climbed to the top of the ladder and saw the man with dead eyes, staring at him as he did before, now from under a layer of hay. He crossed to him and sat down, moving the hay next to him to place his lantern directly on wood. "We meet again."

The man said nothing.

Xavier suddenly flicked a coin at the man's face. It hit him hard in the forehead before he could react. The man's eyes flared in anger and pain. Xavier was not impressed. "I believe that was yours. You left it on the cobblestones."

"If I didn't take it, it isn't mine."

"I've had enough of your riddles. Why did you watch them beat me, only to ambush them later? It wasn't to steal what they took from me. You gained nothing. Seemingly you helped me, but you truly did not. I could have been dead on the stones for your concern, correct?"

"What do you want?"

"I want to know why."

The man inhaled slowly, and exhaled. He looked away, then spoke, "What did he say to you that night? Something about not returning to Tours."

"Yes."

"You, and your barges."

"Correct."

"It was what he said, how he said it. You were not some villain who had dishonored a woman. They were not the starving poor, waylaying a mark to feed their children. They did it because they could, for an increase in their benefit. They reminded me of the field overseers, hired by the nobles, who had no aim but profit, at any cost. Such motivations can be a rock that starts a landslide of horror and tragedy. I decided to catch the rock before it hit the slope."

Xavier had calmed. "How did you defeat five armed men?"

"I have always had a way with such things. With my hands, with movement. I don't know why or how."

"You had no fear."

"I have nothing to fear. And nothing to lose."

Xavier nodded, as if the man had passed some kind of test. "I do not believe in God, nor am I sworn to a King. My loyalties lie with my family, my friends and my business. I believe in the power of man, and the beauty of just law. I am an honest and honorable man. I never steal and I never cheat, except my taxes, and only when I can safely do so. My reputation and standing amongst men is of paramount importance to me. I plan to be a slaver, as soon as I am able. The African slave would like nothing more than to conquer and enslave those who conquered and enslaved him. He simply lost a battle he would rather have won. There is no injustice in their minds, only a negative outcome, one that I will soon exploit. I wish to benefit from their savagery."

"Why do you tell me this?"

"Because you must know everything about me."

"Why?"

"I want your undivided loyalty. And I cannot have it if I lie about who I am, and what I wish to do."

"Why do you wish my loyalty?"

"I want you to be my right hand."

"Why?"

"I don't know," Xavier said truthfully, surprised at his lack of inner discernment in the manner. "Truly, I don't know."

"I am nothing."

"No, you are simply forgotten. And I now wish to remember you." Xavier, without knowing why, was suddenly filled with compassion. He spoke again, only now softly, "None of us choose to be born, or reborn for that matter. But you are now returned."

"Yes." And in that one word was lifelong loyalty: to grave, gold, victory or ruin.

"What do I call you?"

"L'Oublié."

The Forgotten.

Later it occurred to Xavier that the man had smiled. He would never see such a thing grace his face again.

1832

Jake

Chapter 6

Jake was roughly shoved awake. He blinked at the white light of dawn, and found himself looking at a middle-aged Bavarian he had never met. The man tapped his gun, then pointed south over the barricade. Jake's heart began to beat like a drum in his chest - a now familiar rhythm. He slowly stood, and cautiously looked over the barricade. In front of him ran the last fifty feet of Rue de Charenton, ending at the narrow crossing street of Petit Rue de Reuilly. A block to the north on Reuilly, a much-wider continuation of Rue de Charenton ran south-southeast. It emptied into a square at the Paris gates, and then continued to the village of Charenton.

With the defenses fifty feet from the intersection, the enemy had to advance down Reuilly, or up Charenton, then make a complete turn under fire in order to engage the barricade. It forced an action at point-blank range against prepared defenses, with no hope of using supporting heavy weapons. The zig-zag urban canyons gave attackers no other tactical choice.

Jake saw a knot of his men at the northeast corner, who peered south, down the continuation of Charenton. Whatever was worth seeing at this ungodly hour was most likely coming from that direction. Jake climbed the barricade to see for himself.

The day before, after Jake's men had been issued their Charlevilles at the cart rendezvous, they were hastily trained to load and clean them. The fifteen comrades at the cart were young but confident, aged within ten years of Jake at the outside, except for one man. A short, bearded badger of a man, who must have been fifty if he was a day, was the firearms expert. He was dressed in all grey with a grey hat, looking like nothing so much as a hairy tent, and his name was Citizen Loys. Although gruff and profane, he seemed very solicitous of everyone, and gave advice that appeared sound. His instructions on the Charleville were top-notch, and he tried to explain as much of real battle as he could. It seemed to boil down to finding oneself in complete ignorance of all surrounding events, being devastated by noise and friendly casualties, and still trying to do what one was supposed to do, without knowing precisely what that was. Pascal was duly issued a tricolor flag, and, without firing a single practice shot, they trooped to their barricade location, and began tearing up the street. Jake bought food and drink from the locals on Charenton, starting a raucous block party. The neighborhood came out, and dumped furniture on the barricade, and sang songs with the men. Most were shop owners or craftsmen. They were hard-working people who grew no food - they were hard hit when the price of bread went up. A local cooper said, "We spend too much of our *damné* coin on bread as it is anyway. *Être foutu tout les messieurs!* Long live the revolution!" Hearty cheers followed. A group of prostitutes came by and demanded weapons, and soon joined in the singing and drinking - weapons forgotten. A carriage was stopped, and Cyril asked for orders, "Jake, what do we do? Can we confiscate it?"

Jake thought about it, "Where is the driver from?"

"Montreuil."

Just outside of Paris. *En enfer* with him.

Jake spoke, "Yes. If the driver isn't from Paris, confiscate everything."

And so it went. Drivers were stopped and, if the driver hailed from outside the city or a non-republican neighborhood, their goods were confiscated, their carriage destroyed, and the debris added to the defenses. Two drivers managed to talk themselves back on their way unscathed, with horrible stories of tragedy and poverty. The second had five of Jake's men sobbing for a good minute, even after he left. It was utter chaos. They were pirates, except to the good citizens of Saint-Antoine, to whom they must have been like naughty, armed children with plenty of gold to spend, a barricade to build, and lots of songs to sing.

The barricade seemed solid enough. There was a good few feet of earth and paving stone at the bottom of the barricade, which spanned the width of the narrow street. Above the earth and stone was a jumbled mass of timber from demolished vehicles and furniture. Above it all, the tricolor waved on Pascal's flagstaff. A brazier continually boiled cleaning water some feet behind them. Loy's words on the subject of cleaning had been dire, "The Charlevilles will become so dirty they'll be impossible to load."

After fifteen shots, as a matter of fact.

"When they do," continued Loy, "Run to the brazier, change out the plunger on the loading rod for a screw, stuff wads of tow, these flax fibers here, throughout the spirals of the screw," and he did so quickly and expertly, "Soak the tow in the boiling water, then clean the barrel with the soaking tow," and he did so, with an efficient and practiced manner, "Then run back to your post - hopefully after you remembered to change out the screw for the loading plunger. If you didn't, you'll find out your mistake soon enough."

The moment Jake ran out of tow fiber or hot water, every one of his men was suddenly on their last fifteen possible shots and counting with every pull of the trigger. That wasn't even a tactical problem - that was just cleaning. Maybe the rags of a torn-up shirt would work in a pinch. Jake had no idea how the actual fighting would go. Loy did, "You'll like combat as much as the smell of another man's *merde* in your chamber pot. Just do your best, and try not to lose your life or, more importantly, your *foutu* loading rod," he said, with an empathy and gentleness that belied his words.

But now it was the cold of the morning after, and, presumably, the dawn of battle.

Jake reached the other side of the barricade with only minor scrapes, and went over to the corner. "Good morning, Gutek," he said.

Gutek nodded back, "Take a look."

Jake peered around the corner. Perhaps five or six blocks away was the square holding the city gate of Porte de Charenton - and an anthill parade of red and blue Parisian National Guard. There must have been hundreds. Rows of soldiers, cannon, and officers on horseback were poised for the upcoming battle. Jake was impressed and resentful. They looked magnificent, well-trained and organized.

Jake turned, and saw the Bavarian staring at him over the barricade. Jake made a gesture: "*everyone*", then "*shake them awake*." The Bavarian nodded, and disappeared from view. Jake turned and peered back at the soldiers. Nothing was really happening - yet. He spoke to Gutek, "Keep me abreast of any movement."

Gutek nodded, and Jake ran back and climbed over the barricade. After a few moments, his heart stopped trying to leap from his chest. With a subsequent drop in adrenaline came realization. It was a cold, dank morning. It was early, but somehow still too bright. Jake felt greasy. His mouth was full of dirty cotton. He felt a weird, high-pitched kind of angst, one that only comes from lack of sleep, and too much drink the night before. He made it to the friendly side of the defenses, and saw Franck. "Good morning, Citizen," offered Jake mirthlessly.

"I don't know what's good about it. I feel like bird droppings dried on a roof, and buttered with dew."

Suddenly, all heads turned at a sound. Most of Jake's command was now awake, thanks to the Bavarian. They all heard it.

Battle.

It came from somewhere in the neighborhood, one of a half-dozen nearby barricades. Everyone instantly perked up and eyes went wide. The sound was almost like rain - but the sound of a droplet hitting the ground was actually the report of a musket. The rain started slowly, gaining frequency and intensity, until it was a torrential downpour. Jake had no idea how many muskets had to fire in order to produce such a sound. It was sobering to think that the muskets were in the hands of real people, all aiming at each other, all thinking and acting quickly and effectively in their quest to kill each other. It was intimidating to think of battle in such a way, that both sides had equal chance and opportunity to die or be slain.

There had to be a skill to it, like all things. Skill came from talent, training and experience, then factored by passion. Jake's command had neither training or experience, and their opponent had both.

Franck shook his head in awe and wonderment at the sound. He turned to Jake, and they shared a look. Both knew, in that moment, that neither one of them had any idea of what was going to happen. Somehow, they were going to face events as best they could. In spite of such grim thoughts, Jake no longer questioned why he was there. He simply was, with these men and women, and that was all. He could only give everything he had in service to them and the cause. Everything he had happened to be not much at all, but that could not be helped.

One of the prostitutes; thirty, thin as a thirteen-year-old boy, a nondescript brunette with big, crooked teeth, jumped on the barricade and turned with wild, cruel eyes.

"Rain clouds of red and blue,
Come make your sound with us!
I'll show my hate for you,
With smoke 'n fire and lust,
I'll eat your heart with eggs,
And pull your guts to tie me bust!"

The defenders cheered and laughed. The prostitute cackled with her crazy eyes, the very personification of insanity and contempt.

"So, no breakfast?" yawned Franck.

Jake didn't say anything. Gutek, from the corner, turned and yelled, "A mounted officer bearing a white flag now comes."

"Let him pass!" Jake yelled, then he turned to the barricade defenders, "Do not fire at this approaching man without my order! Do not fire!" Jake heard his command repeated down the line.

There was a long moment of waiting. Jake became nervous and restless. He turned to Pierre, and handed him his coin pouch. "See if you can't get us coffee, and some breakfast. Boiled eggs, or *croissants au beurre*. Something. And some water and towels to clean up with. I feel disgusting." Pierre ran off. Jake had no idea how much time they had before the shooting started, but felt better giving orders. He saw Zacharie further down the line. Jake spoke again, "Zacharie, wake up the street. Get everyone down here who wants to fight." Zacharie nodded and walked off, screaming at the top of his lungs.

"Citizens of Saint-Antoine! Come defend your neighborhood!" he yelled.

Jake heard a horse approaching, and his attention became focused. Soon an officer carrying a white flag appeared, and pulled his horse to a stop. He was a *Chef de Bataillon*, a Major, was in his late forties, had a round face and a bushy mustache. He was clean-shaven otherwise, but his cheeks were black with the beginnings of stubble. He came within twenty feet of the barricade. "That's far enough, Major," said Jake.

The Major stopped, and looked them over. "How are you addressed, Monsieur?"

"I am Citizen or Commander," said Jake with a revolutionary zeal he didn't particularly feel at the moment.

"Very well, Commander. I am Major Marie-Pierre Alphonse Roux. Good morning to you."

"What do you wish, Major Roux?"

"What I wish, I do not think I will receive."

"Are you *Poissard*? Or have you decided to speak in riddles?" Jake said, and his men laughed.

Roux was not angered, "No, Commander. I am not *Poissard*, and it is not my intention to be obtuse. I simply do not wish my countrymen to die this morning, but I fear they have already. I especially do not want you to die, not young men and women such as yourselves. I am an old soldier, and I assure you that battle is no respecter of youth. Quite the opposite."

"Speak your message, Major," Jake said. He heard a stony hardness to his own voice.

The Major replied, "You are hopelessly outnumbered, tactically and operationally. You have no choice but to honorably surrender, in order to prevent the needless deaths of your command and mine."

"You don't understand what is about to happen. We have fifty-thousand muskets. You are about to fight all of Paris, Major."

"No, Commander. We control all outlying districts and the left-bank. The city has not risen against her King."

"The day is young, Major. And my orders are to hold. And I will, come what may."

After a moment, the Major removed his hat and held it above his head. "Then I salute you, as a fellow soldier of France. We will give you an honorable death."

Cyril spoke, "Not if we can beat you to it, old man."

"Quiet!" barked Jake. He turned back to the Major, "You have come to us honorably, and you will leave with your honor intact. But know this, we are true sons of liberty. We stand for the rights of man - to determine his destiny, and govern himself. Win or lose, we die for freedom. Long live the Nation! Long live the Fatherland!"

Jake's men went cheered with full throats. The Major saluted once again, and rode back the way he came.

That was a very French moment, thought Jake. *I think I must have gone completely native.* The Gaul loved war and everything about it. They fought and dueled over minor slights. They argued over politics, art, philosophy and food. Jake wondered what people back home in Wellesley, the home of a literally opposite temperament, would think of his hot-blooded theatrics.

His men behind the barricade broke spontaneously into the *Ça Ira*.

"Ah! It'll be fine, It'll be fine, It'll be fine!
Aristocrats to the lamp-post!
Ah! It'll be fine, It'll be fine, It'll be fine!
The aristocrats, we'll hang them!
If we don't hang them,
We'll break them.
If we don't break them,
We'll burn them
Ah! It'll be fine, It'll be fine, It'll be fine!"

There were other versions of the song. The one they sang belonged to the revolutionary *Poissard*, the Paris *Sans-Culotte*. Jake looked out over the barricade. Gutek and the scouts still peered south down the continuation of Charenton.

Franck turned to him, "Do you know where that song comes from?"

"From the True Revolution."

"Not exactly."

"We'll have no more nobles nor priests!
Ah! It'll be fine, It'll be fine, It'll be fine!
Equality will reign everywhere.
The Austrian slave shall follow him.
Ah! It'll be fine, It'll be fine, It'll be fine!
And their infernal clique

Shall go to hell!"

Franck spoke again, "Benjamin Franklin was in Paris, during the American Revolution. Whenever someone asked him about the rebels getting defeated, he'd always say, "*Ça Ira! Ça Ira!*"
It'll be fine! It'll be fine!
Franck continued, "He was so popular, we turned it into a song for our own revolution."

"Amazing." Jake was glad Franck was talking. That was most likely the exact reason why he was talking, he just realized.

Gutek gave Jake hand signals – "*many come.*" Jake waved him back, and soon the scouts were being helped as they climbed over the barricade. Jake heard drums beating a march. They were on their way. People were going to die very soon.

Yesterday, Loy had pulled Jake to one side, out of earshot of the men, "A frontal assault against a prepared position is the most difficult task a soldier can face. That particular is in your favor. But there are plenty of other factors. There is only a short distance between your attackers and the barricade once they make the turn. That is good and bad – mostly good because it eliminates artillery. The King has many experienced men within his ranks, and all of them were trained to fire at least three volleys a minute. Your men are virgins to battle in the majority. Their only training was for a few minutes, and most of them have never fired a gun in their lives."

"We will do what needs to be done."

"I am not admonishing you. You're a commander. Leaders motivate troops, but must deal in reality when talking amongst themselves. I talk to you alone, to speak words only you should hear. Your refugees, the foreigners, know only defeat, at the hands of similar regulars from their own country. Your only hope, for sure and steady hands, will be in the older natives of Saint-Antoine you convince to join you. Hopefully, some of them have seen action under Napoleon, the kings, or the revolutionaries. And that is a hope, not a certainty. Scramble for any advantage, Commander. This will not be an easy fight."

And today, behind the barricade, waiting for battle in the cold, white light of morning, were precious few recruits from Saint-Antoine, of any age.

Jake had an idea of placing snipers in houses, but could not find any homeowners willing to take the risk. He was under strict orders not to alienate the neighborhood, so he did not force the issue. They had the barricade, but would it be enough?

Franck spoke again, "Ben Franklin would show up at Versailles dressed like a farmer. He charmed everyone. He was Rousseau's new man, a sophisticated savage, the freedom-loving individual who has returned to nature. You took advantage of that, a little bit, didn't you? With your stories of the frontier and the Indians and so on?"

"Yes. I actually have no idea what sophisticated savagery entails. I suppose I treated everyone to my pretended version of it."

"Have you actually met any Indians?"

"I am from Wellesley. It is as far from the frontier as one can get, and still keep one's feet dry."

"*Zut!* I knew it!"

"Truth be told, *mon ami*, I consider myself French. I wouldn't return if my life depended on it. I can't even remember the last time I wrote home."

"Well, if it's any consolation, you sound like a native."

"Really?"

"Yes. Like a native-born Parisian, maybe with a dash of Bretagne."

"Ah! It'll be fine, It'll be fine, It'll be fine
Aristocrats to the lamp-post
Ah! It'll be fine, It'll be fine, It'll be fine
The aristocrats, we'll hang them!
And when we've hung them all
We'll stick a shovel up their arse!"

The drums suddenly beat triple-time. From the corner, and without warning, trotted out at least a hundred soldiers, and the song died on the rebel's lips. The soldiers ran to take up a three-row firing position across the entire width of the street - and half of Jake's entire command fired at once without orders. Jake was immediately deafened. The others took the volley as a signal, and began firing as well, just with enough interval to render any shouted orders ineffective.

Jake silently cursed. There had been no thought at all as to how orders would be conveyed once the shooting started. Apart from going to every man himself, or sending a messenger man-to-man to scream into deaf ears, Jake was at a loss. Still standing, he looked around at his men, as the battle began to rage in earnest. In spite of their brave song, he saw many nervous eyes. There was no yelling or screaming, just intense and quick action, albeit clumsy and untrained.

Jake looked out, and saw the enemy had finalized their position. Perhaps ten of them were wounded or dead lying on the ground. Their first rank suddenly fired in unison. Like deadly insects, he heard the sound of musket balls snapping past him. It was the most intimidating sound he had ever heard. His first instinct was to drop to the ground, to get as far from those deadly bees as he possibly could. Instead, he closed his eyes. He took a moment to fight himself, to overcome, forcing himself to stand tall and in danger. He opened his eyes again and looked out forward. The second rank of soldiers advanced and fired. Two more of them fell. The third rank advanced even further and fired. One more went down. Squads of medics and stretcher bearers ran out to help the wounded. Jake saw a few of his own men on the ground, shot in the head or arms, caught trying to take a shot over the barricade. He also noticed many more were squatting completely behind the barricade, and making no move to load or take position to fire. The air was already thick with acrid smoke. The enemy was nearly obscured, even though they were closing quickly.

The prostitute jumped on the barricade, her lips curled in a feral, hateful snarl. She lifted her skirt to the soldiers in contempt, her screamed *Poissard* insult lost to the tumult. The next volley riddled her body. She fell, and collapsed to the mud of the torn-up street, her broken limbs at impossible angles. She was a pile of blood and innards, hair tufts and cloth, like an alley refuse pile shared by a tailor and a butcher.

Another man fell, writhing on the ground in agony. Jake saw others moving away from the barricade at a crouched run. Franck was yelling something at him, but he couldn't hear it clear enough to make out its meaning. As they advanced, the enemy was now aiming and shooting at individual targets. More of Jake's men fled or were down - wounded, dead or terrified, he couldn't tell. Hale men bent over wounded, slowing their volume of fire even further. Franck was trying to pull Jake behind the barricade, but he resisted it. He needed to see what was going on, so his mind could work, so he could come up with a plan. He could almost see defeat rolling out toward him like a dark ocean wave.

Jake took out his pistol. If something wasn't done quickly, they would be fighting hand-to-hand over the barricade. With his pistol's quick action and twenty-round capacity, Jake outgunned everyone, at least at close range. Once he could shoot effectively, he might be able to turn back the charge himself.

Franck started as if hit with a club. The back of his head flew off into pieces, like a china saucer of tomato soup landing on tile. He fell backwards, and his arms bent at the elbows, pointing his hands straight into the air. His eyes were open, vacant and completely red. A pool of crimson quickly spread from his head, as if it held gallons of blood. Jake bent over him in disbelief. He held Franck's body, totally oblivious to the battle around him.

Jake had no idea how much time passed before he became aware of what was happening around him. His senses were muted, as if he were witnessing a spectacle on the street from a table inside a café. His men were running away, or sprawled on the ground in postures of surrender, death or agony. Soldiers were crawling over the barricade, and shooting over the top of it. There were screamed commands and barked orders from enemy leaders. Jake couldn't discern their meaning, as if he had suddenly forgotten every word of French he ever learned.

A soldier brought the butt of his musket into the back of Jake's neck, knocking him unconscious. He crumpled over Franck, and was kicked until his unresponsive body was prone on the ground.

***

Over the course of the day, the surviving rebels retreated south and west, and collapsed into positions in the maze of narrow streets in the city center. They made their last stand in the old church buildings on the Cloître Saint-Merri. By dusk, it was over. The revolution had been crushed in a little over twenty-four hours. The army and national guard lost seventy-three men to the reaper, and sent three-hundred and forty-four to the hospital. Ninety-three revolutionaries were killed, and two-hundred and ninety-one wounded. The fighting went into the history books as *The June Rebellion of 1832*, and was lucky to get a page or two - if the book was thick.

The twelve students of Louis-le-Grand captured as rebels were somewhat of an embarrassment. These young men were the best and brightest of France - indeed, of the world. The students were shocked and traumatized over their brush with mortal violence, and those in authority sensed that whatever revolutionary fervor they possessed had been mostly extinguished. All of them, save one, were remanded to the school without further ado of any kind. Their participation was erased from memory.

Only one particular student was chosen to be put on trial for sedition and rebellion. It was strange because he was not even French. He could have simply been deported, and saved everyone time and trouble, and averted a potential diplomatic incident with his native land - a friendly sovereign state. But, again, for some unknown reason, against all advice - and seemingly the will of the powers that be - Jacob Esau Loring, Jake to his friends, would go on trial with eighty-two other rebels chosen for their keystone positions within the revolutionary ranks and their contribution to events.

For those eighty-two men destined for trial, the best they could hope for was life in prison. Some would surely be executed.

1832

The Time of the Heirlooms

1779

America

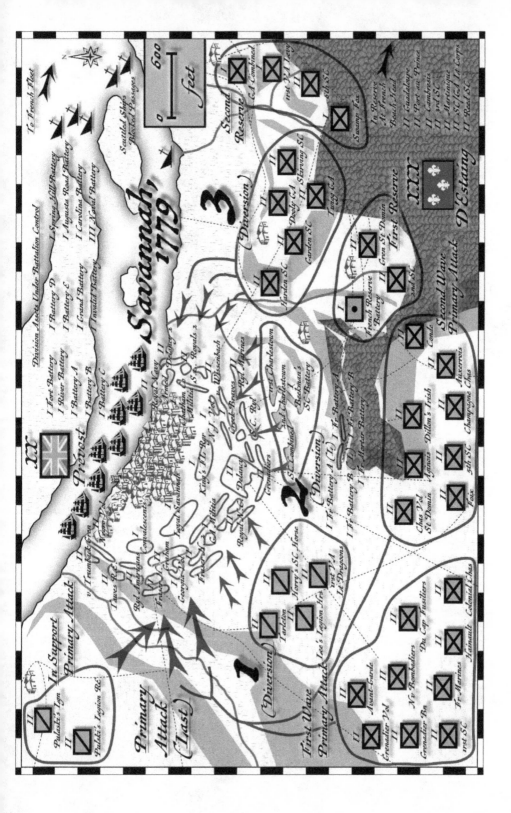

Savannah, 1779

Chapter 7

Colonel Comte Curt von Stedingk hailed from Swedish Pomerania. He was close friends with King Louis and Queen Marie-Antoinette of France. He came from a celebrated military family. He was sharp, competent, experienced and cool-headed.

Today, he led the second wave of the main attack against the defenses of British-held Savannah. His command was an international force of thousands. There were parts of General Ben Lincoln's First American Division from Charleston, French regulars from the storied Irishmen of the 87th *Dillon* Infantry Regiment, elements of the 16th *Agénois* Regiment, the 106th and 109th French Colonials, and also a unique band of five hundred soldiers of the *Chasseurs-Volontaires de Saint-Domingue*, who were mostly freemen of mixed black and white heritage, called *gens de couleur libre*.

The first wave had already attacked. Its energy was spent, but a wide swathe of trenches, earthworks and revetments - taking up the first and second rings of British defenses encircling the western part of the city - were now French. But the enemy fortifications were extensive – three more inner rings of trenches, revetments and forts were still held by the enemy. The weather was fair, and Savannah was full of slaves who had nothing else to do than build British defenses in the preceding days and weeks.

It was now up to Von Stedingk and his second wave to penetrate the last three rings of British defenses and liberate the city.

Von Stedingk and his command reached the first trench. Wounded men from the prior assault were struggling back. The dead seemed to be scattered everywhere. Of the enemy fallen, of whom he was assured only American loyalist militia held the sector, he recognized the uniforms of Fraser's Highlanders, the crack British 71st Regiment of Foot.

The plan had depended on surprise. They had none. The French and American forces of the first wave marched through swamp and marsh and had arrived predictably late. The site for the primary thrust through the British defenses had been chosen for the lack of good units manning the defenses - and that gamble had now proved a failure as well. The overall commander of the French forces, Comte d'Estaing, was a mediocre officer. Ironically, the British commander was a Frenchman as well - Major General Augustine Prévost. He came from a Huguenot family, French Protestants, who had emigrated to avoid religious persecution. The Prévosts were originally from Poitou, a region well-known to produce excellent soldiers. Augustine was proving to be no exception.

French forces began landing on the twelfth of September. It was now the ninth of October – and only now was Comte d'Estaing growing impatient. Had he been impatient in mid-September, the city would have been liberated within hours. Now, with the city fortified, impatience was suicidal. At the course-of-action meeting, every officer had been opposed to a frontal assault. All were in favor of oblique operations improving their overall position, with an eye toward gradually making Savannah untenable. When d'Estaing issued his orders for the attack, it became abundantly clear to Von Stedingk why d'Estaing had never won a battle of any consequence. He had wavered when he should have been strong. Now, when he should be more strategic, he was unwavering. Apart from some supply issues, and sickness brought by the fetid, tropical swamp, everything was in their favor. Hurricane season was ending, the fleet was safe, and time was on their side. There was no need for the butchery of a direct assault.

Yet here they were.

A Polish aide-de-camp rode up and saluted. Von Stedingk returned it. "Colonel, the first wave has taken the primary and secondary lines of defenses. I'm afraid Comte d'Estaing was been hurt."

Von Stedingk nodded sagely. *No great loss.*

The Pole continued, "Comte Pułaski has also been wounded, but I'm afraid his wounds are mortal."

That was a blow. He was an outstanding officer. From Poland as well, renowned for superior horse soldiers, he was training and leading the American cavalry. He had even personally saved George Washington's life. Von Stedingk shook his head, "Is someone with him?"

"Yes, Monsieur. Comte de Benyovszky."

The Hungarian. Good man.

"Very well. Give him my most sincere regards. Tell him, in the interests of our cause, that I will immediately initiate the attack of the second wave."

"*Oui*, Monsieur." The aide-de-camp saluted, and rode off.

Von Stedingk had no illusions about the rest of his day. He could attack cautiously and judiciously - and make defeat an absolute certainty - or he could attack savagely and ferociously, sacrificing his men, but having a slim chance of penetrating the enemy defenses and rendering their entire forward positions untenable. He really had no choice. He had to attack with everything he had, and as quickly as possible. In order to justify such a sanguine plan to himself and to God, he had to lead the assault himself. His men then could do no less than to follow. He turned to his signals officer, "Sound double time attack, if you please, Lieutenant." The man nodded, and turned to issue commands.

Von Stedingk had issued orders to his officers last night, instructing them how they should proceed according to certain signals. Within seconds, the musicians would sound the attack. Within a minute, the entirety of his command would be ready to assault.

He dismounted and handed his reins to the flag-bearer, who in turn gave him the colors. Von Stedingk turned to the rest of his staff, "You are now the rearguard. If I fall, and the attack fails, command the retreat - but only if both conditions are met."

His Executive Officer, Major Marquis de Flaine, saluted. "God be with you, hero of France." He turned his horse, and led the rest of the staff down the column.

Von Stedingk turned to face his forward soldiers. He spoke in a brazen voice, "I am personally leading the assault. I need a man to carry my colors, so everyone can perceive the direction of the attack. I need a man of iron will, one who will not fall back or become frightened. And, if I succumb to wounds, to carry the impetus forward still without me. And I need other men to pick up the flag and lead, if this brave man falls."

A man stepped forward. He was tall, perhaps six feet or more. He had the twisted muscles of a fit, thin man - but more muscles than a thin man would ever have. He was deeply tanned, but the shade of his skin was strange, browner than it should have been. His hair was golden brown at the roots, and gold at the tips, and his eyes were the same color - gold. His features were small and sharp, like a Dane or a Frisian. He was a Sergeant Major, and wore the uniform of the *Chasseurs-Volontaires de Saint-Domingue*. That explained it: he was part black, enough to make his complexion unique. Standing behind him were other men of color, ranging from pitch black to caramel. The Sergeant didn't look scared, or even focused or stern - the opposite, in fact. He was grinning, "I will carry your flag, Monsieur Colonel. To Purgatory or Port-Au-Prince - whichever is hotter and further." The soldiers behind him laughed.

Braggadocio in a tavern around wide-eyed whores was one thing. But they were about to engage in a frontal assault against hardened troops and prepared positions. Most of the men were probably praying for courage and trying not to soil their breeks. It was inconceivable that a sane man could have a tavern attitude on a real battlefield – yet, *voilà*. His attitude had even rubbed off on his men.

Von Stedingk spoke, "What is your name, Sergeant?"

"My name is Sergeant Major Féroce Guerrier, Monsieur."

Ferocious Warlike? What a name!

Von Stedingk kept his face neutral. "Have you ever faced your own death, Sergeant?"

"*Oui*, Monsieur. Many a time. But the devil won't have me, and God keeps a clean heaven."

Mon dieu, more wit!

"Step forward," said Von Stedingk, and the man came before him. Von Stedingk held up the regimental colors, and they performed the drill of a formal exchange. Von Stedingk kept his voice low to travel only between them, "To hell and back, Sergeant. Our life means nothing this day, yes?"

The Sergeant winked at him, as if he was having the time of his life. Von Stedingk smiled back at him, as if he was as well.

He wasn't.

Von Stedingk drew his sword and pointed it at the heavens, and shouted with a booming voice, "For King Louis, and for France! For American freedom! VIVE LE ROI!" and with that he turned, and charged.

He heard a thousand throats scream behind him – "*VIVE LE ROI!*" The battle cry was six-hundred years old – and belonged to the victors, many more times than not.

Von Stedingk ran the last steps to the first set of defenses. Huge clouds of smoke billowed from distant enemy positions. A moment later, he heard the deep, impossibly loud sound of cannons – the long-range guns, rifled twenty-eight pounders taken from warships. At this range, they fired solid balls. As they bounced across the ground, anyone in their way would be crushed like matchsticks, their lives and limbs torn from them like doll parts.

Von Stedingk reached the first trench. The first assault had taken it already, and there had not yet been a counterattack - at least Von Stedingk's second assault then was somewhat timely. He slid into the trench and began climbing up the other side. Out of the corner of his eyes, he saw a few dead and wounded from both sides. Some fusiliers from the first assault had fallen back here and had taken position.

But then he was up and on the flat ground on the other side. Loud insects seemingly buzzed past his head at incredible speed, near misses - musket balls. At this distance, they could only be fired from sharpshooters using long rifles.

They could easily pick off officers and flag-bearers at this range. Anyone in a white uniform with gold trim would probably not survive the day.

More steps - double time. Faster, faster.

Then cotton balls appeared across the enemy line, followed by a demonic roar seconds later - they were now in range of the smaller sixteen and twelve pounders, and the more-forward placed four pounders.

Suddenly, a musket ball hit his hat, and twisted it down over his nose - hard and painfully. He fell, tugged his hat back up - and saw the Sergeant sprint past him. Strong hands helped him back up.

"Are you quite all right, Monsieur?" A Corporal from the *Agénois* inquired.

"Quite well!" shouted Von Stedingk, "To the attack, Corporal!" And he took off running as fast as he could. He wanted to pass the Sergeant. This was his assault, his responsibility. He needed to be first. The insects buzzed his head again. He heard other soldiers behind him fall with grunts and screams. The Sergeant reached the second trench - the last taken by the first wave. Von Stedingk ran as fast as he could, and nearly jumped into the trench. It was considerably more occupied with soldiers from the first assault, for this was as far as they could go. They traded shots at the enemy in the third trench. Von Stedingk yelled, "Make way! Make way!" as he climbed up the other side. A cheer went up from the soldiers in the trench. But Von Stedingk paid it no heed, he had found something to occupy his mind, something to keep it from dwelling on his eventual fate - he was going to beat this *förbaskad* Sergeant to Savannah.

Von Stedingk was ahead and first. The Sergeant was not as mobile in the climb, since he was carrying the colors. Suddenly the air was alive with musket balls whizzing past him, and his clothes tugged everywhere from hits, even between his legs. Von Stedingk was absolutely terrified. Being first, he had drawn fire from the entire enemy position - it was a miracle he was not dead. He turned to see where his men were.

His assault was not nearly as strung out as it could have been. There were at least a hundred soldiers cresting the second trench, the remnants of the first assault were supporting them with volleys as best they could. The Sergeant was right behind him. Von Stedingk held out his hand, "Wait."

The Sergeant stopped mid-stride and stood next to him, looking back as he did, only waving the flag back and forth. The man was completely without fear - fifty muskets must have trained on him in that moment alone.

Von Stedingk raised his sword and shouted, "Do not stop until we reach Savannah! With me!" and then he turned, and ran toward the third trench, held by American loyalists and tough Scottish regulars. He saw long bayonets were on the end of every enemy musket, making them into spears, longer than his arm and sword together. He had no idea how he would enter the enemy trench without being run through. But, suddenly, after firing a last volley, the enemy began to scatter left and right, leaving the trench directly in front of him nearly empty.

Von Stedingk jumped into the trench. He heard and saw men to his left and right do the same. He quickly began climbing up the other end. He hoped that commanders to the rear had enough sense to order the defense of this trench section they had just taken.

He continued his mad sprint across another deadly section of level ground. The Irishman running to his right suddenly disappeared in a puff of red mist. A moment later the enemy works erupted in smoke and belated noise - another cannon volley. Von Stedingk had no idea how many others had been wounded or struck down, but there was nothing for it. He gritted his teeth, lifted his sword and screamed. The insects whizzed passed him again. He hoped his death would not stop the charge, that the mad sergeant could keep them going, and someone as equally mad would pick up the colors when the sergeant fell.

The fourth line of fortifications approached. It was not a trench, rather a wall, a high mound of earth. A wide and shallow trench was on Von Stedingk's side of the mound - a coverless obstruction, and a hindrance to climbing the revetment. The British on the other side of the trench were firing good, organized volleys, loading and shooting from a standing position. A few holes in the mound offered nothing but the mouths of four-pound cannons, probably loaded with anti-personnel grapeshot. Enemy drums and pipes erupted into song, the colors of the British Crown and the 71st Regiment were raised, and a throaty roar went up from the defenders – "*CAISTEAL DHUNI!*"

This time there was going to be a fight.

Von Stedingk could see the uniforms of the *Dillon* Irish, and the blacks of Saint Domingue to his left and right. Scattered amongst them were *Agénois* and a few Americans. The opposing Fraser's Highlanders had proven themselves at the battle of Stono Ferry, they were tough and battle-hardened. Von Stedingk had no idea how his motley force of blacks, Irish, French and Americans would fare against them. It was his duty to strengthen and sturdy them. He turned, and screamed with everything he could muster, "*VIVE LE ROI!*"

The sound of his voice was animal, terrifying - even to his own ears. The Sergeant, who was perhaps ten feet away, grinned at him, and gave a bloodthirsty howl of his own. A roar, like a charge of wolverines, buffeted his ears as it escaped the mouths of his soldiers. Von Stedingk's heart burst with pride. He would throw himself on these Scotsmen, in admiration of his men's bravery, come what may.

He turned back and ran forward, increasing his speed. His chest hurt even through the adrenaline, his breaths were ragged. Cannon and musket fire buffeted him. He was so far unhurt, but he knew there were others who were not so lucky.

He was fifty feet away from the wall.

Through the smoke, he saw a young redcoat right in front of him on the other side of the mound. He was reloading, and staring right at him. Von Stedingk focused on him.

I am going to kill that man and climb the barricade, or he will kill me.

Thirty feet.

The Scotsman leveled his rifle, and aimed right at him, cool and calm.

Fifteen feet.

He fired. Von Stedingk suddenly heard sound differently from one ear - then realized why: it was completely shot off from his head. The redcoat began to reload, on instinct but not wisely.

Von Stedingk ran him through, and the man dropped, nearly pulling the sword from his hands. Von Stedingk climbed the barricade and could feel and see others doing the same, engaging the Scotsmen with bayonets and bare hands. Von Stedingk climbed to the other side of the mound, and saw the British color bearers and musicians - most of them quite young - all of three strides in front of him. He ran at them screaming, swinging his sword in wide arcs, back and forth. He hit two or three in a swing, opening wide gashes. With panicked and wounded screams, the color guard and musicians broke. There was no one ahead of him now, only the no man's land leading to the final set of defenses before the city of Savannah. Von Stedingk turned back to the melee and slashed at two soldiers' backs who were engaged with his men. The area around Von Stedingk quickly belonged to the French. He looked around for the Sergeant - and found him nearly right beside him, covered in blood and black dust, but still calm and in high spirits. He cocked his head as if to ask, *"What do you wish of me?"*

"In a moment, we press on," he said in reply to the gesture, then in a louder voice, "Officers! Officers, to me!" But no one appeared. He repeated his command, and still no one came. His officers were not cowards. Most likely they were dead or wounded, picked off by the riflemen he was so far lucky to have escaped.

Von Stedingk appraised the last set of revetments. They were the tallest of the lot, and held the highest caliber of artillery, which would now be firing grapeshot, basketfuls of metal that would tear through huge swathes of men. They were well-manned, and would, at this point, probably be reinforced by use of the enemy's good interior lines. If they made it to the final defenses, and won the resulting fight, the entire siege would be over. If they didn't, they would have to do all of this again, perhaps might fail again, and all the lives lost so far would be for naught.

He turned to the Sergeant, "Wave the colors, Sergeant," and then to the men, "Prepare for the next advance, repeat my commands rearward!" Voices shouted his command down the ranks. Von Stedingk looked in either direction. A hundred feet of the wall had been taken at great cost. It was enough. It was now or never. "Men of America, men of Ireland and the Kingdom of France - with me now!"

Von Stedingk turned and ran. He heard no cheers, but he heard his men follow. At this point in the battle, there was no more need for inspiration. The men who had the rocks in their craw were with him. Those who did not were left by the wayside, somewhere far behind.

There was a moment of quiet. All Von Stedingk could hear was his own ragged breaths, odd and directionless from the missing ear. Suddenly the enemy revetments were obscured by huge billowing clouds of smoke. Von Stedingk was lifted off his feet, and he fell forward.

Dazedly, on the ground, he maneuvered to a sit. He noticed his sword was bent nearly in half. On instinct, and not feeling, he swiveled to look down at his legs. A good-sized chunk was taken out of his left calf. For some reason, it neither hurt nor bled. He tried to stand, and realized the wound was crippling him out of proportion to its lack of feeling. He managed to get to his feet, but could no longer run. He tried as best as he could to straighten his sword by pushing a knee into the center of angle. He limped toward the enemy, as fast as he could, with his bent sword raised in the air. The Sergeant ran passed him, then turned.

"Go!" screamed Von Stedingk, with dark anger. The Sergeant simply nodded, and kept running. Other soldiers passed him. The attack had transcended his authority, the men attacked without fear and without thought. But they were cut down mercilessly, one after the other. Von Stedingk tried to walk faster, resisting the urge to use his sword as a cane rather than a beacon. He was suddenly hit, and fell again, but now there was pain. A ball had made a deep groove in the flesh between two of his ribs on the right side. One of the *Dillon* Irish pulled him to his feet.

"Come on then!" the Irishman said cheerfully, right before his head disappeared, and his body fell to the ground. Von Stedingk composed himself, and kept walking. He now saw a huge melee at the last ramparts. A stream of his men, narrow at the top and wide at the bottom, fought their way up. The regimental colors waved somewhere near the top. Von Stedingk forced himself to move faster. He screamed in rage to hide his screams of pain. Musket balls whizzed passed him, but he forced himself onward. His presence, and that of the colors, was now the sum total of military authority propelling the charge. He reached the bottom of the revetments. Wounded men were everywhere. He began to climb, using the dead to help his ascent. He bled everywhere upon them, from his ear and from the chest.

He made it to the top of the mound, and saw a brutal fight below. American Tories and Scotsmen fought for their lives against American rebels, French, Coloreds, Irish and, now, a Swede. Von Stedingk let himself slide down the mound and used the momentum to swing downward with his sword. Things moved faster than the mind could register. It would take years of bad dreams to make sense of the ensuing fight.

It was over in minutes. There was a carpet of dead, nowhere did one stand where it wasn't upon the slain. There were no more British – and only a handful of Von Stedingk's men remained. The revetment mounds had been constructed so that enfilade fire, parallel sideways fire, did not rake the entire line, and would hit dirt after fifty feet. Von Stedingk had command of one of these sections of fifty feet. Enemy were on both sides of it still, trying to fire into his position. Enemy were in the upper stories of the Savannah homes and buildings, firing down, but inaccurately, into their position.

Von Stedingk turned and looked over the embankment, back in the direction he had come. There were no more French troops advancing. There was a wide carpet of dead and wounded leading to the fifth line. Part of the fourth line of defensives was occupied by his men, but they too were fighting British on their right and left. He turned back to his remaining men, "Count of able bodies, Sergeant."

The Sergeant Major turned - with a smile - and spoke, "We have twenty men, twenty-one including yourself, Monsieur, and none hale or whole."

Von Stedingk looked them over. Every man was indeed hurt in some way or other. All of them were covered in blood, dirt and gunpowder. They looked absolutely fearful, but, in all honesty, if they were clean and pressed, this rugged crew would still freeze the blood. It was a tough bunch of lucky whoresons who stood before him now.

He looked once more at Savannah. There was no way they could charge the buildings. They would be taking fire from the enemy positions to their left and right, plus fire from the buildings. They were stuck here, unless other men somehow made it across the flat terrain from the fourth revetment to the fifth. Looking back, he realized it wasn't going to happen. Twenty-one men had made it to the last ditch, but no more were coming. The attack was stopped, even with the French vanguard occupying part of the last line.

But all would know he made it this far.

Von Stedingk turned to Sergeant Guerrier, "Plant the colors, Sergeant."

Guerrier grinned like a drunk prizefighter, and planted the flagstaff on the highest point of the revetment, heedless of the subsequent fire. Von Stedingk looked at the flag, gently waving above the final line of defenses. It was beautiful, the flag of France. It billowed white as the clouds, sparkling with gold *fleur-de-lis*. He had taken his objective at tremendous cost, but could not keep it. He resisted the urge to cry.

He could not resist the urge to sit. He had a feeling he would not walk again for days, if he survived at all. His ribs hurt ferociously, and the pain seemed to increase exponentially with every breath. There was simply nothing worse than a rib injury.

Perhaps the third day of a gut shot.

Von Stedingk spoke again, "Very soon, they will counterattack and force us out of this position. When the time comes, it will be every man for himself. If you can run, I expect you to do so, leaving those who cannot move as quickly to their fate. The odds of making it back to the body of our assault will be slim, do not make them worse for yourself."

He saw a round of nods, they understood.

Guerrier squinted, "I will make sure you return, Monsieur."

"I cannot run, Sergeant. If it comes down to it, save yourself."

"No, I don't think so, Monsieur."

"Pardon me, Sergeant?"

The Sergeant shrugged, "I think, Monsieur, you are not going to be left to your fate today." The other twenty men chuckled.

Von Stedingk shook his head, "I suppose I should have expected this sort of nonsense, from the lads mad enough to follow me to the end."

The Sergeant took off his hat and held it in the air, "Colonel Von Stedingk! Huzzah!" And there were three rounds of cheers.

Von Stedingk smiled weakly, then passed out. A Dijonnais placed a gentle hand on his shoulder to keep him from falling. Sergeant Guerrier took one of Von Stedingk's hands, slipped the other between his legs and easily moved the Colonel's weight to his shoulders. He walked up the embankment, and yanked the colors from the loam. He turned to the rest, "Let's go."

To the astonishment of the soldiers trapped in the fourth ring of defenses, the twenty-one who made it to the fifth soon came running back. They poured fire into the British lines, in an attempt to keep their heads down or throw off aim to save their retreating comrades. All twenty-one made it. Then, the twenty-one and the occupiers of the fourth line retreated to the third, then the second.

The attack had failed, however gallantly.

* * *

The French and their allies sustained twenty percent casualties across their entire force in one day. On October seventeenth, d'Estaing abandoned the siege. It was one of the bloodiest episodes of the entire war - only not for the British. Point of fact, it was a tremendous British victory. In London, cannons were fired in celebration when the news was heard.

Von Stedingk recovered from his wounds in a stateroom aboard the 80-gun *Deux Frères*. After he was recovered enough to write his dispatches and reports, he described the assault as best he could, and mentioned Sergeant Guerrier by name - a high honor. He felt, however, that he owed the doughty Sergeant a bit more. He soon issued a command for the Sergeant Major to be found, and brought aboard the *Deux Frères* by cutter.

In the meantime, he made inquiries.

Sergeant Major Guerrier happened to be legendary amongst the fleet. He was black enough to redden the hide of an African, but white enough to straighten out a European private without issue. He was known to keep a rowdy discipline amongst the volunteers, and encouraged a rough and tumble culture. It was said he never lost a fight, his pugilistic skills were impregnable, and honed by a thousand brawls. Oddly, Guerrier also had the reputation of having absolutely unassailable integrity. He never broke the rules, or allowed them to be broken. He was law-abiding, authority-respecting and honorable in all respects. One man said you could give him a thousand livre, and retrieve it a year later not a coin short.

Guerrier soon reported to him. Von Stedingk gave him his heartfelt thanks, explained the honor of being mentioned in dispatches, and asked him how he could express his gratitude in a more tangible way. Guerrier's answer was completely in character.

"Well, Monsieur Colonel," said Guerrier, blinking, squinting and chewing his lip, "I'm an octoroon, and a free man."

"And what is an octoroon?"

"I am seven-eighths white. Back in Le Cap, they call octoroons *Métis*, but most outside of Saint-Domingue call all colored *Métis*."

"They have special names for such things?"

"I have the papers to prove it as well, locked up tight in a merchant house back in Cap Français. We started out free, my family. Buccaneers, we were. When Saint-Domingue became civilized, we became civilized right with the times."

"A buccaneer? A pirate?"

"Well, not exactly. It was just a bunch of Africans, French criminals and Arakawa natives running around, mostly hunting wild boar and such, at least before the sugar and coffee plantations came about. My first ancestor to get on the priest's books was a little of all three, I'd imagine. He was a good man, an ambitious man. He was an overseer for one of the first sugar plantations."

"Fascinating."

"We've always been forward-thinking. Always looking to better ourselves, if only by a rung or two. I am an ambitious man, just like my ancestors. Always have been. I married a white woman, completely white, mind you, and my children are fifteen-sixteenths. We call them *Mamelouk* in Le Cap - and they are legally white. My children are white, Monsieur."

Von Stedingk smiled and nodded. Inwardly, he was struck that Guerrier's ambition was to produce something he was not, and could never be. But many men shared a pitiable drive, if they were not spiritually minded, even if they were kings. King Louis himself was, in fact, miserable. He wanted nothing more than to be a clockmaker, with perhaps a field he could hunt in. Queen Marie-Antoinette, deeply unhappy as well, would have liked nothing more than to be that man's wife, and a mother to her children. A soul's peace never comes from dreams stemming from the disquietude of one's own heart.

Guerrier continued, "I started out bouncing drunks from public houses and taverns, to being a policeman, then chasing runaways, to being a soldier. Now, I think it is time to make another change."

Guerrier had also failed at being a coffee farmer, but he had erased the memory. He did not like to fail.

"What kind of change, Sergeant?" asked Von Stedingk.

"It's time to leave the colonies, and give my family some proper opportunity, Monsieur. The kind of opportunity we have earned. The kind of opportunity my children can now have, being who they are."

"Where do you wish to take your family, Sergeant?"

"To France, Monsieur. I'd also like to become a policeman, having experience and skill doing such a thing already."

Von Stedingk nodded. A voyage to France for an entire family would be frightfully expensive for someone like Féroce Guerrier, and a minor expense to a man like Von Stedingk. "It is of nothing, Sergeant. After the war, you and your family will have your voyage to France, and I will personally write a letter of recommendation for you as a candidate for police." Von Stedingk held out his hand. Guerrier grasped it. "You are a brave and honorable man, Sergeant. It was an honor to lead you, and I hope to do so again."

Guerrier smiled, but did not speak. He saluted the Comte, an unprofessional gesture indoors. Regardless, Von Stedingk smiled back, and returned it. Féroce left the cabin, but did not go back to his cutter. Instead, he went to the dark bowels of the ship, where he was alone and out of sight, and he wept.

***

Von Stedingk would die an old man, a Field Marshall, a Lord of the Realm, recipient of the Royal Order of the Seraphim, the Order of the Sword, the Order of Saint Alexander Nevsky, the Pour le Mérite Militaires, the Order of St. Andrew, and the Society of the Cincinnati, though he could not wear the latter by order of the King of Sweden. The vagaries of history found him fighting for and against France, for and against Britain, for and against Russia, and for and against Prussia. He was respected by friends, allies, enemies, commoners, and nobles, alike. He was a hero, in every sense of the word, loyal to his creed and class to the end.

After the war, Sergeant Major Guerrier would go back to Saint-Domingue, to find his family in tatters.

The Time of the Heirlooms

1783

Cap Français

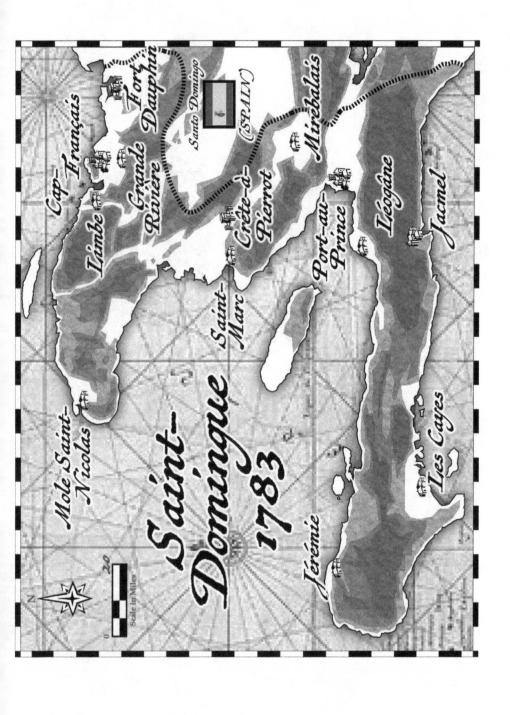

Chapter 8

Seonaidh Guerrier was beautiful, even as she lay dying. Her hair was jet black, her skin pale with a tinge of olive. Her eyes were green, deep-set under large, perfect eyebrows. They were tilted sharply at the corners, giving her an almost Asian exoticism, especially paired with her high cheekbones and fine features. She was slender, but feminine and youthful-looking, even after five children - two living and three dead.

She was nauseous and in agony, her every joint ached, and she was shivering cold in the oppressive, humid heat. She had been sick before, nearly every Summer since she was taken to the Americas as a girl. Every time she was struck down, no one expected her to survive. Somehow, she always did.

This time was different.

At the point in which she should have been getting better, she was getting worse. Most whites had a short life expectancy in the tropics. She had cheated fate for years. She had prayed for her own death so many times in the past, she thought she almost deserved it now, when it was inconvenient and unwanted. She laid in her bed, in her little five-room house made of wood, daub, and plaster, on three high acres just above and outside the walls of the hilly port of Cap Français, Saint-Domingue.

Two sets of eyes watched her carefully, for she had asked for them to come. They were her surviving children, twins, a brother and a sister, edging on fifteen. The Ó Brollachain clan, from whence came Seonaidh, were known for twins, though none of them ever looked alike. Seonaidh's brothers were twins. She last saw them as infants, long ago, and far, far away. It still hurt to think about them, and about that time.

Seonaidh looked to her son, Guillaume, for she could almost feel his eyes burning into her. She could see nothing of his father in him, at least physically. He was Seonaidh in male form - green-eyed, black-haired and handsome. He was usually sullen around her and Seonaidh had to admit she did not know him well. Since his long jaunts to Cap Français, he had calmed, but one look at her and his hate for the world returned, smoldering off his body like inky, black smoke. His anger scared her, and amused his father. She smiled at him, and he did not return it.

She felt she deserved his contempt. She was not a good mother, and Féroce was not a good father.

She looked at her daughter, Estelle, who smiled brightly at her. Estelle looked nothing like Seonaidh, and nothing like her father, either. She had curly, thick, chestnut hair, and alabaster skin covered with big, brown freckles. She was already buxom, and thick everywhere else, although certainly not chubby or fat. Her eyes were brown, and quite large - in fact, all of her features were a bit oversized. Her teeth were even big, and had noticeable spaces between them. She wasn't ugly by any means, in fact, she would make an attractive woman. But she would only just make the border of it, and would never be described as beautiful. But there was something indescribable about Estelle, there always had been. Although she was neither loud, nor in need of being the center of attention, she was known wherever she went. Estelle was perceptive; as smart, but differently gifted, as her brother; kind, and strong - but she struggled with things. Sometimes a darkness enveloped her, in spite of herself.

They were both very special, her twins, although it had taken Seonaidh a long time to realize it.

"How are you feeling, Maman?" Estelle asked.

Seonaidh didn't feel like speaking in French. She had spoken to them in *Gaeilge* since they were born. It was their secret language, one their father did not speak. Seonaidh delighted in keeping their words from him, although now she was filled with regret for being so cruel. "Let us speak in our secret tongue."

Guillaume's face twisted.

"Please, Guillaume. I am dying."

Guillaume calmed, his face went blank. Estelle began to cry.

"Please do not cry, Estelle. I need both of you to listen."

Guillaume spoke, "No more of your stories. I have no interest in feeding your hunger for pity." His words were as cruel as the ones she had used on him in the past.

Such as, "I wish you had not been the one to live, and I still had my Ruairí."
Seonaidh found it completely inconceivable that she had said such a thing to her
son - but she had, and much worse things beside.

Seonaidh sighed, and spoke, "There are things I would have you know. I do
not ask for pity, only indulgence."

He looked down and did not speak.

"I have told you how I grew up in the forest of Ards, in the ruins of the
Kingdom of Tír Chonaill."

Guillaume tensed. He hated it when his mother spoke of her past. He
couldn't tell if she was mad or sane, whether the stories were true or false. She
couldn't read, couldn't write, and her head was full of superstition, like an African priestess. In some places they had lived, the blacks were afraid of her and
called her a witch. Now, his mother's eyes were burning with fever and sickness.
Whatever she was about to say could not be trusted.

Estelle felt the opposite way. She kept and studied every word that her
mother spoke, sifting it for nuggets of gold, for insight into her family's past, of
which she knew little. She believed that family history was important, and could
provide insight into many present things.

Seonaidh continued, "A priest came to clan Ó Brollachain to bless my
mother, when she was gravid with me. There had been no live births among the
clan for six months. The priest came with dire words. He said I was under a
doom of *cinniúint*."

"What is *cinniúint*, Maman?" asked Estelle.

"It is your fate, your luck, your destiny. The wonderful and horrible sur-
prises of your life. The priest spoke in front of the entire clan. I was called *drochthuar* ever after."

"What is a *drochthuar*, Maman?" asked Estelle.

"It is a word I swore I would never use. But I called Old Leather a *drochthuar*, in Montserrat. He became my dearest friend. He was an ancient African.
He perpetrated every evil, and had in turn every evil perpetrated upon him. He
was very wise and very kind."

Guillaume knew of Old Leather. Maman always spoke about him - Old
Leather this, Old Leather that. He had no idea if he existed, or if Montserrat was
an actual place.

She continued, "A *drochthuar* is an evil harbinger of doom. A bearer of dark
magic, affecting one's *cinniúint*."

Guillaume stood, he had his fill.

"Please!" Seonaidh begged, "Please hear what little I have to say."

Estelle made a subtle motion to Guillaume. On her face was a gentle mixture
of love and frustration. He sat down.

Seonaidh continued, "I hated that priest. I hated God, and the church, and
the cruel children of my village. But every word the father spoke came true."

With effort, Seonaidh turned in bed and reached for a thin cedar box she had retrieved earlier. She slid the latch open, and raised the top. Inside were tufts of loose wool. Probing through them, her fingers found *the necklace*. The children had only seen it a handful of times, and each time was vividly remembered. A first impression offered an explosion of scarlet stars. Sparks flew everywhere, red galaxies spinning over the walls and ceiling. Second, one saw the nearly translucent cross, glowing red unless seen in the proper light, when it was revealed as milky white. Christ was in gold on the cross, so too were the settings and other details. It must have been made by angels, for one could stare at it for hours. Seonaidh whispered. "I am dying-"

"No, Maman," said Estelle gently.

"Everyone dies, child. So do I," and, with that, she handed the necklace to Estelle, and wrapped the chain around her hand.

A tear made its way down Estelle's cheek. This was her mother's most prized possession - as well it should be, for it would have been the most vaunted of a Czarina. Her gift could only mean one thing: her mother would soon be gone.

Seonaidh spoke, "I have changed. I have looked back at my life, and where I once saw horror, I now see beauty. Of Montserrat, once I only remembered the beatings of the Ó Conchubhair daughters, now I remember the animals who were my family, the exotic tastes of meals, and the words I shared with Old Leather. However ill I was treated by Captain Eltis, I emerged with a priceless treasure, that I now pass to you." She could see Guillaume getting impatient again and tried to talk faster. "I have come to love life again, and to love God. An understanding has come to me."

"And your time chained in the hold, what treasure did that bring to you?" asked Guillaume, for he knew, from her own past words, that there was nothing but unimaginable horror in that hold. She had been brought to Montserrat in the bowels of a ship, and still Seonaidh woke every morning, wet and screaming, from a nightmare where she was back in chains, lying in her own filth, unable to move or escape. Guillaume asked the question to thwart her, to be ornery and contrary. For a moment, she was lost - there truly was nothing good in that hold. But then the answer came to her like the sudden, gentle break of dawn. She smiled and laughed.

"Why, if not for the time in the hold, I would not have you, Guillaume, nor your sister, and you were always my greatest treasures of all."

Guillaume looked down and breathed deeply. Estelle teared, but held strong.

Seonaidh smiled, "Life is so achingly lovely. A journey of pure wonder. I find myself thankful for having been alive. I wish that I could have weathered my suffering with a stronger soul, and the eyes I now possess. God is glorious, his plan is a celebration. I am so thankful he gave me the insight I now have. I long to finally embrace him, and thank him for my life."

If there was one thing Guillaume knew of his mother, it was that her history had been one long and epic saga of tragedy. She had been forced into a ridiculously bad life - and she had taken every ounce of that suffering and taken it out on them. For a time, she had discovered drink. He remembered her drunk and ranting in French at her father. "You took advantage of me! Captain Fabre told you to take care of me!"

"I married you, Seonaidh, right honorable, in a *damné* church!" shot back Féroce. He would yell and scream at her, but he would never strike her. He sometimes hit his children, though.

She ranted on, "You married my color, not me! Fresh off the boat, I was! I was scared, I was gravid, I was young as a spotted fawn - what did I know? If I knew a soup bowl of what I know now, I would never have had a thing to do with ye. You black macaque! I never would have married you, and had your *putain* children *de couleur!*"

She was speaking of four of her other children, two mercifully dead, but the other two - Guillaume and Estelle - were listening, and had always listened.

Féroce snarled, "My children are legally white, you *salope vérolée*! I may be colored, but at least my line has always been free. You were a *putain* slave, and the only white baby you ever had was the get of your master."

"Don't you speak of him like that!" she screamed, "God returned my dear Ruairí."

"Aye, and he killed him dead from the Summer sickness, as well, didn't he?"

"Shut up, you *merdique nègre!*"

And so it went between Maman and Papa, each slinging hateful words like well-thrust blades. The twins didn't fully understand all of the references, but they got the gist. When Maman spoke the secret tongue, she sounded like a poet. When she spoke French, it was more like the pidgin oaths of a foreign-born dock-whore.

Strangely, Maman and Papa were absolutely true to each other, regardless and always. It was good they had each other, for they had no one else. There was no other family, they scared the neighbors, and they had no friends.

Seonaidh coughed from her bed, and continued, "I love you both so much. I'm sorry I was ever cross with you."

"I forgive you, Maman," said Estelle. She had long waited for such signs of love from her mother. She was as grateful for her mother's words as she was to forgive.

"I do not want your forgiveness. What I want is for every wound I ever inflicted to heal. I want you to know how I have always felt, not how I made you feel. I love you, my beautiful children. Please know this."

She fell silent.

Then she died.

A loud wail escaped Guillaume's lips, surprising Estelle. He had unraveled, broken in a thousand pieces. "Maman! Maman!" he cried. He held her limp body, cradling her head and shoulders and sobbed.

Estelle hoped Maman was looking down from heaven. Guillaume, deep down in his soul, was good and loving, Estelle wanted to believe. He would have many choices before him - he could extinguish his light or turn his lantern brighter - but right here, right now, he was good. His mother had died, he loved her, he was inconsolable. Estelle was terribly stricken as well, but she knew the tragedy belonged to herself, and to the other living, and not to Maman. This was the best thing that ever happened to her, and, at the end, she saw the beauty and wonder of her experience. Maman was missed, but not mourned, by Estelle. She knew her mother was in a better place than this humid, molten-hot, daub shack outside Le Cap.

Guillaume's piercing wails interrupted her thoughts. She put her arms around them both, and rested her head on her brother's back. He was all she had now. Unfortunately, for Estelle, he could not say the same. It was only a matter of time before he would leave.

Guillaume found his second family when he was nine. It was a difficult time. They had moved back to Le Cap after living in the mountains, uphill from Milot, on their coffee plantation named Champ-Élevé. They were happy there. They all went their separate ways during the day. Maman mostly spent her time under-water, in a cool lagoon beneath a waterfall. She would never dry off, and would roam about wet. No one could understand why she would want to be wet all of the time, it was cold enough in the mountains as it was. She would mutter to herself in *Gaeilge*, and sometimes utter strange curses, or hex people with the movements of her hands. The Africans were terrified of her, they called her *le Sorcière d'Eau* - the Water Witch. It was perhaps not too far from the truth - Maman's people were a magic-believing, superstitious lot.

Guillaume roamed the hills, everywhere and nowhere, alone. Estelle did not understand why. He said he just liked to think. and to see what there was to see. Estelle tended her garden, and cooked and cleaned with Bue-Bue, their house slave. Estelle would have rather helped with the coffee trees. Plants spoke to her. Even if no one told her how to grow something, she could suss out what was needed just by seeing the leaves react to sunlight, water and temperature.

Papa had many wonderful qualities. He was a born leader. He could size up men quickly and know their hearts. He was fearless, jovial and capable. He could find a runaway slave in a jungle, and convince him to return to a whipping. He had never found his equal in a fight, but never hated a soul. Unfortunately, he was also self-consumed and arrogant. He knew next to nothing of farming, and absolutely nothing regarding the growing of coffee. That would be an odd attribute for a plantation owner, much less an on-deck farmer. But Féroce had tremendous acumen in all his prior endeavors, and had saved some coin. It was then his to spend.

Saint-Domingue belonged to the plantation owners. The planters had the status, wealth, and power. Féroce wanted all three, so he bought the biggest plantation he could with the money he had - a mistake in and of itself, for he had little left over for random misfortune. He had no reason to doubt his abilities, he had never failed at anything. In any case, self-doubt was incapable of penetrating his overwhelming narcissism.

Estelle knew more about coffee just by smelling the fields than Féroce would ever know in a lifetime. She tried to help. "Papa, the beans can't be harvested all at once."

"The insects eat the beans if left on the branches."

"We have to inspect the trees as much as we can, and remove the beans where the insects have laid their eggs. But we cannot harvest the beans all at once because they ripen unevenly."

"So, coffee just happens to be the only *damné* plant in the whole world you can't harvest all at once?"

"No, Papa. There are others."

"Such as?"

"I don't know. Lemons?"

And he would roll his eyes and do it his way.

"Papa," she said, "You cannot hunt the birds and the bats. And you cannot kill the good insects that eat the ones that are pests."

"Good insects? *Mon dieu*, what next? Estelle, quit riding me like a saddle gelding."

"Papa, I can only tell you what I see plainly. I only want to help," said Estelle, becoming upset and nervous.

"Estelle, don't put yourself in a fit. You know how you get. You're not even ten Summers old. Let me handle the affairs of the land."

And poor Estelle went back to her flourishing little gardens, and Papa failed at his coffee trees.

They finally ran out of money. Papa's grand adventure as a plantation owner had failed. They sold their land and their slaves, and returned to Le Cap, so that Féroce could do the work he did best: hunting and policing men. The lowland weather of Le Cap drove Maman insane, even with the ocean breezes, and made her sick every Summer. Everyone but Féroce was miserable.

Féroce, of course, was soon very busy and successful, and even received a police commission.

One day a fancy letter was delivered to the house. As he could not read it, Féroce went to the Le Cap cathedral, made a donation of alms and asked a priest to read it to him. Féroce soon found that one Monsieur Pinceau, a plantation owner living in Le Cap, had a serious problem. Slaves had escaped from his sugar plantation outside Valiere, and into the mountains above them. They snuck back regularly, and helped others escape. Monsieur Pinceau had lost nearly a hundred-thousand livre in slaves, and harvest was almost upon him. He needed someone to go into the mountains, break up the den, and return his slaves - precisely the kind of work for which Féroce was known.

Guillaume, meanwhile, had developed a skill of his own. He would collect news pamphlets and posters that contained engravings of soldiers. He would cut them out and, using bone glue, give them a backing and stand of frond fibers. He was outside in the yard, in the process of painting his latest creation - with paint he mixed himself - when Papa crossed to his rock. That, in and of itself, was highly unusual. Papa never took an interest in his children's activities.

"Papa?" said Guillaume in surprise.

"Want to go to Le Cap?" asked Papa.

"With you?"

"With who else, jackass?"

"Yes! Yes, I do!" said Guillaume excitedly, for he worshipped his father like a curly-headed god, and was never able to spend any time with him at all.

"Well, put on your good clothes, and come to the cart."

Guillaume had one nice outfit. Some would call them church clothes, but they never went to church because Papa was a pagan and Maman hated God. After he changed, they were on their way. If they threw a stone from their southernmost property, it would practically land in Le Cap, but between them were steep cliffs. The road meandered down at a more suitable angle, before turning south and then east into the city gates. Papa waved at the guards, who were his subordinates, and into Le Cap they went.

Cap Français was charming - quite beautiful actually. The streets were wide and well-planned. The houses were large and winsome, each floor supporting wide verandas, with arches of ornamental wrought iron and hanging plants. The women, mostly whites with a few mixes, were dressed in the latest Parisian styles. The men, mostly white, were dressed with equal magnificence, and the manners and etiquette of Versailles were plain to see. There were many working people, slaves, and sailors about, but most homeowners had money.

In fact, they had a tremendous, gargantuan amount of money.

It was quite simple: anywhere in the world, if one sipped coffee, rum, sweet liqueur or Champagne; if one ate a forkful of cake, any kind of tomato sauce, candies, jams, or preserved fruits; the sugar or coffee necessary to produce them most likely came from Saint-Domingue. Saint-Domingue was the envy of every empire, and the jewel in the crown of France. It was a global center of commerce and Le Cap, as it was called, was the cultural center of Saint-Domingue – the colonial capitol of Port-au-Prince a far distant second.

The self-made nobles who ruled the island colony mostly lived in Le Cap rather than on their lands, and had created a polite society worthy of the courts of Europe.

As they rumbled down the wide avenues, Guillaume would occasionally run through traffic and take posters and news pamphlets from their approved spaces on walls and fences. Féroce laughed as he watched his son dodge the other carts and horses on the street. Onlookers tried not to faint in fear for the boy.

Finally, they came to an elegant four-story villa surrounded by manicured grounds and a tall fence of wrought-iron spears. Féroce turned to his son, "This is the home of Monsieur Pinceau. Mind your manners."

"Yes, Papa," said Guillaume. He had actually been taught a bit of good manners, for Féroce had taken the time to learn, considering the knowledge of etiquette to be essential for advancement. Unfortunately, Guillaume was usually taught in a harsh manner, and during dinner. When called to meals, he usually felt anxious and fearful rather than hungry.

They parked and braked the cart on the street, opened the wrought iron gates, and crossed to the high wooden doors. Soon they were admitted by the butler, and stood inside.

The foyer was dark and cool. The ceiling was two stories high, and was ringed by a balcony, accessed by a wall-hugging, balustraded staircase. The house slaves looked upon them with curiosity. Race was every bit as important in Saint-Domingue as wealth or title. At the very bottom of the social ladder were full African blacks, perhaps better described as the mud upon which the ladder rested. Whites were sand castles, sculpted by a master, to be admired and enjoyed until the waves of disease and climate swept them away. Sand castles cannot inherit what they build, and white women hardly ever stepped foot on the island. In no time, another group came to equal the whites. The true nobles who claimed ownership of Saint-Domingue became the mixes, the *gens de couleur libre*, the free people of color. Le Cap may have been mostly white, but the more south one traveled in Saint-Domingue, the more colored those in power became. The lowest noble caste, the metaphorical barons, were the *Mulâtre*, half-black and half-white, usually the freed offspring of a master and a slave. Next came the dukes of Saint-Domingue, the *Quarteron*, which Monsieur Pinceau happened to be, who were one-quarter black. Further up were the kings and queens, the *Métis* - one-eighth black. There were names for every mix in between. *Marabou* were five-eighths black, *Griffe* were three-quarters, and *Sacatra* were seven-eighths. But high, high above them all were the archangels: the *Mamelouk* - one-sixteenth black. They were legally white, but black enough to be claimed by the coloreds. They were therefore perfect. They could pass in any city in Europe. They could withstand the sun and climate of the tropics. They were as beautiful, smart and creative as the whites, and as strong, spiritual and musical as the blacks - at least according to the mores of Saint-Domingue. Mankind ever seeks to separate cream from milk, then creams from creams, and then label and grade the layers. The ways of Saint-Domingue were different from other places, but only in its means of separation.

This tidy arrangement found itself sullied due to one simple fact: nearly nine out of ten people in Saint-Domingue were pure black African slaves. Everyone else, of any label, was a hopelessly small minority.

In any case, Féroce was obviously part black, but the young man with him looked white. Could that be his son, could he be one of the legendary *Mamelouk*? The answer was yes, and, of course, this was precisely why Féroce brought his son to the meeting. Guillaume and Estelle were his greatest achievements and elevated his status with the landowning *gens de couleur*. Estelle did not like Le Cap, nor dusty cart rides away from her gardens. Guillaume was fearless and adventurous like his father, albeit more introverted. Guillaume was therefore here, and Estelle was not.

Monsieur Pinceau looked over them unseen from the second-story balcony. He had wide African features, but his skin was the color of leather. His hair was slightly less curly than a true black, but was even a lighter color than his skin and was streaked with grey. Looking down, he saw Féroce was everything he was rumored to be. He radiated capacity for violence, control, and a soldierly good-humor. Guillaume was obviously a *Mamelouk*, and the same age as his beloved only son, Raphaël.

Raphaël was all that was left of his wife, Adèle. She was a gorgeous, lithe *Métis*. Perhaps the French blood was too predominated, for she was claimed by the Summer sickness a few years ago. Monsieur walked down the stairs, capturing their attention, "Monsieur Guerrier, welcome to my home, and thank you for coming."

"It is my pleasure to finally make your acquaintance, Monsieur Pinceau," said Féroce, as he bowed.

"And who do we have here?" Monsieur said, as he smiled at Guillaume. Guillaume smiled back.

"This is my son, Guillaume."

Guillaume bowed, "It is an honor to meet you, Monsieur."

"I am enchanted. You will be happy to know that you will not have to listen to the adults converse."

Guillaume smiled and bowed. It was what he was taught to do if he did not know precisely what to say, or if an answer was not required.

Monsieur Pinceau took notice, and nodded his head in return, "To explain, young Monsieur, my son is upstairs with his toys, and happens to be exactly your age. I invite you to go upstairs, turn down the hall to your left, and then knock on the last door to your left."

Guillaume said nothing for a second. Monsieur Pinceau's son should have been called, they should have been introduced, then gone off together to play. This seemed odd.

But Féroce's strong hand nudged him toward the stairs, and he was smart enough to take his cue. "Thank you, Monsieur Pinceau. I will do exactly that, and I thank you for your hospitality." Guillaume went up the stairs, while Pinceau took Féroce into his downstairs study.

The upstairs was dark. It was unusual for a house in Le Cap to have interior rooms with no windows - most rooms in Le Cap seemed half outside, and some could only be accessed via doors on the windswept verandas. But the Pinceaus were wealthy and emulated Paris in their architecture as they pleased. Guillaume went down the dark hallway, and finally stood before the last door on the left. He listened, and heard nothing. He finally knocked.

"Come in," came the voice of a young man.

Guillaume entered. The room was quite large, but held only a bed and wardrobe. Guillaume's attention went immediately to what was scattered across the floor - miniature lead soldiers, horses and cannon arranged for battle, all perfectly and brilliantly painted.

Guillaume went to his knees for a closer look. They were the most interesting things he had ever seen. His paper soldiers were a joke, a ghost of these masterful miniatures. He recognized the well-painted uniforms: Musketeers of the Guard, the *Régiment Royal-Suédois*, artillery companies, dragoons, and cuirassiers.

"Don't touch those," said the voice.

Guillaume turned, and saw a boy lying in bed. He was pale, but obviously *couleur*, with African hair and features. He was short and thin, sweating and sickly. "Why not?" Guillaume replied.

"Because they are mine," he said.

"You aren't playing with them," Guillaume retorted.

"But I do play with them. Why do you think they are scattered across the floor?"

"How do you play with them?"

"I have battles."

"Who against who?"

"Last week, I had a battle of the Musketeers of the Guard against the *Régiment Royal-Suédois*, as you can plainly see."

"Can I? Who won?"

"The Musketeers."

Guillaume made a dismissive sound, "That plainly illustrates your total lack of knowledge of anything important."

His comment was knee-jerk, a youthful and arrogant reaction. It was not designed to begin the argument of his life, profoundly alter his experience, and change nearly every aspect of his life, but that is precisely what it did.

Monsieur Pinceau and Féroce were soon interrupted by the sound of argument, as the boys' yelling shook the walls. The men rushed upstairs. Féroce was horrified, even scared, at how his plan to bring Guillaume along had misfired. Monsieur Pinceau, on the other hand, felt rising excitement, and an optimism he didn't dare believe. But when they opened the door to Raphaël's room, the facts were plain to see. His boy, his beloved boy, who ate food only to lose weight, who was bedridden and doomed to die, who could not be helped by the best doctors in the new world or the old, was out of bed, standing, and screaming at the top of his lungs at the godsend, young Guillaume Guerrier, who was trying his best to drown him out with counter arguments of his own.

Féroce managed a croak, "Guillaume, what have you done?" and the boy paled, and looked terrified.

Monsieur Pinceau had to salvage this situation, and quickly. He smiled, "Messieurs, over what do we argue?"

Raphaël spoke quickly and intensely, much to the delight of his father, "He says the *Régiment Royal-Suédois* could easily beat the Musketeers of the Guard."

"Interesting," said Monsieur Pinceau, "Over what terrain does this battle take place?"

The boys went silent.

Monsieur Pinceau shrugged, "Terrain is very important in battle, is it not, Monsieur Guerrier?"

Féroce nodded. He had no idea why Pinceau wasn't tossing them both out the door, but he was smart enough to adjust his cannon fire on the spot, "Yes, terrain is extraordinarily important, Monsieur."

Guillaume could only take so much. "Yes, but the courage and ferocity of the Swiss Guard has been legendary for centuries."

Neither could Raphaël, "But the King's Musketeers were the best, when France undoubtedly had the greatest military in the whole world.'

"Yes, yes," said Pinceau, "but this answer is not day or night, nor yes and no. Over a hundred battles, the Musketeers would not always beat the Guard, and the Swiss would not always beat the Musketeers. Correct?"

They both nodded, thinking hard upon it.

"Both units are equally well-armored, but the Swiss would have an edge when it came to hand-to-hand combat, being better and heavier armed. Let us say the Musketeers would have the better odds during an exchange of muskets."

Guillaume nodded, "Then the Swiss would have the edge in a forest."

"But not in a field," Raphaël said quickly.

"But not in a city," Guillaume shot back.

"Unless it was a city like Le Cap, with long, wide streets," offered Pinceau. "Please stay here, for a moment," and off he disappeared.

Guillaume forgot his father's prior look, and turned to him, "What do you think, Papa?"

Féroce had forgotten his prior feelings as well, "Well, they are both right tough outfits. I would want to know who had the best equipped and most skilled supply officers, and who had the most artillery. Cannon wins battles. Don't let anyone tell you otherwise. In the modern age, it's man's tools that win the field. Grit alone is not enough. And a good supply train, with plenty of powder, clean water and good, hot meals."

Both boys nodded - it was wisdom.

Monsieur Pinceau returned with paper, pen and quills, and a coin. He sat on the floor, and quickly lined up opposing Swiss and Musketeers, "They are at a distance, but closing. Each side has time for only one volley. Let us say that, at range, the Musketeers have a one-point advantage. Three flips of the coin. Two or more heads fells a Swiss, three tails levels a Musketeer."

And then Monsieur paired up the lead figures, flipping the coin to determine the outcome of each pair, and tipping the loser to lay on its side.

When it came down to hand-to-hand for the miniatures, the boys started arguing again, this time over math. Pinceau offered the paper and ink when they needed to write down a particularly difficult equation, or some complex detail too hard to remember. Féroce was shocked to find Guillaume could both read and write, and knew basic math. He had no idea how he came to know such things. It would have surprised him even more to know that he had taught Estelle.

When the boys were utterly consumed with the numbers behind their mortal combat, Monsieur Pinceau stood and motioned to Féroce. Both men quietly left the room and shut the door. Féroce had no idea what to say and kept his mouth shut.

Monsieur Pinceau spoke softly, "My son is sickly, Monsieur. I have not seen him this well, and this long out of bed for over a year. I beg you, Monsieur, to allow a friendship to develop between your son and mine. I have already determined that you will help me in my business, as a partner performing what I cannot do, from now until the end of time. Now, let us allow our progeny to become brothers, for that is what God wishes them to be."

"Uh, certainly, Monsieur," said Féroce.

"And while he is here, I promise he will be fed, clothed, educated - all his needs will be met, as if he was my nephew. Let him spend the night, as a gesture of goodwill. He will be returned tomorrow, and will always be welcomed here, whether for a day, a night, both or forever."

Féroce honestly did not care. The situation between the boys was of no account. He had the job. It was time to close the deal. "Of course, Monsieur," he said politely, "Let us conclude our contract, and I will assemble my party and be headed south within forty-eight hours."

Monsieur Pinceau offered a hand, which Féroce readily took, "Well and done, Monsieur Guerrier."

From that day, Guillaume spent far more time in Le Cap than he did at home. Estelle missed him terribly. Maman did not seem to care, and Féroce was never home. When Guillaume did return, he was better-dressed and fatter, and usually brought a book for Estelle. His visits were never too long, for when he returned Maman and Papa suddenly did care that he was gone, and there were bitter arguments. To Estelle, these confrontations seemed to have no point but the exhibition of rancor. Perhaps Maman and Papa were tired of berating each other and, needing a change, found Guillaume's return convenient.

Estelle was always grateful for the books, but found her tastes were different than her brother. She implored him to bring her something she would like, perhaps poetry or a play. Guillaume could not understand her tastes and thought he was doing her a favor by ignoring her choices.

One day he brought her the oddest book. Half was composed of excerpts from the Bible and other great works written by philosophers, mathematicians and jurors. The other half, however, was composed of satirical essays – in fact, there was an essay to follow every excerpt. Each essay was in the writing style of the excerpt, only exaggerated to poke fun at each one. The essay authors all had fanciful names: Adelgunde, the Knight of the Rose-Cross, Aristobolus, the Sibyl.

The essays were poetic in nature although usually not in style - virtually incomprehensible on a literal level. They assumed much of the reader, that she was brilliant, witty and well-educated. Estelle realized the excerpts were there only to help the reader better understand the essays. These essay authors, whether Adelgunde or the Sibyl, were ferociously in love with irony, which made things interesting but much subtler. Whether the writers were making fun of someone ancient, contemporary or even Biblical, there were spiderwebs of ideas, images, poetry and parable.

The nature of the work was a mystery, but there were two clues.

Adèle was signed on the inside cover in a female cursive. In the same hand, much larger and on the cover itself, was written *Johann Georg Hamann*. Estelle suspected correctly that Hamann was the one who wrote all the essays under fanciful pen names, and someone had simply taken the time to put them together, include the objects of satire, and transcribe it all into French. Presumably this was *Adèle,* who deserved an Olympic laurel for the effort.

Estelle loved that book. She begged Guillaume to ask Monsieur Pinceau for a longer loan, and Monsieur promptly gifted it to her, unknowing of how it even came into his collection. It became Estelle's most prized possession. She studied every word, and slowly began to understand.

Hamann was convinced man shouldn't be too confident in his intellectualism. Even the best minds and ideas were hopelessly flawed. Mankind's only hope was to put his faith in God, eschew fanaticism of any kind, and have great patience with people of different ideas, and even faiths. He skewered the confidence of most intellectuals - in Estelle's opinion, rightfully so. But she was biased, very biased indeed, for she had developed a mash, a desperate crush, on Monsieur Hamann. It was silly, a flight of fancy, but sometimes she could think about him for hours. She imagined him as a handsome, young man - who became more and more concrete in his features as time passed. Estelle couldn't breathe when she thought about him. She would become utterly taken, as if by a fever.

Estelle had no idea why the world was not as in love with his ideas as she was. It was so clear to her that patience and faith, perhaps coupled with a love for creation, a joyful spirit and much laughter, was a good medicine for most ills. It was simple: society's troubles came from the collective spiritual sickness of *individuals*. Man's laws and punishments did not modify the human spirit. True transformation only came from individual's internal decisions made of free will. Helping to incite change in others required a close relationship, love, and investment of time and energy – especially with others holding dissimilar beliefs. Only through one's own example of action, and investment of love, do people notice other points of view. Anything else was a dangerous shortcut, it seemed to Estelle, when she dreamed of her conversations with the handsome Johann.

It took up a lot of her time, these talks.

Johann would sigh, and lean back against an imaginary tree and say something profound. Perhaps he would talk of finding himself in the body of a cane slave, and how difficult it would be to find happiness. But did wealth and freedom bring happiness? Could happiness come from outside one's soul? Truly, he would say, even a landed duke could find himself joyless. But if the harder task were achieved, that of besting one's own heart and surrendering to God, true joy could be found. True joy emanated from the heart and affected others. To Estelle, all of this was common sense - Christian, good and decent.

She would tell Johann that the greatest thing to which a human could aspire was to be incapable of evil toward her fellows - and that was the sum total of her aspirations… although that was a lie. She very much wanted to be married and have children as well, and with him, with *Johann*, who was nearly the opposite of every man she had ever met. Papa and Guillaume had some wonderful qualities, but sometimes being around them was akin to continually stubbing one's toe on a steel block - unforgiving and painful. Estelle wanted a man who was like a warm blanket on a cold night. She wanted someone she could trust and love safely, and therefore beautifully.

It would never happen.

Estelle knew she would never leave Saint-Domingue. This island, and the hard men upon it, were her lot. So far they had wanted nothing to do with her.

Then something unexpected happened - France went to war with Britain.

And Saint-Domingue decided to raise a unit of volunteers to send off with their colonial regiments. A motley assemblage of whites, blacks, coloreds, freemen and slaves answered the call - including Papa, who was given sergeant's stripes. Marching to their ships, they were a wonder to behold. Estelle wondered how anyone could possibly stand against them.

That was years ago. Many of them had died, but not Papa, who could not die, who was larger than death and life, and could not be bested by normal means.

And then poor Maman, ripped from her home as a child and sold into slavery, a victim of rape, the chain and the whip, unable to acclimatize, mad and sick from the heat, finally passed from the earth with a quiet celebration of thankfulness, responsibility and love. And there was Guillaume, the toe-stubbing firebrand, who now realized he was simply a thing of flesh and feeling on the earth - one who loved his mother.

A breeze blew through the window, and it was soft and cool.

Guillaume spoke, "I'm going back to Le Cap."

Estelle wanted to scream and hit him. Instead, she replied calmly, "We have some pressing matters we must attend to first."

"Such as?"

"We must bury Maman."

"Do not the priests do such things?"

"Perhaps they would. But no one attends church in this family except for me."

"You still attend church? I did not know."

"I do not think anyone in Le Cap will help us, Guillaume. I think we must put Maman on a cart, and go see Father Jozef." Father Jozef was from the United Netherlands, a priest for the slaves at Quartier-Morin, the largest plantation outside Le Cap.

To Estelle's astonishment, Guillaume did not argue. Instead, he turned and held her. "I love you, Estelle."

Estelle broke in an instant, wailing and completely despondent. She was taken with her emotion, thought of nothing and had no control, but soon the moment passed to the pressing responsibilities of the present.

Estelle bundled her mother in her sheets and blankets, as Guillaume hitched the horse. Both of them carried Maman, who weighed but little, to the back of the cart and placed her there. It was less than three miles to Quartier-Morin, and away they went.

They arrived at Quartier-Marin without incident. They were stopped a quarter of a mile within the plantation by a slave overseer on horseback. He was concerned at their trespass, but was cordial enough after they explained why they were there. When Father Jozef was summoned and met them on the road, he was far less hospitable. "You should have gone to Le Cap," he said, "I have neither the time nor the coin for this."

"Father," said Estelle patiently, "We do not require your money. As for your time-"

"My flock is the cane slaves of Saint-Domingue. Do you have any idea how indescribably horrid is the life of a cane slave? Did your father tell you? The one who retrieves them from the hills, to be returned to torture, and sometimes death?"

Estelle grabbed a handful of fabric from the top of her brother's trousers. If he attacked the priest with words or actions, they accomplished nothing. But Guillaume did not move. Estelle smiled, and spoke again to Father Jozef, "I understand, Father. But we are all here together, united in worldly flesh and in Christ. There are likewise some tragedies that unite us all. As we mourn the death of cane slaves, we mourn the death of any man or woman, being of equal value to God. As, recently, myself and my brother mourn the death of our mother, leaving us alone until our father returns to us from war."

Father Jozef teared, "My goodness, child. And such words I offer you. I am so sorry." Father Jozef put a hand on Estelle's cheek. "Forgive me, I am here for you."

And he was. Guillaume, Estelle, the Father and two slaves dug a grave for Maman. She was then buried in a proper Christian sacrament. Estelle cried again, but Guillaume did not. They ate with the Father, and slept on the floor of the church. But later that night, Estelle woke up in a panic, with her heart beating out of her chest.

She pushed her brother awake, "Guillaume!"

He woke, "What is it?"

"What if Papa returns, and we are not there?"

"He wouldn't notice - until you weren't there to make his breakfast."

"Guillaume, do not vex me. If Papa returns, no one will be home. What if he goes off looking for us, worried over our state."

"Then he goes off looking for us."

"No. No, we must return at once."

"It is the middle of the night."

"Yes, I know."

"Estelle, it is not feasible."

"I don't care. We must return."

"Estelle, you will get our horse bit by a snake. Then we will have to walk, and we will get bitten as well."

Estelle cried in the corner of the church.

A few minutes later, Guillaume hitched the horse. Father Jozef heard the commotion, came out and gave them food, and some good torches of pitch and resin.

After thanking the Father, they soon headed home.

Papa was not there.

In the morning, Estelle made them breakfast.

"Estelle," said Guillaume, "you must return with me to Le Cap."

"No, I have to be here for when Father returns."

"The first place he will go searching, if he doesn't find us here, is the Pinceau residence in Le Cap."

"But you don't know that."

"Then leave him a note."

"He can't read."

"He takes the notes to the priests in Le Cap."

"But what if he lights a fire to cook, and uses the note as tinder?"

"He's terrifically clever, our Papa. He would not do such a thing."

"But he might."

"Estelle, listen to me. I am going to Le Cap. I am not staying here. If Papa does not return, I am never, ever coming back."

"How can you say that?"

"Estelle, just come with me."

Estelle realized there was nothing she could do to change his mind. "I will stay here for Papa," she said.

"You can tend the gardens of the estate, and have any seeds you wish to plant."

"It isn't the gardens. I-I have to stay here for Papa."

"I will not visit here. We have no family friends, no relatives, and even our neighbors shun us, for Maman was crazy and Papa was cruel. You will be completely alone, do you understand that, Estelle?"

"Please don't leave me here all alone."

"Come with me. You will be the daughter that Monsieur never had. You will be welcomed like family. You will forget that we were ever tied to these people in any way."

Estelle darkened. "Honor thy father and mother."

"Come with me," he replied gently.

"They are our parents. They made us. We are who we are. We cannot be anything else, we cannot change in this manner. I am staying here because this is the Guerrier residence, I am a Guerrier, and it is my home. It is where Papa will return."

Guillaume sighed, and looked sad. "Goodbye, Estelle."

She could tell by his voice that he very much would have wanted her to come with him. They held each other.

"What if something happens to you?" he said.

"Nothing will happen to me, Guillaume. I'll be fine. Enjoy your time with Raphaël."

Guillaume nodded, they said their goodbyes, and he left.

Estelle spent the next day on the kitchen floor, sobbing and terrified.

The next day she cooked and cleaned, and drew water from their well.

The next day she tended the garden, and hitched their mule, named Abruti. She went out looking for wood and kindling, for she had no money to buy charcoal. Abruti needed to eat as well, and all of the plants she tended were for her. There were no other animals at the Guerrier residence, not even a cat or dog. Perhaps it was because Papa was never home, and Maman had given up.

They had animals when they lived in the mountains at Champ-Élevé – even goats, chickens, and sheep. At Champ-Élevé, Maman sometimes helped Estelle in the gardens, where she proved to have every bit the grower's mettle of her daughter. With the animals, Maman was even better.

When Estelle returned from feeding Abruti and finding tinder, she tended the garden. She had found her routine. Days and weeks passed. Sometimes the fruits and vegetables ripened just as the last crop was harvested, but sometimes they didn't. When they didn't, she would become hungry if there wasn't anything left over from the last crop.

One day she hitched the cart, and headed to the ocean. The coastal rocks outside the city were always filled with dark African men, mostly poor freemen who were hungry. She joined them. They adopted her on the spot, and soon became her Uncles. They were very kind to her and showed her how to fish. It was very important to them that she respect Agwé, the Vodoun loa who rules over the sea. Estelle would always throw a bit of fish back for Agwé. Afterwards, she would pray the rosary. After a time, her Uncles began to pray it with her.

The followers of Vodoun believed a great god created the universe, but the Great Creator was unapproachable by man. One gained the attention of the creator through his subservient loa spirits. Estelle told them about Christ, wholly man and wholly God, and how he came to Earth to die for the reconciliation of Creator and created. They were appreciative, having never heard the story of Christ in such a way, and would pray to him, from then on, as Loa-Pappy.

Estelle was never hungry again.

***

The room was unrecognizable as a place where humans slept. The bed was gone. A chalk line separated a four-foot by twenty-foot section of the room, and included the interior door. This small section was heaped with blankets and clothes, combs, belts and hose - and whatever lead soldiers were not being used. The rest of the room was dedicated to the game. Heaps of dirt had been brought in. The dirt was covered in painted moss, and bits of twigs and leaves made to look like miniature trees. The landscape was dotted with homemade toy houses, little fields and plows, lead horses and carriage - and hundreds upon hundreds of soldiers, complete with regimental colors, signalmen, musicians, supply carriages and mounted officers. The walls were covered in tacked-up papers, scrawled with rules and equations. In fact, papers were strewn about everywhere. Gambling dice were in cups, which rested in small throw boxes.

The boys constantly searched for any knowledge that would help them. They had both fired muskets and pistols, waved about polearms and swords, and tried to run horses at a gallop. They had spent time observing ships, and frequently asked their officers about cannon and shot. They had made their own lead soldiers with clay molds, but, admittedly, the ones Monsieur Pinceau purchased always looked better. When the game's rules needed to be updated or changed, the house would rock with loud argument. When the battles came down to the wire, or when one boy surprised another with a devastating move, the house would shake with mercurial, titanic anger. The servants were confused, when they were not frightened. Monsieur Pinceau loved every minute of it. The boys came down for breakfast and for dinner every night, and they always had something to talk about.

Monsieur Pinceau realized that Raphaël's health was all he really cared about. One day he freed all his house slaves, and put them on generous salary, and didn't really know why. A few weeks later, Marie-Lynn, a housemaid, meekly came to him in his study, and subtly hinted that perhaps he could be so generous with his field slaves.

He could not.

But a week later, he sent a message to his three plantations that all of his slaves were now indentured servants working for their freedom. After ten years of labor, a slave would be freed. Better work equaled less time spent in bondage. Laziness, or dereliction of duty, would result in fines and more time. Unfortunately, if cane slaves survived three years it was a minor miracle, but hope springs eternal. As proof of his intentions, all slaves who had already earned their freedom were placed on salary - mostly overseers and cooks, and those who had been taught a trade.

Monsieur fielded all sorts of complaints over this edict, from his field supervisors to his neighbors. He fell into a mild depression over it, shocked at the intensity of contention regarding his breech with custom.

The complaints from his supervisors slowed and stopped. After the harvest, he learned that the sugar output was seven percent higher than it had ever been before. His neighbors did not emulate him, but they now respected him, as some sort of financial wizard who made something work that they could never attempt. Monsieur Pinceau also came to talk to his dead wife nearly every day, as if she was in the same room with him. It gave him great happiness to do so.

Life was good.

Then, one day in January of 1783, Féroce Guerrier knocked on the door and was shown into the foyer. Monsieur Pinceau had forgotten that he had even existed at all. Féroce didn't look a day older, but his eyes were different - fiery, even commanding. For some reason, his presence gave Monsieur Pinceau great unease. "Monsieur Guerrier, you are most welcome."

"Thank you, Monsieur. It is good to be back. Although I am leaving this afternoon."

"I see. Where are you going?"

"To France."

"This afternoon?"

"The opportunity presented itself, and there is no time like the present."

"I see. Well, perhaps we can give you a good lunch before you go."

"I'm afraid my chests and my daughter are waiting on the street. Where is my son?"

"Upstairs, with Raphaël."

Féroce, without further ado, bounded up the stairs like a goat. Concerned, Monsieur Pinceau followed him. This was all happening too fast. Every second, Monsieur Pinceau realized how little he wanted Féroce to take Guillaume from the house. He had come to love the boy. As time passed, Guillaume's anger and resentment had come to dissipate. As it did, a startling change came over him. Guillaume was actually quite tender-hearted and happy-spirited. The initial bellicosity in both boys had slowly given way, in good measure but not perfect measure, to mutual enthusiasm. When he saw them at meals, their excitement was contagious, and there was laughter, more and more as time went on.

Féroce made the hallway and came before the door. He rapped twice, then opened it. Monsieur saw the boys inside, sitting in their miniature empire like surprised titans. Both of them had wide eyes, and Guillaume looked terrified. Féroce spoke, "This room stinks. Pigs live better than this," he locked eyes with Guillaume and snorted, "You've gotten fat."

Raphaël stood, "Good afternoon, Monsieur."

"I believe it's still morning. Are you Raphaël?"

"Yes, Monsieur."

"Pleasure to meet you. Guillaume, stow your things. We're leaving in three minutes."

Guillaume looked to Monsieur Pinceau as a son would look to a father - for protection. Monsieur's heart broke, he was powerless – the boy's true father was the one from whom Guillaume wished to be saved.

Guerrier shrugged and grinned, "Get your things, or go with one set of clothes, I care not."

"I don't want to go," Guillaume answered quickly.

"Guillaume," said Féroce harshly, "police up your *merde*. Now."

Guillaume did not move. Fast as a cat, Féroce moved to Guillaume, picked him up, and moved quickly into the hallway and toward the stairs. In one moment, Monsieur Pinceau became aware of two things. He heard Guillaume's protestations, pitiful and desperate, at the same time he looked down and saw an immense boot-print in the landscape of the little kingdom. Cracks radiated out from the depression across the countryside, things were broken, half of the soldiers were down. In one action, Féroce had managed to disrupt everything. Monsieur moved quickly to follow him, "Monsieur Guerrier, the boys are so happy together," he said.

"It appears that way, Monsieur."

"It would be no trouble to send him later."

"That would be an expense I do not wish to pay back."

"I will cheerfully pay it. It is of nothing."

"That is very generous," Féroce stopped moving. He suddenly turned, scaring Monsieur Pinceau, who tried not to show his fear. "Monsieur Pinceau, through my actions, my family has...," Féroce searched for the right word, "*transcended* Saint-Domingue. We are now headed home, back to the Fatherland."

Monsieur Pinceau tried to smile, "Good luck to you and your family. Safe journey."

"Thank you!" said Féroce, and he was out the door. Guillaume's eyes went to the second story balcony, where Pinceau knew his horrified son now stood.

"Goodbye," said Guillaume, and the door shut.

"Goodbye," said Raphaël.

Outside, Estelle sat on the cart. When Guillaume appeared, dragged by her father, he looked more distraught than even she had imagined. She prayed that he did not blame any of this on her. Soon they were on the cart, Papa sitting between them. He turned to Guillaume, "I don't want to hear any of your braying and neighing. And I don't want you jumping off the *damné* cart, either. Any sheep-straying from you, I will drag you to the mud, and put the flat of my hand to your arse. Do you understand?"

Guillaume said nothing. Féroce lifted him by the shirt off his seat, "I said, 'Do you understand?'"

"Yes, yes!" screamed Guillaume.

"Don't you yell at me, boy. I said, 'Do you understand?'"

"Yes."

Féroce threw him into his seat, then gently shook the reins. Abruti began to walk.

Guillaume softly cried. Estelle noticed they were heading south, as if they were going home - not east toward the harbor. "Papa," she said gently, "You are going home."

"No," he replied, "We are going to get Maman."

Estelle had told him they had buried her. "What do you mean by 'get Maman?"

He looked at her with a mixture of disappointment and contempt. She was shocked, and wondered what she had done wrong.

***

The cart ride was unbearable. Soon they passed the gates of Quartier-Morin. The overseers galloped to them, one after the other, to challenge the trespass. But as soon as they were close enough to see Féroce Guerrier at the reins, they simply waved and rode off. Guillaume had calmed. He was actually completely calm, even lost in concentration or a daydream. Estelle felt sick to her stomach.

They came to the church. "Where is she?" asked Papa.

"Papa-"

"WHERE IS SHE?" screamed her father.

Estelle sobbed.

"WHERE IS SHE?" he yelled even louder.

"Over there!" she pointed.

"WHERE? SHOW ME!" he screamed.

Hysterical, Estelle left the bench and walked to her mother's grave, where her name was scratched on a wooden cross.

"What does that say?" he asked harshly, pointing at the cross.

"It says her name."

"Move. Go back to the cart."

Estelle went back to the cart just as Father Jozef came out of the church with his two helpers. Estelle couldn't look him in the eye. "What are you doing here?" he asked of Papa.

Papa grabbed a spade and began to dig.

"What are you doing? Stop that at once!"

"And who is going to stop me? You? If you took this shovel with both hands, but I did not let go and we struggled for it, how long would it take for you to run out of breath and let go?" Papa said, grinning.

"This is outrageous. Do you honestly think you can come here and begin digging on holy ground?"

"Frankly, I do," grinned Papa.

Father turned to his helpers, "Let's go." The Father walked away, and soon the three of them were left alone once more.

Estelle was astounded at how little authority Father seemed to have over Papa. Most people were very respectful and even afraid of Father Jozef, who was a strong and forceful presence. In any case, no one returned, neither Father Jozef or anyone else.

As the hole was dug deeper, the stench of rot became more apparent. Estelle was sickened, horrified that the smell emanated from her Maman, who was being disturbed in her eternal rest. Papa sweated in the heat, but his pace did not slow. Soon Maman's wrapped body was thrown up from the pit, to land unceremoniously on the ground. The sheets and blankets of her burial shroud were stained brown from mud and putrefaction. Papa soon emerged from the hole. He wiped his hands together, then threw her body over his shoulder, walked it to the cart, and tossed it in back. The smell was overwhelming. He sat back on the bench, took the reins, and, with a quick "tsk-tsk", Abruti turned the cart.

But they did not go north, back to Le Cap. They headed south. Guillaume said nothing. He had not spoken for hours. Papa seemed immune to the smell. He looked around at the scenery, occasionally becoming animated when he saw a rare animal or a pretty sight. "Look at the caiman!" he would say, excited, as if he had never been cross a day in his life.

A little less than fifteen miles south of Le Cap, the foothills started to rise from the river valleys. The cart headed up into the mountains. It was the road to Milot - the way to Champ-Élevé. Papa gave the reins to Estelle, for Abruti did not really know Guillaume. He walked behind the cart, giving it a push when needed. Sometimes he talked with Maman, "Remember this tree? I don't know where all the leaves went on the east side of it. Although it is still gorgeous, isn't it?"

They made camp in the late afternoon and started a good, smoky fire to ward off the insects. The next day there was no breakfast.

They were past Milot in the late afternoon. It was a small town, and there were not many people about, mostly coffee slaves doing errands. Estelle recognized some of them, who gave them a wide berth. The Guerriers carried bad mojo, as the Vodoun Mambos would say, and today they also brought a bad smell.

Two hours later they were past Champ-Élevé. Papa engaged the brake on the cart, placed rocks behind the wheels, and unhitched Abruti. He tied Maman to the mule's back, and, wordlessly, they all began to hike up the hill.

Night was about to fall when they reached Maman's waterfall and lagoon. Estelle was tired, Guillaume's breath came in ragged tufts. Papa was still as fresh as when he got off the cart. He gently took Maman's body and swam her out to the middle of the lagoon, then returned and stood on the muddy bank. Her body floated on the water, making a slow, lazy spin with the waterfall's current.

Papa looked out over the lagoon, and spoke to his wife, "It is not the forest of Ards, but I know you loved this place," he said quietly. Her body, right at that moment, began to sink. Papa nodded, then used the water of the pool to clean himself and Abruti.

They made a fire on the ridge of the lagoon. Papa did not say anything until Estelle and Guillaume were almost asleep. "I cannot believe you buried her on a sugar plantation. What on earth were you thinking? What if I had not come home?" Papa shook his head, and looked back into the fire. Estelle was ashamed and did not know why. Guillaume was silent and calm, just as he had been for the last day - and half of the one before that.

They were up early the next day. They ate in Milot and continued. Downhill was much faster, and soon they were back in Le Cap, at the large, crowded harbor. Féroce pulled the cart to a magnificent three-masted merchantman, still being loaded with sugar, named *La Petite Princesse de Nantes*. Féroce was ebullient and grinning with the men on the docks, "Buy a cart and mule for two livres? One-time chance for a steal, *mon ami*."

In minutes, half the street stood around Féroce, laughing and talking. Soon Papa sold his cart and horse - for more than two livres - and they were aboard the ship. Three long hours later, she moved away from the dock. Féroce and Guillaume were almost mirror images of calm thoughtfulness as the ship was towed into the bay. Soon, her sails were unfurled, and they were finally away.

It was then - when no sane Captain would have turned the ship around - when Guillaume made his move. He launched at full speed across the deck, and jumped over the side. The plan was perfect: Papa could not follow without Estelle going to France alone. It would have been masterful, save Féroce caught him by the ankle as he jumped. "You think me a fool, boy. I knew your plan before you did." As the sailors chuckled mirthfully, he pinned Guillaume to the deck. Guillaume was then like a feral animal, his prior calm gone as he snarled and screamed. "Have the sailors laugh at me, will you?" hissed Féroce quietly, as he pulled Guillaume into the air, and slammed him into the door leading below. Guillaume, hammered against the wood over and over, reached down and opened the door to prevent further injury. Féroce carried him down the hall and threw him against their cabin door, forcing Guillaume to open it once more, then tossed him against the bulkhead inside. When Guillaume hit the floor, he pinned him there. He tied his ankles together and his hands behind his back. A sack went over his head.

He gave Guillaume the thrashing of his life - with his belt, his hands and his feet. Neither was Guillaume prepared to bear the beating, being soft and accustomed to a sedentary, interior life. It was a long, drawn-out affair, designed to break his spirit. "Did that feel good?" Féroce snarled, "I bet you liked that one, didn't you, fat man?" Guillaume was screaming in agony at the top of his lungs, and could not answer.

As Féroce was leaving, Guillaume finally spoke, "I hope you die, and go straight to hell," he said, through the sack, and still tied.

Féroce smiled, "You and ten-thousand redcoats. But the ten-thousand and one of you have *merde* luck and worse aim, so I'd come to terms with your lot, if I were you."

Féroce took a bottle of Champagne, and went above decks. The sailors were not laughing. They had snickered at first, when one heard the screams and told the others - but the beating had lasted too long. Even a sailor wasn't whipped for such a time.

Estelle stood where her father had left her. Her eyes were downcast, she was in a dark mood.

Féroce grinned at the sailors, "Are you lads ready for a show?" They grinned weakly, not sure what he meant, but certainly not about to gainsay him.

Féroce went to the bow, and poured the champagne into the water for Agwé. He began to dance and sing, to gain his blessing and protection for the journey.

Féroce was accustomed and knowledgeable in the ways of men, yet his actions were mostly objectionable to those onboard. But Féroce knew what he was doing. He was purposefully confrontational. He was forcing every man-jack among them to either accept him or confront him, and acceptance was obeisance. Féroce was marking his territory - he was in charge and it was going to be his way.

Estelle looked over at the sailors, and saw some of them glanced at him, but nothing more. Papa was too strong to confront, too charismatic to outmaneuver. His feet were planted firm in savagery and civilization, black and white, jungle and city. He was intimidating and unknowable.

When Estelle fished, she threw a bit of the catch back to appease her uncles, then told them about God. That was one thing. This was another. This was blasphemy and nonsense, and from her Papa, no less. And there was a part of her that very much wanted to punish him.

Estelle took out her rosary, and began to pray in a loud voice that carried over the deck. Soon some of the sailors joined in. After the first glorious mystery, half the men on deck were praying along with her at the chorus couplets. After the second, all of them were. Soon her father stopped his ridiculous song and dance, and looked at her with an even, uncomprehending stare. In a few minutes, with a scratch of his head and a shrug, he went below decks. Estelle finished her rosary. The sailors smiled at her. She shyly smiled back.

Her father commanded men. He intimidated them. He could enforce his personality upon them with his fists. But Estelle had just beaten him for the allegiance of the crew, and he wasn't sure how she did it.

1832

Jake

La Cour d'Assises Spéciale, 1832

Court President
Sworn Judge
Judge Advocate
Sworn Judge
Sworn Judge
Judge Advocate
Sworn Judge
Sworn Judge
Sworn Judge
Clerk
Bailiff
Accused
Defense Attorney
General Council
Witness Stand
Prosecutor
Press Box
General Public

silhouettes by EK Duncan

Chapter 9

The oldest and most defensible part of Paris was the Île de la Cité, the largest island in the middle of the Seine river. The ancient Frankish Merovingian kings had put everything there they didn't want burned or stolen by the Vikings. The fortified royal residence, the Palais de la Cité, housed their monarchs from the late 800's. The site was renovated and enlarged, and soon became quite grand. Five, six, seven stories of castle, tower and palace soared in grey stone and blue slate. The True Crown of Thorns, and a piece of the True Cross, taken by Crusaders, was placed in the new Sainte-Chapelle, a wonder of stained glass and arches - a forest of light, the most entrancing space ever created by man. On the eastern end, the awe-inspiring Notre Dame, the first Gothic cathedral, took the place of an earlier, less-impressive church. Businesses, residences and ministries populated the spaces between these palaces of royalty and God. By 1358, defense was less of a concern, and the Valois kings finally made a permanent move to the Louvre, downstream on the right-bank. When that happened, a concierge was placed in charge of the palace complex, which was therefore renamed the *Conciergerie*, and it became an administrative hub holding ministries, judicial courts, the former Parlement of Paris, and a prison.

And that was where Jake currently found himself.

Nearly all of the prisoners interned with Jake were brother rebels of the barricades. All awaited trial in the *Cour d'Assises Spéciale*, tribunals where the fate of the prisoners was determined by a majority decision of seven judges, rather than a jury. On appeal, they would be judged by nine.

When first captured, Jake drifted in and out of consciousness for a full day. It took the better part of a month for the last of his headaches to subside. It still hurt to breathe, even when the headaches were gone. He was depressed and mournful, and achingly regretful.

Franck was dead.

How much fault now rested on Jake's shoulders for this horrendous tragedy? For an additional four days, Jake stayed in bed for no real reason. Finally, he was sent from the Salpêtrière hospital to the Conciergerie prison.

Jake purchased a furnished cell, called a *pistole*, for 15 francs a month, which was costlier than a room at an inn. It was about the same size and style as his dorm room, just without sunlight or fresh air. He was allowed to roam the prisoner gallery and the men's courtyard for several hours a day. He mostly slept for the first week, and only ventured out of his cell for meals. He was questioned peacefully and rationally, by a faceless ministry of detectives and officials; so often and for such lengths that it began to feel bellicose and illogical. The bureaucracy quickly produced reams of forms, statements, and reports regarding every aspect of his public being. During his second week, to preserve his sanity, he spent more time in the prisoner's gallery. He found it chocked full of panicked strangers who planned fictional alibis and cooked excuses. At first, they all seemed rather pathetic. After a while, the ubiquitous terror seeped into Jake's normally indomitable character.

They were all going into combat once again. More precisely, their lawyers were going into combat. Only their lawyers would not be wounded or killed or suffer hardship. It was the defendant who would stand in proxy, and take all penalty and discomfort of battle for them. If the lawyer made a mistake, he would only shrug - but soon after, the defendant would be dead or shut behind bars. There was a powerlessness to this, a sense of being utterly outgunned and small. They were separated out from their battalions, forced to fight the might of judicial France as lonely individuals. Even the bravest men, who looked down the barrels of barking muskets, were breaking and willing to sell their principles for courtroom victory - or even leniency. Jake himself began to panic as the rebels went to trial. One after the other, all were judged guilty and received long sentences, often the rest of their life. One man, who was thought to have waved the red and black flag, received the penalty of death. Jake had clearly seen the man waving the flag - and it wasn't him, it wasn't even the right man! More and more, the trials were turning out to be a second rout.

In spite of all of this, Jake had no desire to feel sorry for himself. At least he had a life. Franck did not. His family would never see him again - although Jake's family might well never see him again, either. He had begun a letter to his father at least five times, and five times balled up the paper and burned it.

Sometimes he wished his father to swoop in and save him, but that was childish. Jake was eighteen. He was a man. He had led men and women to their deaths. The court of France saw him as a man, and men should handle their own problems. Jake had, however, done absolutely nothing in this regard. He hadn't looked at his case, sought representation, or even asked questions of the guards. Neither had anyone told him anything in regard to the process. Jake half-hoped that someday a guard would ask him who he was, Jake would tell him, and the guard would inform him that all records of his existence were lost and he was free to go. Considering the amount of paper generated by the system in regard to Jake's case, it would take a citywide fire to destroy it all. Regardless, a part of Jake believed he could wish this scenario into concrete reality by simply ignoring his plight with studied indifference. Jake found himself questioning his sanity - his lack of industriousness already beyond any debate. He had completed only one letter during this entire process. It was to the Despres, Franck's family, and he begged their forgiveness for what happened to Franck. He had not sent it.

A part of Jake wished he would be sentenced to death. In his mind, the sentence would have nothing to do with sedition or rebellion, rather it would be an appropriate absolution for the death of his best friend, amongst others. He could forgive himself far more easily if he, too, was to die. Perhaps that explained much of his present behavior.

Jake sat at his usual spot in the prison gallery next to the tailor Prospel, and the two brothers Joseph and Casimir Roussel, who had fought together at the Passage du Saumon barricade. Prospel knew a card game that could be played by four called *Doppelkopf*. It used a German deck with suits like bells, hearts, leaves and acorns. Instead of aces, there were *daus*. *Obers* and *unters* took the place of queens and jacks. There were bids, trumps, *ansagen*, *absagen*, *kontra*, *keine* and *schwars*. It was confusing, but they had nothing else to do.

"Monsieur Loring?"

Jake looked up, and saw a guard named Corporal Pechegru with another middle-aged man he did not recognize. This unknown man had a fat, round face with small, pudgy features, and unkempt, curly, brown hair. He was well and finely dressed, and had a thin, spry build that belied his cherubic face. Jake excused himself from the game, and went over to them. "Good morning, Corporal," he said.

The stranger bowed at the waist, "It is a pleasure to meet you, Monsieur Loring. I am Adolphe Crémieux."

Jake bowed back, "Likewise, Monsieur."

The Corporal walked off, and left them alone. Jake, confused, turned back to Adolphe, who smiled, "I would be your lawyer, if you would have me."

"Are you qualified?"

"Mildly so, I suppose."

"You say that as if you are abundantly qualified."

"I am. Could we walk as we converse."

"Yes, of course," said Jake, as he motioned the direction to begin an amble, "Tell me of your qualifications, Monsieur."

"I was a lawyer in Nîmes for a time. I am now an advocate for the Court of Appeals."

"I haven't lost or won my case. Why would I need an appeals lawyer?"

"I have deigned to represent you now, and then, if need be."

"Why?"

"Because I am a Freemason, and a member of *The Society*. I was asked by a man you know as Citizen Bouche to help you. He is following your case very closely. You are highly placed in the movement, one of our splinter-group cell leaders, are you not?"

"I am." Jake heaved a sigh of relief. He had thought he was totally alone in this. "Please help me. Be my lawyer."

"Done and done, Monsieur Loring."

"Please, call me Jake."

Crémieux narrowed his eyes. "A boy's nickname."

"I'm afraid so. But when people say Monsieur Loring, I have no idea to whom they are referring."

"Very well, Jake. Please call me Isaäc."

"Isaäc? Are you a Jew?"

"I am. Is that a problem?"

Jake thought about it. "All the Jews in America were on the side of the revolution. Your people are generally reliable revolutionaries. If religions were neighborhoods, I suppose Judaism would be Faubourg Saint-Antoine."

"Ha! I will spread your words. How amusing! But now we must begin." With that, Isaäc was all business, "You gave all the orders: to construct the barricade, to engage the enemy, and so on."

"Yes."

"You had a parley with Major Roux."

"I did."

"Wherein you were vocal in your Republican sentiment and your will to resist?"

"Yes."

"You were caught with an ultra-modern pistol with a capacity of twenty rounds."

"Yes."

"Wearing a green cockade."

"Uh, yes."

"I will be frank with you, Jake. If we go to trial, it will not go well."

If? thought Jake. "Is there a chance we will not?"

"I'm surprised you're here at all."

"What do you mean?"

"The administrators of Louis-le-Grand, not to mention the alumni, want you to be deported. The American ambassador wants you to be deported. Our friends of the radical left within the government want you to be deported. And our enemies on the radical right want you to be deported as well."

"If everyone wants me to be deported, why am I not on a ship?"

"That is the question, Jake."

"I don't understand."

"Neither do I. Jake, how do I say this?"

Jake stopped and looked at the man. What on earth was this all about? What was he talking about?

Isaäc continued, "It is almost as if someone very powerful decided to single you out for trial, for a specific reason currently unknown to us. Have you angered anyone powerful?"

Jake was shocked into silence. The idea was absurd - but Isaäc was dead serious. There had to be some kind of merit to the idea, but, even in the face of it, the idea of someone powerful believing that he was worthy of a conspiracy was laughable.

"Jake?" Isaäc said gently.

Jake couldn't think of anything. He shook his head. "My best friend was killed."

"Franck Despres, of the Bordeaux Despres?"

"Yes."

"You were not the reason behind his death. Neither could the Despres family engineer what has happened, even if you were."

"And Citizen Bouche is on my side, and does not wish that I go to trial?"

"Yes, of course, and, no, he does not."

"Then I must tell you true, Isaäc. I have absolutely no idea who could be behind this plot, if plot it is."

"Perhaps we will know more at the trial. I will request an earlier date than anyone expects. We might as well face our true accusers sooner rather than later, and know our real battle."

"Very well."

"Our business is then concluded, at least for now. Is there anything else?"

"Two things, if you please."

"I am listening."

"The man who was sentenced to death, the flag carrier. He isn't the right man."

"Yes, we know, of course. We will reveal the proof when it suits us, to sully the proceedings. What else, Jake?"

"I wrote a letter to the Despres family, but did not mail it."

"I would keep it for now," said Isaäc in an even tone.

"I don't understand. Can you not mail it for me?"

"Your correspondence is intercepted. By the authorities, and then by myself and *The Society*. Madame Despres has sent you a letter."

"Well, where is it? Wait - who is intercepting my-"

"The letter was written by a mother in the throes of deep grief, and it is better left unread. Hopefully, she will come to a better place in regard to this. It will perhaps take years. For the nonce, it is better if there is no further contact. In fact, she has specified this. Do you understand?"

Jake was overwhelmed. He had spent every Summer and long holiday with the Despres family. They were a second family. "I understand," he managed to say.

"Then I bid you adieu." Isaäc bowed and smiled, then turned and left.

Jake walked to his room and sat on the bed.

He cried. He sobbed like a child, for the first time in years. In fact, Jake realized he hadn't cried since his mother died. He cried for himself, for poor Franck, and for all this miserable business. To his astonishment, he realized he cried the most for his lost mother. He was shocked. To his recollection, he did not think of her often.

He just wanted it all to be over. Truthfully, he now wished it had never begun. But he knew, deep down, it was only now just beginning. Decisions are like seeds, except the harvest can be hurtful, and last for decades - or even end your life.

Jake was about to find out what he had planted, and he did not look forward to the results.

***

The beautiful Conciergerie courtroom of arched windows and soaring stone ceilings was vast, and filled with people. The buzz of noise, hum of energy, the looks, smiles and mood, all helped to create an atmosphere of judicial theater. The business part of the room, the stage, so to speak, was semicircular, with a table, in the same shape, lying in the background, crowning the room like a dome.

The Presiding Justice was seated front and center at this table, with clerks to his left and right. Two sets of three judges served as the rest of the jury, and flanked them on both sides, to total seven judges altogether. Jake sat far stage right, surrounded by bailiffs, in an impressive box for the accused. The Prosecutor General was in an equally-grand box, directly across from him. More lawyers, advocates and bailiffs sat and stood next to tables surrounding the boxes. Isaäc - now back as Adolphe Crémieux - was seated there with his clerks near Jake. A second semicircle, formed by a high wooden bannister, mirrored the judge's table and stood as a podium for witnesses. This half-circle was fore-ground and center stage, the gas spotlight mark for the lead actors of the play.

Major Roux was currently onstage. He stood in the witness box, resplendent in his dress blues, still looking as if he needed a shave, when one knew he had just come from the barber. He was relating, with nearly perfect accuracy, what had transpired between himself, his men, Jake, and the defenders of the barri-cade.

"...at that point, the center portion of the barricade had been cleared by my men, and I was able to ride through to the other side," he said in an even voice.

"Major, were you able to see the man with whom you exchanged words before the melee?" asked the Prosecutor.

"Yes. He was lying unmoving, next to another rebel. There was a Lefau-cheux and a Charleville near their bodies. I asked that the weapons be policed, and the two downed rebels checked for their vitals. The Commander was alive, but the other was not. I asked my aide-de-camp to ensure that the Commander was taken to the hospital, and identified as a rebel leader, to all necessary parties as he traveled."

"Was Monsieur Loring searched before he was taken to the hospital? And, if so, was anything of note found on his person?"

"Yes, Monsieur. We found a green cockade, extra cartridges for the Lefau-cheux, and a bayonet in a leather scabbard."

"And do you remember the casualties of this short, but sharp, engagement?"

"I do, Monsieur. We lost nine good men, and seventeen were wounded. They lost seven dead, and fifteen of the twenty-one captives were wounded."

"Nearly ten percent of the casualties of the entire rebellion happened at this barricade?"

"Yes, Monsieur. We had to take their position in order to use cannon on the main Rue du Faubourg Saint-Antoine barricade. But once we did, the entire rebel position was jeopardized."

"Thank you, Captain." The Prosecutor General turned to the Presiding Jus-tice, "I have no further questions, Monsieur *le Président.*"

The Presiding Justice turned to Isaäc, "Do you have any further questions for the witness, Monsieur *l'Avocat?*"

"I have only one thing to say to the witness," said Isaäc as he stood.

"Then he is your witness, Monsieur."

Isaäc regarded Major Roux for a long moment. His expression was almost paternal. He suddenly turned and spoke to the crowd, "We are humbled. We, our nation, us – France, once the greatest nation on earth. We, *mes amies*, are only the remnant of what was, an upright pillar standing alone in a ruin."

There was only silence, as if his words were a prayer at a funeral.

He continued, "To humble us, nearly every nation of note had to band together. Now the world's policy in regard to France is simple. We are to be contained. We are not to look past our own borders, at least in Europe. We are the perpetrators of great evil, who have unleashed what should not have been unleashed, and now we are to be penitent - chastised for the promulgation of poisoned thought. Yet, there are those who still stand for our nation, who are willing to fight and die for France." He suddenly turned to Roux, "Thank you for your brave service to the Fatherland, and to us all, Major Roux."

Roux nearly teared, "I am at your service, Monsieur."

Isaäc sat.

"Major Roux," said the Judge, "you are free to go."

Roux snapped his heels and left the room. The crowd stared at him as if he was Horatius One-Eye after holding the Sublicius bridge.

Isaäc stood again, "Monsieur *le Président*, I wish to interrogate my client, for the record."

Jake's head snapped up. He did not expect this. His mouth went dry.

"He is your witness, Monsieur," replied the Judge.

Isaäc turned and faced Jake. Jake was shocked to see a stern, disapproving visage on his *avocat's* face. "Monsieur Loring," Isaäc began sternly, "You will address me as Monsieur, or Monsieur *l'Avocat*. Do you understand?"

"Yes, Monsieur." *My God, he really is angry. What have I done?*

"Why are you here?"

"W-what?"

"What, *Monsieur*."

"What, Monsieur?"

"Why… are… you… here?" Isaäc turned, and faced the crowd, "You are an American, yes? Specifically, from the United States. Why are you here? In France, in Paris?"

Jake's thoughts were awhirl. What did Isaäc want him to say? He was from Wellesley - staid, boring and plain. His house was filled with silence, the vacuum left by a dead woman somehow ironically taking up the space. His father was a ghost, only the creak of his footsteps on the wooden floors announced his presence. The servants whispered, as if there was some kind of an unspoken rule to avoid signs of life. Wellesley was ten fingers around his throat, cutting off his air, choking the life out of him.

"Allow me to give you a hint, Monsieur Loring," said Isaäc dryly, and the spectators laughed. He crossed to a Bailiff's desk and, at the exact moment the laughter ended, flourished an old piece of parchment into the air. "Physical Exhibit Fifteen, Monsieur," he said respectfully to the Prosecutor, who nodded respectfully in turn. Isaäc turned back to Jake, "Do you know what this is, Monsieur Loring? Rather, what is written and drawn upon it? Does this jog your memory, or your tongue?" More laughs from the courtroom.

"Yes, Monsieur."

"Then what is it? Explain."

"It is an order from the headmaster of Louis-le-Grand."

"The current headmaster, Father Daniel?"

"No, two headmasters ago. The headmaster from 1805, Father Martin."

"And what does this document reference?"

"It instructs any future headmaster to admit a boy on full scholarship, regardless of his circumstance, who arrives at the school with a certain pewter cross around his neck."

The courtroom exploded into whispers.

"*Mon Dieu!*" Isaäc exclaimed, "Is this in regard to your cross, the cross around your neck?"

"Yes, Monsieur." Jake took his simple cross from around his neck, and showed it to the court.

Whispers were heard again, frenzied but quieter. No one wanted to miss a word.

Isaäc shook his head, "You have a little Cross of Nantes, one that has availed you a tiny treasure! I have a thought! The melting point of pewter is lower than gold. Perhaps it *is* the Cross of Nantes, simply covered in pewter to disguise its true nature!"

"As you can see, Monsieur, my cross is but a thin, small thing. Nothing could hide inside of it."

"And what is engraved upon this cross around your neck?"

"L-L-L-G-10-17-05-4."

"Meaning what?"

"*Lycée* Louis-le-Grand, the date of the seventeenth of October, 1805. The last number, the four, references the fourth document drawn up on that date by the headmaster, which happens to be that very paper in your hand."

"This must have caused quite a stir."

"It did. Uh, it did, *Monsieur*." Jake was beginning to feel better. Isaäc had a plan - he was subtly telling Jake where to move the chess pieces.

"Why on earth would you, sight unseen, be entitled to an education at the most selective school in the world?" he asked.

"My grandfather was a war hero. I did not know him well, but it is said he served with French Marines during the Revolutionary War, and was thus rewarded."

"I would have thought a soldier would have preferred a cask or two of brandy," said Isaäc, and the courtroom chuckled.

"The gift was meant for my father. He taught himself fluent French, which he then taught me. My grandfather spoke no French at all. I'm afraid I have no idea why the gift was so late. The war ended in 1783. The letter was dated twenty-two years after the war."

"There is a curious design upon this paper. It indicates that your cross would have the same design engraved on its surface."

"Yes, Monsieur."

"Could you describe it please?"

"It is small, but it resembles a young woman, lying in eternal rest on a boat which, in turn, lies on a river, headed toward a city on a hill."

"That sounds extraordinarily specific. What does it mean?"

"When I was younger, I thought it was an image of my mother. She passed away when I was a child."

Now the courtroom properly buzzed, as the audience whispered amongst themselves. The interruption ended quickly – everyone was far too interested in what was being said.

Isäac turned to Jake again, now more pensive, "And now? Now what do you think it means?"

"It is Elaine of Astolat, I believe. From *Le Morte d'Arthur*. She was Lancelot's true love. He betrayed her for Guinevere, the Queen, therefore toppling Arthur, and destroying Camelot."

"You are a far more interesting person than anyone could have possibly imagined, aren't you, Monsieur Loring?" Isäac waited for a moment, then continued, "Has this happened before? Have scholarships at Louis-le-Grand been granted for wartime service in the past?"

"No, Monsieur. Never. Although, sometimes, the children of wartime heroes are given special consideration."

"I see. This is most unusual then."

"The document had attained legendary status by the time I arrived. Half of my first day was spent answering questions of the faculty and staff."

"I can well imagine. And did your family simply put you on a ship for France?" More chuckles from the crowd.

"No, Monsieur. They sent a letter to the school, asking for confirmation that the scholarship existed. When a letter was sent back, explaining that indeed the document existed, and the promise would be honored, I was placed in a coach bound for Boston harbor. I have said the gift was meant for my father. My father has never left Wellesley. His loss, as I said, was my gain."

Isäac turned, and addressed the courtroom, "I come now to explain why this line of questioning is important and germane. I appreciate the respect given to me by the prosecution, who trusted that my line of questioning, however unusual, would prove itself to be indispensable, and appropriate, to the defense of my client." Another respectful nod from the Prosecutor, and Isäac continued, "So Jacob Esau Loring was the grandson of a revolutionary, a war hero of America. This man served with French forces with such distinction that a reward of a unique nature - a scholarship to Louis-le-Grand - was given to him, for a relative, or friend, of his choosing; anyone to whom he bestowed the pewter cross, as it were. The very presence of my client, in France, was predicated on the revolutionary credentials of his family. And, presently, he arrived here, to see our own revolution in tatters, our government and society in chaos. Our king overthrown two years ago, war in Algeria, and cholera stalking the streets. And here is Monsieur Loring. As an American, eternally grateful to our nation, eternally indebted to the revolutionary movement, raised and educated in the mores and advancements of the Age of Enlightenment. And suddenly, suddenly, *mes amies*, the streets of Paris are alive with gunfire and barricades and riots and life! *Messieurs et Madames*, at that point, there would be only one question: is he a coward, or is he not? For if he were a coward, he would hide under his bed, and think of nothing else but his skin. But if he were not cowardly, if he was his grandfather's grandson, if he were the correct recipient of this scholarship, if the blood of heroes flowed through his veins, the stuff that could fight side-by-side with French Marines, well, he would come to the streets of Paris, to fight for the people of France! Long live France! Long live the Nation! Long live the Fatherland! *Vive la France!*"

Now the courtroom went berserk with shouting and cheers. Isaäc was saying more, something, shouting it, but was easily drowned out. His huge gesticulations were almost like those of a conductor of an orchestra, but Isaäc's musicians were the courtroom spectators, now turned proper mob.

But there was one man in the courtroom, unseen by Jake, who did not stand or cheer. This was Monsieur Tyran. After an unbelievable, and unforeseen, setback - which was the capture of his prey by the judicial system - things were now going precisely the way he wished them to go, and, actually, far better than he could have dreamed.

To no one's notice, he silently got up from his seat, and left the courtroom.

1783

La Famille Guerrier

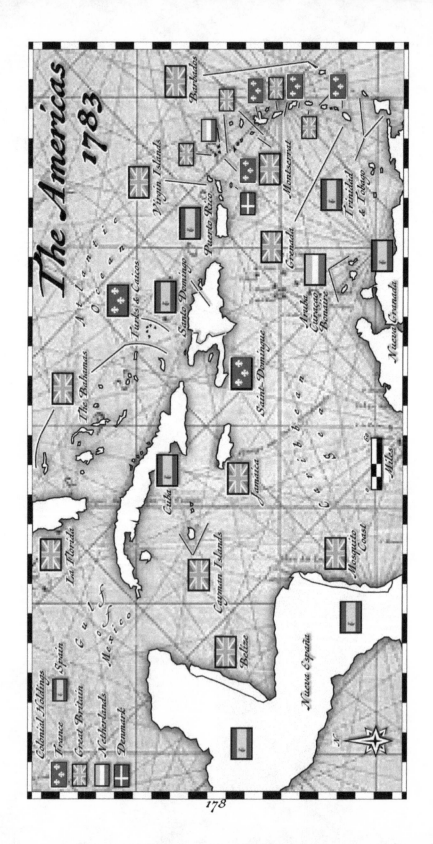

The Americas
1783

Atlantic Ocean

Barbados

Virgin Islands

Montserrat

Trinidad & Tobago

Grenada

Puerto Rico

Turks & Caicos

Santo Domingo

Saint-Domingue

Aruba Curaçao Bonaire

Nueva Granada

The Bahamas

Caribbean Sea

Miles

Cuba

Jamaica

Cayman Islands

Mosquito Coast

Isla Florida

Gulf of Mexico

Belize

Nueva España

N

Colonial Holdings

France   Spain
Great Britain
Netherlands
Denmark

Chapter 10

The *La Petite Princesse de Nantes* left Saint-Domingue just in time to catch the north Atlantic storms. Estelle was miserable, sea-sick nearly every minute of the three-month journey. Guillaume and Papa seemed immune, as long as they were lying down, or on-deck and feeling the salt spray in their faces. Guillaume would spend long hours sitting in the bow, staring out to sea. She wished he would spend more time with her, alone and laid up in the cabin as she was. He would come down at night, and they would talk until Papa came down. Guillaume never talked around him. Papa noticed. He didn't seem guilty or regretful, only thoughtful. He did not deign to try to say anything to him either.

Papa would make Estelle eat and drink, which seemed like torture, especially after all the fresh food onboard was gone. The briny water, weevily hardtack and salted pork made her even more nauseous.

Estelle understood the earth, the soil, and what grew upon it. She knew the rhythm of the seasons and the seeds. The ocean was a terrible mystery to her - there was no pattern that she could discern. She tried to talk to Guillaume about it. He understood her words, but he was comfortable with the sea, and found its mystery captivating. He missed Raphaël and Monsieur Pinceau terribly, and found the ocean a comfort.

Finally, one morning, Estelle woke to the sound of gulls, men's shouted voices, horses, and the creaking of wood and iron machinery. They had arrived in Nantes. There were no more waves, the river current was steady and familiar.

Estelle dressed for the first time in months, and weakly made her way above decks. The light overwhelmed her, but the sun was weak in the sky, and it was cool.

The sight of the city was something she would never forget. There was land close at hand to both starboard and port. But there was no ground to be seen. Everything was stone road, building or wall, wooden dock, platform, or house. What little was left over was of iron or twisted hemp. It was as if two far larger vessels of man were to her right and left, rather than earth bank and river island. Ships were everywhere, of all size and description - ocean and river traders, war-ships and pleasure craft. There were more white people than even in Le Cap. This intimidated Estelle, and she wondered how race and status would be ac-corded here, and whether it would be in her favor.

Soon the ship was towed to dock, built out from an industrialized island south of the city center. Across the river to the east was a huge castle. To the north laid walls, docks, buildings, canals and more rivers - flowing from the north and joining the Loire. The small family packed their things, and took a decrepit, shaky ferry to the city proper. Féroce received directions from a police-man to the commissariat, took their two sea chests and put one on each shoulder as if they were down pillows. "Stay close," he said to the twins, and off they went. They walked east across the city to the huge, squat castle, the Château des Ducs de Bretagne. It was a mile and a half of docks, warehouses, buildings, stacked goods and docked ocean-going sail ships - which eventually changed to river barges as the water became shallower to the east. Even with Féroce carry-ing the two great chests, the children had to hop and skip to keep up with his pace. When they finally arrived, Papa showed a letter to a well-dressed guard at the drawbridge. The guard disappeared, returned, and escorted them inside the castle.

The gatehouse opened into a huge, flat, sandy-colored bailey. Thin, long, elegant Mannerist keeps stood against the walls. There was a small orchard and garden interrupting the sand of the bailey, giving the castle an even grander feel. Papa stacked the chests on the ground. "Stay here!" he barked, as he followed the guard through the gatehouse.

Estelle and Guillaume sat on the chests, cold, hungry and bored. Less than an hour later, Féroce emerged. His brow was furrowed and his lips pursed. He walked quickly to the chests, "Follow me," he said, as he shouldered their be-longings and crossed to the drawbridge.

"Is everything right and well, Papa?" asked Estelle.

"Nantes is full of idiots."

Estelle counted to ten before she spoke again, "Where are we going then?"

"To Angers."

"Oh, I see."

Estelle made sure there was at least an equal count of ten between her questions, for she had many and she didn't want to annoy Papa. The answers came slowly. Papa had a magic letter to become a policeman in France. But the Prefect of Nantes needed an officer who could read and write so Papa was not qualified. They were therefore going to Angers on a barge, being cheaper than a coach, but still taking most of their remaining coin. Angers was fifteen leagues away, nearly forty-five king's miles, and the journey would last several days. Estelle had much to say regarding all of this, but wisely kept it to herself - at least for the nonce.

Soon they were at the docks again. There were many barges; most offering flat, open decks stacked with goods. To their astonishment, the best barge, which was covered with a canvass roof - and even had a sail mast that swiveled up and down to pass under bridges - charged the same price for the journey as everyone else. It had a crew of three, whom Papa confronted, "Why do you charge the same price for a better, faster barge?" he asked, suspicious.

The young captain shrugged, "We are going upriver with or without you. Our tent is to protect the goods, the sail to speed their transit. The price assures we get your coin, instead of another barge. We are a Traversier ship, Monsieur. Neither guild nor prelate determine our price. We could undercut the other barges if we wished, but have no need."

"*Merde*," said Féroce, "Good enough for me." He turned to the twins. "Get aboard."

Within minutes, the sailors gave them wine, cheese and bread, and soon all three were fast asleep.

The trip was uneventful, but beautiful. Everything was so different. The Loire valley had but few plants and trees in common with Saint-Domingue, and once out of Nantes, there were no colored people or blacks at all.

To travel upstream, huge ropes pointed taut from the barge to oxen crews on the bank, who towed them against the current. Their craft was so fast it overcame other barges. Cries of "Slack your lines!" made the slower barge loose and hold their cables, to sink underwater until the Traversier ship could pass.

Estelle kept wondering why the situation in Angers would be any different than Nantes. Her father could not make the same mistake twice, they would then be completely penniless. Her curiosity had to wait until night, when everyone was asleep. "Papa?" she asked.

He woke and replied, "What's wrong?"

"Do you remember the house on the river?"

"Which one?"

"Remember the bargeman, the first mate? The one with the blonde hair-"

"Robert Alain Verne."

"Yes. He said the monks planted Lebanese cedars all along the banks, and he pointed one out to us. The house was-"

"The house after the cedar was a quarter mile downstream from it on the right-bank. It was painted blue with *guède* and lime, but was decrepit."

"No one could remember that, Papa, except for you. You remember everything."

"Why is the house so important to you now?"

"There is really no reason at all for the Prefect of Angers to know that the Prefect of Nantes did not want you."

Féroce did not reply.

"Anjou is quite beautiful, is it not, Papa? I mean to say, if you had known how beautiful was the land of Anjou, this would have been your first choice for your appointment. Not Nantes."

"Perhaps."

"I can read and write."

"Can you?"

"Yes, I can. Perhaps I can write all of your reports, at least until I teach you to do it yourself. With such a memory as yours, and with such dedication as you possess, Papa, you would be an asset to Angers."

"I should hope so," he grumbled.

It was a long journey. Guillaume did not speak. The sailors were busy. Estelle had a long time to subtly work on her father, and she made sure there were many talks, expressing the same ideas in different ways.

Soon they turned off the Loire onto the Maine. Nearly every roof was tiled in black slate, and sometimes even bricked the walls. The city of Angers was called the Black City, for it was completely roofed and half-constructed of the dull, ebony slate. The Château d'Angers, the gigantic, squat castle on a ridge high above the Loire, was wholly constructed of it - layer upon layer of flat, black stone and mortar. On the cool sunny day they arrived, they walked up to the gigantic black fortress on the plateau over the river. The inner keep was enclosed by high walls set with no less than seventeen towers.

After crossing the moat and being admitted into the bailey, the children were again left to their own devices. But the interior of Angers castle was quite different than that of Nantes. A wall divided the bailey in half, and an imposing gatehouse was set halfway down the wall. Beyond the gatehouse was the ancient keep, long hall and practice yard. On the children's side of the wall, every space had been turned into an orchard or garden - even with herb and vegetable plots growing upon the ramparts of the walls. Féroce was taken to the Prefect of Police, Monsieur Bernier - his letter from Von Stedingk ensured no lesser a personage would be involved. Guillaume sat on the chests, transfixed by the soldiers and the spectacle. Estelle picked apronfuls of fruits and berries for them to eat, for Spring was upon them. No one seemed to mind. Sometimes the adults even smiled or winked at them as they passed.

Finally, Papa walked out of the gatehouse with a uniformed officer, both of them smiling. The officer disappeared as Féroce crossed to the children.

"What happened, Papa?" asked Estelle excitedly.

"When I sat down in front of Monsieur Bernier's desk, I repeated word-for-word everything he had said to me from our meeting, along with conversations I heard along the way to his office."

"That must have impressed him!"

"I then described, in full detail, everything I had seen since entering the prefecture."

"What did he say?"

"Monsieur Bernier is no idiot, I can tell you that. He was impressed to his brass buckles. I explained to him that it is fairly common for those who cannot read to develop such skills. And before he could say anything, I told him that you were teaching me to read and write, and would be writing my reports until I was skilled enough to do so myself."

"Are you now a policeman of Anjou, Papa?"

"Of Anjou, but not of Angers."

Estelle jumped up and down, and clapped her hands. This was good news indeed.

Guillaume slowly turned, and looked at Féroce with burning eyes, "Where are we then going, if we do not stay here?"

Féroce said nothing for a moment, then spoke softly, "We are going to Saint-Florent-le-Vieil. There is but one officer there now, a Sergeant Durain. He is completely alone, but there is no crime at all - none on the left-bank from the Loire to the Vendée, they say."

Estelle smiled, "That is perhaps good and bad for you, Papa."

"Oh, I'll be busy enough. The police are agents of the Throne, and the Throne regulates and preserves just about everything. I'll be in charge of cataloging the fields and animals for tax purposes, as well as making sure enough grain is being produced to feed everyone. Although where we are going, there is far more latitude, being so far from Paris. Monsieur explained that Sergeant Durain is getting too old to ride around the countryside. As soon as I am fit and able, Durain will be pulled back to Angers for lighter duty."

Just then a black coach appeared, bearing the coat of arms of Anjou. It was enclosed with forward facing windows, and had an upholstered bench seat that could easily accommodate them. The driver jumped down, opened the door, and lowered the carriage steps. Féroce smiled, "This is us, in you go."

And in they went. Unfortunately, the coach only took them to the banks of the river. The bridges in Angers across the Maine would only bring them to the right-bank of the Loire. To get to the left-bank, they would need to barge down-river - which was thankfully much faster than upriver. The journey to Saint-

Florent- le-Vieil was less than twenty-five miles, and they would be there before nightfall.

***

The new Guerrier residence was in the countryside, a little place called L'Ouvrinière, part of the parish of Saint-Florent-le-Vieil, which was only ten square miles itself. It was a small but very quaint country house surrounded by young beeches and oaks. Estelle fell in love with it, and planned her beanstalks and trellises on the spot. Guillaume disappeared into the darkness of the forest and rarely returned. Papa was promptly gone, sometimes for days. He would return with boxes of chic clothes, hats, scarves, ties, and belts - all for him, all of highest quality - but had to be constantly reminded to fetch food and seed. Estelle mostly ate fish, as she waited for her shoots to break the soil. She caught perch during the day, and carp at night. A self-respecting Frenchman would have been up in arms at such a diet, but Estelle was easier to please, and was fine as long as there was a bit of oil and salt in the house. Fishing was regulated by the powers that be, and her Papa happened to be the local official in charge of en-forcement. Despite this, she fished often and half-hoped he would see her. Papa finally purchased chickens and a nanny goat, which Estelle named Joliefille - then they had eggs, milk and *chèvre* butter - with cheese on the way. Guillaume would not eat, usually - or speak. He was a ghost.

They were not there for very long when they received a group of three vis-itors. Estelle knew that this must have been planned in advance, and she was resentful that Papa did not tell her so she could receive them properly. Sergeant Durain was one - a likeable, forgetful old man who had nothing but good inten-tions for the world. The second was a fat, red-faced gentleman who was dressed like a plaid jay bird, who ended up to be the Mayor, Monsieur de Lefleaur. He was pleasant enough, but seemed full of poorly-disguised guile. But when Es-telle saw the third visitor, she experienced the most strange and unique moment of her life.

The third man was none other than Johann Georg Hamann, the German phi-losopher.

But, of course, that could not be. Johann Georg Hamann was in his fifties, and her visitor was less than ten years her senior. He was not Hamann - only exactly alike the man she had always pictured in her daydreams. Estelle was dumbstruck, and she slowly fell, until her legs and hips rested on the ground. And it was him, Johann Georg Hamann, who ran to help her. The closer he ap-proached, the more familiar he looked to her. His hair was blondish-brown, and tied with a black ribbon. He had a long, clean-shaven face, and a strong chin. His eyes were grey, and they twinkled with intelligence and good humor. He was slender and tall, and soon he was by her side. "My goodness!" he said, "Are you unwell?"

184

She knew everything about him. There was nothing in him that was unfamiliar. He had to remember her - they had to have dreamed of each other. "Don't you recognize me?" she burst out. He looked at her uncomprehendingly. "It's me, it's Estelle. Don't you know my face?"

"You are from Saint-Domingue, are you not?"

"Yes! Yes, I am!" Estelle said excitedly.

"Mademoiselle, nearly my entire life has been spent within a day's ride of this very place. I am afraid you mistake me for someone else."

Estelle felt like a fool. She tried not to cry, "Well, that is all very well and good, but I am going to call you Johann for the rest of your life anyway."

He narrowed his eyes, amused, "Well, my name is properly Father Jonathan Courgeon, so at least it's close."

"Close? They are practically the same!" Estelle said, her hopes rising once again.

He smiled kindly, and spoke gently, "Jonathan means 'God has given.' Johann means 'God is merciful.'"

He was a priest. He had sworn oaths to God. To be anything but sisterly toward him would be an act against Christ and the church. It would put her soul in mortal jeopardy, insult her Father in heaven - and Estelle really did not care. She felt like kissing him.

Guillaume made a brief appearance, and was punctiliously polite, but made a fast exit after introductions. Estelle did what she could for her three guests as they socialized with Papa. The wine was poor and watered, there was nothing to feed them except buttered perch with herbs and wild greens, but all three seemed appreciative and ate their fill. Estelle overheard Father Jonathan, "Monsieur Guerrier, I am at your disposal, truly. Transitions can be difficult, and you have come a long way. Please come and see me at any time, for any reason." Féroce did not ask for help, but soon after he did start attending mass. If everyone went to mass, so did he. If everyone sacrificed chickens to the spirits, so did he. He was a law and order man.

It was Estelle who went to visit Father Jonathan the next day. It was for a good cause, but she knew in her heart that there was only one reason - she simply wanted to see him. She went into the beautiful, white chapel of the abbey, and introduced herself to an older deacon, who ended up to be one Monsieur Falaise. He fetched Father Jonathan, and they sat down together on a pew near the narthex door. "Father Johann, I desperately need your help," she said, once they were alone.

He smiled at her promised nickname. "I am at your disposal, Mademoiselle."

"It is my brother, Guillaume. He rarely eats or speaks. He is wasting away from melancholia."

"He did not seem so," he replied, but then thought better of it, "Why do you think this has come to be?"

For some reason, in that moment, she felt like lying or distorting the truth. She shrugged off the feeling. He was a priest, a bearer of secrets. She would simply tell him what she thought. "My brother is handsome and smart - a *Mamelouk*, legally white. He attracted the favor of the powerful in Saint-Domingue. Before we came here, he might as well have been a young nobleman. He was stolen from a better life."

"I see."

"He does not get along with my father, who is a different sort altogether. My father is akin to a boulder from a gravel pit, only surviving because he was too big and too hard to break. But now he relies on his lithoid qualities to see him through everything."

"Is Guillaume as intelligent as you are?"

"I am not considered intelligent."

"Estelle," he said patiently, "You are quite bright. I offer your metaphor as proof."

Estelle's heart burst. "Thank you, Father," she said, forcing calmness into her voice, "Guillaume is far more intelligent than I, in most ways one would consider a subject worthy of intelligence. My talents lie in areas usually classified unworthy of the appellation. But it does not matter. Here and now, I can survive, and Guillaume cannot."

Father Jonathan nodded, "You are an oak, and he is an ebony. Trees of equal beauty and stature, but the oak can grow anywhere. The ebony requires a certain, specific clime."

"Your metaphors are beautiful as well, Father. To continue it, please help me find suitable soil for my brother."

"Would your father object to Guillaume going off to school?"

"Object? Heaven's no! He would barely notice! Goodness Father! That would be perfect! That would solve everything!" Suddenly Estelle realized she was totally wrong, "No, of course he would notice. He would have to pay for it, and he never would. He would come up with an excuse that only made sense to him. He would scoff and say Guillaume should pay to educate himself, or something equally..." Estelle almost said *stupid*, but stopped herself.

Honor thy father and mother.

Jonathan spoke, "Well, every self-respecting university school in France offers scholarships to poorer students. Even Louis-le-Grand has a sizable percentage of students who come from the most common of backgrounds. These schools happen to rely on parish priests to identify the children who are the most talented, and the most in need."

"If Guillaume could be educated without Papa having to sacrifice anything, this could succeed, Father."

"Then I would meet with your brother, to see if he is suitable."

"You are welcome any time."

Jonathan stood. "There is no time like the present."

And, to Estelle's eternal gratitude, off they went, out the doors of the abbey. But Father Jonathan suddenly stopped. He closed his eyes, and tilted his face toward the sunlight for a moment. He then turned, and looked out across the river. The abbey was at the top of the mountain, which was properly a very tall hill, and the view was magnificent. In fact, everything on the top of the hill was beautiful. It was all trees and gardens - châteaux that seemed whimsical and dignified at the same time. Estelle sighed at the beauty of the Loire, and its islands below her, and finally spoke, "I'm glad you stopped for a moment. It is so important that we enjoy and appreciate creation."

"I agree wholeheartedly."

"If I had created a magnificent gift for someone I love, I would appreciate it so much if the gift was enjoyed, and taken in the proper spirit. And what greater gift than creation, and what greater love than that of God."

Father Jonathan's eyes narrowed, impressed by her sentiments. They soon turned and walked down the hill, descending the narrow cobblestone road braced by ancient buildings. With every step, Estelle felt the weight of the world leave her shoulders. She fervently believed that men such as Father Jonathan, were they more common, would solve the problems of the world with no more effort than a snap of their fingers. What she did not realize was that he was beginning to think the same of her. "And what of the oak?" he said as they walked.

"I'm no oak."

"Well, you're no ebony tree, either, are you?"

"I suppose not. I can fish. I'm good with animals, and the leaves talk to me in their way. Such people are never completely lost, as long as there is a bit of soil and rain."

"Honest, worthy pursuits. How else do you occupy your prodigious mind?"

She couldn't look at him, but spoke as she stared straight ahead, "I end up doing all of the cooking and cleaning, but it is better that I do so, for the men in my family have no skill at such things, and my mother has passed away. I love to read, and to daydream. I would also like to travel, which is odd, for all my other passions seem to involve a home, a place where things grow. I also get very seasick."

"You are quite different than the young ladies of Saint-Florent."

"How so?"

"At your age, they are getting married, in not so long a time, and they are all secrets and plans for the unsuspecting young men. But they have known each other their whole lives, and there is nothing unwholesome in it. There are few couplings that the eldest did not predict, when the girls and boys in question were but children."

"I suppose being an outsider in such a place offers little prospects for a girl such as myself, especially with no dowry."

"Have you considered joining an order?"

"An order? To be a nun or some such?"

"Yes. You seem the type."

If only he knew, thought Estelle.

He continued, "Sometimes we think clergy must be perfect, or composed of men and women who are half-angels - at least, at one point, I did. But that is not the case. We are all just people, dedicated to a cause, and to a community. We give up little with our vows, and gain much - very much indeed."

Estelle had an idea. She spoke as innocently as she could, "Perhaps we could talk of this further. Or even better yet, we could meet from time to time, and talk about catechism and scripture."

"That's really a wonderful idea, Estelle. As you can see, around this time I am dedicated to community affairs. If you were to come at the precise time at which you came today, we could study for a half an hour together. Let us say, Monday through Thursday?"

"I will be as regular as a clock for our appointments."

"I am very pleased, Estelle. I look forward to it."

***

Father Jonathan saw Guillaume through the trees. He was sitting on a rock, slack-jawed, nearly catatonic. He crossed quietly to him at an angle, so that his appearance would not be a surprise. "Good afternoon, Guillaume," he said with a smile.

He stood, "Good afternoon, Father."

"No, please, sit. I will find a rock." Guillaume sat back down, as Father Jonathan spotted a fallen tree trunk, and sat where there were no ant trails. "I have been told you are an educated man."

Guillaume turned and looked at him. He was no more than thirteen, but his eyes pierced and burned - quite different than when he was putting on a show for houseguests. He spoke, "I suppose. Who told you that? Estelle?"

"What is your favorite subject?"

"Military history."

Jonathan knew next to nothing about military history. "And what else?"

"Drama, math, chemistry. Animal husbandry. Navigation and sailing. Metalworking."

Jonathan chose the subject he knew most about in order to continue, "I see. And who is your favorite playwright?"

"Shakespeare."

Terrible start. "And who is Shakespeare?"

"He is British. He wrote during the time of Good King Henry. Mostly poetry and plays, both with a remarkable talent."

"And what do you like about him?"

"There is no *damné* singing in his plays. And his verse emulates speech, though it is pleasing and well-thought. His characters are akin to real people, and the situations taken from history. It isn't stylized - it is lifelike. There is super-natural aplenty, but real supernatural, and frightening, like ghosts and such. Plenty of blood as well. Poisonings, ravagings, war and politics. One can learn of life reading a Shakespeare play."

"Do you like French playwrights?"

"They are *merde*, Father. Stylized, never an attempt to be true to the time or mores of the stories. Entertainment, supporting the *status quo*, abutments for the establishment of thought, nothing new, nothing challenging, nothing *real*."

Father Jonathan nodded, "What is the square root of x?

Guillaume rolled his eyes, "*Y.*"

Jonathan laughed, "Go on.*"*

*"*It is y, if y to the second power equals x."

"You need to be in school, Guillaume. Your mind is wasted, sitting on that rock."

Guillaume looked down, and nodded.

Jonathan pitied him. When a fish is out of water, it is a totality of dearth - the fish is consumed with compulsion, it only knows it needs water, and can feel or see nothing else.

Guillaume turned to Jonathan, and his eyes were now those of a completely different person. They were deep, these eyes - they knew pain. He spoke softly and evenly, "There was a boy my age in Saint-Domingue. He was probably a dark *Mulâtre*, if not full-African. He may have lived on the streets, I don't know. I saw him in the same place, coming from the same avenue, every day, as I walked to my friend Raphaël's house from my home. This boy, who had no name, beat me with his fists and feet, every day, for no reason at all. He was so angry. Just looking at my face, he would become angry. He would yell and scream and run at me. He was so thin, but still fast and strong. Every day he beat me. I never told anyone, because my father would have whipped me for getting beaten. My mother would have hated me, and told a story of what it is to truly suffer. There was only Monsieur Pinceau. But I dared not tell him, for he might forbid me to walk to his home, for fear of my safety. One day, I decided to fight back as hard as I could. We fought for a long time, and I tired of it, and still he beat me. I did not visit Le Cap for several days, and I became distraught and angry. Finally, I steeled myself and walked there again, and I saw the boy. We ran at each other, and we fought. We fought all day, and ended up in the alleys by the cliffs. I took a rock, and I hit him with it. I hit him again and again. I killed him, in fact. I murdered him. I left his body in the alley. I cleaned myself in the ocean, as I always did after my fisticuffs, and went to see Raphaël. When I walked home, I went by the alley, and the boy's body was still there. Everyone just walked past him. But they also walked past when we fought, only sometimes did they take notice, and laugh or curse at us. The next day, his body was gone. I never saw anyone look for him, or mourn him, or wonder where he went." Guillaume took a deep breath and sighed, "That is Saint-Domingue. That is the place where I am from, *Abbé*. That is where my father is from, and my sister. My mother was a slave of the British, and she hailed from Tír Chonaill, though I do not know if that was a real place or not, or whether her tales were true."

Father Jonathan had never heard such a story as this, in the first person - ever. He nodded, as he did in the confessional, but found himself searching for something to say. He finally spoke, "How old were you?"

"I was eight."

"It is hard to bear secrets such as yours, Guillaume."

Guillaume nodded. *Yes.*

"There have been times and places in France that have been equally savage, but that is not this place, nor this time. We must work toward a brighter future, you and I, and toward bettering ourselves."

Guillaume nodded.

"Let me ask you: would you rather not have crossed paths with this boy, that he be alive, and left to learn, and perhaps better himself?"

Guillaume nodded twice.

"Then God forgives you, Guillaume, and now you must forgive yourself. You must also now realize the different world in which you find yourself, and how it will allow you to be. There are different rules that you must follow."

"Yes, Father."

"We must get you to school, with other boys who share your interests. It is not fitting to have only one friend. Speaking of whom, we must get you writing him. There is no reason that Raphaël should be dead to you now."

Guillaume burst into sobs, and threw himself on Father Jonathan, holding him with a strong grip. Jonathan, shocked, managed to put his arms around him.

What a cruel world, thought the good Father.

He was right about the world, but wrong in his opinion of Guillaume.

Guillaume was indeed brilliant, handsome and forceful. He was charismatic and ultimately capable of being pleasant and enjoyable company – but he was also, in more than small measure, self-absorbed, self-righteous and self-pitying. He was fearless and could be violent. He did not care a whit for the boy he murdered. He wished he had never met him - or the boy had never been born. He opened his heart to Father Jonathan because of an unconscious impulse to be comforted, not for absolution.

He wasn't beyond redemption, but only time would tell what the mélange of conflicting qualities inside of him produced. Such people are never to be envied. Their path is always difficult – the only question is how much of that pain will be shared unfairly with others.

1832

Jake

La Conciergerie, 1832

Chapter 11

Jake laid on his bed in his *pistole* cell.

Isaäc entered his room without knocking, and shut the door behind him. Jake felt numb, lost in incoherent thought. He did not sit up.

"The verdict will be announced, and then, immediately afterward, the sentence. Both are being determined as we speak," said Isaäc.

Jake's manners finally overrode his mood, "Thank you for everything, Isaäc. You are quite a brilliant lawyer. It must be difficult to defend someone as guilty as I am."

"Guilt does not determine difficulty."

"What will happen at the sentencing?"

"Jake," began Isaäc, saying nothing more for a moment. When he continued, his voice was soft and empathetic, "My sources have told me that you will be found guilty and sentenced to death."

Jake sat up.

Isaäc continued, "This will be overturned at the appeal, most certainly. It will be overturned, and your sentence commuted to prison time. After your sentence, you will be deported and, most likely, suffer a lifetime exile, a ban from ever returning to France. *If* you are released. I suppose I have gotten ahead of myself."

Jake closed his eyes.

Isaäc continued, "Something unusual has been requested. We have been asked to attend a closed sitting of the court tonight. The public will not be allowed, and there will be no word-for-word transcription, only general minutes made after the proceedings."

"It sounds like a secret tribunal."

"Perhaps, yes. Albeit a powerless one of little account."

"Is that legal?"

"Strictly speaking, yes. We have not been ordered to attend, only requested. There will be no legal ruling possible in this venue, but we could arrive at some sort of deal."

"So, this meeting is simply in addition to the normal legal process?"

"Effectively, yes."

"Is this unusual?"

"It is unique. It is only a request. We can turn it down, and wait for court."

"Why is it happening at all?"

"I think your verdict and sentence were leaked purposefully, in order that we attend this meeting."

Jake thought of Isaäc's prior suspicions, and realized he had moved the trial forward to bring about this very outcome - to force this exact meeting. "My mysterious malefactor will be revealed here, won't he?"

"If our instincts were correct, and there actually happens to be one, then yes. I think so, Jake."

"Then, of course, we must attend."

"Yes, I think we must." He sat down on the chair and leaned forward. "You will want to speak. Do not. Do not, unless I ask you to speak. This is very important, Jake. Do you understand?"

"Yes, of course," he replied, wondering why such a demand needed to be repeated twice.

***

Jake and Isaäc were escorted upstairs by eight guards; three to each side, one vanguard and one rearguard. Despite himself, Jake found his mind marveling at the architecture, illuminated by the flickering fire of the oil lamps. The ceiling was composed of high gothic arches, billowing like cloth tent panels, but made of Lutetian limestone. They ascended a staircase, one that seemed to flow like liquid around a carousel of pillars. Their escort ended at a beautiful carved door, reinforced and inlaid with iron. It was opened and both entered.

Inside was a large room, graced with high arched windows that probably illuminated the room brilliantly during the day. It was sumptuously furnished, and well-lit with lamps and hanging crystal chandeliers iced with white candles. All seven judges were there, plus a full complement of bailiffs and clerks, the prosecutor, and four other men Jake had never seen. The first was a thin, weasel-like creature, dressed somberly, but expensively, in black. He was either an undertaker or a banker. To his left and right, behind him, and staring somewhere near the ceiling, were two tall, well-built men dressed formally, but not expensively, in voluminous cloaks that belied the warm weather - and perhaps hid a few pistols and knives as well. A medium-sized, iron-bound chest sat on a nearby table, its contents conceivably necessitating the presence of the tall men, who could only be private guards.

The last unknown man was quite different from the others. He was dressed in finery, and wore considerable amounts of jewelry - more so than was fashionable. Every possible article he wore that could be adorned bore the appropriate and expensive accessory. He was an ugly man, a foul-looking malevolent creature, but was clean, well-groomed and smelled pleasantly of expensive citrus cologne. He was older, perhaps in his fifties, but was well-built. He looked brutish, but also wealthy and powerful; a physically and spiritually intimidating presence. Jake found himself staring at him. The man looked back, and Jake immediately turned away from his gaze. Nearby, Isaäc was exchanging pleasantries with the court, a low bubbling in his ear.

There was a shuffling of chairs. The room was being made into the shape of a little *Cour d'Assises* by the clerks and bailiffs. Isaäc did not pay any attention to Jake. Jake did not allow himself to be affected. He was now convinced Isaäc was all tricks and traps. Instead, Jake sat in the chair that most resembled his usual spot in the defendant's box. Very quickly, everyone else did the same, except the banker, his guards and the evil-looking man. None of the four had yet moved or spoken.

The Presiding Justice began, "We will call to order this supplemental tribunal. The purpose of this tribunal is for the facilitation of arbitration only."

Arbitration, thought Jake, *Interesting*.

The Judge continued, "The clerks will note that all seven judges assigned to this case are present, along with Monsieur *le Procureur*, Monsieur *l'Avocat* and the defendant. Messieurs, I would inform you that we have arrived at a decision in this case. We have found the defendant guilty of high treason, sedition and rebellion against the Throne and Constitution of France. We have also arrived at a sentence, which will be public execution by guillotine."

Isaäc smiled, "We will appeal, of course."

The Prosecutor spoke, "Monsieur Crémieux, even if you appeal, the sentence will be commuted to life in prison. If you appeal again, and win again, your client will still spend years behind bars, and suffer exile afterward."

Isaäc narrowed his eyes, "You sound as if you are trying to convince me of something, but you have forgotten to tell me as to which course I should change."

The Prosecutor and the Foul Man exchanged a glance. The Foul Man spoke, "If it pleases the court, I would speak on this." His voice was a warm honey, matching his subtle, pleasant smell, rather than his loathsome features.

Isäac shrugged, as if the case revolved around the sale of a used carriage, "And who might you be, Monsieur?"

"I am Monsieur Tyran."

"An alias? Come now. A man's life is at stake. Perhaps we can use our real names?"

"I'm afraid my real name would avail you nothing. I was anonymous, and then I was not. When I was not, my name was Monsieur Tyran."

Jake could detect no foreign accent. The man was certainly French, probably from Marseilles. Tyran meant *despot* or *tyrant*. The name now matched his cruel face, but not his voice.

"Well," smiled Isäac, "since we are all here, I suppose I have no objection to Monsieur Tyran speaking on this subject."

The Prosecutor turned to Monsieur Tyran, and nodded once again. Tyran stood, "What a terrible business, this rebellion," he began, "Seventy-three brave soldiers of France killed by their own countrymen, and over three-hundred wounded. Such a tragedy." He paused, and looked around the room, "And for the surviving rebels, eighty-two expensive trials. Such a waste of time and money - and lives. I feel I should... do something. Help, as it were. Yes, yes, indeed."

The Presiding Justice pursed his lips, "And how would you help, Monsieur Tyran?"

The question came too quickly. All of this was rehearsed beforehand, Jake realized.

Monsieur Tyran spoke, "I believe that one-hundred francs might help to pay for a trial. Let us say also, in a godly world, the family of a brave wounded soldier should receive one-hundred francs as well."

That sum could easily fund a middle-class family for a season.

Monsieur Tyran rubbed his chin, "And the families of the fallen would receive two-hundred francs, I think."

The Presiding Justice was quick with the resulting sum, "That would be eighty-two-hundred francs for the trials, thirty-four thousand for the wounded and fourteen-thousand-six-hundred for the dead. Fifty-six-thousand-eight-hundred altogether."

The Weasel Banker unlocked the chest and opened it. From a seated position, no one could see what was inside of it.

Monsieur Tyran spoke again, "Part of me wishes to upend the contents of this chest upon the stones in front of you." His voice was different. He spoke slowly, but with an edge. "But I will spare you any coarse theatrics," he continued, "and simply say the chest contains exactly sixty-thousand francs. Slightly more than enough. But what is three-thousand-two-hundred francs between friends?"

"My goodness, the chest contains only slightly more than the exact amount of which you spoke," said Isaäc, "What an amazing coincidence."

Monsieur Tyran continued, as if the sarcasm eluded him, "I tell you true, Monsieur *l'Avocat*, that the remarkable coincidences pertaining to your client will only now begin to come to light."

"I am sure I don't understand."

"You said yourself that Monsieur Loring is in France because of a little Cross of Nantes around his neck. A little cross begetting him a tiny treasure - something to this effect. Yes?"

"Yes," drawled Isaäc.

"The year engraved upon Monsieur Loring's cross is 1805."

"Yes, the year Napoleon proclaimed himself emperor, if I am not mistaken."

"You are not. But 1805 was also the very year the Cross of Nantes went missing for the second and last time."

"I wouldn't know. I am no expert on the Cross of Nantes."

"But I am, Monsieur. It went missing for the first time in 1754. Miraculously, it made its way back to the Traversier family during the Revolution, and was lost again in 1805."

"You sound preeminently educated on the subject. I will take your word for it."

"Messieurs," continued Tyran, "I have found a unique document regarding the Cross of Nantes, recorded during the first time it went missing. The Cross, you see, appeared in Saint-Domingue in 1763, in the last months of the war that engulfed the entire world - on the neck of a young woman, no less. It is the only record of the Cross between 1754 and 1788. There are no mentions of this woman at all, in any record I am able to find. No record of her at all - except in the aforementioned, newly-discovered documents."

"Then your search has ended by necessity, Monsieur Tyran, for the people of Saint-Domingue have murdered all the Europeans on their island, and would not take kindly to more. They do not even deign to use the name of Saint-Domingue, rather they call themselves the nation of Haïti," Isaäc said gently.

"No, Monsieur Crémieux, you are wrong."

"Am I? I thought this was common knowledge."

"The people of Saint-Domingue killed all of the *French* on their island. Not all Europeans. I assure you there are still pockets of whites left on the island. Germans, I know for certain. I believe there are Poles, as well."

"Let us speak plainly, Monsieur. Are you actively searching for the Cross of Nantes?" laughed Isaäc.

"I am."

"*Mon Dieu!* Monsieur Tyran, I do not mean to be insulting, but not a year has gone by when someone hasn't found new evidence regarding the Cross, and gone off on some *sangréal* quest to find it. Frankly, if it was possible to find this thing, it would have been found already. No, I'm afraid the directors of the Traversier Trust will be determining their own salaries for the foreseeable future."

Monsieur Tyran slightly raised his voice, and the tone became softly angry, even deadly. "Do I appear casual in my pursuit, Monsieur? Do I seem... poorly-funded?"

Jake felt danger from this man.

Isaäc laughed gaily, "Monsieur Tyran, you mistake my meaning. I am simply confused. What is it that you wish? We dance from subject to subject, but there is no common melody to the tune. The theme alludes me, sir."

"What do I wish? I wish him," and the Foul Man, Monsieur Tyran, pointed at Jake, who felt for all the world as if he had just been marked by the devil himself.

"My client?" said Isaäc, happily shocked.

"Indeed, Monsieur. And at the risk of sounding mad, I will say this: I would have him search for the two Crimson Heirlooms, and the Cross is but the first. There is a magic to the Cross of Nantes, a magic that becomes even more apparent with the study of its history. If it makes you feel more comfortable, say providence surrounds it. Call it cursed, call it holy, call it what you may. But make no mistake, the Cross has claimed Monsieur Loring. It is his destiny to search for it."

"I see. You have some strong thoughts on this subject, Monsieur," Isaäc said, with perhaps more humor than was suitable.

Tyran ignored his tone once again, "It is no coincidence that he speaks French, but is not French. It is no coincidence he can search for the mystery woman of Saint-Domingue, and not be killed or hurt because of his very nature. It is no coincidence he wears a little cross stamped 1805, nor is it coincidence that your client has two choices before him now: to serve me, or to serve the sentence of the Throne."

Isaäc nodded sagely, "For how long? For how long would he serve you?"

"For five years, or until I find the Cross. And he will not starve on his journey, I assure you."

"And how does the court feel about this?"

The Prosecutor nearly whispered, "The sentence of death would be immediately commuted to five years of penal service under the honorable orders of Monsieur Tyran. After the sentence, there would be no further punishment."

"No exile?"

"No exile. As long as Monsieur Tyran's generous offer of compensation for the Fatherland's troubles remain, the Throne's offer will stand for your client."

Isaäc turned to Monsieur Tyran with a gay smile, "And how long does your offer stand, Monsieur."

"You say yes or no before you leave this room."

"I suppose then, I have only one more question."

"I am listening."

"What is the second Crimson Heirloom? You said there were two, yes? We are not just searching for the Cross?"

Monsieur Tyran looked pensive, even distracted, then nearly whispered, "I will tell you this, and nothing more - I saw the devil dance and heard his song. If you only knew the horror of the sight, as I do, your sleep would be haunted forevermore. I witnessed the very moment the dark demon was let loose from the cage of hell - when he became free to roam the earth. He is still here, and will be - from that fell moment, until the day of judgment itself. He cannot be sent back, Monsieur. He is here, now, everywhere, in this room - I can hear him sing that infernal song when the sun goes down and the night is still." Tyran calmed, and continued, "Some little light I would have shine in the darkness, in which we now find ourselves. I seek salvation and forgiveness - and nothing more, nothing else, truth be told. The Crimson Heirlooms are but a means to this end. I cannot be more honest."

Jake forced himself to show no emotion, but his mind reeled:

Monsieur Tyran is insane.

He didn't need Crimson Heirlooms. He needed one of Guilleret's straight-jackets. He was as mad as an outhouse rat.

Isaäc smiled, and spoke gently, "You would make a good advocate, Monsieur. You have spoken a great deal, and have not answered my question."

Monsieur Tyran's eyes flashed, and he spoke quickly, "The second Crimson Heirloom are the words of the devil's song, as he danced across the blood-drenched hills of the Vendée Militaire."

The Vendée Militaire was a place, named after the Vendée River, which was little more than a stream. It was composed of parts of several regions of France which rebelled against the True Revolution. Jake knew nothing else of it.

Isaäc spoke quickly as well, all business, "The second Crimson Heirloom is - are, rather - lyrics, then. The lyrics to this song. To be clear and concise, the devil's song of the Vendée Militaire. I am assuming we can call it that, there being only one such song. I think it is important we establish that. Yes?"

"Yes," replied Tyran, "There is only one such song, it cannot be mistaken."

Isaäc, calm as sabbath morning, turned back to the Prosecutor, "So the official sentence, the official ruling of the Throne, will be five years of honorable penal service, to be carried out under the orders of Monsieur Tyran, with no further punishment. And, of course, automatic commutation of the remainder of the sentence, if the Crimson Heirlooms are found sooner than anticipated."

"That is correct, Monsieur *l'Avocat*."

Isaäc turned to Jake, "Well, what do you think, Monsieur Loring. A pewter cross has brought you here. Now a gold one beckons to take you away."

Jake knew Monsieur Tyran was completely insane. Most likely, he was dangerous and violent. But what choice did he have? He turned to Tyran, and cleared his throat, "For better or worse, Monsieur, I am yours to command."

Monsieur Tyran did not smile either, "For sixty-thousand francs, you had better be."

1784

Xavier

Le Château de La Baronnière, 1784

Chapter 12

For Xavier, it was the day of a short but extraordinarily important journey. He was developing his first contact on the left-bank of the Loire. Through an exchange of letters that had lasted several weeks, a meeting had been arranged for later this day in the afternoon. The left-bank was dark territory, its own animal, so to speak. His father wrote of it.

> The land between the Loire and the Vendée rivers might as well be another country. This area, delineated by its customs and not by its political borders, encompasses parts of Brittany, Poitou, and Anjou. It is rolling hills, bocage, marshland, and forest. It is clannish, traditional if not backwards, and distrustful of outsiders. It is also far more fertile than the right-bank, and the farmers and drovers are not only relatively well-off, but also known as trustworthy and loyal. I could not penetrate this land, and did not make proper use of its resources. I'm not sure why. Perhaps I needed an ambassador. In any case, it is unknown territory to most of the other merchants in Nantes, so I did not suffer by comparison.
>
> In this land, we see the young men go off to fight the wars of France, their drovers walking the cattle to the cities, and

*the teamsters bringing their crops to market. Then all go
back home, to live a life that is utterly mysterious to us all.*

Xavier had pulled all of the resources he was able to reasonably access, by
water or road, out of the right-bank of the Loire. Prices were tightly controlled,
and buyers for farmers' goods had already been prearranged for the greater part.
He was scavenging for table scraps, and working around established harvests.
He now needed more, his own prearrangements, to evolve to the next step of his
plan.

He had found someone who could be a worthy ambassador for the left-bank,
with whom he was meeting today. He had to be sharp, but that very morning, of
all the mornings fate could have chosen, Madame was in one of her moods. The
servants, the few who were still employed, made it a point to stay out of her way.

Monsieur Fidèle, the new maître d'hôtel, had even found the courage to
speak to Xavier regarding her behavior, "Monsieur, Madame DuBois told me
Madame hasn't been this bad since 1754. And we all know what happened then,"
and then more pointedly, "And what she *said*, Monsieur."

Madame DuBois was the curmudgeonly chef de cuisine, employed for decades. She was a tome of Traversier history.

Xavier sighed. He was not a superstitious man. Traversier was not a house
given to spiritual hysteria of any sort. His mother, however, had broken the mold.
Sometimes she had spells - she became convinced her intuitions and obsessions
were foretellings of the future. Xavier found this to be embarrassing, and somewhat shameful. Unfortunately, during her worst spell, in the year 1754 in question, she had been absolutely right in her premonitions. Those who knew of this
ancient, accidental bullseye had a kind of religious respect for her when she went
mad. Everyone, that is, except Xavier.

She was his mother, however, and he promptly went to see her. She was
pacing in her room, with a frantic, crazy look in her eyes.

"Mother, are you quite well?"

"Where did you say you were going this morning?"

"To Anjou."

"Yes, yes. Where in Anjou?"

"Specifically? Just outside of Saint-Florent-le-Vieil."

"Last night, I wrote this." She handed him a crumpled piece of paper. Xavier
sighed.

"And this is?"

"Open it!" she said, with imperious command.

Xavier smoothed out the paper. Upon it was scrawled *DROWNED*. He made
no outward sign of his irritation. "You think I am going to drown?"

"No," she said quietly and pensively.

"Then I don't know what this means."

"Saint Florent le Vieil," she said in such a tone that he thought she would trail off into catatonia. But soon, with rising excitement, she spoke again, "Saint Florent le Vieil was the brother of Saint Florent le Jeune. They were Roman soldiers who converted to Christianity, and were sentenced to death. They were both to be drowned in the Enns river, with stones tied around their neck."

Xavier was back to silently cursing again. He nodded interestedly, to keep her calm.

She continued, "But an angel appeared to Florent, and asked him to rejoin Saint Martin in Tours, which he did, leaving his brother to the torments of martyrdom. Saint Martin himself ordained him, and he then performed several miracles. In Candes, a child had been at the bottom of the river for three days. He prayed, and the child awoke, and returned to the bank. Florent died on Mount Glonne, the highest point of the town of Saint-Florent-le-Vieil, where the abbey now stands."

"And how do you know this, Madame?" asked Xavier, now unable to hide his irritation.

"Nantes has only one use for Catholicism. It is used to scare young girls into chastity and obedience. I assure you, in my youth, I was both chaste, obedient and knowledgeable of my saints. Especially the patron saints of the towns of Brittany, and those on the banks of the Loire, be they of Anjou, Touraine, or anywhere else."

"Well, I am not going to Saint-Florent-le-Vieil, I am going somewhere near it. To be precise, to the château of Charles-Melchior Artus, the Marquis de Bonchamps. It is called the Château de la Baronnière, and I assure you it has nothing to do with drowning."

She stopped pacing and sat down. "Sit with me."

Xavier sat down, and she put a hand on his thigh.

"Do not make light of this," she replied calmly. "You are somehow connected to this place. Not just Saint-Florent-le-Vieil. Everything around and surrounding it. The Loire. Sacred death, martyrdom by drowning."

"I see. Well, your miracle town of Candes lies at the confluence of the Loire and the Vienne. Precisely which river is to have these drowning miracles?"

"The Loire." She said it with such confidence it bordered on conviction.

"I think you are still a Catholic, Mother." he replied with dry mirth, "For only a Catholic could be truly convinced of the integrity of such inanity."

"Perhaps," she replied calmly, "But please heed me. There is something very special about this place. Be aware. Be receptive."

"Madame, I promise you this: if the angels of God come down and speak to me, as they did to Saint Florent, I will listen."

Xavier rose from his seat. His mother's hand snapped on his wrist, with a strength he would not have thought she possessed. "My darling," she said calmly, "think upon this. Only make that promise if you mean it."

"Which one?"

"About the angels, my son."

It took a moment for Xavier to remember what he said, for he did say it casually and in jest. Xavier supposed that if the angels of God indeed spoke to him, it would mean God exists, and the Bible is truth. He was a man of reason. If such a thing were true, it would be the duty of all thinking men to become religious and faithful. If the angels of God came to him, he would indeed listen. It would also never happen. He could promise this. "Mother," he said, "If the angels of God come down and speak to me, I will listen."

She let him go. "Have a safe journey, Monsieur Traversier."

And that was that.

Unfortunately, there was no easy way to get to Saint-Florent-Le-Vieil from Nantes. Xavier Traversier sold his coaches years ago. He traveled by barge or on horseback, if he did not hire a coach.

He decided on a ride up the Loire on one of his barges, for the ten-odd mile journey to Varades. It was always beneficial to be seen by the lowest caste of workers. It made them conscientious, and gave them *esprit de corps*. He would then take a ferry across the river to Saint-Florent-le-Vieil and hire another coach to take him the final mile or two to the Château. Bonchamps, the man he was meeting, was a noble - a real one, not some bourgeoise with a purchased title - and the presence of L'Oublié would probably scare him senseless. He would leave L'Oublié in Varades.

Xavier had dealt with a refuse slew of personalities in the course of building his business. He wasn't surprised by anything, much less intimidated or possessed of anxiety. People could be dishonest, rude, ignorant and selfish. Ominously, sometimes they could be all of those things and yet pretend they were not. But Xavier could usually size them up. Bonchamps might be all four, or none of them, or a host of other negative qualities that were equally common. Xavier would find out soon enough.

Of course, when the time came to travel up the Loire, they were fusilladed by a cold, driving rain that was not completely thwarted by the canvass tent over the barge. They were both dressed finely, and all in bourgeoise black, their wardrobes being more-or-less identical at this point. No one would ever mistake the henchman for the scion of the house, however. The English say the clothes make the man. The French say *bon sang ne saurait mentir* - good blood cannot lie.

Xavier lived in a perpetual state of exhaustion. Even with the rain, he was able to sleep the entire way to Varades. L'Oublié staked out their rooms for the night, while Xavier continued the wretched journey.

The ferry from Varades across the Loire was also a nightmare. It was just a small cutter, and Xavier was totally exposed to the elements. The cutter was, however, expertly maneuvered by the two ferrymen. "You are good sailors, you two," he said to them.

"*Merci*, Monsieur. What brings you to Saint-Florent-Le-Vieil?"

"Business. I am meeting with the Marquis de Bonchamps."

"The Marquis de Bonchamps!" the ferryman said excitedly. "Now there is a sailor!"

"Really?"

"Yes, Monsieur. When he returned from Paris with his young wife, not too many months ago, there was a storm the likes of which you've never seen. No one would take the two of them to the left-bank. But Bonchamps convinced us he himself could take us across."

"And what happened?"

"We've been sailing this river our whole lives, and we found ourselves in school, like children. He was tranquil as a pond, speaking softly, pointing things out we had never seen."

"He was a ship Captain, then?"

"No, Monsieur. He was a Marine, and is still a Grenadier Captain in the Anjou Regiment. He served on ship and shore in India. A war hero, commended by the Duc de Damas himself."

"He is my age? The Marquis de Bonchamps?"

"Yes, Monsieur. Perhaps even younger."

Bonchamps did fit the mold. The French military, both Army and Navy, was led by nobles from old families who were rich in honor, and usually poor in gold. They had a deserved reputation for gallantry and ferocity, and sometimes even intelligence or acumen. For a time, leading to the wretched defeat of 1754, these officers were also corrupt, undisciplined and pleasure-loving. But this Bonchamps would have been the product of the subsequent reforms. It would be rare indeed for any of them to come from a major city, or from anywhere near Paris. They crawled out of little towns, like the approaching Saint-Florent-le-Vieil, and remote areas like this one, western Anjou, able to shoot out a falcon's eye at a hundred paces, and out-point a master fencer. They spoke like courtiers, dueled over spilt wine, and would charge the devil himself for King, altar and country. But this Bonchamps seemed a bit more civilized. "You say he was soft-spoken and patient?"

"No one has ever heard Bonchamps raise his voice, Monsieur. He is the most noble, most gentle of men. The greatest thing I could ever say about him is that he is a true noble of Anjou."

"And how would you describe such a thing?"

"A gentleman who spurns the lure of Versailles and Paris. He stays in his ancestral home. He does not take a fixed rent from his farmers, rather a percentage. Because of this he becomes a partner with his charges, and not their oppressor. If an extra hand is needed, he gives it. He leaves only to serve his country, or at the request of the King himself. On Sundays and Holy Days, the entire parish is seen at his château, dancing and feasting and celebrating God. That, Monsieur, is a true noble of Anjou."

"He must be unique."

"I tell you, where you are going now, things are different. Peasants do not curse the nobles on the left-bank of the Loire, Monsieur. They bless them, and greet them by name. Here, and in Poitou and Brittany, as well."

"Until the peasant dares hunt on the noble's land, I'd wager."

"Then you would lose your wager, Monsieur. The peasants hunt on the lord's land all year long - and the lord would only ride to join them with his musket, and drink from the same wineskin."

Xavier didn't quite know what to think. The ferryman's words sounded farcical and fantastic, like something out of a story concocted by the King's secret police. The man himself, however, believed every word coming out of his mouth. "If what you are saying is true," Xavier said cautiously, "he is noble indeed, and a gift to France, and the world."

"You have made a friend for life, Monsieur. I am at your service," he replied.

Xavier smiled, but was inwardly skeptical. It seemed the ferryboat was taking him into a different world. People here still believed in God and went to mass. The nobles considered their title to be a mark of responsibility, and not necessarily of privilege. Peasants hunted on their lord's land. Landowners took a percentage of yield - and oversaw their own fields. In most of France, the feudal system had never worked as innocently as the ferryman now described it. Through most of history, the lords, and often even clergy, made life difficult for the peasants, and were characterized by social and financial ambition. Usually the nation seemed hell-bent on creating men such as L'Oublié - used, broken, and thrown aside.

When he got off the ferry, Saint-Florent-le-Vieil was almost totally obscured by rain and low clouds. The town nearly went straight up from the banks, onto the sides of Mount Glonne. At its base were only a smattering of buildings, and, past them, fields. The streets on Mount Glonne were stone - and everything to the south, where he was going, happened to be mud. He realized, looking about, that there was probably no chance at all of a single enclosed coach anywhere.

Xavier saw a public house, and ran over to it as fast as he could. It was mostly full of farmers, not rivermen, and the patrons turned to see who entered. Xavier noticed that most of them wore slippers carved of wood instead of shoes or boots, and had straw rather than hose or socks. Xavier took off his hat, and humbly addressed the crowd, "God bless all here, and good morning to you." All of them returned his greeting - it was the perfect thing to say. He continued, "I have a meeting with the Marquis de Bonchamps. I'm afraid I stepped off the ferry with only my two legs. I would be chagrined to muddy the home of the

Marquise, whom I have heard is a kind and faithful servant of God. May I pay someone to take me to the Château, on a cart or coach?"

A man stood, "I will take you on the bumpiest cart in Anjou, if you'll have me."

"You have my gratitude, Monsieur."

"I will not accept payment. Any guest of the Château is treated to the best meals and warmest hospitality one could hope to receive. It will be payment enough."

"You have my gratitude. But if it rains this hard the entire way, I'm afraid I must insist."

The man took his hat and coat off the peg, and made to leave, "Only if you insist, Monsieur. Wait here, and I will hitch my horses."

Xavier walked out into the rain. "Allow me to help, Monsieur." It was the perfect thing to do.

Soon after, the cart made its way through the town. The cart driver was found to be the garrulous and faithful Étienne Roitelet, who provided Xavier with all of the innocent gossip of Saint-Florent-Le-Vieil that he could properly hold in his head. Étienne was barely thirty-five, blissfully married for twenty of them, had five children, and his eldest was having Étienne's first grandchild in the Summer. Xavier found himself envious of the man, and a bit saddened and self-pitying. The driver seemed happy, surrounded by love, accepted and assured of his purpose. Xavier felt none of those things. Xavier appeared most assuredly-assured of purpose. But he was not, and he knew it. Xavier, rather, had faith that being purposeful would someday make him assured.

And then, he saw them. A tall, thin man holding the hand of a teen girl, both bundled up against the driving rain. When they got closer, Xavier realized the man was a young priest.

"Hello Father Jonathan!" said Étienne.

The young priest smiled, and waved, "*Bonjour*, Étienne!"

Time seemed to stop for Xavier.

There was a driving rain. The clouds were low, but probably continued far into the sky. It was nearly dark, and not yet noon.

Yet, a red light glinted off the neck of the young girl - and then they were rumbled and sloshed past them through the mud. The sparkle of light was a lustrous red akin to luminescent, glowing blood. It was unmistakable, unmissable - like the spark of a match fire in the dead of night. Xavier's heart began to beat faster as he wondered. Perhaps it was his mother's ominous words, perhaps it was because he grew up in a house of old paintings that commemorated the heirlooms of his house. Whatever the reason, Xavier could only think of one possibility for the startling sight.

That young girl wears the Cross of Nantes around her neck.

It was an absurd thought. But was it? Whatever light source caused the spark had to be distant, for it was not obvious. What could take a random flicker and turn it into fire? There was only one thing - perfect diamonds of ultra-rare crimson hue, cut by a master. There was nothing else capable of a shocking display of chromatic reflection on such a dark day.

Xavier calmed himself. He was being idiotic.

The Cross of Nantes was worth millions of livres, it was lost to the British thousands of miles away. It could not possibly appear on the neck of a girl in a little anonymous town in the middle of the Anjou countryside as she walked down a muddy mess of a street. Besides, how did it catch a reflection at all? Did she wear the Cross on the outside of her coat? Or did her coat part for just an instant - and her underlying garments for that matter - just for him to see the priceless ornament tease him with a spark? Xavier thought he had to be the greatest simpleton in France: it could not be - any more than Florent's angels talking to him from the clouds.

"Father Jonathan is from Botz-en-Mauges, one parish over. It has to be that way. No one wants to confess to a man whose nose they once wiped. He was a good boy, all say. Smart, I tell you. He knew how to read before he could walk." Étienne noticed Xavier's mood. "Are you alright, Monsieur?" he asked.

"Yes, fine, thank you."

"It is not too much longer."

They drove on. The quaint town soon disappeared, and fields took the place of houses and buildings across the gently rolling hills. Fields soon gave way to trees.

They crested a small hill and outbuildings, a pond, a corral of horses, and a château of white stone and blue slate roofs came into view. Xavier was surprised at how small it was. The Meilleur, original house and addition together, was easily six times its size. The château was also taller than it was wide or long. Along with pointed towers and arching roofs, it gave the appearance of childlike fantasy. It had an intimacy of scale and a whimsical, fantastic aura. A dark, handsome man with curly hair ran from the doors holding an overcoat over his head. "Monsieur Traversier, please get inside! Monsieur Roitelet, you as well! We will have others put the horses inside and rub them down. Just put the brake on. Yes, yes, there you go!" And with that, all of them ran inside, and the door was shut to the cold.

It was warm inside, and smelled of coffee, roasting chicken and browned butter. It was rustic and homey, filled with old, worn furniture. Bonchamps took their hats and jackets himself, until a young servant girl came out to help. Soon even the pregnant Madame, the Marquise de Bonchamps, came out to assist. She was very young and physically nondescript. Xavier tried to properly introduce himself, but she would have none of it, "I am not in Paris anymore, Monsieur! This is Anjou! You are wet, cold and hungry, and we both know each other's names, do we not?" Xavier could only laugh. He could not believe that a Marquis and his pregnant wife were helping servants take his jacket – and the jacket of his driver. He had lived a short journey from this place for his entire life, and the morning had brought nothing but new experiences.

Soon they found themselves at lunch. Chicken fricassée - halfway between sauté and stew, cooked first in butter - was the main course, but not the only course, of the lunch. The Muscadet was from the new Loire vines, introduced after the Himalayan-worthy freeze of 1709 wiped out the native grapes.

Étienne was soon called to the kitchen to gossip with the servants, and the three of them were left alone. Bonchamps listened rather than spoke. Xavier found that his curiosity trumped his better judgment. He decided to switch his investigative efforts toward Madame. "How did you meet? Yourself and Monsieur, that is?"

"Oh, I do not wish to bore you, Monsieur."

"Please understand, I am actually hungering for your story. You and your husband, both. Although I have already tried to pry that mussel from the rock, and was not successful."

They smiled at each other, then she turned back to Xavier. "I was born Marie Renée Marguerite de Scépeaux. You will forgive me, for I am extraordinarily proud of my family, perhaps because I never truly had one. My line is from Maine, and of ancient origin. One of my paternal ancestors, Françoise de Scépeaux, was the Marshal of France under Henry the Second. Several others of my line have served at court in various positions, and were rewarded by their sovereign, for which I am eternally grateful and proud. I was born near Anjou, but was soon to spend my youth in convents, for I had the misfortune to lose my father and mother in the same year. My last guardians, Comtesse de la Tour d'Auvergne and Madame Marshal d'Aubeterre, sent for me to Paris, and I was placed in the convent of Belle-Chasse. It was there I was visited and befriended by Madame de Bourbon-Penthièvre and Mademoiselle, who were very kind to me and solicitous of my welfare."

Madame de Bourbon-Penthièvre was properly Louise Marie Adélaïde de Bourbon-Penthièvre, Duchess of Orléans, the richest woman in France, who was married to the King's brother, Louis Philippe. For a young girl to be visited by such a personage, even in charity, was unheard of. Not only must her line have been extraordinarily honorable, but Madame herself must have built a reputation as a young lady of impeccable manners and character.

Xavier smiled, "And then you met."

"Indeed. I donned my veil, and was given a bouquet of flowers by my good friend Roseline. I was escorted into the chapel by Mother Adela and walked to the altar, where waited Monsieur and Father Gerald. He then married us, we were wed, and then we spoke for the first time."

Her eyes were on her husband, as if the story were the most romantic tale in the whole world, and not some frighteningly personal imposition. "You were arranged to marry then?" asked Xavier.

They both smiled and nodded their heads.

"Were you scared or apprehensive?"

"Why would I be either?" replied Madame.

"Because you were marrying a man with whom you had never even traded words. It sounds… well, to be honest, a bit disconcerting, if not terrifying."

She looked confused, then gave Xavier a piercing stare. Finally, she spoke, "Do you know what love is? True love."

Xavier shrugged, "I have never experienced it."

"Your answer lies in that statement."

Xavier understood, "True love is an emotion then."

She smiled, "But it is not. No, indeed, Monsieur Traversier. You are very wrong."

"I beg to be corrected, Madame."

"There are few people who are honored with the joy of meeting God - few who have experienced the rapture of the Heavenly Presence. Yet, there are many who believe and have faith, and take great comfort from it. There are many who love God, yet have not seen Him. As we take our lessons in life from Our Father, we must take our lesson regarding earthly love."

"Love is faith, then."

"Love, Monsieur Traversier, is a *decision*. True love, then, is a decision undertaken by individuals of pure moral character, with impregnable integrity, who maintain their decision through any trial, with the help of God."

"You made a decision to love Monsieur."

"I was destined to wed him, so I knew of him. I knew he was a man of impeccable character and faith. I knew, come what may, that he would marry me, and when he did, he would make the lifelong decision to love and cherish me, regardless of circumstance. I, too, strive to live in Christlike fashion. I too, come what may, decided to love and cherish Monsieur once I was his wife."

Xavier would have doubted her words, had they not both been so obviously happy and in love. They were happy because they could rely completely on the foundation of values and trust provided by the other. As she spoke, an inner strength and unshakeable faith became more and more apparent. To Madame, Christ was as real as the floor beneath her feet. Xavier had no conception of how such a thing could come to be, or why a human being of such intelligence could stomach something so irrational as religious superstition.

It was so different, the lives of these people. To Xavier, it seemed there were two nations living side-by-side, with almost nothing in common between them. He did, however, genuinely like them both, and hoped the feeling was mutual.

Two hours later, the Messieurs retired to the library with coffee and cognac. Xavier would have given an arm for a good American cigar, but he knew if the nobility did partake of tobacco, it was usually as snuff. Bonchamps, in any case, did not seem to partake at all. The library itself was well-stocked. It was, of course, nowhere near as large as the one in the Meilleur - which could have fit most of the entire château. Xavier looked over the books, surprised to see *Candide* by Voltaire. "Are you a student of the Enlightenment, Monsieur?"

"A student, yes."

"I am surprised. I would have thought that Enlightenment philosophy would offend you."

"What would give you such an impression?"

"Admittedly, it is more of a bias than an impression. The Enlightenment wishes change. I assumed you would not wish change."

"Reforms are always needed, and corruption must always be sought out and eliminated. I am very much for those kind of reforms, and so are most minds of the Enlightenment."

"It is anti-noble, and anti-monarchical, quite often."

"Yes, and oddly, most nobles in France adore it all. I study the Enlightenment because it exists, it is a reality and influences the times I live in. I personally have found that knowledge, absorbed by the right kind of mind, is rain on fertile soil." He paused, then repeated himself, "To the right kind of mind."

"You have an excellent library."

"Thank you. I'm afraid half my books are loaned to the village. Well, a quarter to Father Jonathan, and a quarter to his young protégé Estelle Guerrier."

"And what do you think of these ideas? Those of the Enlightenment?" asked Xavier. Part of him thought bringing up the subject was ill-advised, based on the purpose of his visit - but part of him simply wanted to know. He found Bonchamps to be engaging, and his thoughts coming from a different perspective that he wished to understand.

Bonchamps shrugged, "I think the Enlightenment is already over. I think Rousseau brought the end."

"You begin with your finale," laughed Xavier, "How so?"

"The Enlightenment produced many interesting ideas, but one could say all of them are summed up by Descartes - 'I think, therefore, I am.' All knowledge should be gained solely through observation of fact. *Tout court*."

"Before Descartes. Bacon and Empiricism."

"Indeed. But Rousseau's ideas have nothing to do with fact tested through scientific observation. His ideas are those of an artist. They are emotional, subjective - almost... *theological*, in tone. Rousseau is anti-Enlightenment. He is intuition and emotion over reason - but is mistaken for being the current primary proponent of the Enlightenment."

"An interesting thought."

"But do you see the danger, Monsieur?" Bonchamps asked with an earnest intensity, "We are in a time when people assume the philosopher must speak from fact - and here has come this influential man who speaks from emotion, and it is mistaken for observation. Rousseau is more of a prophet than an observer. No, something has changed. The Enlightenment has become a religion, replete with dogma, fanaticism, prophets and clergy. It is a movement that has completely lost its objectivity. It is now simply a faith, which has relabeled all of its trappings - and claims to despise religion, and those self-same trappings! All this with adamantine self-righteousness, and absolutely no sense of hypocrisy whatsoever."

Xavier was surprised that Bonchamps was such an exploratory thinker, and even more shocked to realize he might be partly right.

Bonchamps continued, "After the Protestant Reformation, there was a Catholic movement, a Counter-Reformation, that has consumed our art and thought to this day. Although now they are best described as Counter-Enlightenment, although that is a grim appellation on its face. To be honest, I find these new Catholic thinkers far more interesting than the current Enlightenment thinkers. There has been a theological revolution right under the nose of the empirical philosophers."

Xavier had never heard of such a thing. "What would be an example of this thought? Who are its greatest minds?"

"*Abbé* Fleury, Hamann, Vico, Pluche, Déguig?"

Xavier searched his mind. None sounded familiar in the least.

Bonchamps continued, "The Pastor of Gap? No?" Xavier smiled, and shook his head. "Moliniere, Massillon, the Bishop of Meaux? No?"

"I'm afraid not, Monsieur. But I am intrigued. Is it possible to briefly summate their theories?"

"I will try," said Bonchamps, with a thoughtful whisper. He sat, and placed his hands below his chin. "Catholicism has given humanity an encompassing world view, but it has provided more than that. It is a way of life. It delineates the days, gives time for rest and work. Its customs, rules, sacraments and traditions are building blocks for the communal life of individuals and communities. It creates a sense of well-being, independent of anything else."

"I will take your word for it."

"Did you know there is no crime here, from the Loire to the Vendée? It is unheard of. Here is truly an environment free of trouble and worry - simply because of the advanced state of mind of its inhabitants. If one were to consider humanity as a type of animal, akin to farmers considering chickens or horses, one would say Catholic village life is the correct way to raise people. People do well in such an environment. They are happy and fulfilled and content."

"Perhaps some people."

"Most, let us say."

"Then let us say most."

"But there is the problem," continued Bonchamps, "What about the few who need something different? In the past, these different few always understood why the lives of the many should be this way, and let the peasants live their lives. But no more."

"What is different now?"

"Why... it is you," Bonchamps said with a smile.

"Myself?" said Xavier, delighted with the conversation.

"Why yes, you, François-Xavier Traversier, deacon of the church of the bourgeois Enlightenment, the few, the vocal, the powerful. Unless I have sussed out your heart incorrectly."

"No, you are quite correct, Monsieur," Xavier admitted.

"The majority of people do not need or desire independence. Independence is hurtful to them. If most people were granted independence from the community of the church, they would be the worst enemy of themselves and their communities."

"Am I an enemy to myself then?" Xavier said with a smile.

"Only to your salvation," shot back Bonchamps, lightly and with a smile. "You are not the group I am referring to. You are the new group, the new man, who confounds and alarms the church. The bourgeois wish to have what they are able to earn, they want nothing to do with a church that professes equality, however imperfectly and hypocritically. You desire knowledge based on hard facts and observation, and have an almost fanatical bias against the supernatural and the mystical - and the basis of the church can only be described as such. You wish no part of a church that wishes to take away your prerogatives as a thinking man, that would prevent you from questioning God and his servants, and you demand explanations placed within a context you deem worthy."

"And we do not accept the church as suitable for any man."

"Indeed. You believe all men should be free from the church, even though, from a purely objective standpoint, the church is obviously the habitat of man. Simple faith, the faith that does not rely on argument or intellectualism, is the savior of the majority. Yet this new man wishes to kick out the crutch, so to speak, and have those who cannot walk on their own crawl, to appease the dogmatic tenets of the bourgeois. The bourgeois are willing to throw the majority of mankind into the stewpot of sacrifice, if only to erase a possible enemy to their own way of life."

"I cannot argue. Most of your words, both dire and agreeable, seem to ring true."

"The presence of life is supernatural. It cannot be explained. The very existence of the universe cannot be explained. It is also therefore supernatural. To force oneself to not believe in the supernatural requires tremendous faith. In other words, you have faith in not having faith. How does the church reach such a man?"

"Perhaps it is impossible."

"Are you happy, Monsieur Traversier?"

For some reason, Xavier did not find the question objectionable. Perhaps it was simply because he liked Bonchamps. The young Marquis did not judge him, seemed to like him, and would probably give him the shirt off his back, if he required it. It is difficult to be offended by such a man. He answered, "No, Monsieur. I am not happy. You find yourself happy, presumably?"

Bonchamps smiled, "At the moment, yes. But, more importantly, I am at peace. Something terrible could happen, and most assuredly I would not be happy. But I would still be at peace. There is an important distinction, I think."

"But to defeat me and those like me, Monsieur, you cannot simply point out that we are unhappy. You must destroy our hope in our dreams. All of us pursue lives that we believe, in our bones, will give us love, safety and security - eventually. We scoff at you, for we have faith in our path."

"Well-spoken."

"Also, it is difficult to understand how such positive things emanate from your dogma. How does one live in fear of breaking the rules - and then find serenity? How does one fear hell and judgment only to find joy? How does one surrender free will and feel anything but the yoke of slavery?"

Bonchamps nodded, "There is a prayer, adopted from the gospels. 'Lord, I am not worthy that you should enter under my roof. But only say the word and my soul shall be healed."

Xavier nodded, "The Centurion. He wanted Christ to heal his servant."

"Yes. The prayer is different from the scripture. Not to horrify the Protestant, but the prayer, to me, is even more impactful and relevant. In saying this prayer, I acknowledge my flawed nature, I turn to God, the fountain of all good, and beg for redemption through him. We are forgiven – indeed, we are loved beyond measure. Our nature is pleasing to our creator, who revels in us and takes joy in our being – and has given us forgiveness and grace. Everything is as it should be. No man should wake in the morning with anxiety upon his heart - but I do not begrudge you the freedom to do so." They both exchanged grins, then Bonchamps was pensive once again. "There is much in the Enlightenment teachings with which I agree. But its anticlericalism alarms me, and I believe it to be shortsighted."

"How so?"

"Religion, for all of its faults, has also been a moral brake on power and authority. Rulers of Christian nations must at least pay lip service to Christian ideals. Their laws and abuses can only go so far before the church is forced to castigate them."

"I will concede your point. It is mildly put, and agrees with what I know of history. But there is something else I know of history, Monsieur, and that regards the corruption of the church itself. What happens when these spiritual gatekeepers are the perpetrators of abuse?"

"Yes, and I must concede that point. But imagine this, *mon ami*. Imagine an empowered government, filled with men who have no true values, who eschew any moral authority whatsoever, except their own. A powerful state, trailblazing its own morality, as it sees fit."

Xavier did imagine it, and realized there was some truth to Bonchamps's fears.

The Marquis shook his head, "Even under the best of circumstances, man succumbs to temptation. When the church rots, some say 'down with the church.' What they should actually be considering is that if man can corrupt the church, he can corrupt anything and everything - nothing on earth is exempt. If love of God does not provide a check on power, we must be sure that our laws do this, somehow. But I do not understand how law can have power if it has no true moral authority, and is based on no true ethical code."

"Well, if the law is backed by force, it has the ultimate power of authority. One would argue that force is the only authority that truly matters to the corrupt. To say that the law is more powerful with God behind it is perhaps naive. Law is fundamentally based on the threat of the bayonet."

Bonchamps rubbed his chin, "I concede your point, Monsieur. I think you might be right." Bonchamps was quiet for a moment, then spoke again, "I do not think modern thought will lead to much good for mankind. Our philosophers define man as a perfect creature waiting to burst through the bonds of oppression. In other words, man is solely affected, and need only concern himself, with economics and law. It is as if every other aspect of our being will sort itself out perfectly, and without attention."

"Man is good in his natural state."

"Yes, which is, of course, nonsense. Man, in his natural state, is savage. Spirituality, culture, relations between the sexes, community, and even the traditions of family are simply ignored by the modern. These aspects of our existence are seemingly not important. Yet, are they not the most important aspects of our lives? Law and economics serve those aspects, and not the other way around, do they not?"

"Again, it is your villain Rousseau. Without oppression, man is perfect, so why concern oneself? Unburden man through law and economics, and everything else will sort itself."

"Have you read Rousseau's *Confessions*?"

"His autobiography? I'm afraid I have not. Surprisingly, for at one point I devoured his work."

"Does knowledge offend or scare you, Monsieur?"

"No, I take your tack with it."

"And your tack is, shall we say, full-sail with the wind?"

"Indeed, Monsieur."

Bonchamps stood, and slipped the book from its shelf, gently, as if it were gunpowder. "I wish to give this to you. I would very much like for you to read it. You are quite intelligent, Monsieur Traversier. I would simply have you draw your own conclusions."

Xavier stood, and took the book from Bonchamps. "I will, Monsieur Bonchamps. I thank you for the gift."

Bonchamps indicated a chair for Xavier, then took his own. "I have taken up your valuable time. You have asked to meet with me regarding your business. I am at your service, Monsieur."

"I am here because I was told that you have the respect, and the ear, of the farmers of the area."

"The area?"

"I do not know what to call it. Perhaps you described it yourself - from the Loire to the Vendée. The land that is different that has no name."

"I know many of the farmers here. I know lords and priests from other parishes and communes, as well."

"I have been spinning linen thread of the highest quality, little by little, since 1776. This thread has been treated with lavender oils, exposed to sunlight, and packed in airtight containers. I have purchased the most modern kind of textile looms, the Vaucanson loom, which utilizes punch cards to program patterns into the fabric. My linen thread must now be dyed, in order to be woven into fabric. In addition, I do not see my demand for linen or dye becoming anything but more voracious. But, most importantly, I need red, blue and yellow pigment, post haste. I am preparing this dye myself. I am doing everything, except the very growing of the roots and flowers."

"Which you now need."

"Yes."

"So, you need guède, garance, and mignonette. By the cartload."

"Yes, Monsieur."

"How much linen?"

"I have nearly 40 tons."

"By what date must your linen be dyed?"

"I have recently purchased an ocean-going vessel. My ship needs repairs and additional outfitting. My goal is to leave in exactly twenty-four months. In addition to paying full-market price for pigments, I will give one-hundred and fifty feet of good rope for each cartload. For now, and forever, I need any and all hemp and flax, not processed, simply pulled with its roots from the ground. To be quite honest, I have come to buy flax and hemp from eastern Europe, my demand being so great. As a businessman, and as a Frenchman, this will not do for long, and I wish to find better long-term solutions. But the pigments, those I need as soon as I can get them. Now and for the foreseeable future."

"I can certainly be your ally in this. It will be beneficial to the farmers to grow more flax."

"I am relieved to hear that. And I agree."

"I do have an important question before I commit, however."

"Of course."

"Does this need have anything to do with the slave trade?"

Xavier was surprised at the question. In truth, every single activity in Nantes had something to do with the slave trade. There was nothing totally clean of it. It was a city built on salt and deep water, but also sugar, coffee - and the black flesh needed to farm them. "No," Xavier easily lied, "No, indeed. The Traversier family does not engage in the slave trade."

Bonchamps smiled. "You will have what you need for your dye, Monsieur."

"I would like to give you something in return for your help."

"That is not necessary. What benefits Anjou benefits Bonchamps."

And that was that.

Xavier was sad to leave the enchanting little château. Monsieur and Madame graciously bid Xavier and Étienne farewell, and they were on their way. The rain had finally stopped, and the sun had emerged.

Outside the glow of company, Xavier felt villainous - like a malevolent spirit who entered this place on false pretenses and had infected it. But there was nothing for it. He had his purpose. And he was assured that his purposeful action would someday lead to assurance. For now, his faith in his dreams was ablaze, and enough.

***

As for the book given to him by Bonchamps, Xavier would not read it for years, but when he did, it would be disconcerting to him, and philosophically untimely.

1832

Jake

La Conciergerie

le Point du Jour

Encre et Charbon,

1832

Chapter 13

The Conciergerie courtyard was very small, but still sported benches, walk-ways and a small patch of grass and flowers. It was pleasant enough, except for the five-and-six-story walls completely enclosing it, creating an effect akin to a stone vase. Jake sat on a bench, his eyes closed, and his face pointed to the sun. The rules no longer applied to him. Everyone in the Conciergerie knew he was a free man, and he had his way of the place. He was waiting for paperwork, and that was all.

There was a shrine to Marie Antoinette, the former queen who stayed here until she was beheaded. He had to pass it on his way outside. It unsettled him for some reason, but the sun was worth the journey.

Isaäc entered the courtyard with a sheaf of papers under his arm, "There he is – in the sun no less!"

"Isaäc!" blurted Jake, quite happy to see him.

Isaäc sat down and handed him a letter, "From Monsieur Tyran." Jake noticed the seal was already broken. He opened it:

> *Monsieur Loring,*
>
> *You will have no more contact with your lawyer, your rev-olutionary chain-of-command, your friends, your family or anyone else from your old life. Indeed, consider our liaison*

*to have recreated you without history. You are reborn
wholly unto me, and exist to serve only myself, and the
search for the Crimson Heirlooms. Do not seek to thwart
me in this. You will not be ordered to do anything untoward,
and will end your service with me with some coin in your
pocket and your honor intact, I assure you.*

*You come from a good family, and you are a well-educated
man. I expect that you will conduct yourself as a good and
honorable businessman, in regard to our legal arrangement. You will be entrusted to perform tasks alone, and you
will be, at times, in possession of considerable funds. You
will keep a good accounting, be an independent, self-moti-
vated worker, and scrupulously honest in your reporting of
any findings.*

*Find with this letter two items. The first is an excerpt taken
from a ship captain's log. I wish you to become as knowledgeable as I in regard to its contents. The second item is a
coin purse. Purchase a seat on a coach to Nantes, and any
effects you need for the journey. I will be in the Château
Meilleur, in the west outskirts of the city. Meet me there, as
soon as you are legally able.*

Monsieur Tyran

"*Son-of-a-bitch,*" Jake said in English.

"I do not understand your meaning, but your intent is clear. Monsieur Tyran is indeed well-named, is he not?"

"He is, indeed. Who is he really, I wonder?"

"A question many are asking. Queries have been made. It is thought he is a colonial, of some sort. He has certainly not been living in France – at least for decades. Our sources familiar with the most successful families in the Americas have no idea who he is. If he is from a foreign colony, it could explain our current ignorance. There are also many colonies, and our contacts do not extend to all of them."

"You say this as if an army of spies follows my every move."

"You are not alone in this, Jake. Citizen Bouche has been informed of de-velopments, along with others of his ilk and conviction."

"His orders, those of Monsieur Tyran, they are legally binding, however absurd?"

"If his commands are legal and honorable. He cannot tell you to waylay a coach, or wear petticoats."

"Is there enough in the purse for a voyage to America?"

Isaäc handed him the pouch. "Perhaps. But it has been established that this trip to Nantes might be a test of sorts."

"How so?"

"Could he not wait for you a day? You are both going to the same place, are you not?"

Jake hadn't even thought about it, but Isaäc was absolutely right.

He continued, "If you were in the same coach, there would be an abundance of time to discuss the captain's log, and other things he would impart to you. But now you go alone - along the same route."

If Isaäc was right, it meant several things. It definitely meant Jake would be followed when he left the Conciergerie.

Isaäc seemed to read his mind, "I'm afraid this will be the last time we meet for a while."

"None of this makes sense, Isaäc. Why would Monsieur Tyran go out of his way, and empty his pockets, to secure my particular employment? He could have had better help, a legion of help, for a cheaper price. Sixty-thousand francs! It's absurd. He is either utterly superstitious, or there is some kind of festering motivation he doesn't wish to admit."

"Yes, or both." They sat in silence for a moment, "You have orders from *The Society*, Jake."

"Of course. I am listening."

"You will leave the Conciergerie tonight, too late to find a coach to Nantes. You will go to an inn in the Latin Quarter. Here is the address." Jake accepted a card. "You will ask for the small blue room. Small blue room. It is written on the card. Very important."

"I understand."

"Take these as well," and he handed Jake a small sheaf of official papers, "Keep them on your person at all times. Find an oilskin in which to wrap them, so they aren't damaged by moisture. These documents prove your status as a resident alien in France and your United States citizenship. They will allow you to leave this place, but more importantly to leave France and enter other countries as well."

"And last, but not least."

"And last, but not least. The captain's log," said Isaäc, as he handed him a thin book.

Jake couldn't wait to read it. It was days to Nantes by coach. He would force himself to wait and read it on the way.

***

Jake

The Inn, *Le Poney Piquant*, was well-chosen. It was a quaint three-story "country-style", a crossed timber and plaster Renaissance affair. Only one wall was shared with another building, the rest was free-standing and surrounded by gardens. It catered mostly to students and their families, and was precisely the kind of place that Jake might have frequented in the past. It would arouse no suspicion if he stayed there preparatory to his coach to Nantes.

Jake entered, and saw a smattering of people sitting in tables to his left, and the Innkeeper and his family to the right. The Innkeeper seemed a likeable sort. He was youngish, fat but brawny, and handsome. His family was laughing with him when Jake entered. As soon as he requested the small blue room, everyone stopped laughing. He felt grim, and wanted them to laugh and be gay again, but it was not to be. He was taken to a room on the second floor.

The Innkeeper opened the door. The small blue room was not blue, had a bed, tall armoire, and a small fire burning in a large fireplace. Jake entered, and - to his surprise - the Innkeeper followed and shut the door.

Jake watched as the Innkeeper opened the armoire, quickly removed the bolts from one of its door hinges and leaned the door against the wall. He then reached down into a bucket resting inside the armoire, and pulled out what looked like a sopping calfskin. The calfskin was placed on the door and smoothed flat, and Jake noticed nails were already in place for the purpose of securing it to the wood. After the Innkeeper bent the nails to keep the wet skin in place, he lugged the door over to the fire. Wet-leather-side-down, the door went into the fire and rested on a small ledge inside the fireplace. The other end of the door was lowered to the floor. For all intents and purposes, it now looked as if a ramp into the back of the fireplace had been created. The Innkeeper turned to Jake, "For the sake of my family, please tell no one of this. Not even those you trust. Please."

"Of course."

The Innkeeper did not look convinced, but instead simply turned and picked up the poker. He hit the back of the fireplace three times - the blows sounding on thick metal instead of stone. To Jake's astonishment, a small section of the back of the fireplace slid open into another room. It was some kind of secret hatch.

Jake realized it did not lead to a secret room within the inn. It led rather to its adjacent building. Whoever entered this secret room from the inn side would never be connected in any way to whoever entered the adjacent building – yet the two parties could meet together, with no one the wiser.

The Innkeeper turned to him, "Do not touch anything save the door when you climb through, or you might receive a burn. Rap on the metal a minute before you wish to come back. I am putting the door back where it belongs until then."

Jake wanted to ask a million questions. Instead, he simply nodded, and crawled across the door over the fire, and into the other room behind the secret iron hatch.

The other room was much darker. He couldn't see anything for a second, but he heard a voice, "Shut the trapdoor. Use the towel soaking in the bucket."

Jake turned, and saw the iron trapdoor set in stone with a bucket beneath it. He reached into the bucket and felt a towel. He wrapped it around his hand, then pulled the trap door up until the latch snapped into place. He tossed the towel back into the bucket, and finally turned.

And there was Citizen Bouche, in all his glory, wearing his ermine cloak. There were six other men in the room, standing and sitting. Some were as young as Jake, and others twice as old as Citizen Bouche. They were all dressed richly, and mostly in black. They still wore their top hats indoors and - between brim and high collars - sported costume masks. The only one who wasn't masked was Citizen Bouche, who sat to one side. The man sitting directly in front of Jake was thin, old - but alert as a king cobra with the cold eyes to match. He sat with his legs spread, his cane resting upright, its crystal pommel topped by his palm, which grasped two black lambskin gloves.

Citizen Bouche spoke quietly, "Sit down, Citizen."

Jake sat in the only empty chair, placed directly in front of them. He had probably spent too much time in the *Cour d'Assises*, for it reminded him of nothing so much as the witness cage.

Citizen Bouche continued, "How are you feeling?"

"My ribs still hurt. I miss my fallen comrades."

"Of course, he does," said a man sitting to the left. His tone was odd, as if they were just talking about him, and he now gave an answer to a former query.

This bizarre, masked group did not feel like his brothers-in-arms. They felt like self-interested, dangerous plotters.

Citizen Bouche spoke quietly once again, "Be that as it may…"

The Old Man who sat front and center spoke. His voice was strong and crisp, "Citizen Loring, you may call me Citizen Director. I am one of the Great Nine, of the Supreme Council of *The Society for the Rights of Man*."

"Good evening, Citizen Director."

"Good evening. How are your revolutionary sympathies?"

"Pardon me, Citizen?"

"You have been through quite an ordeal. Defeated in combat, wounded, judged, sentenced. How are your revolutionary sympathies?"

Jake was intimidated. He was in debt to these men. They had aided him in his time of need. Now he was going off with the madman, Monsieur Tyran, like some sort of legally-bound Sancho Panza, and these sinister men were the only ones who could help him. "My morale is a bit low, Citizen Director. But, I assure you, my revolutionary sympathies have not abated."

The Director leaned forward, "That is an interesting statement, Citizen Loring."

Jake panicked. Had the Director read his mind from an unwitting expression? Jake forced himself to meet the man's gaze.

He continued. "It is an interesting statement because you placed your life in danger for the revolution. You placed yourself, quite literally, on the firing line, did you not?"

Oh, dear lord, what does he mean by all of this?

"I did, Citizen Director."

"To you, your life is worth less than the revolution."

"I suppose that is one way of putting it, Citizen Director."

Surprising Jake, the men all laughed. The Director shook his head, "Do not be so humble, Citizen."

"What do you wish of me? Is there to be another uprising?"

Jake's words killed whatever mirth was left in the room. Everyone shifted in their seats, and looked at each other. Finally, the Director spoke, "This setback has caused a momentary suspension of operations. We lick our wounds, and look for another opportunity."

Another voice from the back, "If the king lasts a year, it will be a miracle."

Citizen Bouche spoke sharply, "It won't be a miracle. If anything is done, it will be done by us, through hard work and persistence. Otherwise, he will stay in power, until the very day he dies."

"Well said," snapped the Director, in a tone that silenced the room. He turned to Jake, "If anything is done, it will be done by us. Yet our resources are exhausted. We are looking for ways to shorten our projected timelines."

"I see," replied Jake.

"Citizen, do you think there is any chance that Monsieur Tyran will actually locate the Cross of Nantes?"

Jake couldn't believe his ears. *The Society* stood for order, education, knowledge and reason. How could a leader of *The Society* be so desperate as to believe in the foolish quest of Monsieur Tyran? Jake spoke carefully, "Citizen Director, I don't think anyone will be able to locate the Cross of Nantes, ever."

"Why do you say that?"

"Well, as Citizen Crémieux pointed out, if it could be found, it would have been found already."

The Director looked at Citizen Bouche, who answered his unspoken question, "The lawyer. The Jew from Nîmes."

The Director nodded, and turned back to Jake, "The Cross was in the hands of Xavier Traversier in 1805, when he stipulated that its owner would inherit the Traversier Trust. It was lost purposefully, Citizen Loring. That means it wasn't lost at all. It was *hidden*. Hidden, and meant to be found. There is quite a difference."

Jake had to admit that there was.

The Director continued, "And this Monsieur Tyran, he is motivated by greed?"

Jake shook his head, "I'm not sure. I would have to say there is a very good chance he is not. This man effectively paid sixty-thousand francs for my services - an absurd, almost inconceivable sum, you would agree. And he didn't seem overly perturbed to be parting with it. He could have hired twenty good men for five years. Instead, he has only one."

"But he wishes the Cross."

"Yes, Citizen Director. For an unknown purpose."

"If Monsieur Tyran inherited his fortune and was some kind of idiotic spendthrift, we would know exactly who he is, and where he got his gold. He is, therefore, not. He earned his gold, somehow, somewhere. And those who sweat and bleed for gold do not part with it with nonchalant indifference. Most assuredly, there is method here, however impenetrable."

"I'm not sure I completely understand. Do you think he truly knows where the Cross of Nantes is located?"

"The Cross of Nantes is worth millions. The mercantile empire of the Traversier Trust is worth millions more. *Millions*. Do you understand? If somehow you were necessary to his plan to retrieve the Cross, sixty-thousand is a pittance for the favor."

Perhaps this isn't a wild goose chase after all.

"Citizen Director, here is what I know: I have been given part of a captain's log, and I am to go to Nantes. I also know that it is almost a surety that I will be followed."

The Director leaned forward once again, "Do you know why you are here? In this room."

Jake remembered being embarrassed at the trial when asked such a question. This time, he was ready, "Yes, Citizen Director."

"Go on."

"You want me to find the Cross of Nantes for *The Society*, to fund the next uprising to overthrow the King."

"That is exactly true."

"If Monsieur Tyran is currently better funded than *The Society*, such a thing might be problematic. I don't know how we will even communicate."

Citizen Bouche spoke, "You will be followed by our agents. You will never see them. If you need to communicate, you will drop a letter to any innkeeper. *Any* innkeeper. You will tell him that you found a saint's medallion, worth nothing but sentiment, and for the innkeeper to present the letter to anyone who asks for it."

"Yes, that might work." Any innkeeper meant *The Society* would be following his every move, knowing when and to whom he would drop his missive.

"You will also write in code, one indistinguishable from a normal letter, in case Tyran's spies suspect something, and happen to read it."

"I cannot keep a code book."

"It will be a simple code." Citizen Bouche turned, "Give it to him."

A young, masked man handed Jake a Bible.

Citizen Bouche spoke, "That is the Ostervald translation, published in '44 by Abraham Boyve and Company. It is widely available anywhere French is spoken."

"What is this for, Citizen Director?"

"You can carry it anywhere, even in plain view, and no one will be the wiser. Now listen very carefully. The code is simple, but it must be accurate."

Jake listened. It wasn't really simple at all, and would take ages to communicate a short message, but it would definitely work.

More importantly, it would arose no suspicion.

1785

Estelle

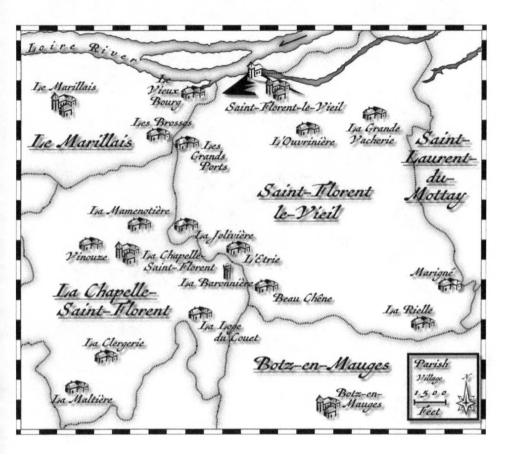

Chapter 14

Estelle, sitting next to her father in the packed chapel of the Abbey of Saint-Florent for high mass, had only seen the stained wood of the pew directly in front of her, when her eyes were open at all. A finger was firmly tamped in each ear, so she could not hear.

She was a young woman, and she was in love. Her feelings overwhelmed her. Sometimes, when she was taken with them, she could feel her heartbeat drumming through her eyes, and her breath would come raggedly, as if she had run up a hill. She was sick to her stomach and her pounding blood wanted to slush through parts of her body she would rather not contemplate. Estelle felt like a sinner unable to hide - a sorcerous green-burning fire on a moonless night. What made it infinitely worse was that she enjoyed the feeling as much as she hated it.

Her brother had sent her a letter. She tried to focus on the memory of reading it -which was difficult since it was not in front of her.

Dear Estelle,

Do you remember the brook near our little cottage when we lived in the mountains? We used its water for everything, and it sang us to sleep every night. I didn't think too much upon that stream when we were there, but when we left I felt its loss very keenly. I still dream about our little creek. Sometimes I just dream the sound. I think you are like that brook. I didn't know how much you meant to me, and how much I relied on you, until I left. I very sincerely miss you. We have been through a lot together, you and I. There are things no one understands but us. You are really an amazing person, Estelle. I felt good around you - you brightened every place. I'm glad I don't dream about you, as I did the brook, for you are horrifically ugly and troll-like, and the nightmares would scare me, and destroy my ability to ingest food the next day. Ha-ha!

Please excuse the paper this is written on. Paper is quite expensive, so I tear down news flyers and posters from the walls. If you soak them carefully, you can get the ink out, although the paper is thereafter an odd color, and tears easily. I have enclosed several sheets for you so you can write back. PS - if you have no ink, just use beet juice, it works just as well. So does charcoal, if you add water and crush it until it is of uniform consistency and will stick on the quill. Mud does not work, nor wet clay.

Raphaël says hello! Can you believe such a thing! I am so happy that my friend is back in my life. It's like he's been resurrected. It takes something akin to six months for my letters to arrive. I always make a copy, for I do not need to be told that the journey is perilous, and some letters may be lost. So far, all is well, however. I write him constantly and he writes me. We are playing a game over mail, and I must wait six months before writing my next move. We are hashing out the rules in the meantime. I have told him all about you, and he says he wants to marry you. I told him he's mad, but he is very serious. I will continue to try to dissuade him. His last letter was dictated, and written by Monsieur Pinceau. I'm not sure why. What do you think? It vexes me.

Grenoble is so beautiful. It isn't as big as Nantes, maybe not even Angers - perhaps Le Cap. It is an ancient, walled city on the Isère river. We are surrounded by snow-capped peaks, and it is breathtaking. The city is so dense, all big buildings and narrow alleys, but they are all very winsome. The French like to live right on top of each other. If Le Cap was like this, everyone would boil on the stones. But it is nice and cool here, so I suppose they have a need to keep heat, and not dissipate it as in Saint-Domingue. Everyone here seems to be in the glove business. That is a very strange thing to say for a town, but there it is. At least Grenoble is not beset by ironworkers banging on anvils. Can you imagine the noise ringing out over such a place? The sound of sewing needles I can bear gladly, for there really is none.

I'm starting to make some friends, but it's hard. Everyone in my class was at school several years before I arrived. The University is ancient. Everything is old. I guess Grenoble was a crossroads of sorts, for armies and trade moving into northern Italy, Vienna and so on. They consider themselves the capital city of the Alps. The Alps could do worse!

I have come upon a strange thing, Estelle. I will try to explain: there is nothing I learned from Maman, Papa, or Saint-Domingue in general, that has any kind of relevance here. For example, when someone crossed Papa, he became angry or threatening, and then he promptly got his way because people were scared he would hurt them. Neither the students, professors, or townspeople act this way. Sometimes they raise their voices in agitation, but that is all. Perhaps it is different when they are in their cups, or dishonored or something, but on a day-to-day basis, you never see anyone - anyone - act like Papa. That is only one example. What I am beginning to realize is that Papa, Maman, and Saint-Domingue are more a part of me than I'd like to admit. Sometimes when I see a student or professor, I say to myself, "He is soft!" or "Someone will steal that boy's clothes, and leave him naked in the street." But, of course, no one does. I am some sort of hybrid creature belonging to nowhere, and feel as if everything I've ever learned has no worth whatsoever here. It vexes me greatly, Estelle. I do not act in a fashion conducive to social interaction, not naturally. In fact, I would say I completely lack social instinct for successful interaction. I have no skills pertaining to people, and feel my inadequacy keenly. In addition, in my categorization, I am neither this nor that, straight down the column of possible identities. Am I Saint-Domingue? I should hope not. Anjou, Saint-Florent-le-Vieil? By what right?

Grenoble? Not a chance. Am I tough, soft, physical, intel-
lectual, white, black, fierce, or calm? I am altogether con-
fused, that is what I am. I do not believe in God, yet I attend
mass... a metaphor for every aspect of my life! I beat a
classmate with my fists. The other students looked at me as
if I was a savage, wild beast. My reputation still hasn't re-
covered. In Saint-Domingue, I would have gained status. It
was a terrible mistake. It hurts me that people I respect and
like so much, do not respect or like me.

Which brings us to the oddest thing about Grenoble. They
are madly in love with dolphins here. I don't know why.
Dolphin images, statues, whatnot, are everywhere here -
even on the flag. In fact, the whole province, Dauphiné, is
named after dolphins. There are no real dolphins anywhere
here, nowhere in the entire province. You can't find a dol-
phin for leagues and leagues - not until you reach the sea.
We are in the damné mountains here, Estelle! What makes
it worse is that an old king of Grenoble, who merged Dau-
phiné with France, did so on one condition: that the heir to
the French throne be ever after called the Dauphin. So, the
princes of France are dolphins, too - because of dolphin-
crazy Grenoble! Madness.

Things are not quite how they are in Anjou, when it comes
to the people of the city. It is more like Saint-Domingue. The
gap between rich and poor is the space between the bottom
of the sea and the clouds in the sky. The farmers and such
are very poor, really actually wretched, some of them. I see
them at the market, and they are mostly barefoot in the
snow. The priests who perform the sacraments (I have to go
to mass, more's the pity), are the usual sort with holes in
their vestments, shivering in their thin cloth on cold days.
But all the rest, the higher priests and such (you would know
titles better than I) you can't tell from a noble. They dress
like marquis, ride around in coaches, live in mansions, and
the bishops even call themselves "The Princes of Greno-
ble." All the café gossip centers around the brawl between
the nobles and the clergy for power, women, and successful
court litigation. Disgusting! I have studied the Middle Ages,
and I know all about how nothing was ever achieved in
France except by the Estates General - composed of the

three estates, the elected nobles, clergy and commoners. That was out of order - second estate, first, and third, that was. Did I tell you about this already? I have never really seen these "three estates" in action, so to speak, and had no frame of reference. Here the struggle between these classes is as real as Roman concrete, and everyone seems to strongly identify with their caste. It is odd to see, and playing out so plainly to boot. There is such animosity. The least of it seems to come from the poor peasants, who probably have the most to be angry about, but somehow are not. The middle-class townspeople are the ones who are frothing at the mouth, like street dogs in Le Cap - so are our professors, who are mostly poor priests. I suppose if I was some glove maker, worked hard, and had expectations about my life - as in, I walk to the bakery, and there is bread, much less bread I can afford - I would be angry if they were not met as well. The glove makers are taxed to the gills, treated like milk cows for government, and when the grain harvest is ruined by rain or cold, they starve regardless of how much coin is in their pocket. Sometimes I think half of France would do better in Le Cap, where plants can bloom on the raindrops before they hit the ground... then I remember everyone here is white, and would probably not last a year. What a curse, to be stuck in a place with such a swing between dearth and plenty. I am fairly disgusted with the nobles here and the upper clergy, having seen better examples of them in Anjou and Le Cap. They mostly try to run people over with their coaches and bark insults or commands, if they even notice you at all. I feel sorry for their peacock servants, who must take their merde *like cheerful chamber pots. From what I am learning, this country has always been a coach at speed - with the wheels not properly attached to the axles. It has always been a mess, and probably always will be. There have been many times when the wheels fell off this national coach, and open war has broken out in the streets. There have been six legitimate wars this century already, and probably as many riots and rebellions. If war breaks out roughly every ten years, it seems we are due, at least for another riot or rebellion. Who knows? I suppose a little bit of blood on the cobblestones would break up the monotony of school work, we'll see.*

Miss you dearly,

Guillaume

PS - Now that I think upon it, the troubles here might have something to do with the fact that everyone can read. That may seem like a strange thing to say, but I will explain. There are pamphlets, leaflets, posters, and newspapers everywhere. You simply cannot escape information. It is a million times worse than Le Cap, and you know I never lacked for paper soldiers there. Everyone in Grenoble is bombarded with information. Everyone knows what goes on, but depending on what you read, you get a different version of it! If things get bad, there are wholesale lies being told everywhere from every viewpoint imaginable. Some of them are quite ridiculous and unbelievable, but you would be amazed at what people can accept. It is as if widespread education has led to a whole new level of ignorance. The unavoidable, constant exposure to the printing press has put people in a fever pitch state regarding nearly everything in the political sphere. One never knows what to believe. Perhaps that is why the peasants are the happiest - they can't read the lies. Much love!

Guillaume had an ambivalent relationship with violence. The scales tipped with his unhappiness and anger, and it was always directed toward men. His young friend from Saint-Domingue was dying, but Estelle did not want to be the one who reminded Guillaume of Raphaël's illness. It distressed her that Guillaume had not found friends. Guillaume was a full-scholarship student, which made him a rare species at the University school. He had no money at all, and wrote on used posters, and was probably close to starving most of the time, which made him an uncommon race of that rare species. He was also a feral *Mamelouk* from Saint-Domingue. Although there were plenty of colored from Saint-Domingue going to school in France, all of them were the sons of planters: rich, connected and aristocratic. Even they would have little in common with him, his friendship with Raphaël notwithstanding. Raphaël, like Guillaume, was a unicorn. In any case, friendships were rarely struck outside of social class, but hopefully things would look up for him. Overall, he seemed to be in a good temper.

Estelle, through the corner of her eye, saw the three young Nicolas daughters staring at her. One of them made a motion - *Why do you plug your ears?*

Estelle immediately put her hands in her lap. She must have looked utterly ridiculous. It would not do. The young girls were watching her, because young girls are always curious about older girls. Estelle straightened in the pew to a normal posture.

And there he was. Father Jonathan Courgeon stood at the pulpit for his sermon. He wasn't speaking. He was simply staring into her eyes. Estelle could do nothing but what came naturally - and what came naturally was to smile, for she delighted in his being. When she smiled at him, his face lit as if hit by a ray of light. And that was the problem - and that was why Estelle had not attended church in Saint-Florent-le-Vieil for over six months.

She had traveled to La Chapelle-Saint-Florent, the parish bordering Saint-Florent-le-Vieil to the southwest, and had started a conversation with a young lady on the street. The girl she chose looked a bit awkward and was alone, and perhaps in need of a friend – and that is precisely why Estelle chose her. Her name was Solange Guigou, and she was indeed all three. She was thin and tall, possessed of long, stringy light brown hair, and grey eyes. Her features were not unpleasant, but plain. She was of average intelligence, displayed no special abilities or skills, but was a kind, good-hearted sort who possessed an abundant supply of patience and selflessness, especially around children and infants. Estelle did not particularly identify with Solange, or have interests in common with her. But she showered Solange with love and affection, and was very attentive of her, and soon Estelle was the best, and only, friend of Solange Guigou.

Estelle found that Solange was the seventh child of eleven, and had been given more responsibility than attention, being nearly a second mother of the family. But she loved her family very much, though she was unappreciated. She had no graces, no knowledge of beauty, and was overlooked by the boys.

Solange soon loved Estelle like a sister. Estelle had a fondness for Solange, but nothing more. She kindled the friendship for one reason, and one reason only: to find a legitimate excuse, that would arouse no suspicion, as to why she no longer attended mass in Saint-Florent-le-Vieil. If her best friend was Solange Guigou, it made sense that she attended mass in Chapelle-Saint-Florent. Despite Estelle's motives, she was a good friend to Solange, and helped her do better things with her hair, dress more attentively, and look at herself as an honorable woman worthy of attention and love. She even tried to teach her to read, but was not successful.

Unfortunately for Estelle, her friendship opened Solange like a budding flower. She began to wear a smile, to talk more, and to be more open with her neighbors. Her relationship with her family and parish changed nearly overnight. Soon Estelle's time with Solange was spent with a growing group of her friends. Again, Estelle really had nothing in common with any of them. But Estelle was giving, kind and attentive, a good listener and empathetic, and all of Solange's friends adored her. The problem came when suitors started to arrive as well.

Estelle's heart fell, but she helped Solange as best she could. Estelle explained that these new arrivals found Solange attractive, and her manner pleasing. Solange was dumbstruck and excited. Estelle explained that she must be patient: it was up to Solange to discover the true temper of these men, and whether they were compatible with her own innermost self. She had to discover whether they could provide for Solange, and care for her future children in a good Christian manner.

The young men certainly took a liking to Estelle as well - but always in a brotherly fashion. She did share many qualities with the young women of the parish: she was faithful, honorable, self-sufficient, hard-working and good with plants and animals. But there was something altogether different about Estelle - nothing objectionable, simply alien and otherworldly, and she was sometimes a bit aloof. She was wise beyond her years, educated, well-travelled and intelligent.

Estelle thought of herself as the most boring person in Christendom. How she could now be perceived as some kind of Turkish princess was a complete mystery to her, but somehow, in Chapelle-Saint-Florent, she was as exotic as a veil dance.

To Estelle's dismay, Solange was soon betrothed. The young man was named Jean Vanier, and he was completely unobjectionable. In fact, he was perfect for Solange, and worshipped the very ground she walked on. Solange and Jean were soon married, with Estelle being the maid of honor, and being mentioned at the wedding nearly as much as the bride and groom. The problem was that Jean Vanier lived with his family in La Boissière-sur-Èvre, the parish just to the southwest of Chapelle-Saint-Florent, in a little place known as La Colle, which was in the very southwest of the parish. For Estelle, it would be more than a fourteen-mile round trip to attend mass with Solange after the wedding. She could no longer plausibly justify her absence from Saint-Florent-le-Vieil. But it had been a long time since she had seen Father Jonathan, she thought, and perhaps things were different.

Father Jonathan, for his part, was also considered to be a bit exotic by the people he met day to day, being a man of the cloth. He was also intellectually curious, delving into science, mathematics and philosophy. These subjects brought up questions regarding the nature of the universe. Father Jonathan eagerly tried to solve them – and delighted in the fact that every answer he found brought him back to God. Like most priests between the Loire and the Vendée, he was born a neighbor to his congregation. However different, he was, ultimately, one of them - they knew his family, and they certainly knew him. Everyone realized he was destined to be a priest from a young age, for he was whip-smart, ethereally-minded and moral, and he was treated differently by his peers and their parents alike. His duties were worthy of his talents, but he felt alone, even being always surrounded by people. There were nine other brothers at the abbey, but they were all much older, and had no interest in discussions of faith or philosophy which involved inquisition or change. They were Black Monks - Benedictines - who had taken oaths of *conversatio morum*, and were dedicated to a routine of prayer, worship and study. It was Father Jonathan's job to interface with the community at large. The monks appreciated Father Jonathan, for he did precisely what he was supposed to do, and did it well - but they did not understand him as a person or priest, nor the intellectual curiosity of his age. Jonathan enjoyed the company of the Marquis de Bonchamps and the Marquise, but the Marquis was often away with the regiment, and the Marquise had an increasing obligation to her growing family as she had more children.

To build community and encourage Christian debate, Father Jonathan had organized a meeting of local priests every Monday. Father Denis from Botz-En-Mauge, Father Cyrille from le Marillais, Father Méthode from Saint-Laurent-du-Mottay, and Father Aurélien from Chapelle-Saint-Florent would find their way to the abbey upon Mount Glonne. In the refectory, they would argue and talk about the state of Catholicism in their parishes, and in France as a whole. Sadly, Father Jonathan had to admit that the meetings blurred together in his memory because all of them nearly went the same way. Mostly Father Jonathan would become irritated and frustrated. "Faith encompasses every part of man. Not just his heart and soul, but his body and his mind. His intellect."

Father Aurélien would always shake his head, "You are young." Aurélien would always say that, in exactly the same way. It simply did not need to be said after the first time, and it annoyed Jonathan to no end.

Then Father Denis would chime in, "The people do not wish to know the theological apologetics behind the rejection of the concept of the Elect, Father Jonathan. Neither do they wish to debate the finer points of catechism or Aquinas. They love God. God loves them. Their faith is a beautiful and simple thing."

Yes, yes - *but*.

Father Jonathan would also be thwarted in his criticism of the church, "It is ridiculous that the church tithes are obligatory for all Frenchmen - and these funds are paying the salaries of the sons of nobility, who do not perform the sacraments – or any other clerical function, for that matter."

There was never a quick reply after such outbursts. Usually either Father Cyrille or Father Méthode would speak first after a pregnant silence, "It is best to not speak of such things."

"Yes, but why?" Father Jonathan would say, nearly shouting, frustrated, aggravated, annoyed at the corruption and lack of desire for change.

"Power and greed corrupt," Father Aurélien had once said in reply, "France is a Catholic nation, by decree. Therefore, the church is powerful, and has access to mandatory tithes. These things are like the scent of blood to the unscrupulous. But this does not affect the congregation, for the lower ranks of the priesthood serve God, and not themselves."

"How can it not affect the congregation? How can the congregation perceive a corrupt institution, and find it in their hearts to believe in it – or us? How can the corruption of the church be the will of Christ?"

Feet shuffled, throats were cleared. Father Cyrille spoke, "It is best to not speak of such things."

Father Denis, the smartest of the lot - but just as conservative – always spoke last, "Father Jonathan, we do not mean to insult Christ. It is simply this: the congregation gains too much, being the beneficiary of a moral Christian state. Attracting corruption is a small price to pay. If we were not a Christian state, imagine the disintegration of culture, the resulting social chaos, and the true suffering that would ensue. The nobles who take high titles in the church do not come anywhere near a congregation. They perform no work, affect nothing, and they are never seen. We are the church, not them."

"Do the ends then justify the means?" asked Jonathan, trying as best he could to keep his voice down. "Are we then Machiavellian, serving God in the devil's way?" There was another silence, but Jonathan broke it himself, "I am always told that I read too much, that I am a good son of a horrible age, and rather should be one wholly of the church. But reform should be ever minded, as repairs on the foundations of buildings are never ignored, except by the most impoverished or lazy. Are we so penniless or lethargic that we ignore our own foundations? We must always weed out corruption. We must always be mindful of our spiritual foundations. To do otherwise would be to betray Christ. The moment we believe any kind of corruption should be tolerated, we completely undermine the reason for our existence. For if the congregation does not trust us, we can fulfill no function in their lives. The goodwill of the congregation must always be paramount, even if we are the ones sacrificed on the altar to achieve it."

Aurélien spoke again, "You are young."

Jonathan's blood was pumping so hard he could barely see. He nearly whispered, to hide his rising emotion, "How so, Father?"

"We are at war. The devil has only one goal - to destroy the church. There are certain accommodations to be made in the winning of it. We must be strong, and close ranks, for he will use any opening to destroy us, even an attempt at reform."

Jonathan rubbed his face, "Can he not use corruption and complacency to do the same?"

Father Cyrille spoke, "We have other, more pressing problems. Some of the peasants, while attending Mass, are using the Orans Posture during the *Our Father*."

The Orans Posture was to stand, bend one's elbows, and hold your palms facing skyward. It was utterly inoffensive - except in regard to the most esoteric, legalistic arguments of theological minutiae regarding the sacrament of the Eucharist.

"It's shocking, but it's true," admitted Father Méthode, "I have seen it with my own eyes. Not only that, when questioned, they do not know why it is wrong, and argue."

Father Cyrille's eyes went wide, "It is the dreaded double ignorance of Socrates! It is not being aware of one's ignorance while thinking that one knows!"

Father Aurélien spoke quickly, "All of you are missing the point. The congregation should not be saying the *Our Father* during Mass at all - only the celebrant priest. Our Bishop should be ashamed. It is preposterous."

It was no use.

But there was one person with whom Jonathan met where great things were discussed, and the process was neither irritating or frustrating. Estelle Guerrier's mind was sharp, and she could disagree in a way that favored more discussion and argument. They would laugh frequently and learn from each other. She had begun their relationship hanging on his every word, and reading every book he mentioned. She had now practically surpassed him in knowledge and organization of thought. He was not threatened by her amazing ability - no one could ever feel threatened by Estelle Guerrier. He was rather proud of her, and honored to be her friend. He talked with her after his disastrous meeting.

"Yes, you are right, Father. But things must move slowly," she said with her beautiful smile, showing the gap in her teeth.

"Must they?"

"Slow is always better, even if it is frustrating. Important actions must be undertaken… like the building of a roof, with patient attention to detail. A roof needs to last a long time, and has an important purpose that is difficult to achieve. Or, better yet, think like a farmer."

"In what way?"

"A farmer cannot simply say 'water is good for crops.' There are some plants that can take all the water you can give them, others will die quickly with the same treatment. There are a million types of flora. They are affected by soil, water, sunlight, temperature, altitude, and incline. It is always best to slowly test any change in those factors, or else the plants will die. Change must be slow to prevent hurt - with mankind, even more so than plants, for we are more precious. Yet we neglect ourselves sometimes, because we are so resilient, even whilst we take great care with our flowers," she laughed, and everything was right in the world.

"How does one slowly root out corruption?"

"The problem is not the fact that France is a Christian nation. The problem, I believe, is the mandatory tithe. It is the power to gather money that corrupts the church." She had a way of saying such things that did not offend. From her tone, she was not a teacher, not arrogant or condescending. Rather, she was a mischievous co-conspirator.

He agreed. "Without the mandatory tithe, we can keep everything important, and weed out the salary seekers."

"Yes, but we ask a lot of the cloth. If nearly everyone of high rank in the church is a noble, collecting salary whilst they play cards in Versailles, why would those self-same people rule on the elimination of their own salary? It is their only reason for joining the clergy."

"So, what is the solution?"

"People like you must attain position, and while you do, not be corrupted by the process."

"And which of those conditions is the most difficult?"

"For someone like you, the first. Such a revolution would entail much luck and timing. There must be a legion of Father Jonathans across France, moving in the same direction. You must start a conspiracy for Christ to achieve your worthy goals."

Father Jonathan was stunned. A girl almost ten years his junior had just changed the entire focus of his life. He should not have been surprised - it was Estelle Guerrier, after all.

Father Jonathan came up with a plan, and went to his immediate superior, Brother David. He told him everything. He was excited, and his enthusiasm must - *must*- have been contagious.

Brother David finally spoke, "A generation goes, a generation comes, yet the earth stands firm forever."

He was quoting Ecclesiastes. This did not bode well. That particular part of scripture was a sword into the heart of man's vanity. Was Father Jonathan engaging in vanity?

Brother David continued, "What was, will be again, what has been done, will be done again, and there is nothing new under the sun. Take anything which people acclaim as being new: it existed in the centuries preceding us. No memory remains of the past, and so it will be for the centuries to come - they will not be remembered by their successors."

"Do you prevent me from doing this, Brother David?"

"No. Do as you will."

And so he did. Father Jonathan wrote twenty letters a day - whether he was sick, tired or busy - from that day forward. He wrote to the priests he knew regarding his ideas, and asked them for more names - then he wrote the priests he did not know. He called out for warriors against corruption, men who knew the removal of the parasites would only make the church stronger. The elimination of the mandatory tithe would actually provide a better living for the average *curé* and *abbé*, for the funds would be spent where they should, and not be the ante for a Versailles gambler's pot. Jonathan knew what he wanted would be difficult to achieve, but if anything in life changes, it is circumstance and opportunity. And Estelle was his knight's lady - in his heart, he carried her colors, and could weather the long, hard fight with the inspiration of her favor.

Father Jonathan was a man of ferric moral character. He not only strove to be appropriate in every circumstance, he would judge people and situations beforehand, and prepare himself morally and ethically for any challenge. His actions as a priest, if he were to be judged solely on his actions, had been wholly and completely honorable, if not commendable.

But that would not be the entire story.

He had come to realize that he was in love with Estelle, and had been for some time. Considering how he lived his life, this should not have come to pass - but Estelle was a poniard that had found the space between the plates of his armor. When they first met, she was little more than a child really, but on the verge of womanhood. He had no fear of her whatsoever, for all good men look upon children in an honorable manner without thought or effort. But when she was a young, he had deeply connected with her as a person. He liked and respected her. They developed an easy humor between them, laughed frequently, and experienced joy together. Then, unfortunately for Jonathan, Estelle suddenly blossomed into full womanhood. Her freckled face lost its childhood fat and now had lovely angles. Her breasts were large but well-shaped, and she had wide slim hips. There was no modest fashion, even the burka of the Bedouin, that could hide such a figure.

Perhaps that would not have been a problem, except Estelle seemed to enjoy and appreciate any and all attention he gave her, and - at least in his heart - he crossed a line. He believed only social mores and personal ethics prevented utter chaos when men and women arrive at a certain age. But Jonathan had let her inside his heart, totally and unconditionally, because she was young - and then she became a woman: an object of love, lust, companionship and motherhood. It was only then, when it was too late, that he realized their ages were not so far apart as he had thought, and that he had greatly erred. Father Jonathan had not foreseen the implications of Estelle's age. He found he had no defense, or rather, his defenses were formidable, but she was already past them. He wanted her, he was in love with her - utterly, completely, and totally. It was perhaps the worst thing a priest could realize, but for some reason the terrible reality did not vex him for a very simple reason.

He silently thanked God that it was Estelle Guerrier who had captured his heart. She was a tower of spiritual strength. His vows were safe.

Even fully aware of his feelings, and perhaps growing aware of their intensity, he knew he would not act upon them. But he also knew he was just a man. If Estelle did anything at all to indicate she felt the same way - and, to his mind, to think she did was absurd - he would fall. He would fall hopelessly and be a priest no more. It would be a tragedy, it would haunt him forever, but he knew his feelings. When he was around her, he could be set on fire with a torch - and feel nothing but the joy of being near her. But when she was gone, when the world turned dark once again, the betrayal of his oaths would crush him like a weight falling from the sky - until she appeared again.

That would not be a good life. They both deserved better.

But it *was* Estelle Guerrier, thank God. If he was not strong, she would be. And she was certainly not the type to have such improper feelings as he did.

He smiled, glad to see her again amongst the congregation, and began the sermon.

Estelle tried to listen, but her whole being was elsewhere. Father Jonathan was her dearest friend. He had communicated with every school in France, and finally saw her brother shipped off to the university school at Grenoble. Guillaume had become a different person attending school. How could Estelle ever thank Jonathan for saving her twin? Father Jonathan was the greatest man she had ever met. He was kind, honorable, giving, gentle, intelligent, handsome and compassionate. He was her Johann. At first, it was perhaps her imagination - but she came to realize Father Jonathan was far more precious than she could have imagined Johann to ever be.

After mass, Estelle was besieged by half the congregation, and her father rolled his eyes and walked off without her. The villagers had beaming smiles on their faces, overjoyed to see her again. She had no idea she had made such an impression. Father Jonathan stopped outside the ring of people, "Welcome back, Estelle. You have certainly been missed," he said as he motioned toward the crowd.

Estelle returned the smile, "It is good to be back, Father. I have truly missed all of you as well."

Father Jonathan smiled again, and walked on. To all eyes, everything was as it had always been.

That night, Jonathan could not sleep. There was nothing he could do. He noticed the moon was full, and there were no clouds or wind. He went for a walk in the silvery darkness, bound and determined to exhaust himself so he could sleep.

Two miles later, he passed Estelle, walking quickly with a determined grimace on her face. They greeted each other warmly but curtly, and kept walking in their separate directions. It was strange that two close friends would be so perfunctory with each other.

The next day, Estelle went to Chapelle-Saint-Florent and visited Father Aurélien, whom she knew well. He was tending his garden, and she kneeled to help him. He was patient, and waited for her to speak.

"Father, I am in need. I wish to secure a position. Perhaps as a governess. Something. It doesn't matter."

"In Chapelle-Saint-Florent?"

Estelle sighed, "Anywhere, really."

"Anywhere?"

"Yes, Father. Anywhere but within a league of Saint-Florent-le-Vieil."

He stopped his ministration in the dirt, straightened, and looked at her. "Why? What has happened?"

"Truthfully?"

"As you will, Estelle."

"I am in love. I am in love with Father Jonathan Courgeon, and I think he with me. Our actions have been nothing but honorable, and we have never spoken of this. I don't know if he knows of my feelings, but I have no doubt of his, though he has tried to hide them, as any honorable man in his position would do. Despite his best intentions, they are as plain to me as a sunrise. Please help me in getting as far from his parish as humanly possible, and as quickly as possible, before our salvation is thrown into dire jeopardy by the folly of our sinful hearts."

He nodded, and spoke evenly, "You will be gone before high mass on Sunday. Make all arrangements."

"Thank you, Father."

Father Aurélien nodded, "He is young, Father Jonathan."

"Please understand, our actions and words have been nothing but honorable, as priest and parishioner should be. Father Jonathan is a gift from God to Saint-Florent-le-Vieil."

"I understand, Estelle."

"Please do not think ill of us, Father."

"We are all human, Estelle. But not all humans run from sin like a deer from wildfire. For that, you should be commended. We need speak of this no more."

They continued their gardening in silence, as if they had not spoken at all.

Estelle did not return directly home. She ran several errands before going to the banks of the Loire, where her father usually stood about talking with the rivermen and inspecting cargo. He looked irritated to see her, and took her to one side, "What are you doing here?"

"I have secured a position, and I will be leaving shortly."

"What position?"

"I'm going to be a governess, for an extraordinarily rich family." She added the description because Papa respected ambition.

He nodded, "Make sure their sons ring you before you commit to anything. Don't be a fool."

Estelle had no idea what he was talking about.

He spoke again, "It is not fitting that no one should mind the house."

"I have spoken with Sandrine-"

"The Potato?" He called their neighbor Potato, for she was an old, curmudgeonly sort who preferred to live alone.

"Indeed. I have spoken with Sandrine-"

"Potato."

"I have spoken with Potato, and she has agreed to be your housekeeper. If you are at home for lunch or dinner, she will cook for you if you give her advance notice."

"You couldn't find anyone more pleasing?"

Estelle found someone who would be unaffected by his sharp tongue and ill-manners. "Now, now, Papa, she is willing and close by."

"Who is going to look over my reports before I send them?"

"Your writing has advanced admirably. If you only looked up words in the dictionary you do not know-"

"Pages are missing."

They possessed a used *Dictionary of the French Academy*, printed in 1762, but nearly forty pages had been torn out. Estelle sighed, "There is always Father Jonathan."

"He is a little chirping bird, that one. I think he'd burst into song and dance, if a cloud passed the sun."

Estelle embraced him, "Good luck, Papa."

"All right, then," he said, as he looked down, and shuffled his feet.

And off she went, as if to the market, and not to a faraway place. His reaction did not make her unhappy. She knew him well, and anticipated his tone.

She loved him, in her way. He loved her in his.

1832

Jake

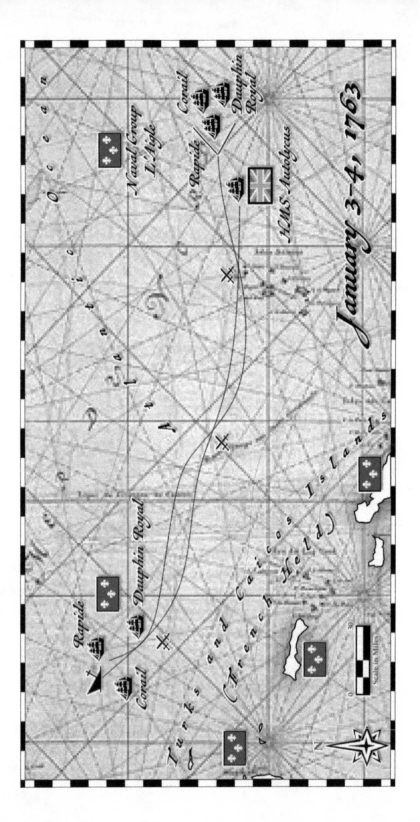

Chapter 15

Jake couldn't sleep at all, although the bed in his new room at the inn was more than adequate. Rather than drink himself into unconsciousness, he simply tossed and turned his way to dawn. In his nocturnal rotations, he came to the conclusion that the best course of action would be, for now, to foster the perception that he was oblivious to the machinations of his observers. It was best if no one perceived him as being too alert or skittish. If he simply went about his ordered tasks without trying to spot his shadows, it would lower everyone's guard - everyone's except his own.

The next morning the grim innkeeper thoughtfully had a basket of food and a cabriolet waiting at the curb. Jake thanked him and gave him a large gratuity for his trouble and risk. After a short shopping trip for oilskins, a satchel, a chest and some clothes, the ride to the southwest of Saint-Germain-des-Prés was grueling. Jake had a headache, was dead tired, couldn't sleep and the traffic was a purgatorial stop-and-go nightmare for the entire, nearly-four-mile trip. Jake thought it would have been only slightly slower to walk.

Jake imagined that if he were in America or England, he might have been able to take a train to Nantes. But there was only one train line in France, going from Lyon to some southern mining town. In typical fashion, France was the first nation on earth to have such a thing as a train line. But soon, in typical fashion, half the world caught up and soon surpassed her. France's one train line remained France's one train line, and it was nowhere near Paris. That alone was not typically French: everything was usually in Paris. So off to the stagecoach ticketing office went Jake.

The coach station at the Barrière de Versailles gate was already filling up. No one there was rich, or they would have their own carriage. No one there was poor, for the coach was expensive. Including food and drink, the passage from Paris to Nantes could bleed one's coin pouch for up to fifty livres. A drunk older man was loudly proclaiming that he intended to be intoxicated the entire ride, sleep soundly and make his water in a bottle. He was looking for others of like mind or those who didn't mind. Jake gave a gratuity to the clerk in order to secure a coach only partially filled with passengers - and specified that they be quiet and not be of savage or drunken mien.

He soon found himself with a window seat on a large coach bound for Nantes. It would not stop for darkness but only at stages where the horses would be changed and the passengers could eat and stretch. The other six interior passengers were all calm young professionals who worked on their papers with charcoal pencils, or read books. Jake had a feeling they all had made this journey many times. None of them spoke to each other except to exchange polite pleasantries. A bedraggled family of four sat on the roof. It was cheaper, wetter, dustier and the seats were less comfortable. In spite of it, sometimes, at least in June, the air and sun could make it pleasant. The coach had a crew of two, a driver held the reins on the top bench, and one man sat postilion on the lead left charger. Chests of mail and parcels bound for Nantes, and points in-between, were stacked everywhere, inside the cabin and out.

Jake was asleep in minutes. He woke up to see they were almost to Chartres and their first change of horses. He felt refreshed and anxious. He had reserved this moment to read the captain's log, given to him by Monsieur Tyran.

Jake had been forced to the quest, he was convinced that Monsieur Tyran was a madman, and he was leery of *The Society*, and their now different involvement in his life. Despite it all, he was intrigued by his mission. The Cross of Nantes was an attractive mystery, and the captain's log was his entré. Whatever information it possessed, very few other people knew of it.

He took the papers containing the log from his satchel. The writing was in a tight, perfect, uniform hand - the mark of a professional transcriber. This was then a copy, but was probably easier to read than the original. Without the original, however, Jake had no way to tell if the document was genuine, or if it had been altered from its text. But whether he trusted Monsieur Tyran or not, he had his orders.

He began to read

FBFW *Dauphin-Royal*, *Téméraire*-class 74
CdV Henri-Marie Jacque Fabre, Comte l'Aigle
In Command of Naval Group *l'Aigle*
Dauphin Royal 74 Gun FBFW
Corail 28 Gun Frigate
Rapide 18 Gun Sloop

January 3, 1763

North Atlantic Ocean, 100 miles NE of the Caicos Islands
23° 00' 52" N 69° 01' 22" W
Choppy seas. Light Haze. Wind 6 knots NE.
19 Officers, 26 Aspirans, 643 Sailors 159 Colonial Marines

At four bells into the afternoon watch, a British Man-of-War was sighted at a distance of 8 miles southwest. She was identified as a 135-foot, 28-gun frigate travelling northeast with the trade wind. The frigate presumably sighted the naval group, and changed to a full-cloth due westerly course.

It was my belief that this frigate was the HMS *Autolycus*, an independent British command raiding our shipping lines, and relying on her great speed to escape larger vessels. She had already been responsible for the interception and scuttling of numerous merchantmen, and also the destruction of the 28-gun frigate *Saint-Malo* in the terrible Winter of 1761. I also believed that our sloop *Rapide* could outdistance her, and engage her with fore-mounted guns during the pursuit. The *Autolycus* would dare not heave to in order to fire back at the weaker ship, for fear of the *Dauphin Royal* and *Corail* catching up and joining in the engagement.

Orders were given to the *Dauphin Royal* to tack west, and the *Corail* and the *Rapide* were signaled to pursue the frigate independently of group command. As a result, the *Corail* and *Rapide* were able to overtake and pass the *Dauphin Royal*, and become the lead chase elements.

Orders were given to the *Corail* and *Rapide* to engage and slow the frigate to force an action with the entire naval group. When dusk fell both the *Corail* and *Rapide* were out of signal range. The enemy frigate could no longer be seen. The *Corail* was five miles away, and the *Rapide* nearly ten.

All through the rest of the afternoon and evening, cannon fire was heard in the very great distance, presumably as our sister ships engaged the British frigate in an attempt to slow her down.

January 4, 1763

North Atlantic Ocean, 50 miles N-NE of Samana Cays
23° 42' 42" N 73° 09' 24" W
Choppy seas. Low Clouds. Wind 9 knots N-NE.
19 Officers, 26 Aspirans, 643 Sailors 159 Colonial Marines

At dawn, no ships were visible from the *Dauphin Royal* but cannon fire was heard in the great distance. At seven bells of the forenoon watch, we were able to catch sight of all three ships. The British frigate had lost her aft mast, which had fallen fore across the deck, and destroyed her mizzen and foremast rigging. She was immobile, and engaged in combat with the *Rapide* and *Corail*, both ships maneuvering to avoid broadsides from the frigate while hitting her with their own.

By eight bells, we were upon her, but the frigate had already surrendered and the battle was over. The *Rapide* and the *Corail* were signaled to stand by as the *Dauphin Royal* pulled alongside the frigate. Lieutenant Petit's three Marine platoons were ordered to secure the vessel as he saw fit, and soon she was ready for boarding.

It was learned that in the engagement only 6 men were killed and 22 wounded between the *Rapide* and *Corail*, and neither craft had sustained significant damage. The striking of the aft mast of the *Autolycus* was a spot of good marksmanship, and slowed her considerably. Subsequent volleys of chain shot had cut the lines holding the mast and brought it to the deck, ripping sails, cutting more lines and nearly disabling the frigate and ending the pursuit. Although the *Autolycus* was willing to engage the *Corail* and *Rapide*, when the *Dauphin Royal* was spotted their captain wisely ended their stand to save the lives of the remaining crew.

I myself went aboard the frigate and questioned the captain of the vessel. He identified himself as Captain William Eltis of Eastleigh, Hampshire County, England. The ship he commanded was indeed the *Autolycus* and he verified that his orders were to disrupt shipping and naval supply. He commanded a small crew of 240 souls, 39 of whom were now dead and 66 wounded. The polite nature of our conversation was interrupted by Marine Lieutenant Petit, who said that there was something that I needed to see below decks.

I accompanied Lieutenant Petit to the captain's quarters of the *Autolycus*. Inside was a pale girl in a torn black dress, of approximately fourteen years of age, who was chained to the wall from an iron collar around her throat. To our horror, she was very obviously European white and from her features could have easily been French. When questioned, it was revealed that she spoke no French, and very little English. Her name, as far as we could understand, was Shinaidah Braucklin and she was from a place called

Ards, or perhaps the Forest of Ards, in the Kingdom of Tierconnel on the island of Eru, wherever that might be. She crossed herself and, through her other gestures and simple words, we determined she was a fellow Catholic, much to our astonishment. Darkly, it was also established that she was the slave of Captain William Eltis and she had been cruelly used in the most dishonorable and lowest fashion by this man for quite some time.

I immediately confronted Captain Eltis regarding this disgraceful discovery, and told him I would see him hanged. Eltis claimed that she was his legal slave, and had the papers on board in his chest to prove it. It was astonishing to me that such a thing could be true, for I associated white slavery with savage Mohammedans from North Africa, and certainly not with the British. It could not be possible that such a nation as Great Britain could countenance such a thing. Captain Eltis, however, did indeed produce documentation proving that the girl legally belonged to him under the laws of the United Kingdom. His bill of sale was from a merchant house in Montserrat, but gave very little information on the girl. I destroyed the papers in front of him, and told him his paperwork bought him his life and nothing more, and that the girl was free.

When she was brought above decks, she attacked Captain Eltis with her bare hands. In the attack, she took from him a pendant from around his neck that proved to be a cross of white stone and gold, bejeweled with red gems of unusual splendor. Captain Eltis was quite angry at the loss of his necklace and claimed that it too was legally his. With the cross, he explained, Captain Eltis planned to buy his nobility and retirement and the girl had no right to its possession. I saw upon the girl's face, however, a glimmer of satisfaction, as if she knew what the cross meant to him. Upon asking for and being handed the cross by the girl, I realized that it was quite lovely, and it was also Catholic, having the Corpus Christi upon it in gold. I told Captain Eltis that it was my belief he stole the cross from a French merchantman, for why else would he have such a thing? As far as I was concerned, the poor girl had more claim to the necklace than he did. Also, the cross was a small price to pay for the treatment he had visited upon her, and I promptly returned the necklace to her as wergild for her troubles. Upon seeing this, Captain Eltis became hysterically upset, and it was no longer my desire to converse with him. He was imprisoned with his men in the hold of the *Dauphin Royal*, and neither he nor any member of his crew received special treatment for rank or status, being we all of like mind in our disgust for them.

I gave full range of the ship to our young girl Mademoiselle Braucklin and proclaimed her the good luck charm of our vessel. I ordered that she be shown the respect and courtesy due her as a young woman of God, and was pleased to see that the sentiment of my orders was embraced immediately by all hands.

Upon inspection of the *Autolycus*, it was revealed that her injuries were such that she would have to be towed to port in order to be repaired enough to move on her own. This was deemed unfeasible under the circumstances and I ordered everything of value taken from the ship prior to her being scuttled. This was achieved by eight bells of the first watch and the *Autolycus*, with her sordid exploits and crew's misdeeds, given to the sea.

I ordered the naval group to change course for Cap-Français in order to transfer our captives to prison barges, and to deliver Mademoiselle to a friendly port.

(January 5 through January 13 omitted)

January 14, 1763

Cap-Français, Saint-Domingue
19° 44' 46" N 72° 11' 50" W
Becalmed. Clear. Wind 2 knots NE.
19 Officers, 26 Aspirans, 642 Sailors 159 Colonial Marines

At one bell middle watch, Graduate Seaman Pierre Leroux died of wounds sustained in his fall on January 6, and was buried at sea before reaching Cap-Français. May God rest his soul.

Upon reaching port, all captives were transferred to the care of Squadron Vice-Admiral Maurice Roland de Chauvirey minus the twenty-three who died of wounds. All flag officers of the naval group were debriefed by Colonial Naval Command Cap-Français.

Resupply, refit and repair was to take six days and orders were given to issue stages of leave time to the men.

Mademoiselle Braucklin had become quite a fixture onboard the *Dauphin Royal* and we were sorry to part with her. She was given one-hundred livre donated by the ship's senior officers, and entrusted to a local freeman named Féroce Guerrier, a law-abiding Octoroon with whom I have had some dealings. He was told to help her, and make sure her honor was kept intact. Although Monsieur Guerrier is an extraordinarily colorful and fierce character, he is completely honorable, and a man of his word. He agreed to make sure Mademoiselle was not lost in the bustle of Cap Français, and would help her in any way he could. He was given additional funds, and initially refused them. He finally accepted fifty livres on the condition it was only spent on the needs of Mademoiselle. When she left the ship for the last time, there were no dry eyes amongst us, and we felt as if we had all lost a little sister.

I moved the naval group headquarters to a rented villa for the time we would be in Cap Français. All of the ship captains were invited to the governor's mansion for dinner, and we duly attended. Governor General Gabriel de Bory de Saint-Vincent and his wife were delightful. We were told that the war would probably be over within months. We were both saddened and gladdened by the news. This conflict has not gone well for the Fatherland. I fear that if a great victory is not won soon, the peace settlement will not be in our favor. French blood has been spilled all over the world, and it calls from the ground to be honored and avenged. We trust in God and Saint Michael for the future.

(end)

The Time of the Heirlooms

1786

Jeannine

Chapter 16

Caroline Lacroix Cœurfroid was once beautiful. She had big green eyes, and a head of full-bodied, light brown hair. Her mouth was big and full, and, when she smiled, she revealed a set of perfect, large teeth. Jeannine Cœurfroid knew this of her mother because there was a painting of her in the foyer hallway. No one, of course, would accuse Madame Cœurfroid of being beautiful now. She had lost the lank of youth, and was beset by ungainly rolls of fat. Her hair was grey and thinning, her teeth rotted out from eating too much sugar, and her face was curled from an infernal, perpetual craving to pester and annoy anyone who aroused her baser instincts.

At least, that was Jeannine's perception.

The perpetual attempt to understand the relationship between herself, her mother and her father would consume Jeannine for the rest of her life. Her parents never spoke of such dark and hairy things, nor the trials of their past, so it was up to Jeannine to piece together the tale - mostly as she pleased. She believed her father, who was kind to her, fell in love with young Caroline because she was beautiful, and he was not - being in the unfortunate shape of a hairy, blonde gorilla. He was rich as Croesus now, but he was not then. He was a non-practicing Catholic, and Caroline was a frenzied Huguenot - a French protestant. Jeannine imagined this gorilla of a man, who sat in the wrong church - when he did at all - who did not have two coins to rub together, was madly in love with this rich, ravishing Calvinist Princess, and simply could not live without her. There must have been an army of competitors as he tried to woo her. His natural cha-risma and force of personality eventually won over the Princess, and they were married. In tales, this was usually the end - Princess and Gorilla would live hap-pily ever after. But life is not a tale. In the broken window of reality, the Princess demanded the Gorilla become a Protestant. He does so, but his lackadaisical at-titude toward religion does not change. The Princess resents this tremendously - but not as much as his poverty. Whatever mist of glamour he placed upon her eyes eventually wore off, and she finally saw him through hateful eyes. Her loathing was magnified by the fact that she was convinced he tricked her into loving him, if just long enough for her to make a decision she could not undo. The Gorilla, somehow shamed by the woman he thought would redeem him, dedicated himself to his work, and found his business grow and succeed - albeit not fast enough to appease the Princess. Little by little, his desire to spend time with the Princess waned; when a spare minute reared its head, it was spent with associates and friends - and not with her. The Princess exacerbated her own un-happiness by reinforcing the troops of her losing battle, rather than changing their position. Their children, as they grew older, saw her as a villain, for their father made no unreasonable demands upon them, and she did. The Princess found herself alone.

And then, just then, her last child, Jeannine, was born. The Princess, ever scheming behind the wall of her conscious thought, laid a base design upon her infant. Jeannine was to be her mother's companion, to provide the love her fam-ily did not, to be a perfect machine dedicated to providing every emotional need to her long-suffering mother.

Jeannine proved to be a frail nothing of a girl. She crawled late, spoke late, and thereafter could do nothing right. Her earliest memories involved feelings - shame, fear, depression, self-hate - as she disappointed her mother over and over. She longed for her father. She loved to hold him and kiss him. She always felt a keen sense of loss when he left the house, and was excited and complete when he returned. Her father loved her, but he was never there, and when he was, mother rarely allowed her to be in his orbit. Jeannine had a foul, boring gover-ness, who died before she was a teenager, who taught her sewing, music, art, and literature. After her death, her mother stepped into her place – substituting judg-ment and cruelty for tedium and offensiveness. It was too much to bear. Jeannine realized she had to find a sanctuary, or surrender her life to the cruel Princess. She opted for a savior, and soon found it.

Jeannine became a liar - a maze within a maze within a maze, her inner-most self a steel cell that no one could enter. Perhaps the only thing inside that cell was a thin, scared, little girl - but that was even more reason to seal the metal, and allow no light. An unwary traveler would be lost within the mazes, and never come close to the truth within. No one would ever penetrate to the sanctum, no one was worthy.

When the Princess - Madame, Mother, Caroline - wanted to go to church, Jeannine was ready early, and chided her mother for being late. When the Princess wanted to leave after the service, Jeannine demanded time to pray in the pew. When the Princess ate little, to fit better into old gowns, Jeannine ate even less, and teased her mother for her piggishness. When asked to play the pianoforte, she would not stop until the early morning, citing the need for practice. Every absurd expectation of the Princess was turned around and pointed against their maker.

The Princess soon spent less and less time with her daughter, although she didn't realize it. When Jeannine was young, the Princess was her torturer, although she did not hate her. As Jeannine became older and cleverer, the Princess had to become less cruel, for she was unknowingly manipulated into doing so - but she also, subconsciously, began to hate her daughter.

Then, something else happened.

Men ignored Jeannine, as if she was invisible. She noticed this because men always seemed to be in the house. Mother, the Princess, was never happy with their expansive five-story townhome, and some kind of improvement was continually underway. Jeannine found herself fascinated with the subsequent tradesmen who would come into their home. She wanted to throw them in a room and never let them out until they answered every question she could possibly ask. She was enthralled with the world of men, and wished to know everything about it, even its darkest, most naked secrets.

Then the men began to be interested in Jeannine. It was innocent, at first. She had simply become a person in their eyes. By the time she was fifteen, they were more interested in her than she was in them. Just after her sixteenth birthday, they simply stared at her, as if the sight was such a privilege they had to stop everything to savor the moment.

Jeannine pondered this, when she was supposed to be praying or going to sleep. There could be only one answer: she might be attractive, like her mother.

But she underestimated herself. Jeannine had grown into a legendary beauty.

The quality of a woman's mien is not easily quantified. She can be *élégant* - sophisticated, her looks reminiscent of high social standing, wealth and power. She can be *frappante* - possessed of an interesting and unique look, standing apart to even the most jaded observer. She can be *sensuelle* - sultry, sexually stimulating, sometimes independent, or at odds, with other standards of winsomeness. She can be *en vogue* - the *ne plus ultra* of how a lady should look for her time and place. Yet, there are women who possess none of those qualities in good measure – yet are utterly magnetic. Of course, the Gaul would never let such a quality go undefined, and they called this attribute *je ne sais quoi*, the undefinable, powerful *something* that lit one from the root.

Jeannine

A woman rarely had all of these words written on her face and body, and perhaps had different ones written on each. But Jeannine had them all in good measure, face and body, hair and skin. In addition, her sense of color and style was impeccable, her grace and carry unmatched. This *savoir-faire* reacted with her attractive qualities like a skilled cut to a gem.

When the staircase was to be remodeled, Jeannine carefully constructed a plan to test the power and strength of her beauty. She needed a man who was happily married. He could not immediately be struck by her appearance. He must be honorable and handsome - at least somewhat experienced in the attention of women. She wanted a hard nut to crack, so to speak.

She entered the foyer where the work was being done. She took a place off to one side, and said nothing until she was noticed, "Good morning, gentlemen," she said brightly, but with strength. A chorus answered her.

The foreman, Monsieur Eugène, spoke gently, "Can I help you, Mademoiselle?"

"Not at all, Monsieur. I am simply fascinated by the practical arts, and would like to observe from a distance, and out of your way." She had not moved from her spot since entering. She was away from everything, and she knew that by not moving, she was implying that her spot would be where she stayed. Subconsciously, the foreman would understand this.

He smiled, "As you will, Mademoiselle."

And then she willed herself to stand in that very spot, saying nothing, day after day. After a while, they became comfortable with her presence.

As soon as they did, she advanced.

She knew the routine of their work and would never get in their way. They could go about their business, slinging equipment and moving as they would, without any fear of hitting her, or bumping into her. They began to trust her ability to move amongst them.

As soon as they did, she advanced.

As they began to speak freely around her, she gained knowledge of everyone in the entire crew - their names, history, and family connections. She knew which of the men would be easy for her to manipulate, and who would be difficult.

Her choice came down to the marble layer - Marcel Courbet, a handsome, quiet man in his twenties who had a pretty wife and an infant child. They both sometimes delivered lunch to him when he worked. Jeannine started her machinations with a feather's touch. She began to converse with him, but only on the most superficial of levels regarding his work. After a while, she would punctuate her speech with physical contact - but kept everything else in shallow waters. She had established physical intimacy in a way that he did not perceive as threatening or untoward.

Then she advanced.

"Marcel, you are so talented. If only you knew how much you truly deserved in life, with such skill in your fingers." It was only about his work, at first. "Marcel, you are so strong. It adds so much to your appearance, and your bearing." If she said such a thing a minute earlier, it would have raised his defenses, been considered inappropriate. But her timing was perfect. She had gained intimacy.

Two days after that, the apocalypse began.

At one hour past midnight, Marcel's young wife came to their door, completely bereft of reason, holding her baby in one hand and a blade in the other. She pounded at the door with the butt of the knife, screaming at the top of her lungs, "Where is the little blonde *prostituée à bas prix*! Come out of your *bordel*, *salope*! Come meet the wife of the man you seduced! Come meet my little steel *quéquette*, you *putain*!"

Jeannine heard her through the window, and hid herself against the wall.

This was not part of her plan.

Beneath the anger in the voice of Marcel's wife was hurt, panic, and fear. Jeannine felt sick. She was overwhelmed with feelings of guilt and shame. It had been nothing but a child's game, a test with results only she would know - her actions weren't supposed to have consequences. She honestly did not think she had the power to affect anything of import. She could hear the servants trying to calm the young wife and mother, then the voice of her father. Suddenly, everything went from a scream to a conversation, and Jeannine could hear no more of it. She heard an occasional tortured sob from Marcel's wife, and the high points of words, but nothing more.

Her mother soon burst into her room, "What have you done?" Jeannine did not answer - she was the scared little girl again. Her mother seemed taller, more vicious and frightening. "Your life, as you know it, is over," she said. Her mother left and slammed the door, and Jeannine could hear her footsteps echo across the hall.

It took the better part of an hour to calm Marcel's wife, and she finally left the street. Soon after, Jeannine was summoned to her father's study. Her mother was standing in the corner, shaking as if from cold - but it was warm in the room. Sitting in his desk chair, her father looked tired. "I have been summoned," Jeannine said meekly.

"Are you still a virgin?" asked her mother through clenched teeth.

Jeannine didn't know what to say. "I-I don't know. How does one not become a virgin?"

"What?" sputtered her mother in horror.

"Caroline," said her father tiredly.

Her mother turned to her and spoke softly, "The entire street knows our shame. You have embarrassed this family. You have made a mockery of us."

"I didn't do anything, Maman."

"You will address me as Madame."

"Yes, Madame."

Her father rubbed his eyes, "What exactly happened, Jeannine?"

"Nothing. I like to watch the workmen make the stairs."

"Nonsense!" barked her mother, "She deliberately set out to seduce Monsieur Courbet. How else could this have happened?"

"I don't think she intended to do anything untoward, Caroline."

"What do you know? She is evil. She is the devil's creature. Her heart pumps snake's venom instead of blood."

"Don't be ridiculous."

"I demand that her freedom be restricted. I demand that she be scourged through prayer and contemplation. This cannot stand."

Her father sighed, "Jeannine, do you have anything to say?"

Truthfully, Jeannine felt wretched. She sat in a chair, and found herself crying. "Can I go to work with you, Papa? I won't be a bother, I swear."

"Do not be fooled," said her mother, "Her heart is dark. If we do not stop this now, she will become exactly what she has been accused of being. She is not innocent."

"What do you propose?" her father asked, beaten.

"When there are workmen in the house, she is retired to the family chapel for prayer and contemplation."

"The workmen perform their duties according to the light," her father said.

"Then she will contemplate God in the daylight."

It suddenly occurred to Jeannine that her mother wanted to lock her up for at least twelve hours a day in the windowless family chapel. She felt a rising panic, "Please Papa, do not do this to me!"

Her mother stepped forward, "You know why this must be done. Beauty is the ultimate corrupting power a woman can possess. Its only antidote is a kind nature, for then she assumes the world is kind to her out of altruism, never suspecting her experience is different from anyone else. But Jeannine is not defined by kindness, rather by cleverness, and she recognized her power just as it raised its head."

Jeannine thought about her mother's words. It almost seemed as if her mother was frightened by her beauty. Jeannine suspected her test had provided unexpectedly positive results, at least in its conclusions.

Her father held up a finger, "She will pray in the chapel, for a time."

Jeannine held her breath, hoping her father's next sentence would start with the word *but*.

"We will find her a companion," he continued, "of pure and moral character, who will be her friend and shadow. I think that will solve much of this. She is bored and lonely."

"I demand her companion be a Protestant."

"If a good Protestant girl is available, she will be Protestant."

And then her mother stormed from the room. Jeannine smiled at her father, but he shook his head, "Go now," he said sternly, "and act in a more mature fashion, and with modesty - for the sake of your family's honor."

Jeannine lowered her head, and went to her room, utterly chastised.

***

Two days later, when Monsieur's valet announced the presence of the workmen - minus Marcel, who had been dismissed quietly and with coin - Jeannine was escorted by her mother inside the fourth-story family chapel. The Princess had such an exultant glare on her face that Jeannine was taken aback. Madame almost looked as if she was going to laugh as she shut the door. Jeannine reached out a hand. "Wait!"

The door stopped. Caroline's face was half-obscured. Her forehead came to rest upon its edge, and her eyes raised to look at her daughter. A smile spread over her face. She looked like nothing but a child half-way through a prank.

"Mother, what if I find myself the victim of nature's call?"

"Hmmm," smiled her mother, "I placed a *Bourdaloue* inside the chapel last night. And a pitcher of water."

"May I come down for *déjeuner*?"

"No. I will bring your food." And with that, the Princess shut the door.

Jeannine sat on a pew and wept. She wept until she realized her mother had opened the door again, and was staring at her with an ecstatic smirk upon her face. With the same smile, her mother exited, and shut the door once again. For some reason, this made Jeannine feel better, not worse. Her status as a prisoner was no longer a punishment, it was a competition. She could not let the Princess win.

First things first. She had to scout the chapel, and see what her new realm entailed.

The family chapel was an odd place. It was windowless, and quite large, very large for a townhome chapel - almost fifteen-hundred square-feet. There were lanterns, lamps and candles, but not enough to make the room bright.

She took a lamp from a mirrored alcove and explored further. Multiple rows of pews lined the floor facing a large altar - holding only a three-foot silver cross that was hopelessly tarnished and grey, resting on an ornate marble dais. To be in such a state, the servants must have been ordered not to touch it. The room was painted in strange colors - blue with black trim. Everything seemed strange, now that she had time to think about it. The chapel had a secret, of that she was utterly assured. The punishment - that became a competition - was now an adventure.

The first clue was the altar dais. The lower marble of the block was white with swirled black veins. The next, smaller block was red with brown veins.

Inlaid into the red marble was a circular labyrinth made of bronze. The end of the labyrinth was not seen, for the altar - a nearly chest-high rectangular block of stone - was placed right in the center of it.

Jeannine knew of the labyrinth, for it was a well-known symbol. Taken from Greek legend, the labyrinth became an emblem of Christian allegory in the Middle Ages. A labyrinth was not a maze, nor a puzzle. A maze was precisely a puzzle - one can get lost in a maze, because there are false directions and misleading paths. A labyrinth looked like a maze, with its circular winds and twists, but there was only one way to go and one destination – the center - the end of the labyrinth. It was a metaphor for life, for all of life's twists and turns led only, and inexorably, to death and God. The most famous labyrinth was at Our Lady of Chartres Cathedral, and was nearly six-hundred years old. It was circular, gigantic, almost forty-feet in diameter. The curving, looping paths led to its center: a six-lobed rosette, an ancient symbol from the east, used to portray the nature of God in Sumerian, Babylonian and Jewish art. Set in the ground, one was meant to slowly walk a labyrinth, pausing often to pray. It was a form of meditation, akin to a rosary.

It was odd to spend such time inlaying a bronze labyrinth into marble, only to hide most of the affair under an altar. Jeannine sat down by the labyrinth and studied it more closely. The bronze was not flush with the surface of the marble. It was rather like a track. It was a half-inch bronze groove in the marble, curving back and forth with the design.

Part of the groove was worn. The outermost circle of the labyrinth showed scrapes and scratches, extreme wear, as if it were the track for a wheel. Jeannine's heart began to beat, for she realized that was exactly its purpose. The labyrinth had been placed in the marble for only one reason - to disguise a track for a wheel. The altar must move, she decided, it must swivel to reveal some kind of hidden place.

She took hold of the stone altar and gave it a strong push, then pulled it. It might have been her imagination, but it seemed to budge a little both ways, as if meant to move, but locked down.

And if it was meant to move, there had to be some kind of secret way to unlock it so the altar could wheel out over the track.

Her first choice was the crucifix on top of the altar. She grabbed it and pulled. The cross moved like a lever with the sound of a mechanical *click,* and the clanking of a chain belt. With rising excitement, she pushed the altar - and it swiveled easily, exposing a dark rectangular hole.

Jeannine took up her lamp and moved it to the darkness - and revealed stone stairs going down. They were dusty, having neither been used nor cleaned for quite some time. Jeannine immediately rushed to extinguish the other lights in the chapel, so it would be dark if her mother unexpectedly returned. If such a thing did happen, Jeannine thought she might hear the door, and be able to quickly return to move the altar back and hide her discovery.

After the room was dark except for her own light, she descended the staircase. On its circular walls there were plenty of alcoves holding lamps and lanterns, but she did not dare light them. The plaster had odd symbols in white and gold randomly patterned upon it. There were curved swords, always pointed to the right. Crescent moons, always pointed down. Double-headed eagles, crosses with superimposed triangles and swords. There were crosses inside seven pointed stars, also compass and rulers, the letter G, and odd triangles pointed upwards with an upward curve in the lower side. Skulls and crossbones abounded, crosses tucked in crowns, compass and ruler superimposed on a book under a halo. Whenever the cross was painted alone, it was always the flat *croix pattée* that the Templars and Teutonic knights used in their heraldry. None of these symbols were from any church, Protestant or Catholic, that Jeannine had ever attended.

The stairs ended in a narrow, empty hallway, going east. It was thin enough to be set in an interior wall and not be noticed - and as testament Jeannine had never noticed anything untoward in her house at all, much less evidence of a secret hallway between the walls. By her calculation, in less than thirty feet, the hallway would simply end, being then at the brick property line of the townhouse. She walked its length, and, to her surprise, the hallway was perhaps ten feet longer than it should have been, and ended at another staircase going down. That meant the stairs were in the townhouse next to theirs, which was the second home of a gentleman who lived in another city - at least as far as she knew.

Jeannine descended. The stairs ended at a magnificent, gabled double-door that proved to be locked. There was a thin crack between the doors, very thin, but wide enough for her to see the doors were barred from the inside with a mahogany plank. If there was no latch on the wood bar, she might be able to get the doors open if she could find something very sturdy and thin. She retraced her steps to the chapel and returned everything to its prior state.

When the Princess delivered her meal, Jeannine was found praying in a pew. Her mother placed the tray down and left. Jeannine ate the meager lunch, then hid the tray on the stairs under the altar.

After her daily jail sentence was commuted for the night, she found the atmosphere at dinner to be awkward. Her parents did not really converse with her, and she said nothing. They looked as if they were expecting her to speak, most likely to beg for reprieve, but she did not. They ate in peace, then Jeannine went to her room.

That night, Jeannine asked a servant to bring her a pair of heavy scissors. The next morning, she hid the scissors in her dress. As soon as she was sequestered inside the chapel, Jeannine cut the thin, metal center from the tray she had hid under the altar. It proved to be thin enough to slide between the mahogany double-doors and sturdy enough to move the wooden plank from its holders.

She slowly opened the doors. The room must have been vast, for when she held up the lamp, there was only total darkness in every direction. Rather than explore, she found a way to shut the double-doors, and replace the mahogany bar from without, using the metal tool she had constructed from the tray. She practiced over and over again, until she could do it quickly. Subterfuge had to be her first priority.

She was praying in the chapel, when her mother entered with lunch. Jeannine prayed for an additional quarter hour, ate, then went downstairs again to the huge, dark room.

This time, she threw caution to the wind. She decided to light all the lamps in the huge room. It couldn't be for long, or else someone might notice an unexplained drop in the level of the oil. She would light them all, then look around, letting the nature of the room surprise her.

And it did.

The room could only be described as a temple. It was gigantic, ancient Egyptian in style, with hieroglyphs and wall paintings aplenty. The floor was a checkerboard of purple and black marble. There was a dais at the far end of the room, holding thrones of various sizes at various levels. Smaller chairs were in two rows around the edges of the room. A stone altar presided in the center of the chamber, ringed by four tall pricket candle holders. The ceiling held an oval inlay, spanning the length of the room, decorated as the night sky with a ceremonial star radiating light. The strange symbols were here as well, although now in gold inlay, and not gold paint, and included zodiac symbology as well. Jeannine was overwhelmed by the mystery. This place was nothing if not totally exotic, and perhaps even a bit eldritch and evil.

There were four doors leading to other rooms - a library; a soundproofed antechamber, complete with hoods, blindfolds and padded earmuffs; a records hall; and a storage room holding a banquet table, silver dining ware, and more chairs. A newer door had been made into the east antechamber wall. That particular door led into the townhouse proper. She took the chance, and explored the townhouse as well.

She quickly realized that no one lived here - the story of the out-of-town nobleman was a simple ruse. There were bedrooms aplenty, but all were akin to guest bedrooms. There were huge sitting rooms with comfortable chairs and well-stocked bars. All was very secure with thick, locking doors separating every chamber. All were unlocked and open, except the front door. Everything was clean, perfectly clean, and ordered - and ready for the next meeting to take place in the wizard's temple upstairs.

The library and the records room gave her all the clues she needed to figure out the mystery.

This was a masonic temple, used by the Freemasons. When Nantes was less liberal, the temple was accessed through the secret stairs in the Cœurfroid chapel. Now they didn't bother, and came in through the front door, and the newly-made antechamber entrance.

The Cœurfroids were Masons, and had been for decades.

The next meeting was in three days. Her father hadn't used the chapel entrance in years - he wouldn't even think to use it, knowing it was not only secret, but barred from the inside.

Jeannine came up with a simple plan.

Her father would leave his front door, walk the twenty paces east to the ruse townhouse, and open the front door for trusted servants to prepare for the meeting. Meanwhile, Jeannine would retire to the chapel to pray, enter the ruse townhouse via the secret staircase under the altar, and make her way to the mahogany double-doors. It would all have to be performed in total darkness to hide her presence. She would hopefully be able to eavesdrop on the meeting.

At dinner that night, Jeannine asked if she could pray in the chapel once more before retiring. Her parents were somewhat flummoxed at why she would want to spend even more time in what was effectively her jail cell.

"I have come to enjoy my prayers, and my reading of scripture. I would only ask for your indulgence."

And, of course, what could they say? One does not punish a girl by not allowing her to pray.

Less than an hour later, Jeannine was through the secret stairs and positioned behind the mahogany doors.

She soon heard footsteps shuffling into place. Suddenly, a booming voice, "Brother Tyler, your place in the Lodge?"

Another voice answered, "Without the inner door."

"Your duty there?"

"To keep off all cowans and eavesdroppers, and not to pass or repass any, but such as are duly qualified, and have the Worshipful Master's permission."

"You will receive the implement of your office." She heard footsteps, and the sound of a bared sword leaving a scabbard - which set her heart to flutter. "Repair to your post, and be in the active discharge of your duty."

Suddenly she heard and felt the antechamber doors being shut and sealed. The meeting had begun.

"Brother Junior Deacon, the first and constant care of Masons when convened?"

"To see that the Lodge is duly tyled."

"You will attend to that part of your duty, and inform the Tyler that we are about to open a Lodge of Entered Apprentice Masons, and direct him to tyle accordingly."

Jeannine had no idea what any of it meant. But it was grand, like the casting of a great, dark spell. The voices reinforced the image - they were bold, loud, and sing-song in rhythm. There was a practiced expertise to all of it.

She very much wanted to be a part of it.

The rites soon changed into some kind of initiation. "Do you seriously declare on your honor that, unbiased by the improper solicitation of friends against your own inclination, and uninfluenced by mercenary or other unworthy motive, you freely and voluntarily offer yourself a Candidate for the mysteries and privileges of Freemasonry?"

Jeannine said the words before the candidate did, "I do." And there was more, so much more. Vows of secrecy and fidelity. Promises of virtue and service.

Then something else.

"Having been kept for a considerable time in a state of darkness, what, in your present situation, is the predominant wish of your heart?"

Jeannine blurted the answer without thinking, "Light."

A moment later, a voice, "Light."

More words, some rose above the others in her mind with their beauty or majesty. There were ornate movements she could not see, secret handshakes, secret words.

"Brother Le Brevet, by the Worshipful Master's command, I invest you with the distinguishing badge of a Mason. It is more ancient than the Golden Fleece or Roman Eagle, more honorable than the Garter or any other Order in existence, being the badge of innocence and the bond of friendship. I strongly exhort you ever to wear and consider it as such; and further inform you that if you never disgrace that badge - it will never disgrace you."

After the rites, there followed a grand meal and a great debate.

"If the nature of man is good, are then our baser impulses good? We are told as Christians that our impulses are evil."

"The youth must be indoctrinated with virtue."

"He cites Cicero! Are we then Romans?"

"The mason is not a Roman, nor a Christian. He is Rousseauian. We are of the Nature God."

"So, what does the Nature God say of this?"

"He has danced off like Dionysius, and left us to our own devices. God is gone. Dead or alive, who knows? There is no more of the supernatural left in our universe."

"Our impulses, Brother. That is the question. Are they good or evil? Is man capable of being virtuous without training and control?"

And then her father answered, "If man is basically good, meaning good in his most basic form, it follows that our most instinctual impulses must also be good, because they are the most basic intellectual reactions we possess. What we think, what we want, what we need, now defines what is good. Virtue is the impulse to support what is right. Therefore, virtue is now defined as the desire to support a state which protects individuals as they pursue their instinctual needs. An individual's needs and desires now solely define what is good."

Jeannine quietly wept, hearing her father's beautiful words. She was not the evil and worthless girl of her mother's imaginings. She was her father's daughter. She was a Mason. She was good. What she thought, what she wanted, and what she needed were good - and she vowed, right then, to always live her life based upon that knowledge. She would be true to herself, and the needs of her soul.

The Freemasons may have been secret, but she was even more secret - for she was a secret Freemason, unknown even to them.

She broke into the lodge storeroom the next day, and stole her badge.

***

Thanks to Father Aurélien, the sisters of Saint-Clément Convent in eastern Nantes were kind enough to give room and board to Estelle until she found a position. The walk from the convent to the townhouse was not so terrible after the rigors of country life. The interview was for a position that was far from perfect - they wanted a Protestant, and Estelle was Catholic - and she did not expect much, but she did not wish to be a burden on the kind sisters any longer than necessary.

Estelle had witnessed the hustle and bustle of Nantes before, but it astounded her once again. Water was everywhere, meaning docks were everywhere, indicating ships and cargo and sailors and carts were everywhere. But the townhome was away from it all, in a very rich and handsome neighborhood in the city center. She knocked on the front door and was admitted. The inside of the home was even more magnificent than the outside. The servants quietly hustled in and out of the room and adjoining hallways. They gave her sour looks, which did not bode well. Estelle was determined to just be herself, to put on no airs and be honest and forthright. Soon Madame came down from the stairs, "You are Estelle Guerrier?" she asked.

"I am, Madame. It is a pleasure to make your acquaintance," Estelle said in reply, with a curtsey and a smile.

Madame looked her over, "You are quite plain."

"I am as God made me."

"Your clothes are patched."

"I'm afraid the alternative was to wear them torn."

"You obviously cannot sew then."

"I can. Unfortunately, fabric is beyond my means. I suppose I could make linen, if I made a loom first. But flax takes ever so long to turn into fabric."

"I see."

Estelle swallowed her impulse to say something rude. This woman was insufferable, but that didn't mean Estelle had to sacrifice herself on the altar of Madame's unpleasantness. Instead, she simply smiled. They both stared at each other, Madame with her look of arrogant judgement, Estelle with her tired smile. But soon Estelle became irritated with the game, "Should I meet my potential companion, Madame?" she offered, as pleasantly as she could.

The woman nearly jumped, as if startled. She nodded, looked right and left, made to go left, then changed her mind, and headed right and disappeared. Soon a servant girl appeared from the same hallway, and bounded up the stairs.

Estelle found all of this quite odd, but she determined to forgive all. She only imagined what someone would have thought if they had visited her in Saint-Florent-le-Vieil and met Papa, had they not a kind heart.

Jeannine came down the stairs. For Estelle, time seemed to stop. Jeannine was so attractive that her presence was overwhelming. Estelle laughed, "My goodness, you are lovely, Mademoiselle. You are a princess of angels!"

The young lady looked as if someone slapped her. She put a gentle hand on Estelle's arm, "Please do not call me that."

"Pardon me, Mademoiselle. I don't understand."

"Please do not call me princess."

"Oh, of course not. I did not mean to offend. I was simply shocked. I have never been affected by a woman's beauty - but I found myself struck as you moved down the stairs. I suppose it is just as rude to comment on such a thing, as any other thing one should keep to themselves. Please forgive me. Let us start over. I am Estelle Guerrier," Estelle said with another curtsey and a smile.

Jeannine bowed, and spoke sincerely, "I am Jeannine Cœurfroid. I am so-," but she did not finish the thought. Instead she started a new one in a far more neutral tone, "Tell me about yourself," and she took Estelle by the arm and led her through the house.

Estelle wondered why Jeannine stopped herself from revealing a thought, but she answered, "I am from Saint-Domingue. I am legally white. I love and serve God, or try to, as best I can. I enjoy everything to do with the raising of plants and animals. I love to read. My father is a policeman, my brother attends university school in Grenoble, and the rest of my family has attained their eternal rest."

"What do you mean by legally white?"

"I am one-sixteenth black."

"Black, as in black from Africa?"

"Yes, Mademoiselle."

"Please call me Jeannine."

"Very well, Jeannine. Please call me Estelle."

"I will. I have never met someone who is black, one-sixteenth or otherwise. Does it mean anything?"

"I do not get sick in the tropics, as many whites do. But some Europeans survive quite well in Saint-Domingue, so I suppose it doesn't mean much at all."

"How interesting." Jeannine thought it was time to test Estelle, just as methodically as she had tested her own beauty. She cocked her head coyly and smiled, "I suppose my mother was as cross as ever to you."

Estelle was off-put. Jeannine seemed to change expression rather willfully, and not subconsciously according to her emotion. "In her way, I suppose Madame evaluated me as a potential companion."

To Jeannine, Estelle reeked of caution, obviously deeply uncomfortable speaking in a negative fashion regarding anyone, even the abominable Princess. This was a good sign. She was a bearer of secrets. Now for the second test. Jeannine gave Estelle a wicked grin, "Are there very many handsome young men where you come from?"

"In Saint-Domingue? I-I don't know. I have not thought about it overly."

It was not the perfect answer. Estelle was discreet, which was good, but could not be a reliable co-conspirator in misbehavior. Perhaps perfidiousness was too tall an order for a companion capable of passing her parent's muster. Boring, however, would not do at all. "Do you have any other interests?"

"I love philosophy, especially Johann Georg Hamann."

Jeannine had never heard of him but nodded enthusiastically.

Estelle continued, "To be honest, I thirst for activity. Any activity, as long as it is not cruel or immoral. We must experience creation. It is there for a purpose, it is a kind of food for the heart and soul."

Things were looking up for Jeannine. "What is your favorite opera?"

Estelle's face lit, "Do you go to the opera?"

"The Théâtre Graslin nears completion. I intend to see everything it offers, opera or otherwise, at least fifty times each."

Estelle smiled, "I'm sorry Jeannine, I would never see the same play or opera more than forty-nine times. I must put my foot down."

A sense of humor! Jeannine had seen enough. She would do. "Estelle, could I lead you back to the front door, in order that you should wait for me? I would speak to my mother regarding your employment."

"As you please, Jeannine." Estelle had no idea whether she made a positive impression. As Estelle was led back to the foyer and left alone, she found herself thinking about her new acquaintance. When speaking, Jeannine was artificial, nearly expressionless - unless the expression was artfully crafted. Jeannine might have been honest and kind under it all, but her manner was off-putting. Estelle was worried about spending time with such a person, but decided that giving love and friendship to anyone was never to be regretted, being ultimately expressions of her love for God. If she was to be Jeannine's companion, she would be her true friend, and perhaps Jeannine would change, as Solange had changed.

Jeannine stormed into Madame's sitting room. "I will not abide that freckled peasant girl one minute longer," she hissed at her mother.

Caroline stood, "Oh yes, you will."

"She is part black. Did you know that?"

"She is your new companion. She will be with you night and day. However much I do not trust you, I trust her. She will put a stop to your wickedness, whether you like it or not."

Jeannine, satisfied at her victory, sought another and changed tack, "I refuse to be seen with her! She is dressed in tattered rags!"

"Then you will take her shopping for clothes and purchase for her a new season of wardrobe, and buy nothing for yourself!"

Jeannine could think of no other action more pleasing in which to spend her day. Her face tightened with anger, and she turned, and stormed out of the room.

Her mother called after her, "I am summoning a coach! Prepare yourself!"

Estelle waited patiently in the foyer. Suddenly, Jeannine burst into the room with an ecstatic smile on her face, like a child seeing a kitten for the first time. "Estelle!" she exclaimed, "You are my new companion! We are to spend every waking minute together!" Jeannine's happiness was true and real.

Estelle smiled at her. "Bless your heart, Jeannine! I am flattered by your joy! We will be like sisters, you and I."

"Yes! Yes, Estelle! And we are going to start by going shopping! I am buying you a new wardrobe!"

"Oh, I couldn't possibly allow that."

"No! No! You can and you will! You will allow me to be generous when it pleases me. You honor and love me with your acquiescence. You must understand: to the Cœurfroid, I am giving you nothing more precious than a mud-pie, and you will take it."

"I don't know what to say, except that I am a bit uncomfortable with this unexpected generosity," said Estelle with a smile, softening her words.

"We cannot be sisters unless you allow me to honor you, or else the entire world will think I am an evil, miserly sister - and I am no such thing."

"Very well then," Estelle said, amused.

"Then let us go!" and, with that, Jeannine pulled Estelle out the door to the waiting coach. She raised her face to the sun and laughed at the sky. Estelle wondered at her. She appeared to be the most innocent creature in the whole world - occasionally possessed by the most cleverly hidden imp.

1832

Jake

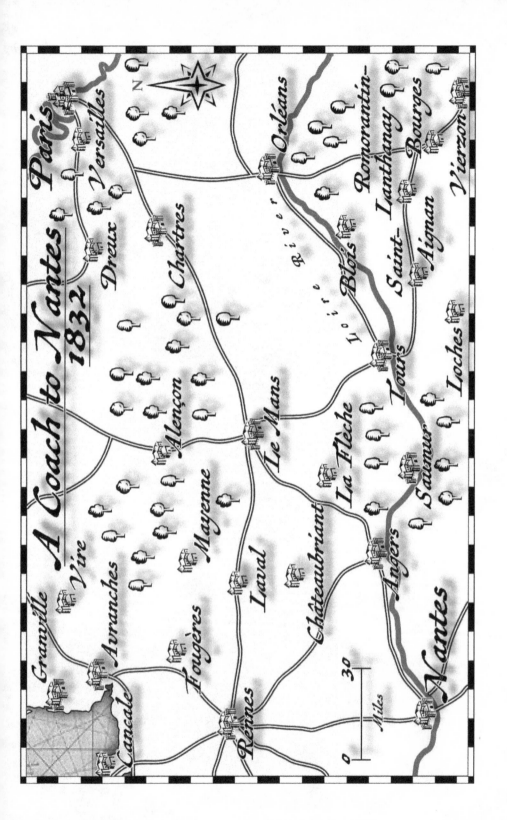

Chapter 17

Jake had enough of horses and carriages to last a lifetime.

He had arrived in Nantes on the morning of the fifth day of travel. The coach had traveled twenty hours a day with drivers, postilions and horses changed at regular intervals. Jake, unfortunately, was naturally stuck for the entirety of the trip. It was, however, a beautiful one. The area around Paris was unending fields of wheat, broken only by the occasional copse of trees, or cluster of stone homes and barns. This slowly gave way, as one traveled west, to the rolling hills and bocage of the Loire Valley. It was handsome and fair, with a mild breeze, and not a cloud in the sky. The architecture was quite distinct, as the Italian Renaissance came early to the Loire valley. Leonardo da Vinci had even spent his last years on the Loire, and died within sight of the river. Stone châteaux built in the Italian styles of the late 1500's dotted the land all the way to Nantes. Little inn towns had developed at the rural stage stops, but Jake determined that walking at the stops was far more important than eating. Sheer boredom had acquainted him with the captain's log until he knew it practically by heart, and he had even taken to reading the Bible the director had given him, at least the parts with bloodshed and battle.

The young slave girl found by Captain Fabre of the intrepid *Dauphin Royal* was very obviously Irish, although it seemed no one amongst his command had the cultural perspective to realize it. Jake knew that there was a language of Ireland, but the Irish of America rarely spoke it. In fact, all of them came to America speaking English, albeit with a motley handful of accents. Admittedly, they were mostly of English and Scottish stock, called Scots-Irish, or Orange Irish after King William of Orange. This Catholic Irish slave girl must have been from somewhere remote indeed. Deep in Jake's memory, he remembered that the west of Ireland, especially the west and north, were as wild and primitive as Comanche plains. So somehow this little Irish girl, from the end of the earth, ended up a slave on a British frigate, then as a guest on a French 74-gun Ship-of-the-Line, and then was dumped in Cap-Français, the old provincial capital of Saint-Domingue, with a priceless necklace around her neck.

Saint-Domingue was now République d'Haïti, and it was nowhere anyone needed or wanted to go. The girl, who was probably Sinead O'Brolin - or O'Broughlin or O'Broglin - was entrusted to an octoroon, whatever that was, named Féroce Guerrier. The name meant *Fierce Warrior* in French and was probably a nickname or some kind of alias.

Jake's presumption was that his next stop, in his quest for the Heirlooms, was probably Cap-Français, which had been renamed Cap-Haïtien after the Haitian revolution, and the massacre of all the whites - or all the French, as the case may be. Jake presumed he'd find out the true proclivity of the Haitian people in regard to his color and nationality soon enough.

But he was now in Nantes, and on his last carriage ride, at least for the nonce. Abutting the river, a gigantic and imposing castle sat surrounded by water at the southeast corner of the city. The city itself was surrounded by high, thick, businesslike walls of stone, although suburbs sprawled out in all directions. The stagecoach road passed through the northeast gate, over moat and through the thick walls.

The coach stopped in the Place d'Oratoire, where Jake hired a cab. The burly, well-dressed driver of the open cabriolet expertly maneuvered him from the coach stop toward the western part of town, and here the city finally began to reveal itself.

Something was not quite right.

Factories and warehouses were ubiquitous. The river was completely bordered by docks and quays. The islands in the Loire nearest the city were carpeted with shipyards. All of the old, wood and plaster Medieval buildings that filled half of Paris were nowhere to be seen here. Buildings of stone abounded, all less than a hundred years-old. Some new source of wealth must have emerged for the city to rebirth itself anew. Only the city walls, the castle and the soaring cathedrals indicated its true age.

But the docks were empty, warehouses composed of grand spaces of air, the factory furnaces cold. People walked aimlessly, as if the original builders of this energetic city suddenly disappeared and were replaced by those who had no idea how to sail, trade or manufacture. It was a populated city of the dead, like well-dressed vagabonds in a kings' necropolis.

Grabbing his attention from the sights, Jake heard a rumbling in the far, far distance. At first, he thought it was thunder from a distant storm. But it was a beautiful day from horizon to horizon, and no such thing was possible. As it continued, he realized it was the sound of war. Cannons, miles away, were firing tremendous volleys. He spoke to the driver, "Where is that coming from?"

The burly driver turned, "From the Vendée, Monsieur. South, across the Loire."

The Vendée!

"Will the fighting come here?"

"I certainly hope not."

"What on earth is going on?"

"When the troubles started in Paris and Lyon, Duchess Caroline of Berry started a war against the King. Her son is Henri, Count of Chambord. He is the rightful king of France, or so they say. He's a Bourbon all right, like the headless Louis of old."

"I see."

"The Vendée is the devil's playground, make no mistake, Monsieur. Whole armies have vanished there without a trace."

The Driver's words left Jake speechless. He finally managed to croak a reply, "Lamarque fought against them."

"At the drop of a starter's hat, the Vendée will rise. They were thorns in the side of the revolution, Napoleon, and now the usurper Louis-Philippe. That is why Caroline chose the Vendée as the place to plant her flag."

"Do your sympathies lie with them, Monsieur?"

"You have never been to Nantes."

"No, I have not."

"The Vendeans laid siege to Nantes. There is no shared sympathy, Monsieur."

The cannon rumbled again. Jake hated the sound. It made him imagine he was there and part of the fighting, undergoing the change, the unnamed change, that happens to a man in combat. Jake, like every soldier in every war, had forced himself to face his own death in order to kill others. He had no idea why there was no word for such a thing in any language he knew. Unless, Jake thought, words like bravery and courage were euphemisms for it.

They came to a massive city gate set in the western wall. The driver turned, "It's not too much further past Porte Saint-Nicholas. The Château Meilleur stands near the abbey, and the Manoir of Jean the Fifth."

Outside the gate, the suburbs continued upward for less than a half mile before farmer's fields, and a smattering of widely-spaced châteaux and religious compounds. The cab headed toward a hilltop dotted with huge Romanesque buildings. The structures were made of a very different kind of stone than the rest of Nantes, or anything else he'd seen in the Loire valley, for that matter. It was dark brown, but shone everywhere with veiny streaks of a metallic, rust-colored mineral. The effect was not unlovely, but it had a more mature and serious look than the cosmopolitan Tuffeau of the Centre-Ville.

The driver pointed at the buildings, "Those two are the Manoir and the abbey. The other four buildings are the Château Meilleur."

The château was then a main house, stables, what was perhaps a servant's quarters, and a newer add-on to the main house, built to match the rest in the curious brown stone, but in the luxurious, more modern, playful Rococo style.

Meilleur, in English, meant *better*. Jake suddenly understood how it got its name: the Meilleur was not only more beautiful and grand than the Manoir, it dwarfed its size. The Meilleur was simply... the *better castle*. As they drove closer, Jake saw that an ornate stone and wrought iron fence encircled the entire hilltop. The fence had impressive arched gates at all intersecting roads. All of them stood open and unmanned.

They passed under the iron arches of the gate, and pulled up to the imposing entrance of the Rococo addition. Wide stairs led to the doors, while huge, curving, balustraded staircases framed the entire château on their way to the second story. The result was resplendent.

"And here we are, Monsieur," said the driver, as he opened Jake's door. Jake exited the cabriolet and strode to the entrance. He lowered the heavy knocker twice.

An older, balding servant opened it, "Good day, Monsieur. How may I help you?"

"My name is Monsieur Loring, and I am here to see your master. I am expected."

"My master? I'm afraid you have the wrong house. There is no master here but me." The Servant saw the Driver unloading Jake's luggage, "Stop that! Stop at once!"

"Monsieur!" Jake said tiredly, "It has been a long journey. Five days over bumpy roads from Paris. I assure you I am at the right place-" Jake stopped short. What if the driver was wrong? "Monsieur, this is the Château Meilleur?"

"That is not its proper name but, yes, it is commonly called the Château Meilleur."

"Then I am Monsieur Loring, and I am here to see Monsieur Tyran."

"*Mister Despot?* Is this some kind of joke?"

Jake was at a loss, then remembered Tyran was an alias.

Monsieur Tyran could very well be playing some kind of mad joke on him. Perhaps this farce was a riddle to be played out. Or maybe Monsieur Tyran was nearby, and sent him here instead of his true location as a precaution. Whatever the case, no one present was responsible for the trouble. Jake calmed and bowed to the man, "Pardon me, Monsieur. If you could but indulge me for a moment.

It has been a long journey, as I said, and there has been some kind of mistake. It has obviously been made by myself or my associates. I humbly apologize."

The Servant nodded, and made to shut the door. Jake put a gentle hand on it, "If I may?"

The Servant stopped his action. "Yes, Monsieur?"

"What is this place? What is the Château Meilleur? I mean, apart from obviously being the grandest house in Nantes."

Jake realized he had said exactly the right thing. The Servant brightened immediately, "Why Monsieur, this must be your first time in the city."

"Indeed."

"The Château Meilleur is the ancestral home of the Traversier family, Monsieur!"

"The same Traversier family from the legends of the Cross of Nantes?"

"The very same!"

"Do they live here now?"

"No, no - only servants, Monsieur. The Trust has never sold the house, and never rented it. The pure line of the Traversier family is extinct, you see."

Jake had an idea, "Fascinating. And you, Monsieur, what is your name?"

"Roquer, if you please."

Jake stared up at the mansion. "There must be tremendous history in this house, Monsieur Roquer. Not just of Traversier, but of Nantes, and France herself."

"Indeed, there is." The Servant narrowed his eyes, "Your pardon, Monsieur, if I could have your name once again?"

"My name is Jacob Esau Loring of Wellesley, Massachusetts. I am recently graduated from Louis-le-Grand and, even more recently, from the barricades of Saint-Antoine and the Conciergerie."

The Servant made a discreet motion in the air.

Jake didn't know what it meant, but he suspected, "I am not a Freemason, Monsieur, but I have been asked to join by Adolphe Crémieux, and I fully intend to do so."

The Servant spoke loudly at the Driver, "Please take Monsieur Loring's belongings to the servant's entrance." He turned back to Jake, "Monsieur Loring, we would be honored to have you as a guest, at least until you are completely sorted out in your arrangements. Please come in."

"Thank you so very much," said Jake as he entered.

If anything, the house was grander on the inside. The foyer was the size of a ballroom and was sumptuously, but sparsely, furnished. The walls were covered with paintings, some dark with great age. Every piece of furniture and decoration matched in style and color, every piece was crafted by a master. The main door was opposite a balustraded double staircase that curved to the second story; which was actually at the height of a third or fourth, the ceilings being so high. The walls were not the brown stone of the exterior, rather textured white Tuffeau limestone, and the floor of smooth Italian Carrara marble. The wall between the two sinewy staircases was dominated by a huge and ancient painting. Other servants, male and female, waited motionlessly behind Roquer.

Jake realized something. If Xavier Traversier wanted the Cross of Nantes to be found, the key to locating it would lie in understanding his motivations. Jake realized this was the headquarters of the search for his secrets - the ultimate resource for his journey.

"Would you like a tour?" offered Roquer.

"That would be wonderful."

Monsieur Roquer turned and, as he moved, spoke to another servant, "Prepare the *Chinoiserie* for a guest, and inform the chef de cuisine we have another for *dîner*." With a curt nod, the other servants disappeared in unison.

Monsieur Roquer crossed to the huge, dominating painting and Jake followed. The ancient canvas was dark in color, tone and shadow, almost morbidly so. It was an angel's view of an older Nantes, the creatures in question habituating the upper part of the canvas. The Loire bled into the ocean to the west, and curved into the city from the east.

Monsieur Roquer gave him a moment to stare then spoke, "It is the work of Jean Cousin the Younger, we believe. It was painted somewhere around the time of the building of the house, so the trip from Paris would have been quite difficult for Jean Cousin the Elder. Their work is nearly indistinguishable, you know."

"So, the painting is from…?"

"From 1576, or thereabouts. The Traversier family was already successful by then, of course."

"When does the Cross of Nantes come into this painting?"

"The Cross of Nantes was finished by 1700. But one cannot understand the Cross of Nantes without understanding the history of Traversier, Monsieur. And I suppose one cannot understand Traversier without understanding the history of Nantes."

"Then I am all listening ears."

Roquer began to walk. "Nantes is the furthest point inland on the Loire deep enough for ocean-going ships. We are at the confluence of the Loire, the Sèvre and the Erdre rivers, and not too far from a handful of others." Monsieur Roquer moved right, into the north wing of the house, and into a three-story library. Jake had never seen so many books in one place in his life, even at Louis-le-Grand. Roquer continued, "The Loire connects us with cities further inland, such as Anger, Saumur, Tours and Orléans. The Loire valley has always been fertile and productive. We eat well when Paris starves."

Monsieur Roquer stopped in front of several ancient framed pieces of parchment, covered in faded Latin, all sealed at the bottom in ribbon and wax. "These are from the twelfth century, but the Traversier family can trace its name in the records of Nantes to the eleventh, when the city was re-inhabited after the Viking occupation. They were successful fishermen and minor traders until the city, along with the rest of the Duchy of Brittany, merged with the Kingdom of France in 1532." Roquer moved further into the library. "At that point, they became proper merchantmen. As Nantes began to grow in size and economy, so too did the legacy of Traversier. By 1576 the original part of this château was completed. We are in the newer addition, completed in 1712."

The Traversier family was extraordinarily wealthy fifty years before the first European settlement in New England. They built an add-on to their mansion before the existence of New Jersey, Georgia, or South Carolina.

When he emerged from the thought, Jake found himself looking at a large portrait. The painted man was stern, even hard-looking. He was large-featured and long-haired. He sported extravagant Van Dyck facial hair and was dressed finely in a black tunic with blue embroidery. Whoever this man was, one could easily tell he didn't suffer fools, he didn't waste time, and he was rich. Monsieur Roquer spoke, "This is a Peter Paul Rubens from 1630. Rubens was in Paris at the time. It was fashionable to travel to Nantes at least once, if one was an artist in Paris. Where there is gold, you will find painters. And back then there was plenty of gold in Nantes."

"Who is the subject, Monsieur?" Jake asked.

"Jules César Traversier, as he was in 1630. He was the first of the family to engage in the slavery and sugar trade. Back then, naval technology was still fairly primitive. It is hard to believe, but the trade was even more dangerous, time-consuming and expensive than it is now."

They went from the library into a series of antechambers and sitting rooms, all bordering a grand, proper ballroom. The tour quickly revealed that the staircase in the foyer was not the only staircase, nor was it the only double staircase. Huge fireplaces proliferated, and the furniture was fit for kings - carved, inlaid, and nary a straight line, but rather made of graceful and impossible curves of wood and metal. Ornate carvings decorated every wall, the hardwood and marble floors were in ornamental patterns. Silk wallpaper adorned the walls, wrapping them like presents for a duchess.

Roquer continued, more interested in history than artifacts, "Slavery is what turned a wealthy family into a dynasty of demigods. The first voyage of Jules César netted a profit of two-hundred thousand livre. The Traversier legacy of status and wealth was born healthy and screaming."

"You are a poet, Monsieur."

"I wish the words were mine. Tours of this house have been given for centuries. Servants have built upon it over the years. I'm afraid my part in the creation of the telling is small."

"Slavery is quite immoral, is it not? Are you quite sanguine about its spiritual implications?"

"No, indeed. The Traversier Trust does not currently engage in slavery, Monsieur. Although with its relegalization, plenty of other merchants in Nantes are guilty of it. Xavier Traversier, the last of them, ordered the practice halted right before he died, although he was a magnificent slaver himself."

"Were they Freemasons, these Traversier?"

"Only the last two."

"I'm shocked that a Freemason would engage in slavery."

"It does seem strange. But Nantes has one god above all others, Monsieur. If one can coax the heavens to rain gold, it is a baptism of forgiveness for all sins. There was no stigma to being a slaver whatsoever. It was legal, regulated and taxed, after the *Code Noir* of 1685. Even the church put its stamp of approval on the enterprise."

"I would have thought that corruption beneath them."

"There was no way of exposing Africans to Christ. Slavery at least could save some souls. At least, that was their reasoning."

"Then they saved by damning. How does any man do such a thing, I wonder? Sell another human being."

Roquer was pensive, "Living in this house, I have thought often about the relationship between evil acts and otherwise good men."

"You indulge in a complex form of philosophical mathematics, Monsieur."

"My pensive meanderings are worthwhile to none, but even birds must pause on a branch to sing."

"May I inquire as to your findings?"

Monsieur Roquer was again thoughtful before he spoke, "Not many of them chose to dwell on the horrors they witnessed. They had a job to perform in order to advance their families. They steeled themselves and they did it. None of them were raving mad, nor were they seemingly evil. In fact, Traversier had an excellent reputation around the world. It didn't matter if you were speaking to the chiefs of Africa, the farmers of Saint-Domingue, or the merchants of Nantes - all would have said the same thing, Monsieur. They were good and honest businessmen with spotless reputations. Although sometimes, at least in the beginning, they were criticized for their lack of religious conviction. But soon the world caught up to them in that regard. For a time, at least. France is now as religious as ever, I suppose."

"They were good *bourgeoise*, these Traversier."

"Indeed, Monsieur. The religious wars raged around Nantes when Jules César was a child. We've all heard stories, but imagine what he saw, being so close in time and space to the atrocities of the Reformation."

"I suppose his moral blindness was cured in this instance by evils close enough to touch."

"Yes, one does pay more attention to one's own backyard, do we not?"

"Indeed, Monsieur Roquer."

They had come full circle to the south end of the first double staircase. Roquer stopped in front of another portrait, also of a man. This one was more recent. The drab tones and simple styles of the Seventeenth Century had given way to the riotous colors and bizarre wigs of the Eighteenth. The man was slim, almost gawky, and wore glasses. He looked intelligent and unwise at the same time, like some kind of misguided academic, or an impotent but benign king. The background was dark, and the foreground was empty, but the man held an object of legend in his palm.

It could be nothing else but the Cross of Nantes.

More time was spent by the painter on the artifact than on the man's face. It was as if he realized the masterpiece demanded the proper obeisance from his own art. The cuts of its crimson gems speckled red stars of light across the canvass and the wounds of the golden Christ upon it. If the real object was even a fifth as glorious as its portrayal, it was fit for the crown of Jupiter. Monsieur Roquer shook his head, "This was done by Gilles Allou in 1703. I realize Gilles Allou is anonymous. But I assure you that back then, he was quite well-respected, and it was thought his work would be remembered."

"The painter was ambivalent toward the man. But not toward the Cross."

"No one, Monsieur - no one - is ambivalent in their feelings regarding the Cross. It was a glorious product of God and man's will in concert, for its materials were the pinnacle of the majesty of creation, and its working performed by the most paramount skills of the mortal craftsman. It was said the crimson diamonds married with the light akin to the ocean as it kissed the setting sun. To see this interplay was to become utterly spellbound, by all accounts. There is nothing that mankind has made that is as valuable for its size and beauty."

"Crimson diamonds?"

"It is a rare and brilliant hue - priceless. Far more spectacular than a ruby or carnelian. There are only twenty-eight specimens so far unearthed by man, and nearly half that number adorn the Cross of Nantes. The cross itself was made of carved stone. Translucent, white Olmec jadeite, to be precise - beyond value in and of itself. The rest, the corpus, settings and adornment, was made of gold."

"Why does he hold it? The man in the painting."

"He is its creator, he commissioned it."

"Was there a specific purpose behind its creation?"

"Yes. In a word - absolution. By his time, no one in the family ever left for Africa, or anywhere else for that matter. The business was left in the hands of their employees. The Traversier were so wealthy that even when it became possible to purchase a nobility, they did no such thing. They could have made themselves princes. But they realized having wealth, and purposefully not becoming noble, made them better than the aristocrats."

"They avoided the empty vanity of titles, for the truer vanity of wealth and fame earned by merit."

"Ironically, the Traversier of this time were precisely titled by birth, and not at all by their own merit."

"The man in the painting, Monsieur?"

"Sevan Gédéon Traversier, then paterfamilias of the clan. He was the only Traversier to ever become religious - although perhaps it is better said he became as religious as his gift of faith allowed. He was also weak-willed, dull and introverted, by all accounts. Sevan enjoyed his wealth and place in society, but he feared for his soul. He devised the perfect plan, at least to Sevan Gédéon, to ensure his salvation but keep his lifestyle intact. He would make a priceless treasure, and send it to the Holy Father, Pope Clement the Eleventh, with the implicit condition that the Holy Father pray for the souls of the Traversier family, especially one Sevan Gédéon, and their dearly departed in Purgatory."

Jake smiled. "Wealth, garnered from the profits of human suffering, used to purchase forgiveness for the venture itself."

"Or so thought Sevan, although his thoughts were more basic and missed the irony entirely. The Cross of Nantes was not large, as you can see. If Clement received the gift he could only wear it with his choir dress cassock. Truthfully, the mission behind the creation of the Cross was perhaps doomed from the start. It was whispered that the artisans knew of Sevan's lack of mental acuity. Counting on his ignorance, they set out to create a masterpiece of platonic perfection, with no effort given to fulfilling its ordered function. If true, they succeeded beyond their wildest imaginings."

"It is lovely. It is actually... disconcertingly lovely."

"You will see better portrayals later." Monsieur Roquer walked up the stairs, and stopped at another framed parchment adorned with seals and ribbons. Jake recognized the crossed key insignia of the Vatican upon it: it was an official correspondence from a Holy Father. "Sevan did not go to Rome himself," continued Roquer, "His salvation, like his business, was entrusted to hired hands, and placed on the Traversier sloop *Caïn le Laboureur*. His agent was the Bishop of Nantes, a family friend and distant relative. With him was the Cross, a large chest of coin, and a parchment note requesting the absolution and prayers of the Father. The Bishop returned two months later with the Cross, a different note - which you see here - and considerably less coin. In a well-wrought hand, as you can see-"

"In beautiful Latin."

"In beautiful Latin, the Pope's secretary politely explained that what Sevan wished from the Holy Father was called an indulgence - and indulgences were no longer given by the church. Pope Clement advised Sevan to go to confession, delve into scripture, and place his trust in God. Through prayer, he would be led to God's Will, and be guided to do the Lord's work. As for the Cross, it was a wonder to behold, and would be a shame to not be available for all of mankind to see. Clement advised Sevan to hang the Cross from the neck of a statue of the

Virgin, at a holy site of his choosing. The Holy Father suggested Chartres, Notre Dame de Paris or perhaps Saint-Denis. Even a cathedral in Nantes would be an admirable choice, and the Cross would not only attract visitors to the city, but increase Marian awareness and devotion."

"Interesting. What was his choice?"

"Sevan did none of those things. He felt belittled by the Pope's reply and didn't understand his reticence in accepting the gift. From his writings, we know he felt guilty and ashamed and didn't know why. He retreated from the church, and kept the Cross in his office desk."

"You're joking, of course."

"In an unlocked drawer, no less. It is said he would often stare at it. He wrote that looking at the Cross never became repetitive or boring - it truly was a wonder to behold." They reached the first landing and Roquer slowed, "At a total cost of three-and-a-half-million livres - at a time when a fully-rigged Dutch sloop could be had for seventeen-thousand livres - it should have been."

That was two hundred ships, give or take.

At the time, a commoner's annual wage was perhaps five-hundred livre.

Jake shook his head, "Did the Cross bankrupt them, Monsieur?"

"The generational wealth of Traversier was not completely exhausted by the commission of the Cross. Remember, the addition to the main house was constructed around this time as well. Sevan could have easily purchased a desk with locked drawers, if that was your thought. Or had one of a dozen previously purchased over the years moved to his office. He never did."

"And the Cross was stolen."

"No, Monsieur. The Cross's time in Sevan's desk passed uneventfully." Roquer chuckled, and continued up the stairs. "Sevan passed away. He was replaced by more apt members of his clan, and the family quickly righted itself. The Cross made its way onto the décolletage of Traversier matrons; knowledge of its original intent forgotten."

Roquer stopped in front of another painting. It was of a stunning woman with a sly smile, wearing the Cross of Nantes around her neck. The artist must have been in love with her, and in love with the Cross. If not, he was certainly spellbound by both. "This was done in 1722 by Charles-Antoine Coypel, the First Painter to King Louis the Fifteenth. Gwenaëlle Traversier first wore the Cross to a ball hosted by the mayor of Nantes, Monsieur René Le Ray de Fumet. She was absolutely resplendent in pink silk, the exact dress portrayed here. This was Coypel's greatest work. He asked that it never be publicly displayed. He painted Madame de Pompadour, the King's mistress, you see. But he was never able to portray Madame with as much finesse. I'm sure you understand."

The Cross easily upstaged the dress. There was something about the white stone that absorbed the light and made it glow. It was becoming more apparent with each viewing, seeing it through the eyes of those who mastered light and color - the stone became alive.

Jake realized Roquer was talking in front of another painting, "-years later she gave it to her sister-in-law, Athénaïs, renowned for her beauty, who proved to the world the Cross looked equally-well paired with white, green and blue. Jean-Baptiste Marie Pierre, 1735. Another First Painter of the King, although not until 1770."

It was a triptych: three identically framed paintings of one woman from the same angle, only the pose, location, light and dresses were different. The light changed not for the woman, but for the crimson diamonds of the Cross. The painter was again in love - and not with her. He had eyes only for the necklace.

Monsieur Roquer was moving further up the stairs. "But in 1749 the Cross made its way into the hands of Philippine Traversier, and its fortunes changed. This is a Jean-Marc Nattier. He was renowned for his portraits of women, but, as you can see, his choices for this work were quite shocking."

In the painting, one could hardly see Philippine's face, for her head was tilted downward. She held the Cross, but only part of it was visible. It was a unique pose for a portrait – nearly heretical in style. A painter could have been sued for such a work.

Monsieur Roquer continued, "Philippine was intelligent, but occasionally possessed of premonitions and feelings from which she could not shake free. In 1754, she had a horrible sense of foreboding that something malevolent was about to be visited upon her husband, Priam Paul. She insisted that he take the Cross for good luck on his next voyage - and so he did."

1754.

Jake's memory stirred. "The beginning of the first war to rage across the entire world. A few previous conflagrations had small skirmishes in far-ranging places, but that one – 1754 - was the beginning of world war in earnest."

"Indeed, Monsieur. Indian Moghuls, Russian Cossacks, Iroquois and Huron braves, Brazilians and Caribes, Swedes, Germans, Yankees, soldiers from across the Spanish, French, British and Portuguese empires, clashing on land and sea. The Seven Year's War - a crushing defeat. We lost Canada, India, everything east of the Mississippi, and our pride. And gained debt, mountains of debt."

"As did Britain," added Jake.

"Indeed!"

"Britain's war debt forced new taxes. New taxes fomented rebellion in the Colonies. France intervened in the conflict to exact her revenge on Britain."

"And, that time, we won." Roquer was intense in his sentiment - even more than a half-century after the fact.

"And America was born of French blood," and Jake bowed to the Frenchman, who bowed back.

"But, in the process, France accrued even more war debt - which, in turn, fomented our own Revolution."

Jake nodded, "1754 changed everything. Our world is still fully a product of that year. Napoleon, German nationalism, American expansion - all of it has its roots in 1754. Mankind has still not recovered from that terrible year, if ever we will."

Roquer continued, "As you probably know, the British started that war with a sneak attack, seizing almost the entire French merchant fleet. Every ship owned by the Traversier family was taken, Priam Paul was captured, and the Cross ripped from his neck by a British captain of savage renown. Priam Paul was stranded somewhere in the islands of the north Atlantic."

They reached the second story - far more intimate but no less exquisite. It was the private quarters of the family, not a space for entertaining. The paintings of lesser-known family members, or lesser known painters, would customarily be placed here.

Roquer smiled and indicated a direction, "Traversier, like France, had experienced setbacks but was not defeated. The wealth of the family sustained them easily through the war. Priam Paul finally returned to joyous celebration in 1758. Although the Cross and the fleet were gone, Priam Paul was possessed of boundless enthusiasm for restoring the family fortunes. He even sired a son, who was born the next year. When the war ended in 1763, much was sold or mortgaged to purchase another ship, and to fill the hold with goods. Philippine had no premonitions of doom for her husband this time. There was nothing but good expectations of their return of wealth and status."

"Interesting."

"It becomes more so, Monsieur. Priam Paul did not return. The ship did not return. No man from the voyage was ever seen again. They vanished as if plucked from the ocean by God himself. The sea is fickle, not to mention some who sail upon it."

Roquer stopped in front of two paintings. To Jake's shock, he recognized the painter - the late Jacque-Louis David, the titan of Neoclassicism. He was the most influential and important artist of his time. Having a David was akin to having a Rembrandt or a Michelangelo. These two paintings should have been in the Louvre - or at least downstairs. They dwarfed everything in the collection, in importance and in value.

"You have two Davids."

"Several more, actually. He was a frequent visitor here, Monsieur David."

But Jake was already lost in the study of the two works. They were both of the same man, and only a few years apart. In the first, he was in his early twenties. One could only see hardness in his visage. His eyes were igneous, his body lean. He was dressed in the plain, but very fine, style of the bourgeois Third Estate, in the years just prior to the Revolution. Jake was reminded of Jules

César, except this more-modern Traversier had a quality which Jules lacked. This man was both hard and desperate: his ambition had an edge, a darkness - a yearning. Jules César had nothing to prove. This man did.

Monsieur Roquer continued, "Priam Paul and Philippine had one child: this man, Xavier. Look closely. Do you see it, Monsieur?" Roquer had a mischievous look on his face, as if he very much wanted Jake to know what he was talking about.

"Yes, he is almost a young Jules César."

Roquer nearly shouted in his excitement, "Indeed! Well done!" he rocked once on his heels and continued, "Xavier was cut from a very old bolt of Traversier cloth, as if Jules had come back from the dead, and created the issue himself. He was hard as stone, smart as drill, and willful. Almost single-handedly, he restored the fortunes of the family to its former glory. By some cosmic accident, the Cross of Nantes even made its last appearance to this man, some say to bless him as the last of his line, before disappearing again - perhaps, this time, forever."

And with that, Roquer took three steps, and stood in front of the second painting of Xavier. Jake was shocked. The man was older in the second painting, but truly not by much. But now he looked utterly spent. His eyes showed the abyss, as if they had stared into hell, and saw the purity of its hatred.

"It is said," Roquer nearly whispered, "Xavier always chose the perfect course of action. I have frequently wondered how someone with this ability could change from the man in the first painting, to him of the second."

In the second canvass, Xavier held the Cross of Nantes. David had purposefully painted the Cross in shadow, as if the sun itself had conspired to rob it of its beauty. But that was David. He would sacrifice his soul, if the loss would but illustrate his theme with slightly more finesse. The Cross was in shadow for a reason. Perhaps David meant its return brought Xavier no joy, no victory.

"Determined as he was," Roquer said, "Xavier died without an heir. He was the last of the true family, male or female. Nantes was rife with relatives and family offshoots, but Xavier was firm in his decision to give them nothing after his death. It was said that when the family fortunes were at their lowest, his relatives turned their back on him. In true Traversier-style defiance of Christian spirit, he gladly returned the favor."

"This painting is haunting."

"David is a master, is he not?"

"Indeed."

"Before he died, Xavier ensured the survival of the business he had rebuilt nearly from nothing."

"And gave its ownership to the future Cross-bearer."

"Yes. Quite an odd request, especially from such a rational man."

"Where do you think the Cross is now, Monsieur?"

"That is a question no one has ever asked me, believe it or not."

"I am stunned, Monsieur."

"No one thinks much of servants. Even the concierge of great empty houses." Roquer stared up at the first David. "He was an interesting man, this Xavier. He traveled the world. He was elected to the Estates-General. He was a soldier, and fought against the Vendée."

The Vendée, again.

Roquer moved to an empty doorway. "But he was unlucky in love. From his history, I suppose I could say, definitively, that no woman now has the Cross. At least, I could if there wasn't one more painting to show you."

Jake moved to the open double doorway. Two handsome, carved, teak doors had been propped open, exposing a magnificent master bedroom. And dominating it all was another David.

The work of Jacque-Louis David would live forever. Long after Jake was gone, crowds would stare at *Oath of the Horatii* or *The Death of Marat*. Napoleon would be forever remembered on David's canvas, painted on his charger at the pass of Saint-Bernard or at his coronation. And yet, with works in the Louvre and in the halls of kings, it was here, in this bedroom, that Jake saw the true masterpiece of the greatest painter France had ever produced. It was of a young woman, still asleep in bed as rays of light illuminated her from the window above. She was covered in bedding and a simple shift. But, between her soft chestnut curls and her freckled chest lay the Cross of Nantes, throwing off a celebration of fire-colored sparks under rays of late morning light. But she - this woman - unlike the subjects in all the paintings to come before, rivaled her prize. She had the aura of an earthly angel, gentle and innocent but mischievous; a personality that easily translated to her sleeping form, either through the power of the subject or the forceful talent of the canvass's creator.

"David," Jake whispered.

"Yes, Monsieur Loring. David."

"She has the Cross."

"Yes."

"When?"

"It was painted in 1788. It is a room downstairs, near the servant's quarters."

Sinead O'Broughlin might have been in her fifties in 1788. The young, freckle-faced girl in the painting may have just had her eighteenth birthday. She was someone entirely different, someone completely unknown. And she wore the Cross in 1788. And was painted by David, in Nantes, at the Château Meilleur.

"Who is she?" Jake nearly whispered.

"We don't know, Monsieur. No one does."

"You can't be serious."

"I'm afraid that I am, Monsieur."

"What is the name of the painting?"

Jake

"It is called *The Mystery of Nantes*."

1832

1786

Xavier

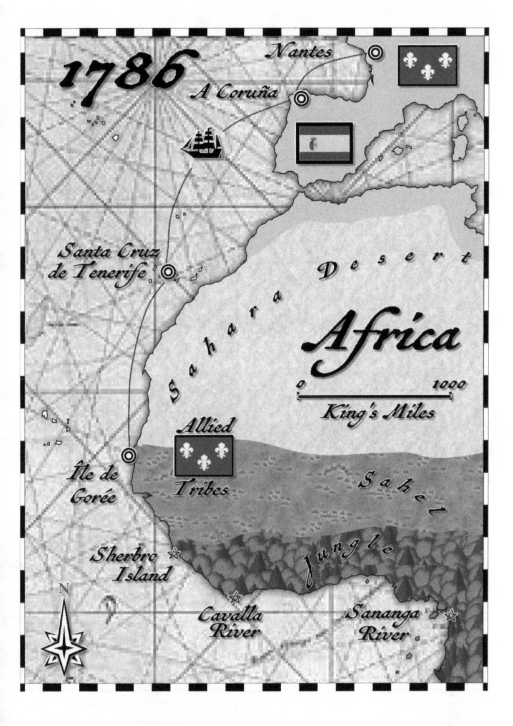

Chapter 18

From the Journal of Priam Paul Traversier:

Traversier has traditionally traded in the northern and western slave lands, as do most French traders. Occasionally, one must travel down the coast of Africa, trading with every tribe one can find, then - if unlucky - continue following the coast east, then south, in order to find enough slaves to fill a boat. It is seldom that one finds oneself in Angola with cargo space, but it can certainly happen.

Africa is hard to understand. Obviously, northern Africa is Mediterranean, her people look akin to Greeks or Arabs, and it might as well have been part of Europe until the coming of Islam. The endless Sahara prevented regular contact with the rest of the continent. In fact, the Sahel (or dry savanna) cultures south of the Sahara have had equal contact with Arabians, who are far to the east but can circumvent the Sahara by sea. Therefore, when we say Africa, we properly mean black Africa - Sub-Saharan and even Sub-Sahel Africa, if you will - not Mediterranean Africa, and not the Arabian and Semitic Africa of the far east and north. In this properly defined place - a vast, diverse, exotic place -

there are simple things we take for granted that are simply not present. We Europeans engage in rapine, torture, slavery, cruelty, and unfairness - but we have values that decry these things, that lead to their condemnation, and, hopefully, their elimination someday, at least amongst Christians. None of these values are present in this Africa, and it is a bizarre and chilling thing. The African engages in rapine, torture, slavery, cruelty, and unfairness as if he were fulfilling the sermon on the mount. There is not a shred of refinement, or civilization. They do not have the wheel. There are no indigenous written languages. What little they have created on their own is invariably primitive, except for the complex rhythms of their music. Life is cheap, meaningless really, and cruelty is so common the African does not have a complaint or argument against it. There is no recognizable moral or ethical structure. The chiefs are only interested in being honored and respected by their fellows, and killing and enslaving their neighbors. They salivate over weapons and ornaments, like vain and deadly peacocks. This Africa is mostly just small tribes that have been at war with each other from time immemorial. The economy, whether that of kingdoms or petty chieftaincies, is wholly based on slave labor. There are elaborate caste systems and good interior trade routes. Empires are scattered few and far between, and are mostly found in the deep interior, and much further east. In the north and western regions, there abounds only chaos. Small tribes constantly war upon one another for slaves, resources and land.

The African has no fascination with the sea, and there are no formal ports or fortifications except what Europeans have built for themselves to protect their interests. The vast majority of the continent's inhabitants have never seen the ocean, and live inland. I have no idea why this is so, it makes no sense to a European, who lives and dies on the waterways. In any case, nearly all whites who have ventured into the jungle to investigate have perished from disease, violence, or other hardship. Tellings of events in the interior is gained only through hearsay. Amongst the dizzying number of tribes and ethnicities, they have an equal multitude of faiths and beliefs. There are two organized religions, one called Vodon and one called Bò. Vodon relies on the conjuring of minor spirits to ask favors of the heavens, through

spirit possession of a medium. Bò has no modern equivalent. It is very African. Simply described as black magic
witchcraft, it is full of curses and dark spells to cause harm.

A form of currency has been adopted throughout the continent, for use between Europeans and Africans, called the
"bar". The bar represents the cost of a bar of iron, much as
the pound represents a pound of silver. Both slaves and
trade goods will be calculated in bars, and an equal barter
is therefore arranged. A bedrock price for a slave is fifty
bars. Never pay more than one-hundred bars. There are
roughly four to five livres to a bar, so a slave costs anywhere
from less than two-hundred-thirty livre to four-hundred and
fifty livres.

The native African traders are an interesting lot. They
are mostly the chiefs of powerful coastal tribes – or inland
tribes who have conquered to the coast. The cultures we
have dealt with so far have been rather extroverted, and
these traders are certainly a product of their upbringing.
When one considers the African from the sole standpoint of
interpersonal communication skills, one finds him on par
with the European – or even his master. Never underesti-
mate an African in this arena. They are camel traders par
excellence. They can outtalk a Parisian fishmonger, and
outhustle a Bretagne salt smuggler. Using every trick from
disgust, anger, physical intimidation, threats, lies of poverty
and need, inducing pity, feigning friendship or slight, they
will drive the hardest bargain they can. The unwary and the
unaware will leave with their ships half-full, and their expensive trade goods long gone. The African has a valuable
commodity in the form of chattel slave labor. But one must
never forget the European has goods of even greater value
on the shores of Africa.

Mostly we rely on past relationships and established
prices. Occasionally our favored merchants die, or another
tribe takes them as slaves, and the process must begin
again. To forge a new relationship, first one must honor the
chief. This involves gifts of beads and other ornamentation.
The chief will take them whether he has slaves to sell or not.
At some point, after being continually honored, the chief
will open negotiation - if he has anyone or anything to sell.
There are no guarantees. The African mostly wishes cloth,
muskets, gunpowder, brassware, iron and beads. Do not

take anything for granted: they are highly particular regarding what they will exchange. Gunpowder is always a reliable trade item, but doesn't bring much in return anymore. Cannons were once a fool-proof barter item, but are now occasionally out of style, and not worth the expense - unless specifically requested. I believe, as time goes on and certain tribes become more powerful, that these traders will be more interested in luxury goods. Red and blue cloth is selling quite well right now, but their taste in these items can be fickle. It can sometimes be difficult judging African desire for goods without having the opportunity for much exposure to their cultural trends and ways. I no longer trade in beads, for once I was left with a large stock unsold - a Portuguese trader having inundated the region previously.

Sometimes slaves are not close on hand in sufficient number, and the trader must go inland to buy more. If this happens, make sure they leave a hostage with the ship's captain - preferably the trader's son or wife. If a hostage is not secured, there is a good chance the trader will take one's goods - and never be seen again. The hostages are called "pawns," and the practice is well-known and perfectly accepted. Do not think it is insulting to ask. The African is usually far more sanguine in their manner than the European in regard to such practices.

Unfortunately, we are forced to deal with these coastal traders once again, since Île de Gorée was captured by the British. It is said they are returning the island soon, but that does not help us now. The island provided a bit of order in an otherwise completely entropic enterprise. If it is ever resurrected, its conditions are far more preferable to trading on the mainland, although prices can be higher. Sometimes convenience and safety trump price. In Africa, this is always so.

***

Trade sailed.

It sailed on rivers and over oceans. Ships were, by far, the best way to get cargo from one place to another.

But war killed ships. Weather sunk and battered them. Saltwater ate the wood of the hull. The nation's boatyards worked as fast as they could, but every aspect of their trade was bottlenecked. Most trees in the country were fiercely protected, and lumber was always at a premium. Masts came from the Baltics, and oak from the Illyrian coast - and every shipbuilding nation vied for their share. Even peripheral needs such as those for iron, steel, brass, leather and salt could sometimes not be met. There were places where ships could be had more easily, and less expensively, such as the United States, but foreign nationals had to establish credit or bring cold, hard coin for purchase - and, of course, compete with domestic needs.

Xavier had agonized over this, and finally decided on a plan. He purchased an old Dutch sloop, christened the *Nooit Sterven,* for nine-thousand livres from a fellow Mason, Jérôme Charles Olivier. A sloop could travel in quite shallow water, and was known for being extraordinarily maneuverable. A sloop rig was at a disadvantage at anything past a broad reach, but they were greyhound-fast running with the winds. It was an ideal craft for the trade routes that followed such winds and the currents.

The *Nooit Sterven* was built in 1761, and had seen better days. Xavier considered the price to be outright highway robbery. Xavier agreed to it, but had a forward-thinking condition placed in the contract: the ship would be drydocked, free of cost, in the Olivier yard, for as much time as need be in order for Xavier to repair the vessel and make her seaworthy once again. Conversely, if Xavier died whilst it was in drydock, ownership of the vessel would revert to Olivier, regardless of its status - which was good for Olivier.

Just to get her out of water and in drydock, there had to be a massive bilge pumping, and quick plugs of her hull. There was a three-foot hole amidships, where the ocean had worn away the chemical surface and wood sheath that protected the hull. That part of the hull, and the rest of the sheath, would have to be replaced, and then resurfaced. It was said the British had started to use copper to sheath their hulls, instead of wood. All attempts in France had failed - the copper had somehow caused a disintegration of the iron bolts of the ship, through some yet-unknown reaction. Xavier decided on an oak sheath. It was the first decision to be made in a long list of needed repairs.

And workmen began on the list, the very day she landed in drydock. Her restoration continued, little by little, as Xavier poured every spare livre into the ship. He angered a whole new host of tradesmen when blacksmiths appeared on his rolls. His hired men were hastily trained to perform a handful of tasks. Soon they were churning out the accoutrements of slavery - chains, cuffs, stanchions and fasteners - as well as needed items for the ship. Xavier sent the Nantes police on another round of peacekeeping. In return, he painted their commissariat and repaired a roof leak.

Soon the work was finished, and the sloop was slid back into the water, fully repaired. Jérôme Charles Olivier came to watch like a proud parent. Xavier still stung from the insulting price he paid for the ship. He was amazed that Olivier had the infernal gall to come at all. Yet there he was, and, to all intents and purposes, acting like he had actually helped Xavier in some way, instead of swindling him. His delight over the repairs was ecstatic and genuine. Xavier realized the man had a gift: a selective and highly-subjective memory, combined with concrete self-righteousness. If the man now believed he was the hidden instrument behind Xavier's success, there was no convincing him otherwise. Xavier put on the warmest smile he could muster, "Thank you, Monsieur. Thank you for everything."

Olivier teared. He actually teared, "God speed, Xavier. Restore your house to its rightful glory."

"With your help, Monsieur, anything is possible."

It was the perfect thing to say.

Olivier looked at him like a son for the rest of his days, and helped him in any way he could. He endlessly repeated the story of how he helped the Traversier family get on its feet. Everyone thought Xavier saw him as the father he never had. Xavier absolutely despised him, and deplored his cheating of a fellow Freemason. In time, the Traversier family became so rich that no one really believed Olivier anymore, and his stories became a joke he unknowingly told upon himself. But in that moment, Xavier had to take the injustice in stride.

On its banks lie fertilized fields, and the river eats its share of dung. The feculence sinks into nothingness within its depths, unable to change the nature of its host in the slightest way.

His mother came to him, smug and imperious. "I would tell you, my son, to return bearing your shield or upon it. But you are quite precious to me, and I would have you return regardless."

Xavier did not believe her. If he did return an abject failure, Madame would not be so tender. "Thank you, Madame," he said.

"Be careful."

"I will."

"Return home soon."

"I will not. It will be a long journey."

She teared, and suddenly flung herself upon him. He patted her on the back. He resented her sudden affection, but said nothing. He was not cruel, and only wanted the moment to pass.

"Everyone who leaves for the sea comes back a different man - when they return at all," she said softly.

"I am touched by your concern." He wasn't. "Thank you for your kindness." It was not kindness, but selfishness, he suspected. "But I have planned this for years, and there is no turning back now. Do you understand?"

She nodded. There was more small talk, then they left each other's company. He deeply distrusted her, and suspected her love was wholly conditional, but appreciated the abatement of her contempt.

Xavier had never been to sea. He had placed himself in a position where his entire life's work hinged upon performance of duties he had never performed before - which was ridiculous, if not hazardous. Xavier found himself overwhelmed at the realization. Xavier did not like to be comforted, however, he rather enjoyed the surety of hard truth. Therefore, he sought out l'Oublié, who only spoke hard truths, being incapable of anything else.

L'Oublié saw the look on his face, and spoke before Xavier could frame a question, "Monsieur," he said, "if the ship encounters a storm, and it sinks, and we two find ourselves alone on the beach of a faraway island, will it break your spirit? Or will you find a way back to France, purchase another ship, fill it with cargo and sail out again?"

Xavier did not take the question lightly. He considered the sweat and blood he had put into this journey. "I think I have enough strength to do this one more time. It will be much easier, after all," he said.

"Then there is nothing to fear. We are prepared for the worst."

"Would not death be the worst case?"

"No. Death would be a blessing," he said, and meant it.

So it went with l'Oublié.

Xavier heard his truth, and was therefore fortified and continued on. He slept well that night, and left with l'Oublié for the docks the next morning.

The ship's journey was a long one, and involved many people besides Xavier. Therefore, the dock was a jam of carts, and a carnival of sailors, family, well-wishers, stevedores, officials, and tax men. Xavier watched as the huge chests of linen were loaded onboard the sloop. The floor of the hold took a layer of chests, and a sturdy shelf above them took more. All in all, there would be around forty-thousand pounds of trade goods - the absolute limit, considering the weight of crew and other supplies necessary for the journey. With Xavier and l'Oublié stood Marc Marie-Florent Avenir – the riverman from Tours, and two new additions: Messieurs Vaux and Deschenes. Vaux was thin and tall, Deschenes was thick, but not short. Both were steely-eyed leaders. Vaux was fiery and loud, getting right in the faces of those who angered him. Deschenes never raised his voice. One heavy-lidded look would send even the most recalcitrant sailor scurrying. Both had captained slave voyages in partnership ventures in the past.

These five men – Xavier, l'Oublié, Avenir, Vaux and Deschenes - had been assembling crewmen for years. Over twice as many men as they needed would be boarding the sloop, and all of them were responsible and experienced sailors - along with the two riverine and two seagoing captains. No one knew why this was so arranged, except these five. A larger crew would only add tremendous expense to an already precious journey.

Xavier had thought long and hard about including Avenir. He had seen to it that Avenir's thugs died a horrible death, and Avenir had watched it all happen.

Since then, Avenir had given him no trouble at all, indeed he had expanded riverine trade threefold. Xavier had aided his efforts whenever possible, and had made him quite successful. This journey would make him more than just successful, it would make him rich - if everything went according to plan. But if Avenir did hold some kind of grudge, it might manifest on the journey, when Xavier could least counter an attack. Admittedly, Avenir was worth his weight in gold in a dozen different ways. Xavier had decided to include him. If Avenir was as smart as he had been up to this point, his presence would only help the overall chance of success.

The Farmer-Generals scoured the ship, and took inventory of everything going up the gangplank. They crawled over the *Nooit Sterven* like ants, cataloging everything. Xavier would owe some taxes before he left, and would pay others on his return. He would owe *Taillon*, a tax for military expenditure, now and later. There was an additional tax for slavers so the French fleet could patrol and maintain the trade routes. He would owe the *Vingtième*, five percent of net earnings, on his return, as well as the exorbitantly high *Aides* tax – a national tariff. Now and upon his return he owed a *Traite* tax – custom duties for the import or export of goods to and from France, or from one province to another. Upon his return, he owed the Nantes *Octroi* – a city tariff. He would also owe the *Dîme*: ten percent to the excremental clergy in a mandatory, nationwide tithe. Xavier was not Catholic, and did not attend mass, and still had to pay. There was a very good reason for this - the politically well-connected nobles, who received salaries for being the bishop of so-and-so, drank, whored and gambled in Paris and Versailles. God forbid if they had to budget or do actual work. Why do so, if there were men like Xavier to do it for them?

Slaves were expensive to acquire, therefore the trade goods carried to Africa were extremely valuable. The ships themselves were precious. The journey was very long, and dangerous - and always deadly, for at least one or more. Because of this, slave expeditions were financed by multiple sources. Corporations, banks and individuals bought shares in the journey. Apart from the Traversiers of old, it was unheard of for any one person to finance an expedition, not even a sea captain with his own ship. But on this journey, that was exactly the case. The ship belonged wholly to the Traversier trust. Everything on the ship was paid for in full, or had been internally generated by Traversier subsidiaries. This was Xavier's fortune to be made or lost.

He still could not afford insurance, however. His father had made the same gamble and lost, leaving the family deeply in debt to the financiers, until Xavier came along and paid the debts in full. Xavier had made sure that if he failed as spectacularly as his father, Madam would, at least, be in much better financial order than she had been after the last cataclysm. There would be no debt, at least.

By the next morning at dawn, all was ready. The oversized crew boarded and took position. None of them were drunk, and none were late. The tugboats rowed them deeper into the Loire and the ropes were cast off. The Loire took them into the Bay of Biscay, one of the most treacherous and feared waters in the world. The storms were horrendous, and not necessarily all in Winter. But that afternoon showed them only a heavy fog, and they plotted course southwest.

And finally, it happened.

L'Oublié came below decks and fetched Xavier. They both went topside. The fog had lifted and become a low ceiling. Xavier, confused, turned to l'Oublié, "I do not see, l'Oublié."

"Precisely, Monsieur."

And then Xavier realized why he had been fetched. They had lost sight of land. In every direction, there was nothing but the grey blue sea, darkened by the clouds.

Xavier moved to stand on the bow of the ship, and reflected. His father had much to say about this particular moment:

> *On the voyage, very soon after its beginning, there will come a time when you and your men are a world unto yourselves, when you lose all sight of God's green earth. One must understand, in that very moment, that civilization, order, and morality are all illusions, and their lines can be crossed, or erased, at any time by you, your men or the people you encounter. At this point, nothing will force men to do anything, or change their course of action, except the artfully-worded promise of future reward or punishment, brute force, or subtle argument - each emanating from a leader's words and actions.*
>
> *You have left the world of women and polite society completely behind. There is no paperwork, no promise, no social castigation that props up the law of the town here, no indeed. At any point, for a number of reasons, the duties and responsibilities of civilization can be forgotten. Your ship, your life, your possessions, your honor, the very integrity of your body, all hang in the balance, completely dependent on your ability to reach down into your own soul, and summon a unique, unnamed power from deep within - a primal, masculine power, the only force that can hold a tribe of savage men to your willed purpose. A good leader will prevent his followers from realizing the illusory nature of regulations and control, his very presence will assure them that these things are very real and enforceable, and the only authority is his alone, and punishment awaits all transgressors – onboard, and perhaps even at home. All power, all rules,*

all purpose - and all of civilization, truthfully - hinge on one thing: the ability of a leader to convince loyal men to threaten violence on disloyal men, in order to perpetuate leadership and achieve the leader's goals. It is this violence, and the threat of it, that underpins all of man's achievements. There is nothing else, and it is a truth that only men can understand. The better the leader, the more he leads by threat of violence and not actual violence. This leader achieves more in terms of his goal - and does not have to spend energy overmuch in self-preservation. If leadership fails in this task, there is only chaos. Violence, to restore order, is always preferable to chaos. Threat of violence, to ensure order, is always preferable to actual violence.

Order is the paramount goal of leadership. Order produces fertile soil for teamwork. Men find purpose in teams, and revel in the excellence of their performance and how it adds to the goals of the brotherhood. Order can only come about through the hard work of a good leader.

As a group of followers becomes more intimate in size, so too grows the need to lead by example. There is nothing more intimate than a ship. A leader's will, and force of personality, must be akin to Valencia steel - stainless, hard but flexible... and sharp.

So it began.

Xavier spent every waking hour learning everything there was to know of sailing. He was exhausted at the end of each day, but was determined not to be outworked by anyone, even the most seasoned hands. There was no time for rest. In a few months, and according to plan, he would captain his own vessel, and there was a world of knowledge to absorb and learn. It took years to become proficient at some of the ship's trades - such as that of a sail master - but hopefully Xavier would know enough to be a captain and delegate to the true masters onboard.

They arrived in A Coruña a week later, topped-off on fresh supplies and water, and quickly departed. There was no need for anyone to become sick, not on this journey, and not this early.

As the days passed, warm days turned into hot ones. The sun was more intense, but did not burn for as long in the sky. Two weeks later, they entered the Spanish port of Santa Cruz de Tenerife to take on more supplies.

The next stop was Africa.

Xavier sought out l'Oublié. "I am nervous."

L'Oublié shrugged.

"Come with me to the captain's meeting. I will be the least experienced man in the room, but what I order must be the way it will be."

"As you wish, Monsieur."

L'Oublié, Avenir, Deschenes, and Vaux met in Xavier's quarters. A map of Africa was spread on the folding table, and all men peered at it.

Deschenes spoke first, "I have contacts on the coast starting in the three-river region east of Sherbro island." Deschenes's finger came to rest on a map point that was perhaps sixteen-hundred miles away from Tenerife. "But this is Africa, you understand. They might all be dead, I don't know. But whatever tribe controls the region, they will have slaves for sale, that I warrant."

Vaux nodded, "My contacts start further north. But the northern tribes know they are closer and more convenient - they can name their price. More reasonable prices begin when the coast turns due east, around the Cavalla river." That was an additional four hundred miles from Sherbro. "At the Sanaga river, it becomes a buyer's market."

The Sanaga was over seven-hundred and fifty leagues distant - twenty-six hundred miles away, the distance from Paris to China.

Xavier's eyes darted. Every day at sea demanded an impressive array of expenses: pay for the crew, food for their bellies, additional supplies, wear and tear on the sails - and an exponential increase in the chance of something going very wrong. The closer they sailed toward the coast, and the more times they did so, the more chances for sickness and death – for the very air of Africa was deadly. Xavier was reminded that, at embarkation, every coin he possessed was hidden in this cabin. The ship and its cargo represented ten years of hard work.

Ten years.

Xavier remembered his father's journal. "What of Île de Gorée?"

Vaux made a face, "*En enfer* with Gorée."

No one gainsaid him. Xavier spoke, "Why?"

Deschenes looked at Vaux, then turned to Xavier, "It is French, a crown holding, with a governor. They have developed close relationships with all of the chiefs on the local coast, and support them with weapons and such through trade. On Gorée, one might as well be in France. But that is not necessarily a good thing, as well you know."

Vaux nearly shouted, "Gorée is price controls, meant to keep the sugar flowing, but benefitting no one."

"Price controls for whom?"

Deschenes answered, "For the colonists. There was a regular route between Gorée and the colonies. I don't know if it exists anymore, or what state Gorée has found itself."

"After the British occupation, you mean?"

Deschenes nodded, "Indeed. It is French once more, but..." he shrugged.

"Monsieur Vaux?"

"Only God knows, and he is silent to the sinner. It is close though, just under a thousand miles away."

Only in Africa could a thousand miles be close. Xavier straightened, "Traversier is not subject to colonial price restrictions. We are beholden to none, and I have the paperwork to prove it."

Avenir spoke, "Then one question remains. Can Gorée legally trade with non-colonials?"

There was no answer.

Xavier spoke, "We want nothing to do with the northernmost traders. Gorée is ten days to the south, and on the way to every other choice. We stop there, to top off supplies, if nothing else. Deschenes, plot a course for Gorée."

"*Oui*, Monsieur," he answered, and left the cabin. Xavier watched the other men very closely - but there was no need. There was no question of his authority or commands.

L'Oublié turned to Xavier, "Your angst availed you nothing, Monsieur."

His words did not bother Xavier. L'Oublié could speak to him in such a manner if he wished, if no one else - and they were alone. "I'll buy a pound of worry over an ounce of ill-fortune."

"As you will, Monsieur."

***

Ten days later, they came to Île de Gorée - an island just off the mainland, in a place called Senegal. Xavier was a different man now. He knew every task on board, was dark as leather and fit as a farmhand.

Looking out, Xavier realized the island was quite small, the entirety of it easily seen from the sea. It was comprised of low hills and sandy beaches. It was humid as an armpit after a day of picking grapes - only much, much hotter than one's armpit could ever be. The heat was searing. The sun had an edge, it hurt wherever it touched - especially the ears and eyes.

The island was uninhabited until Europeans realized it boasted a deep-water harbor, and it bore their marks rather than that of the African. There were small, quaint buildings dotting the scrubby hills, and occasionally a glimpse of color from flowering bougainvilleas, acacias and silk-cotton trees. Rounding the southern end, a series of docks came into view overlooked by a gigantic, squat fort perforated by gun hole slits. A grand, three-masted barque and a brigantine were both at harbor. A small line of nearly-naked human beings, with impenetrable jet-black skin, waited to board the barque. They were seemingly immune to the sun, which would have quickly incapacitated a European in similar undress. Xavier peered out through his telescoping glass, and let Vaux bring the boat in and rendezvous with the tugs. There didn't seem to be many white people at all. In fact, he realized all the Europeans were sailors from the ships. Instead, a host of blacks in European clothes ran the docks, all of whom acted, walked and gestured as if they had lived all their lives in Paris.

The *Nooit Sterven* soon found herself sliding into dock. As she laid down four anchors, blacks in European clothes - speaking perfect French, no less - tied them down to the long, well-made dock. Soon the gangplank was lowered. To his astonishment, Xavier saw another group of blacks - both men and women, and dressed in the latest French styles - saunter up to the plank, talking gaily amongst themselves. Well-dressed black servants, or perhaps slaves, held cloth umbrellas over their heads.

As they came closer, Xavier noticed something peculiar. The skin tone of the well-dressed crowd was not the jet-black of the African, but rather different shades of brown. They were easily distinguishable both by color, and by their sharper features, from the blacks holding the umbrellas. He realized they were *Métis,* the Mixed, also called *gens de couleur libre* - free people of color. It appeared to Xavier that Gorée was run by the *Métis.*

"Permission to come aboard, Captain!" said one of the *Métis* in a friendly voice.

"Granted, of course. You are most welcome, *Mesdames et Messieurs.*"

As they walked up the gangplank, Xavier shot a look at Avenir, Vaux and Deschenes. All of them looked confused. "Clear the deck," Xavier said softly.

Vaux turned, and issued commands. The crew vacated the deck without complaint, despite knowing below decks was a sweltering, hideous oven.

Xavier spoke again, as calmly as he could, "Help l'Oublié bring up the sample chests, if you please. Not the beads - the linen samples." L'Oublié and the Captains disappeared as Xavier crossed to his visitors and bowed.

They bowed and curtsied in return.

"You are most welcome aboard," he said to them, "My name is Xavier Traversier, of the Traversier of Nantes. My family's ships came to these shores quite often in the past, but I fear we are the first since 1754. I have in my possession a notarized and sealed copy of our family's renewed license to engage in the slave trade. In 1632, we were duly licensed by the Throne of France to buy, sell and transport slaves, as legal independent agents beholden to no colonial price restrictions. You will see that this condition is effective in perpetuity." Xavier offered his paperwork, and one of them graciously took it to peruse.

There was a quick discussion amongst them. Soon one of the women stepped forward, "*Bonjour*, Monsieur. My name is Mademoiselle Anne Pépin. We welcome your family back to Senegal."

Xavier bowed deeply once again, and tried to hide his surprise that a woman, and a colored woman at that, was representing the slave traders of Gorée. He noticed the three sample chests of linen had been brought on deck by l'Oublié and his captains. He motioned, and they were carried to him.

Anne stepped forward, "Are these some of your goods, Monsieur?"

"Yes, Mademoiselle. If I could present?" Xavier said as he swiveled them open.

The group bent down over them. One of the men smiled, "What is that wonderful smell?"

"Lavender oil, Monsieur. The cloth is linen, and not favored by the moths, but one cannot be too careful."

"Lavender oil."

"Yes, Monsieur. It is especially important for wool. Not so much for linen, as I have said. The linen is of the highest quality. As you can see, there are three different patterns of fabric. Every pattern has multiple color schemes using white, red, blue, yellow, green, and orange. It has a density of one-hundred-fifty thread count, which I realize seems low for other types of fabric. I can assure you, however, that linen at this thread count is far more durable and longer lasting than wool or cotton of nearly any grade – and will let air pass far more effectively. It will last decades, regardless of use, and will only get softer with age. The dye used was of the highest concentration and the colors will not fade. The chests are also for sale. They are made of oak and brass, with leather seals so as to preserve the linen. They, too, are of highest quality, and are nearly waterproof."

Mademoiselle Pépin spoke, "Why did you not sell this cloth in France? It is certainly of high quality, and would have fetched a good price if you had taken it to Paris. The journey would have been profitable and much safer."

She was right. "Mademoiselle, I am taking great risk for great gain. And I intend to develop relationships that will help me achieve my goals. I am a Traversier of Nantes, as I have said. We do nothing in small measure. We are a great mercantile house, and Paris is too near for our adventurous spirit."

She nodded. "On Gorée, the ocean winds dissipate the vapors of Africa. You will be quite safe here. There are quarters for your crew upon land, if you wish."

"I am sure your offer will be much appreciated."

"There are also quarters for you and your officers, as well."

"Again, I thank you, and accept."

"I am having a gathering tonight, a *salon*. It is more of a *soirée* than a ball. I would like to extend an invitation to you and your officers."

"We would then require your forbearance, for our wardrobe is somewhat limited, but we are honored to attend, of course."

"Excellent." And with that Mademoiselle turned with a swish of her gown and headed to the gangplank. As soon as the other traders noticed, they too hastily turned and left the ship.

Vaux snarled a whisper once they were gone, "What the *foutre merde*?"

Xavier spoke softly, "At the party, all of you will be on your best behavior - as if this *soirée* takes place at the Château des Ducs de Bretagne."

Xavier heard a humble chorus of "*Oui*, Monsieur." He issued his command without hesitation. He no longer worried so much about being obeyed.

He was not as surprised as his men at the trader's behavior. It was the French way - acquaintance, friendship and bond, then coin and contract. Anything else was bad manners. Xavier had been ill-mannered too many times in the past because he was desperate and lacked time. He could not afford to do so now.

***

Mademoiselle possessed the most imposing house on Gorée. It was large, but very simply made and adorned. L'Oublié remained in the grand foyer, and Xavier did not see him for most of the night. The aristocracy of French Senegal came together for the night, eager for news and for company. Most were *gens de couleur* but there were a few other whites, one the well-dressed, bewigged nobleman named Stanislas de Boufflers, the governor of Senegal. In the salon, songs were song, instruments played, poetry and monologues recited. Xavier was inundated with questions about the latest styles and trends of Europe, and found himself to be a woeful herald of such things, having the soul of a businessman and not an aesthete. Avenir and Deschenes luckily picked up the slack in his line, and both proved to be quite popular and charming.

Vaux was buttoned-up tight for most of the night, and Xavier worried that his demeanor might affect some aspect of their purpose. But mid-way through the night, a young colored girl of remarkable beauty played Mozart on the violin. Vaux then stepped forward, causing Xavier to inhale and hold his breath. He asked if there was a cello available, and, if so, could he possibly engage the young mademoiselle in a duet? The cello was duly produced, and Vaux proved to be quite a capable musician, much to everyone's surprise, since he brought no instruments on board the ship.

Mademoiselle flitted in and out of Xavier's company the entire night, as if she juggled him. Her manner was flirtatious and friendly, a masterful coquette - engendering attraction and admiration, while still keeping him at a close, but comfortable, distance. She juggled others, and he intuited that she was probably the governor's lover, from subtle clues regarding her manner with him. Indeed, everyone liked the governor, who was a capable and honest administrator by all accounts. The *soirée* ended too soon, and Xavier and his captains were taken to rooms in a spacious guesthouse next door.

Xavier did not bother getting undressed, but told l'Oublié to sleep. He sat in the foyer and waited. Soon, a well-dressed servant, or slave, opened the front door, and jumped when he saw Xavier. "Forgive me, Monsieur. You startled me," he said, and Xavier nodded. "I was sent by Mademoiselle Pépin, to ask the favor of your company."

Xavier stood. "Certainly. I am at your service, Monsieur."

327

***

Xavier was shown inside the mansion. Mademoiselle's home was still brightly lit, but everything had been cleaned and put away. There was no reason for anyone to be awake and oil to be burning, but that was indeed the case. Pairs of servants, or slaves, were standing like sentries at nearly every door.

Xavier was shown to a breakfast nook near the kitchen, where Mademoiselle sat at a small table eating from a bowl of cubed fruit. She was alone in an intimate room - but with every single one of her servants posted as sentries throughout her house. It was intimate, but for her, safe and comfortable.

Brava, thought Xavier, as he bowed to her. "I am summoned, Mademoiselle."

"Oh, do sit down. And please call me Anne."

"Anne, I would be honored if you addressed me as Xavier," he said as he sat down.

"Xavier then." and she popped a forkful of fruit straight into his mouth, in a complete and total breach of etiquette. But it didn't seem so, for some reason. It was perhaps the most intimate positive gesture that anyone had ever performed upon him, and it simply came off as friendly. The memory of it would return throughout his life, like flowers emerging in the Spring.

Xavier chewed. It was sweet, flavorful, and moist - like the greater, more interesting cousin to the orange. "I don't know what I am eating."

"It is called mango. Isn't it wonderful? We shall eat it together."

Xavier took another forkful. "Was that mango as well?"

"No. That was jujuber. Wait until you try the chocolate berries. They are not at all chocolate, that is just their name." She did not even take a breath. "I would not assume your ignorance, Xavier, but, if you wish, I could tell you how business is now conducted on Gorée."

"I would be most appreciative, Anne."

"We do not trade in bars like savages, rather in livre. We are business people. You have goods to trade, we do as well. We have *arachide*, oil of *arachide*, gold, ivory and slaves. We do not deal in *gomme arabique*, nor would we attempt to trade it outside of the legal monopolies set up by the Throne. You will name your price for your goods, in specie or barter, and we will buy it - or we will not. If not, we bid you *adieu*, and, hopefully, we can welcome you back in the future."

Xavier was impressed. She obviously had business acumen. She was intelligent and polite, but in a way that no one would mistake for weakness. She also came off as honest and forthright. On top of everything, she showed breeding - she was from a good family, that was evident - but she obviously did not stand on ceremony. Xavier found himself bursting with questions he could not possibly ask without being terribly impolite.

"You are married, of course. Do you have children?" she asked.

"I am not married."

"Why, Monsieur Traversier, you are both handsome and wealthy. You must be entirely too busy for your own good."

"I am afraid that is the case. Perhaps we both are."

"Yes." Mademoiselle scraped the bowl, "Both the cloth and the chests will sell well on the mainland. What do you wish for them?"

And, suddenly, there it was.

Numbers ran through Xavier's head. Each chest held four linen bolts. Each bolt was fifty-four inches by fifty yards. There were two-hundred and twenty-eight chests in the hold. The *Nooit Sterven* could hold two-hundred and seventy-five slaves in an empty hold, if they were tamped in like musket balls. One chest and its four bolts would fetch one-hundred and seventy-five livres in Paris, or more. But he was not in Paris. They were easily worth double here - perhaps four-hundred livre per chest, or a cargo worth roughly ninety-one-thousand livre. It was doubtful that linens of such quality were common here. In fact, they were most likely unique. A good price for a slave in Africa was two-hundred-thirty livre. So that would get him nearly four-hundred slaves. At the outside, at a high price for slaves, it would get him two-hundred.

"Anne," Xavier said carefully, "We have two-hundred and twenty-eight chests, each containing four bolts, of identical quality and length, as the ones you have already inspected. We wish to trade for slaves, preferably but not necessarily male. I require two-hundred and seventy-five."

Mademoiselle looked off to one side for a moment. She turned back and smiled, "I'm sure we can accommodate you, Monsieur Traversier. And expect more of your business soon. Can we talk about lavender oil?"

"Anne, we can talk of whatever your heart desires."

1832

Jake

Chapter 19

The dinner was small, but magnificent. Duck breast in port reduction, harvest-ground rye bread - which tasted like something altogether different, steamed vegetables with black truffle parmesan sauce, and crepes with orange liqueur. Rosé champagne was served with the savories, and an exquisite Sauterne with the dessert. Jake retired to the parlor with Monsieur Roquer afterwards for Cognac and cigars.

Despite some reservations, Jake told him his entire recent history, completely and truthfully, from his recruitment into *The Society* to the unusual court decision.

Roquer was pensive, "You have become part of the story of this house."

"It seems so."

If you find it, will the Cross go to Monsieur Tyran, to *The Society*, or to you?"

"*Mon dieu*, I just realized I never thought about it. I never thought it was up to me."

"None of this has crystalized in your mind as a reality as of yet, I think."

"Perhaps not."

"Should I help you, or not?"

"You phrase your question in an unusual way."

"I suppose, what I am asking is whether, according to your own mores and code - which we seem to share, is it beneficial for me to offer assistance to you?"

"I see what you are saying now. You are asking if my cause is worthy. If I should truly pursue it, or consider it to be blackmail."

"Precisely."

Jake sat back in his chair and thought about it, "I have no idea, Monsieur Roquer."

"I say this gently to you, Monsieur Loring, for we are now friends, but you no longer have the luxury of unpremeditated action. Every step must be carefully considered. You must see events how you wish them to happen, and your subsequent measured actions to bring them about must arouse no suspicion."

"I have only partly done so. I must give myself over to this espionage completely."

"I think you are right, Monsieur Loring."

"To answer your question, yes, you should help me. The information I unearth will be filtered before I pass clues any further."

"Then, Monsieur Loring, you have my help."

After their talk, Jake was shown to his room.

Jake's bedroom was the size of most houses. It was the *Chinoiserie*, and all of the furniture and accoutrement were either imports from the Far East, or domestically produced in the distinctive Oriental styles. His sheets, sleeping clothes, slippers, and robe were all made of silk.

He slept like the dead.

The next morning, he woke up to breakfast in bed, with a grand fire already burning in the hearth, and the curtains elegantly tied back from the windows. He had the best coffee, butter, and bread of his life.

Jake felt he could certainly get used to this life, but that was not his destiny. He could not stay here forever. But Tyran had told him to come here, so here he was. He was not dawdling, nor disobeying. He had found himself in the treasure cave of the Forty Thieves. He would attempt to find all possible clues that could aid him before leaving.

Jake went downstairs after he dressed. The stairs led to the south-facing sitting room, with cathedral ceilings and floor to ceiling windows. There were game tables, comfortable chairs, and small, shelved tables for books, cards, and writing implements.

And there was Monsieur Tyran.

He sat in one of the chairs, reading the *Le Breton* newspaper. "Good morning," he said, without looking up.

Jake sat down, near him but not next to him.

Monsieur Roquer came into the room with a smile, "Ah, I see I have come just in time. Monsieur Loring, may I introduce Monsieur Cale. We were expecting him months ago, and were overjoyed to see him appear today."

Jake bowed from his seat, "Monsieur Cale."

Roquer spoke to Tyran, "Monsieur Loring is recently graduated from Louis-le-Grand, and has come here for pleasure."

Tyran bowed from his chair, "Monsieur Loring. Have you been to Nantes before?"

Jake could smell him: first bergamot and rosemary, then lavender. Perhaps under it was cardamom and geranium, and a hint of cedar. Jake could not remember any scent more pleasing. "No," he replied, "I have never been to Nantes."

"You will find it more than amenable to your needs. It is a charming city, with a cosmopolitan population, and many things to do and to see."

Monsieur Roquer beamed, "I leave you both in good company. Messieurs." Then he left.

There was nothing but silence between the two men.

Jake broke it, "How is it that you come to be such an honored guest at the Château Meilleur?"

Tyran spoke as if Jake had not, "I was not there. But I have heard what transpired from many mouths. In 1805, anyone with any kind of power or authority in the Traversier Trust was summoned to Nantes by order of Xavier Traversier himself. They were either housed here, or in luxury apartments downtown. One morning, they were all brought into the main foyer, the Carrara Room. Perhaps you entered there."

"I believe I did."

"Chairs were placed in the room for all, facing the one that Xavier would occupy. He came down the staircase to their right with l'Oublié. He sat, l'Oublié stood."

"Who is l'Oublié?"

"A very dangerous man." Tyran saw the look on Jake's face, and a dark laugh escaped his lips, "You think I am dangerous, do you? No. I am a Summer's day compared to l'Oublié. He is a killer golem. No one knew anything about him, nothing, not even his name. Time has not unraveled the mystery."

"Who are you?" Jake asked quietly, "What is your name?"

Tyran nearly shouted, "Jacques Bonhomme Cale. Does that help you?"

Jake looked downward, "No, Monsieur Tyran, it does not."

Tyran calmed and continued, "Xavier nodded at the recording secretaries who wrote the minutes, his traditional signal that the meeting had officially begun, then spoke, 'I have just received word from the doctors. My illness, that I have heretofore hid from you and the world, can no longer be obfuscated. If the doctors know their craft, and their diagnosis proves accurate, I'm afraid that within a fortnight I will have perished.' It was news to them. As far as everyone knew, Xavier was as healthy as a draft horse. Xavier had to slam the butt of his cane into the marble three times to quiet the room. 'Let us proceed apace,' he said, 'I do not wish to talk of the specifics of my illness, nor do I wish to hear exclamations of surprise or condolence. Let us assume all of it is implied, and get on with more important business."

"Which was?"

"His will, of course. Xavier looked around the room before he spoke again, 'The first order of business is for every man to certify that I am of sound mind and body. Is there anyone here who would dispute this?' He waited long enough for someone to make themselves known. No one did. 'Then the matter is settled,' he said. He went on to describe how he wished to transform the Traversier Trust into what it is today: a mindless, predatory leviathan, ruled by a board of directors whose only concern is that the creature kill, eat and become larger."

"And not trade in slaves."

Tyran said nothing for a long heartbeat, then continued, "Traversier told them the Trust would be given over to the next person who possessed the Cross of Nantes. On its face, the order was absurd. They argued. 'Monsieur, if you give the Cross to an unknown recipient, and he is waylaid in an alley and the Cross taken from him, it is entirely conceivable that the murderer of your heir would come to us, demand his inheritance, and receive it.' But Xavier would have none of it, 'Then he will receive it,' he said. He went on, 'When the bearer of the Cross of Nantes appears, whenever he or she appears, in a month, or in a century, however they appear, be they white, black, yellow, red or otherwise, be they angel or devil, be they hateful, stupid, inarticulate, vapid, dissolute or saintly, you will immediately confer ownership of the company upon them. That ownership will be immediate and unconditional. The Board of Directors will then exist solely to fulfill the wishes, and even the whims, of this new owner, whoever he or she might be, until such a time as the owner dissolves or changes the board, depending on their wish - or whim."

"Was he in a mental state and simply too forceful to be gainsaid?"

"No. Stable as a Greek pillar, he was."

"It doesn't make any sense, does it?"

"None at all. His men argued, 'We have already agreed that you are of sound mind, Monsieur. But one must admit, objectively, that this is an unusual request. Of course, we will fulfill it. But may we ask, for the honor of knowing... why you have made it of us?"

Tyran fell silent. Jake spoke, "What did he say?"

"All parties, with whom I spoke regarding this, remarked on what happened next. It was as if Xavier seemed to deflate. In an instant, he looked ten years older, even beaten. For a moment, it seemed as if he wouldn't speak again. But then the golem, l'Oublié, standing motionless by the stairs, suddenly took one step forward. Every man took notice, as if a stone gargoyle had suddenly come to life. His action changed the air in the room. One step forward, and Xavier's authority remained. Xavier shuddered, then the color came back to his cheeks. He looked up, and gently smiled before he spoke, 'My directive must seem strange, I know. All of you have served me for years, some for decades, and your collective livelihood depends on the Traversier Trust. You deserve to know my reasoning. I'm afraid, however, that my words will not detract from the mystery. I would only ask that what I am about to tell you never leaves this room.' The men silently nodded their acquiescence, and Xavier began to speak. When he was finished, they understood his motivation, but the mystery of the Cross had only deepened, and its eventual destination was still hidden."

And Tyran fell silent once again. Jake spoke, "What did he say exactly?"

"If you find out what he said, it will not be from me."

"You do not know then?"

"I do know. I am simply not telling you."

"That makes no sense."

"Regardless, there it is."

"Are you mad, Monsieur Tyran?"

Tyran thought about it. "No," he finally said, quietly.

Jake calmed, "I suppose I am going to Haïti."

Tyran looked at him with contempt, "Is that what you think? After reading that log?"

Jake was frustrated, "Yes, it is precisely what I think."

"You are a fool, then."

"How so, Monsieur?"

Tyran spoke as if Jake had not interjected, "Exactly one week later, Xavier passed from the earth. L'Oublié was emotionally unaffected – which made no sense at all, for if Monsieur Traversier died, the first action of the board would be his separation from the company, l'Oublié being a frightening monster. This led to the rumor that Xavier was not truly dead, that he had somehow faked his own death. But when Xavier's body was displayed on a mountain of flowers at the Cathédrale Saint-Pierre-et-Saint-Paul, l'Oublié utterly lost his composure. He tried to throw himself upon his master, but was restrained. He did not regain his composure even as he was hustled outside. He ran from the church making wretched sounds, and greatly affected the demeanor of the mourners waiting outside. Traversier had been no friend to the church, and sometimes even its enemy, so the presence of his body in the cathedral was thought strange. But he was the most powerful, wealthy and influential man in Nantes - and he had left extraordinarily specific instructions for his burial. After his display, a huge hole was dug in the grounds of the Château Meilleur, with ramps leading to its bottom at two opposite sides. His casket was placed inside his ebony german, and trotted into the hole. After the horses were retrieved, the entire carriage was buried until only a cairn mound remained where the entire affair had once been. It is here, this mound - outside this very room, to this day."

Tyran pointed out the window, and Jake saw a mild hill, covered with grass and hydrangeas, lying in the expansive grounds.

"He is buried there, then," Jake said.

"Yes."

"Where am I going, Monsieur Tyran?"

"Tír Chonaill, and the Forest of Ards."

"Why on earth would I go there?"

"You are not just looking for the Cross of Nantes, Monsieur Loring, but for the Crimson Heirlooms, in case you have forgotten."

Jake had forgotten, as a matter of fact. The second Heirloom was ridiculous, the product of madness.

"There is something else you should know, Monsieur Loring. L'Oublié may be still alive, although if so he is no longer young."

"He has not been seen since the death of Xavier Traversier?"

"No, he has not. But that fact, in and of itself, may mean nothing at all. There is one other of whom you must be wary. His name is Marc Marie-Florent Avenir, a riverboat captain."

"His presence in all of this seems random."

"Not at all. He is one of the oldest employees of the Traversier Trust. He was present at the last meeting. He is crafty, violent and dangerous. He has carefully followed every search for the Cross, and has been spotted observing its searchers."

"You think he will steal it, if the opportunity presents itself?"

"I think most of world would steal it, if the opportunity presented itself. But not all are as dangerous, nor as smart as Avenir. He would manipulate events to bring the opportunity about, while others would not, or could not. I think he would kill for it."

"Do you think he would kill me?"

"For the Cross? Don't be ridiculous. He would kill you in half a heartbeat, Monsieur Loring."

Jake tried to think. He could not be gullible, he could not rely on anything as fact. He had to see through things, to perceive machinations. His head hurt with the attempt, but it did avail him a thought. He turned to Tyran, "Why were you not at the meeting?"

Tyran, for once, looked off-put, "Which meeting?"

"You know which one. The final meeting, where the captains and presidents of the Traversier Trust were summoned."

"Why on earth would I be there?"

"Because you either worked for the Traversier Trust, or you were a contractor for it, or a friend of Monsieur Traversier, were you not?" Jake was proud and relieved to hear his own voice – he had not heard such steel in his words since the barricade.

Tyran leaned back in his chair, and exhaled. "Your conclusions are absurd. And, besides, it is not your job to investigate me."

"Your very presence as an honored guest of this house proves me right. Monsieur Roquer is not the sort to be bought. He is ideological, and loyal to his duties. You are here. He welcomes you. Why?"

"I could have worked for the Trust after the death of Traversier, could I have not?"

"Perhaps, but your age and success would indicate otherwise."

"There is an easy answer to your question. I lied. I was at the meeting. I did work for the Traversier Trust. You are right."

Jake nodded, as if he was sated. He was not. There were two things that Monsieur Tyran did not want him to know. The first was that he worked for the Trust. The second was his presence at the meeting. Perhaps Tyran had finally given him one truth, in order to keep one lie.

Tyran spoke, changing the subject, "The Forest of Ards still exists, and is called by that exact name, making it easier to discover. I have found it to be a small wood in a place called Donegal, near Londonderry. Tír Chonaill was harder to find, for it no longer exists. But with such clues, it was not impossible. Tír Chonaill was the old Irish kingdom of the area, before the coming of Cromwell's army. Many of their nobles fled to France, but her commoners were left to the cold mercy of the English. They killed or enslaved half the people on the island, the English."

"Enslaved?"

"Indeed. They were sent to Barbados, Montserrat, and Jamaica, mostly. For centuries – but not anymore. In fact, they say black slavery in the British colonies won't last the year."

"At least, in this, the French were ahead of the British. We abolished it in 1794."

"And then we brought it back, as soon as the Revolution was crushed, and have it still. Which is, of course, very French, as well."

Jake said nothing.

"You will take a coach from Nantes to Calais, a ferry from Calais to Dover, then travel by rail - horse-drawn and steam locomotive, as opportunity presents itself - to Liverpool. A sail-steamer could be found to Londonderry from there."

"When do I leave?"

"Tomorrow will be fine."

Ce bâtard!

Jake kept his thoughts to himself. "I think, perhaps, I will do some additional research while I am in this house. I'm sure I will return at some point, but there is much to learn."

"As you will," and with that, Tyran went back to his newspaper.

Jake left his chair, and exited the room.

Foutu le bâtard Tyran!

The coach to Dover alone would be ten days on his arse.

Jake vowed not to think about it. He went to the library, and was soon met by Monsieur Roquer. "Monsieur Roquer, how well do you know this library."

"Fairly well, Monsieur."

"Can we perhaps find records of the final meeting between Xavier Traversier and the principles of the Trust?"

"Easily, Monsieur."

Exactly one hour later, Jake found the lie. Jacques Bonhomme Cale had been summoned to Nantes from Cuba, a Spanish colony, no less. But Jacques Bonhomme Cale had *not* attended the meeting. To Monsieur Tyran, it seemed this was the more important lie to keep.

There were few other records of Jacques Bonhomme Cale, mostly references to communications, but not the communications themselves. He was not an employee of the Traversier Trust, either – exposing another lie from Tyran.

Jake had found just enough truth to make him utterly confused.

1786

Xavier

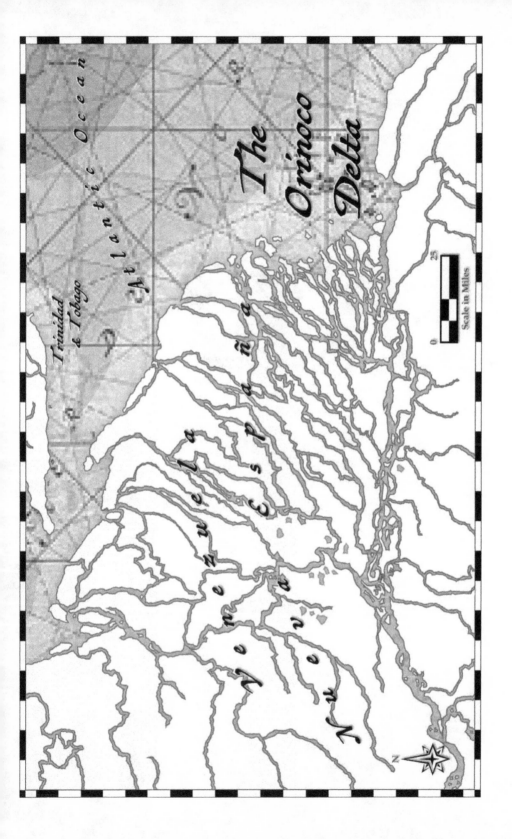

The Orinoco Delta

Trinidad & Tobago

Atlantic Ocean

Venezuela

Nueva Esparña

Scale in Miles

0   25

Chapter 20

It was extraordinarily time-consuming to load a ship with slaves. They each had to be carefully chained. It could not be done quickly, for the slaves were mostly captured warriors. If they saw the slightest opportunity, they would kill their captors and to try to escape. The warriors were from a bewildering array of tribes and peoples, however, and hated each other perhaps more than they hated their slavers. Indeed, they would not have come into contact with Europeans at all, had another rival tribe not captured them.

They were chained together so closely in the hold that they literally defecated on each other. They would have to be regularly taken to the deck in small groups for food, water, and cleaning. As the hold filled, the sound of crying, moaning and screaming gradually became louder. The ship bellowed like a doorway to hell, the unsettling howling of the damned plainly heard.

Xavier said his goodbyes to Mademoiselle. "I am truly sorry to leave; your company is delightful."

"Likewise, Xavier. But the next time you come, do bring more news of fashion and style. And more instruments, and better clothes." It was only humorous admonishment. It brought a smile to his face.

"As I am ordered, so shall I engage."

"Goodbye, *mon ami*."

"Goodbye, Anne."

He kissed her hand, and they parted.

***

They made excellent time to the Americas, using the strong current and trade winds. Nothing else was excellent.

In fact, Xavier found himself in hell. He was stuck on a small ship with hundreds of people, most chained in his hold, like stacked spoons on two levels of shelf. They were given very little to eat, and only when they were brought to the deck. They defecated and vomited and sweated. The smell, and the sound, was overwhelming, and could not be avoided anywhere on board. Barrels of seawater were poured over them to clean and cool them, but conditions were still horrific on deck for the sailors, much less for the slaves in the hold. The Africans began dying on the very first day of travel, and one seemed to die nearly every day they were at sea. After three days, they began to lose their minds, and became loud and aggressive.

Xavier noticed the crew was now loathe to go down and bring up the small groups to be fed and cleaned. He was on deck when a team of three came back, one with blood on his face. Xavier knew this was a bad development, and crossed to the man immediately. He found l'Oublié had shadowed his movements, and now stood behind him.

"What happened?" Xavier asked.

For just a moment, he saw the man's eyes burn with resentment, seemingly at Xavier. But when he spoke, he was deferential, "They kick now. They are insane, and do not care if we punish them, Monsieur *Le Capitaine*. One struck me, and knocked me off balance. I went face first into a bulkhead. We beat him with straps, but..."

Xavier nodded. He turned, and noticed all eyes of the deck were upon him. This was not unusual, for the crew now looked to Xavier for leadership. But Xavier realized he had no idea what to do.

He suddenly found himself in the memory of the Cœurfroid Summer ball. It wasn't his loyal crew who looked upon him - but the young ladies behind their fans. In a heartbeat, he was totally bereft of confidence and filled with shame. A second heartbeat later, a savage wave of anger gripped him like a tentacle of fire. His temples pounded and his vision darkened.

Xavier tried to calm. He could not allow his men to sense his indecision or emotion. He forced himself to nod, "This will be handled, and will not continue. Get your wound some attention."

The man looked relieved, and walked on. The tension left the deck. It was the perfect thing to say, but now Xavier had to back up his words with action - and he had no solutions.

L'Oublié spoke softly, "What do you wish of me?"

"I have no idea," Xavier said, in a voice that carried only to him.

L'Oublié nodded, then simply walked away. Xavier wanted to know where he was going and what he was doing, but he purposefully did not look in his direction - so, to the men, it seemed as if he had ordered him to do what he was doing, whatever it was.

If the slaves did not want to come on deck, they would not eat or drink. They would become needful and weak, and then order would return. But if the slaves were even more poorly tended than usual, disease might rip through their ranks, decimating them wholesale, and perhaps even endangering the crew. The easy and slow way would simply not work.

A moment later, only from the corner of his eye, he saw l'Oublié reappear. His hand came up - he was handing Xavier something. Xavier forced his face to remain neutral, and turned.

He found that l'Oublié had given him an ax, and held one himself. Xavier tried to study the other crewmen without looking around. From what he could tell, they looked impressed. He then spoke so others could hear, and infused his voice with as much confidence as he could, "Let's go," he said.

L'Oublié nodded, and they both entered the hold.

The hold.

My God, this is hell. This is hell on earth.

Black limbs flailed in the abyss, white eyes and teeth blinked in and out of the darkness. Hundreds of voices screamed from the nothingness, buffeting him, like a blow from a board made of human bones.

Xavier realized what he had to do. The solution was radical and uncivilized. It was so radical, and so uncivilized, he feared if the action were performed he would lose l'Oublié. He could not, regardless of what happened. He turned to him. "I would not ask you to stay - or participate, if you decide to stay," he said to him.

"I will stay, and help."

Xavier nodded. *So be it.* "We need one who is not afraid to die."

L'Oublié nodded, and walked down the ranks of the Africans. He grabbed one of them, and from Xavier's viewpoint it looked as if he reached down into a pit of writhing snakes. The chosen man was pulled out as far as his chains allowed. His face was an angry, fearless snarl. He was the perfect choice.

Xavier strode over quickly, and struck before he could think upon his actions. He swung hard with the butt end of the ax – a blunt club - and it hit the African's right forearm. He felt, and heard, the bone break. Suddenly the man's arm wobbled like a rope, as if there was no bone inside of it at all. The man tensed for a long moment, then screamed with a full throat in unfathomable agony. Xavier unlocked his cuffs. "Now his legs!" shouted Xavier over the din.

L'Oublié pulled the man out further, and Xavier gave out a furious yell, propelled by sudden unbidden fury, and swung the butt of the ax into the man's leg. The blow was weak and worthless. Xavier swung again – but still it did nothing. He felt l'Oublié's hand on his shoulder, and he stopped himself. Only now could he see the man's leg was bent and shattered, as he continued to scream in terror and pain. Xavier wondered why he had seen no effect from his actions. Xavier unlocked the ankle cuffs from the man's quivering legs. Soon he was free, only now too damaged and traumatized to move against them.

Xavier grabbed an extra wrist chain, which had hung from the hooks on the mast going up into the deck. He threw one cuff of the chains over a deck beam, so both cuffs now swung in front of his face. "Hold him up!"

L'Oublié dragged the man over, and duly held him up. Xavier clamped the chains on his wrists, and L'Oublié released him. The man now hung limply from the beam, his knees slightly bent, the top of his feet resting on the ground.

Xavier stepped on the bottom flange of the ax blade and pulled the wood haft free of it. He turned to the man, and found his prior anger had returned ten-fold. "*Encule toi, jean-foutre!*" he snarled as he swung the thick, wooden ax haft with both hands, striking the man's arms - again and again and again. L'Oublié moved behind the African and beat his legs with hard, swift strikes. No blows fell on the man's head, and none on his torso. Everywhere else, every bone in his body, was soon shattered into gravel. The muscles of his legs and arms were shredded, his veins pulverized, his tissue ripped. By all rights, he should have been dead in only minutes from an arterial hemorrhage somewhere inside his broken body. But instead, he would live for days, and die in absolute torment. He would moan, and scream, and beg for death. The stench and corruption of gangrene would claim him, finally, as he drifted in and out of consciousness. In the meantime, he would hang from the bones of the ship and suffer, to exist only *pour encourager les autres.*

Xavier finally stopped swinging. He was out of breath, and realized he was sobbing hysterically. The man screamed hoarsely, on then off as he drifted in and out of consciousness. He must have been screaming through the entire ordeal, but Xavier had only now become aware of it. He turned to go.

"Not yet," said l'Oublié, in an even voice.

Xavier understood, and nodded. He noticed that the hold had quieted. He heard crying and moaning, but it seemed to be out of fear and resignation. The terrifying atmosphere of anger, madness and rebellion had dissipated. Xavier had traded his soul in order to reestablish order and control, and had successfully done so.

Finally, the pair of them left for the deck. Xavier was too emotionally exhausted to be surprised when he saw that his men waited for him with water, towels and clean clothes. He did notice, however, that both l'Oublié and himself were covered in blood, defecation, vomit, human tissue and sweat. He washed himself, changed his clothes, was vaguely aware of moving to his cabin, and was soon asleep in his rack. It was one of the few times, for the rest of his life, that he would sleep without nightmares. For most of his future nights, he would dream of the horrific hold, the fearless African, and, especially, his own malevolent actions. Xavier found it odd that such a short incident, within minutes its decision made and outcome achieved, would have such a lasting impact on his life.

Leaders do not lose their temper - ever. Xavier also knew that violence and brutality were not the natural tools of the *bourgeoise*. He knew that proper leadership only used such techniques with extreme caution, if at all. The smell of blood travels far, and violence never works in half-measure. He knew from history that a leadership style involving extreme violence was highly effective, but could also become volatile and self-destructive. Xavier wanted nothing to do with such savagery, and had his sights set much higher. The foundations of an empire must be laid on stone, not on magma. As a result, after what he did in the hold, he made a conscious effort to lower his voice with the crew. He did not yell, or even move quickly. He even tried to smile, whenever it made sense. The crew had to know that what happened in the hold had nothing - absolutely nothing - to do with them, nor would anything like it ever happen to them without equal cause. His men were his brothers and business associates. The Africans in the hold were cargo. One bad apple, however expensive, was sacrificed for the good of the barrel, nothing more. With human beings, such things were not contemplated. The crew was human, the hold was not. For good business to continue, it was the way it had to be.

It was the perfect thing to do. Morale drastically improved all the way around, even in the hold.

Thirty-three days after debarking from Gorée they were within sight of the Lesser Antilles. Their luck did not hold.

Xavier was on the bow, enjoying the wind and practicing navigation with the sextant, when he heard a voice waft down from the crow's nest high above the deck, "A ship due north at twelve miles, Monsieur. A three-mast frigate, full-rigged for windward."

Xavier moved closer amidships. L'Oublié and his captains joined him in seconds. Xavier yelled up to the crow's nest, "What is her heading?"

"She has just changed to south-southwest, running four points to the wind or closer."

Deschenes nodded, "An intercept course."

Xavier yelled up again, "What are her colors?"

"She flies none, Monsieur. None at all."

It was a pirate.

She was already rigged for windward. Square sails were for running with the wind. The pirate had triangular sails on all masts, ready for a windward pursuit. The *Nooit Sterven* was as maneuverable as an osprey with an itch, could sail in a shallow bathtub, and was perfect, and fast, for running with the winds and currents of the trade routes. She was, however, nowhere near as effective as a three-mast frigate in the closer points. The sloop was good prey, and the pirate was pursuing her in a good direction - for the pirate. The *Nooit Sterven* was not without defenses. She had a few cannons, and plenty of small arms, and a good, big crew. But she was also no match for the frigate, in any way whatsoever.

Xavier forced himself to calm. Which one of his captains would know the most about this situation, their geography? He searched his memory. It would be Vaux. "Where are we, Monsieur Vaux? In regard to escaping this pirate?"

Vaux shrugged, equally calm, his overbearing manner now completely gone, "To the north and west lies Barbados, and Grenada to the south and west. Both are British. To the far south and west are Trinidad and Tobago - Spanish both. Below that is jungle - savage and pristine. The vast Orinoco delta, in what is called Nueva Grenada."

A British governor might know this pirate ship's captain by his Christian name - or even be related. A Spanish port might confiscate the slaves, for Xavier had no authority to bring such cargo into a Spanish port. There was nothing for it.

The Orinoco.

If they made it to the veins of the gigantic delta, they could sail upriver. If they chose a shallow offshoot of the mighty Orinoco, the frigate could not follow.

Xavier turned to Deschenes, "Here are my orders: we go south, to Venezuela. In the Orinoco delta, we find a southerly tributary too shallow for pursuit. Once we are upriver, we find an offshoot tributary, one that flows into the ocean at a more northern point. We sail down the northern tributary and exit the Orinoco far from where we entered - and hopefully the pirates haven't seen our trick before."

Xavier looked around. They all seemed to be in accord. L'Oublié gave him a subtle nod. Xavier continued, "Deschenes, you are the most experienced sailor. You are in command of the ship, until we reach the Orinoco. Once we do, you will hand over command to Avenir. He is our most experienced riverine captain. Deschenes, the ship is yours."

Deschene turned immediately and yelled, "Prepare to jibe!"

The ship exploded into activity. Xavier walked calmly back to the bow, and picked up his sextant. L'Oublié soon joined him.

"L'Oublié, my plan is poor."

"How so, Monsieur?"

"All of the delta tributaries of the Orinoco might be deep enough for our pursuer. If we do find shallows, we may hit a mud bar and become stuck there, or hurt the ship with the impact. If we sail upriver, we may not find another tributary leading north for weeks. Even if we do, the pirate might have good charts of the river. If he does, he will know where we will exit the delta before we do."

L'Oublié shrugged. "Your plan was beyond my ken, Monsieur. I follow and obey, as do the rest."

"I would say we need providence to smile upon us. But on our fell errand, perhaps we need the black luck of the devil."

"Providence was never meant to smile, Monsieur. It burns us, so we remember the Winter, and freezes us, so we recall the sun. Perhaps luck is better, however black it may be."

Xavier prayed for both.

They barely outran the pirate to the delta. The frigate was in full view, the *Nooit Sterven* nearly in range of her forward cannon, when Avenir changed course and headed directly into the mouth of an Orinoco tributary. It was not wide, perhaps two boat lengths from bank to bank. The frigate slowed and took fathom readings. The *Nooit Sterven* did not, and entered the river with foolhardy abandon. Soon they were surrounded by tall trees, and the river was as black as the skin of the slaves below decks. They couldn't see much of anything past the next bend through the thick foliage. The trees were full of strange creatures - monkeys, birds, snakes - none of which they had ever seen before. The men began to fish, and pulled even stranger creatures from the water. The noises of the jungle were disconcerting and alien, especially at night. The insects were a plague upon them, the river being too narrow to avoid them. Vaux burned pitch and rope, an old sailor's trick, to ward them off and save the crew from being eaten alive. Xavier didn't know which was worse: choking on pitch or being sucked dry of blood.

They continued sailing up river. Avenir had a preternatural instinct for avoiding the ubiquitous mud bars, and finding the deepest part of the flow. Had he not been present, their journey would have already been over. Bringing him was the perfect thing to do.

It was only four days before they found a wide tributary angling north and east. They raced back to the Atlantic at high speed in the deeper water, and emerged into the ocean at a more northern exit. The pirate was nowhere to be seen. They promptly changed course due north. Most of the mosquito-eaten crew fell sick within days. Luckily, only the cook's helper died of the sickness, and three of their cargo.

The crew, not to mention the slaves, was half-starved. Regardless, Xavier made a bold decision. He would not stop at the first slave port in Saint-Domingue, which was Jacmel. Jacmel was a coffee port and the demand would be far less than at a sugar port. Instead, he made the decision to sail to Port-Au-Prince, in the heart of cane country. Not only was Port-Au-Prince starving for slaves, she was a less popular destination than Cap Français, which was a superior city in every way a city could be.

Four weeks after sight of American land, they were finally towed into dock in Port-Au-Prince. There were two-hundred and twenty-nine slaves left from the original two-hundred and seventy-five. It could have been worse, but it could have been better. The port authorities came onboard and gave them good instructions. Soon the slaves were being unloaded into a local auction house, shore leave assignments were posted, and everyone had some real food in their bellies.

The slaves were sold in groups to various agents and planters of the area. The price was in livre, but would be paid in sugar. Xavier chose sugar because weight was more of a concern than volume. In a sturdier ship, he would have taken molasses. The lowest price they received was two-thousand livres per slave, but the highest wasn't much more.

All in all, the expedition grossed nearly four-hundred-sixty thousand livres. That was nearly three-hundred tons - six-hundred thousand pounds – of sugar, far more than he could hope to put in his hold in ten journeys, much less one.

He filled his hold with forty-thousand pounds of sugar - as much as the *Nooit Sterven* could take - and restocked her with supplies. After a week of shore leave in Port-Au-Prince, they took the seventeen-day journey to Boston.

This was the tricky part.

***

The port authorities of Boston were paid the tariffs on the sugar, but it was not unloaded. A good schedule of rotating guards was put into place. The rest of the men were given shore leave, and told to keep their ears to the ground for certain information.

Xavier and his captains split up. They were looking for shipbuilders, ship owners, and dealers. Xavier had a proposal - an extremely risky one - and was solely relying on his instincts regarding personal character to see him through. His instincts were usually right, but this time they had to be dead-on.

Truthfully, Xavier and l'Oublié dawdled a bit. Boston was a storied city. It had played front and center in the American revolution, which had captured the imagination of the entire nation, and especially the Freemasons. Boston was a hard port town, but only near the docks - becoming exponentially more respectable with every footstep west. They went to the battlefield of Bunker Hill, the Old State House, arguably the birthplace of modern revolutionary ideology, and King Street, where civilians were killed by British redcoats - in an event known as the "incident" or the "massacre" depending on with whom one was speaking. In Xavier's minor dealings, the Yankee seemed like an interesting character. He was completely unpretentious, religious, forthright, provincial, narrow-minded, and fanatically self-sufficient. The forthrightness tended to disappear as one moved higher up the ladder. Tongues became forked, words less trustworthy, and the mental knives sharper.

They found a handful of businessmen and met with them. Xavier didn't like any of them. He remained patient and did no business.

352

One of the riggers, Éric Arthaud, said he had heard something interesting. Xavier and l'Oublié met with him in the captain's quarters.

"What have you found, Monsieur Arthaud?"

"Well, I was in The Green Dragon Tavern-"

"Why? You say that as if it were special."

"It's where the Freemasons meet," said Arthaud, who was a Freemason in Nantes with Xavier. "Also, the Sons of Liberty."

The Sons of Liberty was the secret society dedicated to overthrowing the British king prior to the revolution.

"Go on," said Xavier.

"Anyway, I met a man named James Rodgers. He works for a man who goes by Boston Rag, or sometimes just Rag or Ragwany. We had an interesting conversation over oysters and stout."

Xavier and l'Oublié looked at each other. Xavier turned to Arthaud, "Why those names? What do they mean?"

"Well, here is where it gets interesting, Monsieur. Rag was a trapper when he was young, out in New France, way up the Hudson river. The entire operation was captured by the Tuscarora Iroquois. The Tuscarora set about torturing them, something about testing their mettle as warriors, or some such. The other lads captured with him all broke and begged for their deliverance. The Iroquois promptly obliged them, if only by slitting their throats. Rag kept his mouth shut through it all. Boiling water, hot stones, and the laughing squaws with their wooden needles and knives."

"What is a squaw?"

"I think it's from a tribal word that means *chatte*. It means a native woman. James said one day, akin to any other, the Tuscarora cut Rag loose. They gave him magic beads, new deerskin clothes, a white feather for his hair, and just let him go. When they bid him *adieu*, they honored him, and called him *Rahga Wahgeh Oowah Ryahkkeh Roskerah Kyehneh*. It took me five minutes to get that right, but I insisted on learning it. It means 'Chief of the White Warriors.' He was the only one of his mates to survive."

"*Mon Dieu*, what a story." The experience and title were awe-inspiring. Xavier thought smart men should work hard to never earn either.

"So, after his release from the Iroquois, Rag was no man's minion. It is said he honors nothing but his word, having no faith in God, King or Country. He did not fight in the Revolution, and rather sold his wares unashamedly to both sides. He was clever and tough enough to keep his business, even after the war was won by his neighbors. He deals mostly in weapons and rum. He's got seven ships. He knows all about you, and how we have forty-thousand pounds of sugar just sitting in our hold. He laughs at how you've thrown all the sharp tricksters aside. He likes you from afar."

"It is a sure bet your meeting was no coincidence. But I think I want to meet this man. Set it up."

"*Oui*, Monsieur."

"If we do business with him, there will be a bonus for you."

"*Merci*, Monsieur."

***

They met in Rag's office. Xavier had with him l'Oublié, Avenir, Vaux and Deschenes. Rag had his men as well. Xavier thought if it came down between them with knives and pistols, it would be a fool's errand to call the winner. Rag was of German or English descent, white as rice, with black hair and black eyes, and perpetual whiskers. He had strange scars and burns on his skin - everywhere one could see. There wasn't much small talk, not even the offer of a drink. "Well, what can I do for you, Monsieur Traversier?"

Xavier spoke, "Forgive me, my English is quite poor."

"Prob'ly better than mine," Rag said, ruefully.

"I need ships. I wish to meet someone who can provide me with ships."

"I know of one for sale. A cedar-hulled Jamaican sloop called the *Taino Rock*."

"I do not need a ship. I need ships."

"Well, Rome wasn't built in a day, was it?"

"No, Monsieur. But that is what I want to do. I want to build Rome."

"Don't we all."

"Your Rome is bigger than mine."

"I paid more for it."

Xavier tipped his hat in respect.

Rag shrugged, "I ain't never understood the French. I don't know why so many of y'all came over here and died for us. You have a king and we were trying to get rid of one."

"We were against the British, more than for American freedom, truth be told."

"Interesting. Anyway, I ain't never understood the French. Someone would say me and you are polar opposites. I'm north Maine, and you are east Siam."

"Maine is named after a river in France. Perhaps I am Maine."

"You saying I'm Siamese?" Rag asked evenly. Xavier shrugged. Rag continued, "It don't matter. Because we are not opposites at all." Xavier said nothing. "You're a kindred spirit, Monsieur Traversier. We'd both die for our word. We're tough but generous to our people, and straight as arrows when it comes to business."

"You can tell all of this from the few words we have spoken?"

354

"Nah. I've had men - and women - following your troops, asking questions, getting information from the sober and the drunk. I know what I'm about."

Xavier went with his gut. This man was an American. From his experience, he knew they were indeed the opposite of the French. For them it was coin and contracts, and only then anything else. "I will call you Boston Rag."

"Yep. That's all right."

"Boston Rag, I have forty-thousand pounds of sugar worth thirty-one thousand livres – or fifty-two hundred dollars, if you please. Take the sugar. All of it. I have a lot more in Port-Au-Prince - five-hundred and sixty thousand pounds, to be exact. I'll pay you for your help transporting it here."

"Flying the stars and stripes? What are they gonna charge me down there? As an American, I mean. Gonna tariff the nose right off my face."

"We are going to turn all of your ships into Frenchmen. I have the forged paperwork and the flags to do it. You will keep the paperwork, and turn your ships into Frenchmen whenever you wish."

"Kinda clever of you, ain't it?"

"*Baise la taxe.* I get charged ten percent by the church, and I do not even attend mass. I have no loyalty to the Throne and its war debt."

"So, we get the sugar. Then what?"

"I need to commission the building of at least two more ships. I want a hundred-ton three-masted barque as soon as possible. I'm willing to pay two-hundred thousand livre, up front, for the barque, using the sugar. If you have the contacts, and they have the resources, I will pay for two - up front. I'll pay twenty-thousand for the sloop, and will give you forty-thousand for your transport and agent fees, for finding the ships and supervising the sale, or the building of them."

"Sweetheart, where have you been my whole life?" said Rag, and Xavier and his men tensed. Such a statement could be cause for a duel. But Rag and his men laughed good-naturedly. Xavier made a subtle gesture to his men to stand down. Rag took out a long pipe, "Do you partake, Monsieur?"

Xavier shrugged, "*Oui.*"

Rag started the pipe, "Maybe your ships could be American, if need be. Least I could do."

Xavier smiled. His instincts about this man were right.

***

The *Taino Rock* would sail home with the *Nooit Sterven*. Xavier and Avenir would captain them with two of the four skeleton crews they brought along. They would pay their taxes as if the *Taino Rock* was the only proceeds of the trip, and then load up with linen and other trade goods and return to Africa, Saint-

Domingue and finally Boston once again. Deschenes and Vaux were to stay behind in Boston, with the other two crews, and work for Rag, at least for the nonce. Hopefully, by the time Xavier and Avenir returned in the two sloops, the two barques would be ready. All four ships, captains and crews, would then leave together for Africa. At the end of that third journey, in Nantes, all of the profits from that particular run would be disbursed solely to the four crews and captains, minus Xavier. That would make them all rich men, from sail master to carpenter's assistant. That was the deal that lured four good crews and captains, on one small sloop, away from home for nearly a year, under the harshest of conditions.

After that, things could go back to normal. There would then be a fleet - four ships and counting. They would slowly expand even more as they found good, reliable crew possessed of discretion. They would insure the fleet against loss. They would share profits regularly, and Xavier would allow himself a salary that would enable a lifestyle appropriate to his station. If there was war, they could change colors and be American. Xavier had Boston as a new home, if need be, and Rag had Nantes. Mademoiselle Anne in Gorée would be their permanent contact in Africa.

It all seemed so easy now, and so clear. And yet Xavier realized it had been ten years since he had regularly slept more than six hours a night.

But he could not rest, not now. His regimen was to continue for years to come, though his coffers filled at an exponential rate. Xavier did not stop, did not rest, until his wealth and power were titanic, monstrous things – gigantic spiked towers of basalt and iron.

But somehow, akin to the illusion of the powerless strikes against the African's leg, those towers never seemed to be good enough protection, the architect only too aware of their weaknesses and flaws.

By 1788, he was the richest and most powerful man in Nantes, and Traversier was once again the premier family of Brittany.

But nothing really changed for Xavier, not even then.

1832

Jake

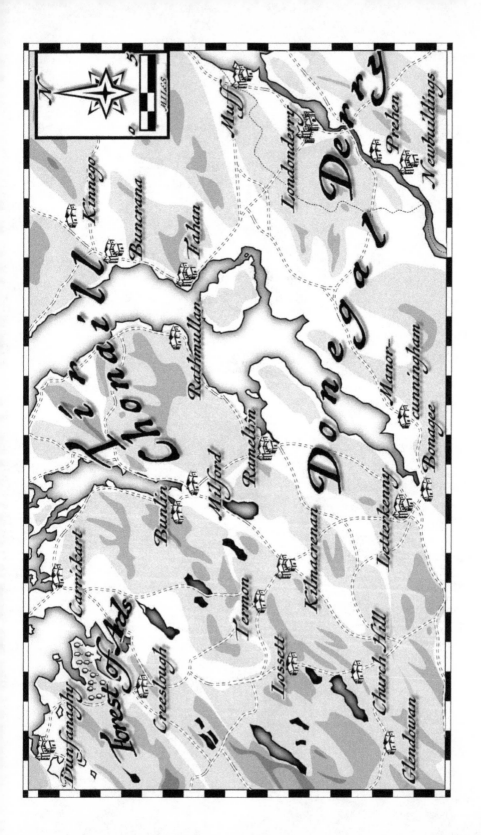

Chapter 21

Jake stared at the man through the thick bars of the jail cell. He was in his late seventies, and looked to be one-hundred-fifty. He was a mass of dirty wool garments; overwhelming beard and long grey hair streaked with white, both impossibly thick and curly. He was awake, muttering and shaking like a leaf on the stone floor. He smelled of alcohol; horrid, slimy sweat - and the privy.

This pitiable specimen was Jake's last hope. If this man was incapable of coherency, this trip would be for naught.

The night before he left the Chateau Meilleur, Jake did not sleep. Instead, he spent the night formulating a coded letter for *The Society*. On its surface, it seemed like an apology to Isaäc, asking for his forbearance in the late payment of his bill. In reality, it spelled one word in code: *Londonderry*. He posted the letter from the Château Meilleur right before leaving for the coach. It was nine days to Calais from Nantes on two separate coach lines, the change occurring in Paris – where he dared not tarry.

The Calais channel ferry took him to Great Britain, to Dover, which was, in Jake's opinion, an amazing place. Huge chalk cliffs rose directly from the beach. At the top of the cliffs were rolling hills – nearly all of which held a fort or castle. It was as if every generation built a fortification above the town for a thousand years, and never was one demolished. The town itself was a grey border port, full of travelers, secrets and sailors.

It was odd to speak English again.

After procuring the necessary paperwork for his journey, he was off. Travelling in Great Britain was a relief, after the muddy lanes and misbegotten coaches of France, for Britain had extensive rail lines. A horse-drawn coach with special wheels could be placed on a rail, and was henceforth nearly immune to bad weather, terrain, and mud. Entering the Midlands, and the industrial heart of Britain, the horse-drawn coaches on rails were sometimes replaced by the marvels of propelling steam engines, called locomotives, that carried one or more coaches at an even faster pace. The distance from Dover to the sprawling port of Liverpool was easily as far as Nantes from Paris, yet it was just shy of a three-day trip.

Jake kept a careful eye for anyone who followed his journey, but no one did. The people who temporarily shadowed his movements in England had not been with him in France. He decided that if *The Society*, or agents of Tyran, were following him, that they were either very clever, or invisible. He began to relax.

Britain was a marvel. Jake had to admit that the countryside of rolling hills and forest copses was even more beautiful than France. The women were lovelier as well. The people in general were politer, more civilized, and more conservative. Every time Jake turned around, he saw something new and interesting. Great Britain was a technological marvel, at the cutting edge of a new age.

The architecture had left much to be desired, however. Every new building in Britain seemed to be made of bricks. Modern architecture was an ugly and atrocious addition next to the graceful stone and wood creations of more graceful times. The cities were dirty, and full of the poor.

A steam-sail ship – another wonder - took him from Liverpool to Londonderry - the three-hundred-odd miles easily eaten in less than two days.

But Londonderry was in Ireland, and Ireland was a different creature altogether.

Londonderry was a small, industrious town composed mostly of sturdy and unimaginative buildings. However bustling during the day, it might as well have been a Roman ruin after dark, there being no life to the city at all.

Jake found out the land called Ards, forest and otherwise, was owned by a local lord by the name of Stewart. Jake arranged a meeting with Lord Stewart, using an interesting lie designed to pique his interest.

Lord Stewart was a florid, arrogant sort. His every word seemed to carry judgement, as if everything and everyone were being constantly reevaluated for propriety. Jake showed him the captain's log, and told him he was working for the heirs of Captain Eltis in an attempt to find the Cross – which was, in this particular lie, simply an ordinary thing of value. Jake explained that the Cross was rightfully the property of the Eltis family, and not that of some ridiculous Irish slave girl.

Lord Stewart seemed to warm to the prejudice.

Jake revealed that he wanted to find out if the girl came home to Ards. Lord Stewart was intrigued by Jake's story, had no designs upon the Cross whatsoever – wishing to see it back in its rightful hands - and promptly set up a meeting between Jake and his Master Huntsman, Lord Ivor MacInnes.

Ivor proved to be old and scary-looking, but otherwise quite similar to the other Presbyterian inhabitants of Ulster with whom Jake had met: religious, dour, staid, and conservative. "Ards is in north Donegal," he said, in a voice like scratchy burlap, "Nearly twenty-five miles away. We will be armed to the teeth, for 'tis Catholic country. We will travel on horseback to Creeslough, then walk the rest of the way."

It took some time for Jake to convince Ivor that he had never been on horseback. When he did, Ivor was helpful and taught him the basic techniques, and minded Jake's horse as much as his own.

It was a cold, wet journey to Creeslough, where they slept at an inn. It was not much better when they woke the next morning, and walked into the forest. They stopped perhaps a mile and a half inside the trees, in a spot that looked like any other part of the forest.

Jake was hungry, cold and wet. Ireland was proving to be a foul, damp, misbegotten place, and he vowed never to return.

"Here it was," said Ivor, "None of these trees were here back then. The Ó Brollachain village was right in this very spot. They wore wool garments woven by their own looms, and slippers carved from white oak."

Jake remembered seeing Irish arrayed likewise on the road on the way up. It seemed these Catholic Irish were all hopeless peasants - dirty, scraggly families of a dozen children or more. Between their wide-brimmed hats and long beards, the men were sometimes hard to tell apart. The women wore wide-brimmed bonnets, flowing long-sleeved dresses, covering their necks to the jaw, arms to the wrist and legs to the ankle. They were mostly black-haired and blue-eyed, but could also be remarkably dark. Their houses were made of sod, wood and thatch, and their small plots offered potatoes and beets. They were a humbled people, a broken and beaten people of no account.

Lord Stewart had previously acknowledged little regard for them, "Allow me to illustrate the nature of the Irish. Despite foreknowledge, and our best efforts to educate in prevention, cholera came to the island last year and spread quickly. Of course, happily, the Virgin Mary came down and spoke with them," his voice dripping with sarcasm, "It seems if peat was taken from a particular hearth fire, and rubbed on the walls of a house, cholera would not strike there. So, they divided it up, and began rubbing it on houses. Oddly, as the turf traveled, its very nature began to change. In one town, it was magic sticks, in another, blessed water. Soon the entire country had a cure for cholera, except it was a different cure depending on how and when the original story was altered through the telling. So instead of moving their dung heaps from right outside their front doors – which would have helped tremendously - they rubbed their huts with magic sticks. This secret conspiracy was so vast, so pernicious, that we thought another rebellion was being plotted. Imagine our surprise at the truth! Cholera has claimed nearly fifty-thousands of these woebegone creatures already. This Catholic superstition was even given a name by the newspapers – the *Panic of the Blessed Turf,* no less."

Jake emerged from the memory, and turned to Ivor, "What happened to the village?"

"It was burned down. Every *Taig* swept from the forest."

"What is a *Taig*?"

"I am assuming you are Reformed Protestant, being an American from Boston."

"I am a man of the Enlightenment, truth be told."

"I dunno what that means, but I assume you take no orders from the Pope."

"No, indeed."

Ivor nodded, satisfied. "A *Taig* is an Irish Catholic."

"Do you know the story? Of what happened?" Jake asked.

"Aye. It's part of the local lore, and is well-known."

"I would hear the whole story, in as much detail as you are able to recall."

"Very well. Do you wish now to dig or search here, in the ruins of the village?"

"Here? Hell's bells – no. No, thank you, no."

"Let us walk back toward the road then," said Ivor as he headed west. "The Forest of Ards, at that time… When was it? 1759, I believe. The forest was part of the demesne of Lord Wray. His estate was far closer to Londonderry, you probably noticed it on the road."

"If it was large and fair, then I did indeed."

"Back then, the Irish were still discontented. The whole island crawled with our soldiers. Our place in the world was far less assured, you see. Nowadays, Britannia fears nothing. We are the greatest power on earth. But back then, the Irish would rise, every time we turned our backs to deal with a threat. They always have, these bastards. Allied themselves with every enemy we've ever had, until we put them down proper in 1649. Even then, the island had to be an armed camp."

"*Le village, Monsieur?*"

Ivor gave him an odd look.

Jake realized why. "If you could please continue, Mister MacInnes."

Ivor did, "Young Lord Wray, the eldest son, was intent upon hunting on his lands in the Forest of Ards. It was a bit far from Londonderry, and they had never hunted there before."

"Perhaps that is why he was so intent."

"The ways of lords are strange, but we obey."

"I'm an American, remember."

"Your people will come back to the crown, someday. Your way of life is not natural."

Jake chuckled, Ivor did not. "Perhaps, but please go on."

"Young Lord Wray formed a hunting party. The Wray hunt master, Rowan Craig, three dozen beaters - farmers in the main - the kennel master, four helpers, dogs – mostly retrievers. Cooks and valets, and so on. The hunters would be the young lords Wray, Gore, Brooke, Hampton and Scott. Off they went, in their fine coaches, which bogged down along the way."

"The road coming here was terrible."

"Indeed, and worse back then, for the weather was colder and wetter."

Jake found that hard to believe.

Ivor continued, "The famers were nervous, for the woods of Donegal were said to hold Irish bandit clans, those who fled to the forest rather than being subject to English rule. The lords were not threatened in the least - they positioned themselves near our inn, which was not there at the time, and the beaters spread out through the trees across the forest's width, perhaps starting a mile in, maybe less, and beating to the west."

"And the Irish attacked them?"

"No. The hunt was west of here, and Lord Wray had a sizable party."

"What happened then?"

"Two Irish boys were playing between the line of beaters and the lords. They were but wee, but they spooked the line, the beaters mistaking them for attackers. Shots rang out. Both boys were wounded so severely that huntsman Craig put them out of their misery with his knife."

Dear Lord, thought Jake.

"Soon after, two crazed *Taigs* attacked the line. Several men were hurt, and three killed, and one of the wounded died several days later. The two Irish were slain as well in their attack. The wounded were sent south in one of the carriages, and the lords had their lunch in a pavilion not too far from our present inn."

Jake was stunned, "They didn't leave?"

"It is said Huntsman Craig informed Lord Wray of what transpired, and his advice was to immediately abandon the hunt. Lord Wray did not."

"Why not?"

"It was his land. When does a lord flee his own land?"

"In that exact circumstance: when there is blood on the ground, the enemy's numbers are unknown, there are wounded, and nothing is lost by retreat."

"British lords do not retreat from their own lands. Such a thing would be ridiculous."

"Very well. So, what happened next?"

"The Ó Brollachain unearthed their ancient wheellocks and arquebuses. They lined up at the edge of the forest, and fired a mighty volley at the hunters inside the pavilion. Young Lord Wray took a grievous flesh wound to the thigh – and he was not the only man hurt. After the first volley, the party quickly took cover and returned fire. There was a stalemate, but the hunters had taken casualties, and this prompted swift action. Under fire, horses were harnessed to carriages. They left everything behind but themselves and their muskets and took to the road. By this time the Ó Brollachain powder was mostly expended, and the hunters were able to escape without further loss. But there was only one casualty who mattered: young Lord Wray. He was from one of the premier noble families of Ireland, much less of Ulster. This incident was now an affront to the Crown."

"An Irish uprising whilst Britain was at war."

"Yes. Back then, we were fighting across the entire world: against France, Spain and Austria. We could not face a second front in Ireland. It would not do."

"Were troops nearby?"

Ivor snorted, "There were more than a dozen regiments across the island. An entire full-strength battalion, over a thousand men with two light cannons, was dispatched from Londonderry to clear the Forest of Ards. Two companies and the heavy weapons were led by the battalion commander up the Letterkenny road, the two remaining companies were commanded by the executive officer, and left by sea. Their orders were to kill or capture every Catholic soul squatting in the Forest of Ards."

"How many were there? Irish, in the forest?"

"Perhaps thirty, if you count the women and children."

"So, a thousand men – with two cannons - against thirty men, women, and children."

Ivor grinned, "Sends a message, it does. The Irish were expecting them by the road. They had a way of weaving branches together into obstacles. They dug pits, placed sharpened wooden spikes, and had rocks and javelins ready to throw. They didn't expect anyone by sea, and the second column took them from behind and burned the village. The rest of them were encircled to the west of it. They fought to the last, they did. None survived that battle."

"There were survivors, though."

"Indeed, a woman, her twin infants, and a girl - her older daughter - were captured by cavalry to the north of Ards. If there were any more of them who lived, no one told of it."

"And what happened to them? The woman and her children?"

"The four of them were sold on the docks of Londonderry, for something over a pound sterling. The infants were taken from the mother and thrown into the sea. She fought her captors, and was brained by a heavy keychain. She never woke from her wound. The girl was sent to Montserrat. If she survived the journey to the Americas, they could sell her for over five pounds. The Irish didn't take well to the tropics, you see, and sold much cheaper than the blacks. Sometimes they were bred together, the black and Irish. It was said the offspring were much smarter than the African, and could still weather the climate."

Jake was absolutely sickened, but he forced himself to show no emotion. He was an agent for the Eltis family, here to retrieve a necklace. "Interesting," he finally said.

And that was that. Back to Londonderry.

Jake found lodging in an old medieval establishment called *The River Inn*. The plump matron, one Missus MacAdams, was quietly friendly, and sat him down for dinner in the main hall after he was settled. He soon found himself in front of a ham and mutton pie, with peas and something called champ – which ended up to be mashed potatoes, chopped scallions, cheese, butter, and cream. He washed it down with stout, and was surprised at the pleasantness of the meal.

He was waiting for dessert, and writing in his journal, when he became vaguely aware of an argument. It did not disturb him until it became quite heated.

Missus MacAdam's voice - quiet and unflappable, "Sir, you are simply not in a suitable state for dinner."

"Thas not true!" shouted a drunken voice, in a thick Irish brogue, "I am a true son of Erin, and thas why you are ejectin' me!"

"No, that is quite untrue, sir. And I assure you that you are in no fit state for company."

"Thiss inn belonged to my people. Not your people! This belongs to the Kingdom of Tír Chonaill! I am Aodh Dubh Ó Brollachain! I am a true son of Ards! *Éirinn go brách!*"

Jake jumped from his chair, and sent it flying. He nearly ran toward the argument.

"Sir, I do not mean to disappoint you, but this establishment was built in 1684, not 1648."

"Oh," said the now defeated voice, "I misread. I'm terribly sorry. May God smile upon ye, beautiful lady, and this fair place. I will get me gone."

Jake rounded the corner, just in time to see Ó Brollachain try to kiss MacAdams good-night. She would have none of it, tugged him by the sleeve, opened the door, and gently pushed him out.

"Fare thee well, Madame," he said with a flourish and a bow.

And the door was shut.

Missus MacAdams turned to Jake, "I am terribly sorry, Mister Loring."

"Please, I must speak to this man immediately."

Missus MacAdams did not even blink as she reopened the door, "As you wish, Mister Loring."

And out into the rain went Jake. He looked around in the darkness, and saw no one. He shouted, "Mister Ó Brollachain!" but there was no answer.

Jake

***

The man in the cell stirred. Jake waited patiently, sitting on a wooden bench padded with coarse blankets. A lantern on the wall gave him enough light to write in his journal, should that necessity arise.

"Where am I?" the man said.

"You are in jail, in Londonderry."

"Again? What did I do?"

"Nothing in particular. You are Irish, as well as a drunk. For a man such as you, in a town such as Londonderry, a stiff breeze would be cause enough for imprisonment. But I will answer your question properly: you are here because I contacted the authorities, and had you brought here."

The man looked at him with innocent incredulity, "Why would you do that?"

Jake sighed, "I finally found you, just outside of town. I begged you for help, and offered you a princely sum for your thoughts."

"How much?"

"A guinea."

"You offered me a guinea for me thoughts?"

"Yes."

"Well, what did I say?"

"You told me to do something obscene and physically impossible."

The man shook his head in wonderment.

Jake continued, "I tried again the next day. I offered you three guineas. You nearly knocked me unconscious. I must say, you are remarkably strong and quick for being so old and decrepit."

"I am woefully sorry, sir. My most sincere apologies. I most likely hit you with a bottle. The weight of it makes up for me age."

"I lost my patience with you, and had the constables bring you here."

The man spotted what rested on the floor next to Jake. "If I could ask, what is inside that keg to the side of your foot, young Master?"

"It is good Ulster porter inside this keg, sir."

"Could I trouble ye for a mug?"

"You can have as much as you want, but it is expensive."

"Please, kind sir. I have not a farthing. And if I do not drink, I feel as if I will die. The shakes are upon me already."

"I do not require money. In fact, if you earn the contents of this keg, I will give you three guineas for your trouble."

"I dunna understand."

"Then I will enlighten you. When you were brought here, you still would not help me, nor answer my questions. I decided to let you stew for a bit. You have not been allowed to drink on purpose."

"You are torturing me for information then?" the man said sadly.

Jake wanted to crawl into a hole and never come out. He kept his face stern, "Yes."

"What on earth would I know, that you would interfere with me life in such a manner?"

"Do you wish to drink, and be free, and be paid for your troubles?"

"I suppose I do, sir."

"Your name is Aodh Dubh Ó Brollachain."

The man's face twisted and turned dark. He did not reply.

"Answer me, sir," said Jake.

"Who told you my name?"

"You did, when you claimed my inn for the kingdom of Tír Chonaill."

"I don't want to answer any of your questions."

Jake wanted to let the man go, but held stern. "Mister Ó Brollachain, you are going nowhere, and drinking nothing, unless you answer my questions. You have two choices before you now. You can aid me, and secure your freedom, or thwart me – in which case I will cruelly leave you be for several hours, and return with my keg when you are truly in dire straits."

The man began to cry, softly, like a child. "I was but wee."

"Your name, sir?"

"I will talk of anything but me past."

"That is precisely what I wish to talk to you about. Your history, but most importantly, the history of your clan, the Ó Brollachain."

"It is a common name."

"You are of the Ó Brollachain clan of Ards, are you not?"

"No."

"I have caught you in a lie, sir. For you have said so yourself, in a drunken stupor."

"I lied then, not now."

"I will leave you be, for the nonce." Jake stood.

"No! No, please!"

Jake kept standing.

The man pulled himself closer to Jake, "Please."

"No."

"You humiliate me. You shame me."

"Do I? Or do I expose humiliation and shame that was put there by another?"

The man seemed to grow even older, right before Jake's eyes. He spoke softly, "The latter, sir."

"Your name, sir?" Jake said, shocked at the coldness of his own voice.

"My name is Aodh Dubh Ó Brollachain, of the Ó Brollachain of Ards," he said, as if he was lost in a daydream and far away.

Jake found himself shaking. Part of him did not want to proceed, afraid that his expectations for this man were far too high.

Ó Brollachain brought him from his thoughts, "What do you seek, young master?"

Jake uncorked the keg, and filled a large mug resting on the ground. He maneuvered it between the bars and handed it to the man. Ó Brollachain emptied it to the dregs in a single draught. "Thank you," he said.

"I seek any knowledge of Sinead Ó Brollachain. Did you know her?"

The most curious look came over the man's face. "Ah," he said, "Your presence, and your inquiries, now make perfect sense.

Jake's excitement almost turned to fear. Something strange was happening. "Why does it not surprise you that she is the subject of my inquiry?" Jake said, in a hollow and shaky voice.

He replied in an even voice, "Her name was Seonaidh Iníongael Ó Brollachain, which means Gift of God, Daughter of the Gaels, of the clan of Ó Brollachain. Of our little clan, there was less than two score, and we all knew each other's hearts like the back of our own hands." He handed the mug back to Jake, "Know this," he continued, "There are many things sacred to the Gael of Ards. We had no books, no theater mummers, just ourselves and the night fire. We can spin yarn with our stories, sir. We have memories like stone cisterns, and magic in our souls for the telling. What you ask of me is sacred to my people, for we are storytellers. You will ask me no questions, but listen to my voice, as I tell you what you seek. Will you do this now?"

He was a different man. Jake nearly whispered, "Yes, I will, sir."

The man sat up, and crossed his feet. His eyes went wide, and his hands came up. To Jake, the man's face was only in outline, as the flickering light of the lantern played upon it. He began to speak, in a bold voice, "To answer your question, I must take ye to a time before I was born. Almost a hundred years ago, in the fell, cold year of Our Lord 1748. His name was Athair Mac Giolla Eoin. He was a priest, but he was also a man of Tír Chonaill, and therefore a Gael. The Gael are an old people, and we are a bit more *draíochta*, more magic, than the newer races of man. We must be mindful of things that could affect our *cinniúint*, the mystical force that determines destiny, fate and luck. A Gael must be cautious not to upset the devil, or even the lesser creatures of mischievous intent.

"Athair Mac Giolla Eoin's flock were the Gael who lived in Ards, a place of meadows, sandy beaches and dark forests. It was thick with the history of the Gael, this place. Ancient forts and tombs lie buried in its loam from the time of stone. A ghost, the Bhiorog Ó Baoighill, prowled the night, and wailed for the dead. In the times of legend, Diarmuid and Gráinne, in their flight from Fionn Mac Cumhaill, took refuge in the stone cairns of Ards.

"But now, I take ye to late Autumn. The branches were dark claws, and the ground spotted with patches of early snow. The wind blew off a cold, angry ocean, and stabbed through clothing like knives of ice. For Athair Mac Giolla Eoin, this hardship had to be endured, for he had no church, and said mass outdoors in the middle of the night, on a special rock imbued with natural *draíochta*.

"He was a priest of darkness by necessity, for he was an outlaw just for practicing his faith. A newer people, called the *Béarla*, had come a century before, and sacked the kingdom of Tír Chonaill with a butcher's grace. What few Gael who survived were shipped across the ocean in chains. This was a terrible irony, for the first prophet who brought the faith of Christ to the Gael had come first as their slave. In memory of him, the Gael had not taken slaves for a thousand years and became the first men of earth to do so. The dual tragedies of butchery and slavery resulted in an empty, lonely land - the population of the entire island of Ériu, not just Tír Chonaill, had been cut in half. Soon a people called the *Albanach*, the allies of the *Béarla*, came from across the sea to claim the land of the Gaels. What few Gael were left had hidden in the deep forests, and only now ventured into the daylight of roads and villages. What they found horrified them. Not only had the language and law of the Gaels been banned, but their ancient Catholic faith as well. Any misstep, any crossing of the savage *Béarla* or their *Albanach* allies, and a Gael found himself in chains, following his ancestors across the ocean. It was a dark time indeed for Tír Chonaill, and the Gael of Ards.

"The Wray clan of the *Béarla* then held lordship of Ards. They did not usually interfere with the Gael, but who would bother what is hidden, and slinks unknown in the dark? No Gael plowed sunny fields in Ards, only the Wray *Béarla* and their oathed men. Half the Gael lived on potatoes and trap game. But it was God's will, come what may. Suffering was the lot of man and the fruit of the world. The Gael did not complain, although sometimes he mourned or became angry. His only recourse was potato liquor. We call it *poitín*, for it is made in a pot still.

"The ears and nose of Athair Mac Giolla Eoin itched in a way he understood - the Ó Brollachain clan expected him, and were growing impatient. But they would have to wait; Athair tarried for a purpose. He had seen omens of *cinniúint* relating to their clan and had to find out what they meant. *Íosa Críost*, the human aspect of God, communicated with his followers through the *Spiorad Naomh*, a mystical, invisible force that touched all things. If the *Spiorad Naomh* spoke to man, it was a matter of faith and salvation to listen.

"Athair Mac Giolla Eoin came to the fairy place. It was a beautiful bramble, a dark corner of the forest where rowan, oak and hawthorn warded evil and shaded the sun; where shrubs and ferns covered the ground. Stones jutted from the earth like teeth at the height of a man. Athair Mac Giolla Eoin knew if white *draíochta*, the working of the *Spiorad Naomh*, was afoot, it would speak to him here. But first, he had to make peace with the place itself. He spoke to it, 'I am Athair Mac Giolla Eoin', he said to the wind, 'A Gael of Tír Chonaill, which is no more. From the time of stones, we have respected and preserved the fairy places. I come in peace to listen to God through the *Spiorad Naomh.*'

"And Athair Mac Giolla Eoin waited. The only sound was that of water dripping from the moss of the trees. Then he heard the whistles of a wren. Just as quickly it was gone. He waited for another call, as a wren will sing forever, but nothing followed. He knew then that he had been answered, and given permission to enter. He walked around the point of the tallest stone, under the branches of the rowan tree. He knelt to see what he could see.

"Lo! There was a bird's nest on the ground. An old collared-dove cock sat in the nest, watching him with a calm, ready stare. A chick, resting in its egg with part of the shell still on the top of its head, looked up at him with nothing more than curiosity. Between them and leaned on its edge, sat a gold coin. Athair Mac Giolla Eoin reached in with two fingers and pulled it out. Yet neither bird moved.

"To Athair's astonishment, it was a piece of eight from 1537, clean and gleaming as if it were minted yesterday. He put it back between the placid doves, then moved away from the nest, and exited the fairy place.

"Athair was darkly distracted. Thoughts ran through his mind: doves did not nest on the ground if there were trees or even shrubs nearby. Doves did not lay eggs when it was so cold. Cocks did not nest the chicks. Doves nested far closer to farmland. Doves did not sit quietly, as one inspected their nest. And then there was the coin. Ships of the Spanish Armada crashed up and down the coast of Tír Chonaill in 1588. It was possible to find a gleaming Spanish coin from 1537 sitting in a bird's nest - but it was only God's will that brought it there.

"Athair Mac Giolla Eoin made his way toward the village of Ó Brollachain, lost in thought. We Ó Brollachain lived in the deep forest, where it was always cold, wet and dark. Where we lived was not always so, but we were now happiest in the cold and dark, and felt ill at ease in a place where the tree moss did not first catch the rain. We built our huts from daub and bricks, and our roofs from thatch. We lit fires under our clay floors on Winter nights. The paths were strewn with chips of white oak, which did not rot from wet, and kept the mud at bay. In a wide, wooded hollow, all sat outside amongst the huts waiting for Athair, holding quiet infants. Children of all ages stared out from the forest, preferring its freedom to the comfort of roofs. A wide pen of woven tree branches encircled the hollow, and chickens, goats, sheep, and pigs ran freely. They stayed to the forest fringes, away from the huts, to avoid the nips of the dogs, who were closer members of the clan.

"Athair had been there before, many times, and the animals did not announce his presence as he came upon them. He had come because there had been no live births amongst the clan for six months, and Ingen, the scarlet-haired wife of the clan chief Eigneachan, was very pregnant indeed. He was there to bless her, and her unborn child, but he had other words to say.

"The fairy places have been alive with messages from the *Spiorad Naomh*,' he said, 'God speaks to you of the *cinniúint* of your unborn daughter.' Ingen made a ward against evil with her hands, but Athair would have none of it - 'Do you ward off the spirit of God, woman? These are no signs under the strife of blackthorn. This is no work of the devil. I tell you your child needs no blessing. It is a girl. She will be born hale and whole, and none of you will live to see her death. What is more, that is only the beginning of God's message to you.'

"The clan was taken aback, but it was only the beginning. Athair raised his hands, 'A chair fell, a magpie flew into my hut, salt spilled. I saw thirteen ravens in a field, silent as the grave. I saw a pool of dead Natterjack tadpoles, and they have never been seen outside Ciarraighe and Uí Ceinnsealaigh - this everyone knows. I saw a *rúad* fox next to an egg - uneaten. I saw a dove cock in a nest with a chick still in its shell, both between a coin of ancient gold. Three *tuar* omen I saw to warn me there was more to come. Four *céalmhaine* omen in the fairy places under Hawthorn bough to tell me what I needed know. The *Spiorad Naomh* has spoken. Your daughter will share the birthday of Christ, you will bear her on the day of Christ's Mass. But that is not all she will share. Your daughter is blessed above all to share in the sufferings of Íosa Críost.'

"The men and women of Ó Brollachain were shaking, white as ghosts. The children had run off into the forest, and their parents would be lucky to see them in a week. Ingen put a hand on her unborn child to steady herself, 'Tell me of her, of this doom of *cinniúint*.'

"And Athair spoke dire words, 'She will suffer and even the sun in the sky will be her torment. The days of the Gael of Ards are numbered. But she does not bring the end. She is no *drochthuar* harbinger of doom. She is the gift that God brings to his people, and that will be her name. Her children and her children's children will have the destiny of those in greater places – but now dark clouds come across the sea. As the children of God have their scripture, now will come the anti-scripture. Now will come the Logos of the devil. His words will burn on the earth. The sundered children-to-be of Ó Brollachain will suffer. Their lands will suffer. They will see the evil of Cain, see what cannot be unseen, hear what cannot be unheard - until their eyes turn to coals in their sockets. But all is in God's plan, though his finger points to the road of pain, where Críost stumbled to his death in Jerusalem. Wisdom and salvation will come to all future hearts where flows the blood of the Ó Brollachain of Ards, even those who perish untimely by the hand of man. And to those who survive, those few who walk through the fire burned but breathing still, they will come upon great power, the wealth of ages, and perform a great healing for God. Here and elsewhere. And Críost's true plan will be revealed.'

"Ingen rubbed the girl in her womb and spoke, 'So you are named. You are God's gift, daughter of Ards. You are called Seonaidh. Seonaidh Iníongael Ó Brollachain. Gift of God, daughter of the Gael, of our clan."

And suddenly, the incredible story over, they were abruptly back in a cell in Londonderry.

The man fell silent for a long moment. His eyes finally came up and met those of Jake, "I am not surprised, young master, at your inquiry, because Athair's words came to life, at least all of them I was party to see."

If Jake did not know better, he would have thought the man's tale was scripted by Monsieur Tyran. In the story, the priest's words could describe the two Heirlooms with only a slight reach – the words of the devil, and the treasure of ages, came to mind.

The priest had spoken of anti-scripture, the Logos of the devil. Logos was an interesting word. It came from the Greek, was used in the New Testament, with no word in French or English to completely satisfy its meaning. It meant *reason, proportion, discourse* – but also *expectation, word, speech, account, ground* and *plea*. Philosophers began to hang mighty weights upon it, five-hundred years before Christ. It came to mean the principle of order – the logic behind an argument, the premise. The Greek Christians added more: an embodiment of universal meaning, the principle of divine reason. Christ was logos – the living word, the embodiment of the ultimate message, which was, precisely, the explanation of the purpose behind all creation.

So, what was anti-scripture, the logos of the devil?

Action based upon emotion, chaos of form, enforced silence to stifle communication, disbelief. Illogical fanaticism, the ultimate lie, the opaquest obfuscation of purpose and knowledge.

The Logos of the devil was indeed the devil's song. But Jake was no closer to the lyrics, and this song was sung nowhere near the Vendée.

Jake looked up, and saw that the man had tears running down his face, but he was lit with a smile. Jake was struck, and said nothing for a time. Finally, he spoke, "There is a necklace, called the Cross of Nantes. It is of inconceivable value. It could properly be called the wealth of ages."

"It came into her possession."

"Yes."

"Do you seek this thing? Is that why you speak to me?"

"Yes, amongst other things I seek."

"Then I would tell you this: whoever now has this treasure also has the blood of Ó Brollachain running through their veins, for that was the revealed will of God."

"Why has your mood changed so suddenly?"

"Because, young master, I know that you were sent here for a purpose."

"Why do you think this?"

But the man left for another world once again, "I was five Summers, when Seonaidh Iníongael Ó Brollachain was eleven, and she was as dark as her mother was fair. Seonaidh knew the forest; she loved her home, and was as much a part of it as the branch moss. It was her kin who vexed Seonaidh. We called her *Míthuar* or *Drochthuar*. Both meant the same; a person of ill-omen and evil fore-boding. But *Drochthuar* was worse, it meant more magic was involved. Our parents called her *Brocóg*. There were fifty words to call a girl in our language. *Brocóg* meant dirty-faced girl. Sometimes they called her *Brocóg-Drochthuar* behind her back. It made Seonaidh feel humiliated and embarrassed to be called such things. She felt she was different, in a place where she should have had the comfort of being the same, insulted where she should have been embraced. But her second cousin was in love with her, and she with him, though both were too young to realize it. He was thirteen, Ruairí was his name, and he fought for her true name. I think they would have been happy forevermore together, had not the *Béarla* come. It was they, those two, who spotted the hunters, and had the village looking for their missing children and livestock."

The man did not speak for a moment. When he continued, there was true sadness in his voice, "We did not expect the *Béarla* to come from the sea. There were but pregnant women and children in the village. I was there, being but wee. All of us ran, in a panic. I came upon Seonaidh and Ruairí, who had surprised Athair Mac Giolla Eoin, as he entered the forest. He told them what I knew al-ready, that the herring fisherman had seen the huge ships of the *Béarla* unloading soldiers all morning. He sent Ruairí to tell Eigneachan. When he was gone, he told Seonaidh it was too late for the village, that the men from the boats must be already to their homes, which I knew to be true. She screamed and cried, 'No! My Mam is back home with the wee twins!' He tried to explain there was noth-ing she could do to help, that she had to save herself, and go with him to safety - but she would have none of it. 'You are the one,' she said. 'You named me *drochthuar* before even I was born.' He begged and pleaded with her, said he named her gift of God, named her Seonaidh, and anyone who called her *droch-thuar* betrayed the *Spiorad Naomh*. But she was angry. 'You turned everyone against me,' she said, 'Everyone looked upon me as if I was painted the devil's scarlet from head to toe. Ruairí was my only friend, and you just sent him away! You are my curse, priest! I call you Athair no more!' And she turned and ran like the wind, straight off the path into the forest. There was no way for him to follow, much less catch her. He called out her name, but she did not stop. It was then when I came out of hiding, and spoke to him. I said I would go with him, and I did."

After a long moment, he spoke again, "All of them died, except her – but she was shipped off in chains to Montserrat. I was then *drochthuar* - the un-wanted, the pest, the extra mouth to feed with no kith or kine. I left for the city soon enough, and have been useless to man ever since. I do not know why I am still alive. The bottle should have killed me dead long ago. I suppose now I know why I lived."

The man did not elaborate, but Jake wanted to know. "Why?"

"Because I was to meet you, and you were to meet me."

"But why, sir?"

The man teared again, but with sadness, remorse, and shame, "I left my mother and father to die. I left all my family, my friends, and my home out of fear. I should have fought and died with them, however young I was. I am a shameful coward. I have disgraced my clan, and my line. I am a blackheart. How can God ever smile upon the likes of me?"

Jake felt as if he had a tremendous responsibility to this man. He wasn't sure why. Somehow the man's words had connected them together. He spoke without thinking, "Because you are forgiven."

The man nodded, then moved from a sit. He laid flat on the floor of his cell, as if it were a bed, and closed his eyes.

Jake stood, and walked out. He had no recollection of interacting with the jailors, as he had to in order to leave the cellblock, but found himself outside.

He collapsed to his knees and wept, and did not know why.

1788

Xavier

The Kingdom of France was hereby created in the year 1180 of Our Lord by the Capetians, in the line of Hugh Capet, the Robertian, a mighty King of Francs.

House of Capet

Philippe II the Augustus	1180–1223
Louis VIII the Lion	1223–1226
Louis IX the Saint	1226–1270
Philippe III the Bold	1270–1285

The Kings of France and of Navarre

Philippe IV the Fair, the Iron King	1285–1314
Louis X the Quarreller	1314–1316
Jean I the Posthumous	1316
Philippe V the Tall	1316–1322
Charles IV the Fair	1322–1328

Woe upon France at the death of Charles, for he was the last Capetian. The Valois were the rightful Kings, but the excremental Plantagenets of England waged war for a false claim. For one hundred years, until the coming of Saint Joan of Arc, French blood fertilized barren fields. There was only darkness.

House of Valois

Phillipe VI the Fortunate	1328–1350
Jean II the Good	1350–1364

Stripped of lands,
these Kings could not bear their true arms.

Charles V the Wise		1364–1380
Charles VI the Beloved, the Mad		1380–1422

By treaty did a hateful English King take the Crown of France.

Henry VI of England		1422–1453

House of Valois
(Continued)

Charles VII the Victorious, the Well-Served	1422–1461

The war ends in 1453.

Never since the ancient land of Israel has the Lord intervened to save a nation. Yet the Lord God did just this, and sent Joan of Arc, the Maid of Orléans, to save France. The French people have been annointed by Christ himself to serve him and his purpose. The sun dares to shine on France once more.

Louis XI the Prudent, the Cunning the Universal Spider	1461–1483
Charles VIII the Affable	1483–1498
Louis XII Father of the People	1498–1515
François I the Father and Restorer of Letters	1515–1547
Henri II	1547–1559
François II	1559–1560
Charles IX	1560–1574

And with the death of Charles, storm clouds gathered. The Wars of Religion came to France, like pitch and fire on thatch. The King's heirs were carried off by accident, disease and assassination.

The armies of the God of Peace butchered each other.

But Henri of Navarre, God bless him forever, converted to Catholicism and became King. He was part of both worlds, and brought peace to all.

He thereby started the House of Bourbon, The greatest line of Kings this world has ever seen.

House of Bourbon

Henry IV the Green Gallant, Good King Henri	1589–1610
Louis XIV the Great, the Sun King	1643–1715
Louis XV the Beloved	1715–1774
Louis XVI the Restorer of French Liberty	1774–1792

Chapter 22

Xavier had more time on his hands. He had finally read *Confessions*, the book Bonchamps had given him, as well as the Constitution of the United States. He wished he hadn't read either.

The Freemasons of Nantes had just inducted the painter Jacques-Louis David into their ranks and, as Xavier sat in a cushioned Sené bergère in the lounge, they were giddy and chatty over the import of the event. David himself was surrounded by brethren, like a prima donna after an opera. Xavier could plainly hear his voice, "*Ertes'ome. Terbalues er'ome. Terrat'n'philosophy cassahadow'n eberting.*" David was getting more and more difficult to understand. As a youth, he had been accidentally slashed in the mouth during sword practice. He had developed a tumor, and it seemed to have grown larger. As a result, conversing with him was arduous. Xavier had no desire to socialize with him tonight. He was always drained after the meetings, especially this one, and the idea of bringing David home and listening to his castrated warbling seemed unbearable.

But David was his guest. It was a long story - of his mother, actually. Even when she could not afford to do so, Phillipa made overtures to the talented, up-and-coming painters of Paris, because that is what the matrons of Traversier did. As a result, several artists had been brought to Nantes, and feted at the Château Meilleur. David was one of these painters, but his status had changed considerably. Art was currently defined by the Rococo style: whimsical, ethereal, and overly-stylized. Paintings were full of chubby angels descending from billowing

381

clouds, to figures in billowing blouses - and billowing bosoms. David eschewed it all, and became a modern Roman painter - blunt, historical, allegorical and deadly-serious. This Neoclassical style was a lit keg of powder in the basement of the artistic establishment.

It was perhaps the humiliating defeat of the Seven Years War, when the nation had to admit she had been eclipsed, when the memory of Rome began to figure heavily upon the French mind. Roman virtue was represented by the *fasces* - a simple bundle of sticks. Each of the rods was easily broken alone, but tied together they were adamantine. *Fascism* was the concept of civic-minded, virtuous citizens coming together as human fasces, and undertaking the responsibility for upholding the state. This was now a French ideal.

Perhaps it was inevitable.

Since the Renaissance, Roman virtues had been taught more than Christian values, Roman history more than French. Even after avenging themselves upon the British, the French spirit longed for Fascism, for national greatness and virtue. The standard by which France judged itself was now the brilliance of Republican Rome. When modern Kings, nobles, and clergy failed to live up to her imagined splendor, there was disquietude. Had David not been, he would have been invented. Fascism and Rousseauian Socialism dove-tailed nicely in the mind of the Freemason. When David, painter of the New Rome, returned to the Meilleur for the second time, he was an international celebrity. Everyone in the city knew David had come to Nantes. Everyone knew he was staying at the Château Meilleur.

L'Oublié quietly moved to Xavier and gave him a snifter of *eau de vie*, and then left him with his thoughts. It would probably take an hour of quiet, and several more refills, before his mind slowed enough to entertain the notion of sleep.

The meeting had been an unmitigated disaster.

After the rites and during dinner, Chapelle, the lawyer, was speaking of America, "The doughty Americans are now ratifying their new, hard-earned Constitution. Thousands of French soldiers, marines and sailors, from every level of society, have returned - besotted with American virtues and dreams of freedom. The American revolution has inspired the nation as no other event in history. In many ways, philosophically and militarily, we are the proud parent of the American newborn."

Cœurfroid interjected, "If they are our children, they are as recalcitrant as my own. They made peace with the British behind our back. We received nothing for our trouble but mountains of debt."

A notary named De Heulee spoke, "And we are now continually reminded of the incompetence of our government, as they fail again and again to bring sanity and balance to the national finances."

Francois-Pierre Blin, a medical doctor. grimly interjected, "We went to war for vengeance, and thought of nothing else. We achieved it. We humbled Britannia, on land, and even mostly on the sea. There is no cost for the return of honor, brothers. No price for the return of face."

Xavier thought that was a contradictory thing for a doctor to say, but it was the times.

"The King must call the Estates-General. Then we will be given political power," said a young voice. The trader, Julien Videment, perhaps.

The Estates General could override the blocking mechanisms of the nobles, such as their regional Parlement courts. The idea of France being composed of the three estates, however, was laughably out of date. Most of the nobles - the greater portion - came from wealthy bourgeois families who had simply bought their titles. The clergy was hopelessly divided. Some were actual religious servants, and others were scions of noble houses who were getting a salary and didn't even necessarily believe in God. The idea of a commoner estate was even more riotous. The vast majority of the people, and an increasing percentage of her wealth, was common. France *was* a commoner state.

Guillaume Bouteiller, an elderly and well-loved retired merchant, spoke loudly due to his deafness, "Wait - what? Aren't we getting ahead of ourselves? What of the Constitution of which you speak? Who has read the damn thing?"

Xavier spoke, "I have."

He came to regret those words.

Jérôme Charles Olivier raised his glass, "Of course you have, Brother."

Xavier smiled and raised his glass.

Bouteiller pounded the table, "Well, stand up. Let's hear it!"

There were cheers of, "America!" "The Constitution!" Xavier stood, and everyone pounded on the tabletop.

Xavier waved them down. "Brothers, the Declaration of Independence, although penned by Franklin, Adams, and Jefferson, could have been written by Rousseau himself."

"Vive Rousseau!" said a voice, then laughter.

Xavier continued, "It followed that their new political system would in fact reflect his philosophies."

"Yes!" shouted the chorus.

"If it did, their system would be possessed of a strong federal government, capable of protecting freedom-loving individuals from others who opposed their ways and views."

"*Urrygut, urrygut,*" garbled Jacque-Louis David from the shadows.

Xavier smiled, "It would be an enlightened, empowered government capable of social and economic engineering at the national level, to ensure the life and liberty of its citizens." Xavier paused, unsure of the proper tack regarding the ideas he was about to express. He decided on a neutral tone, "I have come to realize that nothing is further from the truth. In fact, it is my personal belief that there was a brilliant conspiracy to remove the Freemasons, and therefore Rousseau, from its authorship."

Dead silence followed his words. Xavier should have heeded the warning. He did not.

Instead, he continued, "I believe that Franklin, who was too well-respected and well-loved to move against, was instead made the moderator of the Constitutional Congress, for the very reason of elevating him beyond the ability to directly influence its creation. Perhaps they knew he was too elderly to juggle too many responsibilities, and ensured he had them *en masse*."

Silence.

He continued, "I believe that Jefferson was similarly dispatched. He was elevated out of authorship by being given the seemingly illustrious post of Ambassador to France. Which was a meaningless position, given the American betrayal, and their obvious lack of interest in truly supporting us in any way."

Dead silence.

He continued, "I believe that a brilliant coup promoted the Freemason leadership out of the way, so that men of different beliefs could come to the fore. Two-thirds of the writers of the Declaration of Independence were Freemasons. Two-thirds of the authors of the Constitution were not. One must understand that Montesquieu, not Rousseau, was the philosophical backbone of the document."

There was no more silence. Everyone shouted at once.

"*En enfer* with Montesquieu!"

"He is the antichrist of the Rousseauian ideal!"

"He was a damned noble! Why on earth would they have a thing to do with Montesquieu?"

It was only now that Xavier realized he had badly misstepped. No one here actually cared about the Constitution. They were here for Socialist church - to be told they were right, to find a community, to voice their righteous anger. There was no desire for debate. Debate indicated a stick was outside of the *fasces,* weakening the whole. It was a danger to the virtuous populace, those attempting to move as one.

Montesquieu was a pariah, an untouchable. He departed radically from the Rousseauian model, and was generally despised by Republicans for his noble and wealthy upbringing. In America, he was widely read and respected - here, he was hated and ignored. Xavier wasn't sure how to proceed. He shrugged noncommittally, and continued, "I am simply saying the American Constitution is readily recognized as his intellectual progeny, if not an outright plagiarism."

"How so?" The voice was almost angry. The loud silence continued after he spoke.

Xavier was taken aback. No one had used that tone with him in a long, long time. He wasn't sure who spoke, so he shrugged, and continued, "Montesquieu saw humanity through - shall we say? - a more Protestant optic: man's nature is basically evil, and incapable of change. He saw the conflict between different groups as inevitable, that man would always lust for power and control. Montesquieu designed a government pitting three branches of government - executive, legislative, and judicial - against each other, in a system of checks and balances, in a way that still allowed them to govern, thereby insuring liberty throughout all levels of society. This is exactly what has been created in the Constitution - even in their choice of names for the branches. In addition, the governments of the Thirteen Colonies will remain as strong state governments, therefore providing an even bigger check on national power and ambition, and ensuring the liberty of the people."

A man Xavier's age, Thierry Alain Bedos, spoke with a twisted face, "And yet they still have slavery! It sounds as if you believe all of this – and you are against Rousseau." He had probably blurted it out without thinking, but regardless, it was a public challenge to Xavier's political affiliation – much less his career.

And that could not pass.

Xavier chuckled, "My dear Monsieur Bedos, I know all of the cultural habits of the African Yoruba, but that doesn't mean I'm going to strip naked and bang a drum - now does it?"

Everyone laughed at Bedos, and his face turned red. Xavier stared evenly at him. A look of resignation came over Bedos's face, and he nodded to Xavier - *touché*.

Good enough. The dolt would learn to think before he spoke in the future.

Xavier had enough of the cannon fire meant for Montesquieu, and used the laughter as an opportunity to sit. He didn't need non-religious, religious fanaticism to get in the way of his thoughts, or his approbation.

As the debate raged around him, his mind chewed on another disagreement between the two philosophers. Montesquieu believed that Rousseau's cult of the individual was a myth. Rather, human beings are better defined by their group affiliation. Whether it was family, community, faith, nation or, God forbid, the Freemasons, individuals were always seeking out larger entities to join and identify with. Montesquieu believed that man's true nature was to willingly become part of a community that demanded belief, and the limit of personal freedom in some way, to one degree or another, whether by belief or action.

If mankind is composed of individuals, and not communities, explain the need for ceremony - for example, the rites of the Rousseau-loving Freemasons - and what it then meant.

Xavier had to admit, intellectually, that Montesquieu was right. Rousseau, in the end analysis, was just a dreamer, an artist. But when one gives a speech to the mob, a good speaker plays on emotion. One speaks in songs - and Rousseau was music, a powerful, hypnotic chord progression, a philosophy for the angry and alienated, a justification for the self-righteous to be against whoever they wished to blame for their own imperfection and oppression. His group of followers could, therefore, include basically everyone. It was said the Queen herself was a doting admirer.

Xavier vaguely realized the formal meeting had ended. For him, it simply meant a change of chair. He moved into the parlor, shaking hands and smiling, and slipped into his current seat, to watch the Freemasons pay homage to the incomprehensible Jacques-Louis David.

Xavier shook his head at his own lack of foresight. The intelligentsia of France did not believe Rousseau was a philosopher. They believed he was the *messiah*, a Christ whose words were divinely inspired. Xavier had moved against Rousseau, and felt the ire of his cult. The trouble was, Rousseau was not worthy of idolatry.

That brought his mind back to *Confessions*, Bonchamps's book he wished he had never read. In his autobiography, Rousseau was a self-admitted debaucher, a libertine, the worst sort of scoundrel. His life was filled with mistresses and unwanted children who ended up on the orphanage steps. The shocking odds of such an infant surviving to adulthood were over a thousand to one – his children were as good as dead. Rousseau cared for nothing except his own fame, wealth and sexual conquests. His life was dedicated to himself, at the cost of others. In the end analysis, Xavier did not think he was any more holy - but Xavier was not starting a philosophical cult, nor influencing the minds of the world.

The question was, why had Rousseau written the *damné* thing anyway? Why admit all of this? Xavier thought about it, and found the answer was simple and obvious: Rousseau's true motivation was to create a world where he could do whatever he wanted, whenever he wanted to do it, and he would still be the most honorable of men, and feel no guilt or shame. He was smart enough to disguise this by empowering and validating his readers, imbuing them with self-righteousness, and proclaiming them moral, intelligent and well-educated - for simply agreeing with him.

Rousseau wanted to create a world where his urges were not beholden to his empathy. Rousseau enjoyed being a celebrity, he liked adoration and seducing women into his menagerie of egotism. His needs were wholly selfish, and had nothing to do with anyone but himself. It stood to reason that the perfect society he wished to create would uphold the individual, sanctify the needs of the individual, and create a government that would protect his rights. He wanted to bed women and, when he bored of their company, throw them and any ensuing children on the refuse pile. He wanted people to chant his name, and turn their heads when he walked in a room. He cared for nothing else, and wanted all institutions of mores and custom to tell him he was perfectly noble and within his rights for doing what he wanted to do, when he wished to do it, regardless of who he wanted to do it to.

He was charming, handsome and famous. He was also hated and reviled, fleeing one country only to be exiled from another. He did not, however, want to change things simply to avoid criticism and the law - he wanted to create a world where he was the *ideal*.

And yet...

Yesterday, Xavier had observed a line of young schoolchildren cross the street. His attention was quickly redirected to the other adults who were watching, for they were utterly entranced. There was a smile on every face. Some were even pointing, so others would notice the sight as well. The children might as well have been Naiads dancing toward the sea. It was not the first time Xavier had observed this new attitude toward the young.

France loved her children now.

It was becoming more and more pronounced, this fascination with innocence. It was a change in cultural seas from just short years ago. It astounded Xavier how his society could transform so quickly.

It was due, in large part, to Rousseau.

Xavier saw this change as wholly good. It was confusing, to the point of disconcertion, that Rousseau, and his possible impact, could not be easily classified. It meant that his ideas and opinions had outcomes that could not be foreseen for good or ill – and if Xavier could not see a Rousseauian future accurately, no one could. It was not hubris to think such a thing. It was simply accurate.

A voice broke his concentration: "The irony of it all is that Rousseau and Montesquieu were both French, we enabled American liberty through force of arms - and we're still a despotic Monarchy."

Xavier looked up and saw Maurice Cœurfroid sitting next to him. "Indeed, Monsieur Cœurfroid," he replied.

"You were right, of course. The Americans used the emotional Rousseau to light the fuse. But now the intellectual might of Montesquieu is their compass. But how does a hot-blooded revolution cool its ardor, and begin using its intellect and not its impulsive heart? Plainly our future might hinge on such a change. How did the Americans achieve this so effortlessly, and without any serious internal strife? Such as what you were just subjected to, for example?"

"Precisely." An idea buzzed half-formed in the back of Xavier's mind. The differences between Rousseau and Montesquieu ran much deeper. They were at a much more profound opposition to each other than anyone realized. It bothered him that he could not articulate his intuition further.

Cœurfroid interrupted his thoughts, "My advice would be this: let us put out the fire on our roof, before we rearrange the furniture in our living room."

"The fire being, in this case, the fact that we are still a Monarchy? Is it even realistic to think we can affect such a change?"

"Perhaps now. Our goals may be enabled by just one thing: the American war debt."

"It is said the King is reducing court expenses."

"To pay the debt for two world wars? Marie Antoinette, at her worst, is but a drop in the bucket. I have heard the court's expenses are anywhere from six to twenty-five percent of the national budget, depending on the politics of the speaker. But the court is, essentially, the central government of France. In light of that, the percentage is acceptable. No, the Queen inflames the masses, but a lavish court is only an insult to the poor, not the true problem. The King must tax the nobles – that is the problem. But the nobles have become used to the burdens of state being dropped on the bourgeoisie and the peasants. Bourgeoisie buy titles and avoid tax. The peasants cannot pay our debt alone, not this time."

"The nobles fight the King and his taxes, posing as defenders of freedom."

"And the king tries to tax them, by posing as the defender of the people, and the equalizer of class. Neither realize they both erode the other."

"Do you think the King will call the Estates General?"

"The Estates General would only give a platform to revolutionary views, and legal power to the bourgeoisie. If he is stupid enough to do such a thing, he deserves to be thrown out a Versailles window."

Xavier shrugged. It could go either way.

Cœurfroid smiled, then continued in a more jovial voice, "Where do you hide yourself these days, Monsieur Traversier?"

"Monsieur Cœurfroid, under no circumstances, from now until the end of time, would I ever hide from you."

"I do not worry about our friendship, Xavier. I know you would walk on coals for your friends. I worry about *you*."

Xavier leaned forward, "How so, Monsieur?"

"Man is not an island. It is not healthy for you to limit your social life to these meetings. You must now take your rightful place in Nantes society. You must find a wife, and start a family. It does not do for your poor mother to be alone, either. She must rejoin us."

Xavier was suddenly stuck in a morass of emotion. He wanted to reply, but had no words.

Maurice continued, "I have always seen you simply as my brother Xavier, the individual who sits before me now. My interactions with you have never been influenced by anything else, apart from who we are as men."

"I cherish our friendship, Monsieur."

"But you must understand something. For three-hundred years there have been Traversier, both men and women, who looked down their nose at the lesser families of Nantes. For centuries, these families have tried to be accepted, and advance their social status, and the ultimate judge and obstacle to these things has always been the *Messieurs et Mesdames* of your house."

Interesting.

Maurice shrugged. "People have long memories for slights. One would rather take a musket ball than be humiliated in front of neighbors. Yet Traversier has heaped its share of public scorn. Not always, not all the time. But enough to be remembered. When Traversier was at its lowest, there were the weak and the cruel who decided to seek a petty revenge by excluding you. They slighted you - in the exact way your family did to them."

Xavier found a lump in his throat. He was equally surprised and horrified. He felt like a child too overwhelmed by emotion to speak.

Where is this coming from? Why do I feel this way?

Xavier was twenty-nine years-old. He should have been married long ago. He was a millionaire, and had been for some time. He should have rejoined society by now. Why had he not? He hated to admit it but, truthfully, he was terrified. He was terrified that he would be rejected again, that what he achieved was not enough. He felt that nothing he could do would ever be enough. Deep down, he was still a fatherless young boy who was despised by his mother for no good reason. When he was dismissed by Nantes, it was a sickening feeling, but somehow it made sense – it resonated with the lessons of his upbringing. He once believed gold was the sorcery needed to break the spell. But now that he had gold, he was unsure of its magic.

"You might think this city is a nest of vipers, but you would be wrong. It is just a nest of people. And people are quite strange and humorous creatures, are we not?" suggested Cœurfroid.

"Yes, Monsieur. And I am as well. Strange and humorous."

"As am I. The truth is, the entire city has forgotten its treatment of you. The harsh words, ones that you will probably remember for the rest of your life, are words they have already forgotten they have spoken. The memory of their ill-will and joy at your descent has been erased, as if it were never there at all. The city of Nantes is now wholly concerned with gaining your good graces. Your family is the royalty of Nantes once again, with the coffers to match. Whatever perilous journey you undertook, knowing there was risk of failure at every turn, is now just seen as an inevitable success based on who you are, and where you came from. The past is moot- now, today, the city begs for your presence. And you must be gracious in a way that they were not, and rejoin them. And forget. Marry the woman who was most cruel to you, and see her worship the very ground you walk on for the rest of your life. And if that doesn't suit you, I have unmarried daughters who will certainly vex you for the rest of your life."

Xavier looked downward, "May I admit something to you, Monsieur?"

"Of course."

"I read in my father's writings that he did not like you."

Cœurfroid did not exactly smile, but his expression was friendly. He nodded.

Xavier continued. "I approached our relationship openly but cautiously. I keenly observed our interaction, attempting to find the qualities in you that had aggrieved him. I never found any. You are my dearest friend. His disparagement of your character makes me think less of him."

"Do not allow it. Your father was an admirable man, and he was certainly entitled to his opinions. His behavior was never less than honorable, and he was always well-mannered, and even friendly. He was very proud, your father."

"Yes."

Cœurfroid now smiled, "In exactly one month, I am having a ball. Everyone who is anyone in Nantes will be there. So will you. For you are indeed someone, Monsieur Traversier. And we would all be honored with your presence."

"As you wish, Monsieur."

Cœurfroid smiled broadly, slapped Xavier on the thigh and left his chair.

Soon after, Xavier summoned his coach, and sent a valet to tell David they were leaving. He did not need to look to know l'Oublié was behind him. They both entered the coach, but the door was left open. The coach, purchased last year in Paris, was made of imported ebony with pewter accoutrement, and a black leather interior. It could hold nine people quite comfortably. Its grandeur was totally lost on Xavier, and he knew this, but he had not bought it for himself to enjoy, only for reasons of prestige.

Xavier stared at l'Oublié. He was the oddest man he had ever known, and he still did not fully understand him. For some reason, they simply fit together - or they were two pieces that could fit with no other, and were alone - but alone together. At one point, Xavier asked him if he wished to become a Freemason. L'Oublié said nothing, and simply stared off. Xavier knew from prior experience that this expression meant *no*. Regarding his commitments, l'Oublié carefully considered everything, his caution bordering on the fanatical. Perhaps it was because l'Oublié was as loyal as Leonidas, once committed. Xavier supposed that if one were to have such a ferocious and generous loyal nature, it would pay to have a balancing quality of selectivity. The true question was why l'Oublié had foregone the admission. In any case, he waited in the parlor of the townhome during the meetings and Xavier would not be gainsaid, by his mason brothers or anyone else on the subject.

Xavier spoke to him, "Why do you reject the Freemasons? I ask simply out of curiosity."

L'Oublié said nothing for a long while. Xavier knew that he might answer, or he might not. But he did. "I do not believe in hope."

"It seems strange to ascribe that one word to us."

"Mankind only walks in circles. If we had but a longer memory, we would recognize the scenery."

"And what if we did?"

"When walking on footsteps, it seems wrong to celebrate progress, or the blazing of a trail."

Xavier chuckled, "No one looks too closely at the scenery, or the path, for that matter. We walk desperately in our little circles, do we not?"

"Yes," said l'Oublié, but his voice cracked. "So very desperately, Monsieur."

Jacque-Louis David jumped in the coach, "*Arcunastaynder all night. Gut people'll.*"

"You are always welcome in Nantes, Monsieur. I hope you know that."

"*Izzal'ays anoner to be here.*"

Xavier smiled, and tapped the ceiling with his cane. The coach began to move.

"*Imuzadmit something to'oo. Therza'oom just right'ar' entrance way that has t'mos'magcent light.*"

"Well, we shall have to set your studio up there. Or at least one of them. You are certainly welcome to spread out as you please, Monsieur David."

"*R'generosity's'always appreshtated, Monsieur.*"

David prattled on, and Xavier smiled and nodded when it was appropriate, but his thoughts were elsewhere.

The Freemason lodge was in the city center, looking for all intents and purposes like a large stone townhome in a neighborhood of other large, well-appointed townhomes. At one point, it was accessed through secret passages. There was no reason for that now, with the rapidly changing political climate, so business was conducted through the front door. Xavier, as he gently bounced home to the western part of town, thought about Cœurfroid's words. His mother, when told of the ball invitation, would be both ecstatic and hysterical. She would fret over her wigs and outfit, and worry over every detail, thinking her mental acrobatics could somehow will the evening into perfection. She had been out of society for some years now. He genuinely hoped that the upcoming experience would be nothing but positive, and their lives would thereby change for the better. He would have a month of pure bedlam, however, and he would just have to grit his teeth and bear it.

More merde *for the river. It never ends.*

Between the limestone storefronts and the carriage, a woman came into view, as she violently spun further away. She nearly cartwheeled before hitting the cobblestones. The carriage did not stop or slow. It took a moment for Xavier to realize that one of the carriage horses had probably struck her and thrown her to the side. Horrified, he slammed his cane into the roof of the coach until the carriage abruptly stopped. Xavier was nearly thrown across the cabin, but managed to get his bearings as l'Oublié quickly opened the door. Within seconds, all three men were by her side. She was a young woman, well-dressed, and unconscious. Her face was but a pale moon in the night's darkness. Xavier's horrified driver and footmen bounded over but a second later. "Help me get her into the coach." Xavier said as calmly as he could. Soon they all lifted her inside onto one of the plush leather benches. "Hurry home! As fast and as safely as you can!"

The Driver nodded and soon the coach moved back into the street. Xavier felt for a pulse. "It is strong. Thankfully. But she is still unresponsive."

"That does not bode well, Monsieur," replied l'Oublié.

"No. No, indeed."

"*Wemst hurry!*" offered David.

***

Madame Traversier was led to the room by a maid holding a candle. After the doctor had been fetched, and David safely ensconced in his bedroom, it was time for her to attend to their wounded charge.

Xavier sat next to l'Oublié in chairs by the door. Madame could not stand him, but she understood his connection with her son and tolerated him. "What happened, Xavier?" she asked.

Xavier sighed, "I saw her fly onto the stones as I looked out the far window. I think she was struck by the lead right horse."

"Of your carriage, as you traveled inside of it?" she asked, and Xavier nodded. "I will check on her."

"Thank you, Mother."

Madame opened the door. The young woman was partially undressed for examination, and in bed, still unconscious. Female servants - for the house was fully staffed once again - held candles for the Doctor, who sat by the prostrated woman's side.

"How is she, Doctor?"

"She has no broken bones, but has a very serious concussion. She needs to be bled - extensively, and as soon as possible. Her head must be kept cool, and she must remain in this position."

"Of course. Whatever needs to be done."

Xavier waited, slumped unhappily in the chair, then heard a piercing scream from inside - from his mother, no less. Xavier bolted from his seat, but Madame had already exited the room, and was backing away from the door. "The drowning! It is here! It is here!"

"*Mon dieu*, Madame! What is the meaning of this?"

She could only point. Her mouth uttered nothing but grunts and wheezes.

Xavier walked through the open door. The servant girls stood with their candles. Their faces showed only surprise and concern. They had no idea why Madame was horrified, they were only shocked by Madame's reaction. The Doctor looked equally perplexed.

Then there was a crimson spark, like a nova in the night sky, that suddenly erupted from the bed. Xavier was reminded of his trip to Saint-Florent-le-Vieil. It was the same shock of blood red light, the same explosion of vibrant color. But it was different this time - the sparkle changed angle, shifting in color and density, but did not vanish. It was real, undeniable, and emanating from the bed.

Looking down, he saw the young woman was in her shift. The laces of the blouse were partially undone at the neck. Hanging half-out of her shirt was a necklace. It was a cross of translucent white stone. Gold wrapped around it, like priceless metal ivy. It held the dying Christ in gold, and at its four ends sparkled clusters of crimson red diamonds.

The young woman, whom Xavier struck with his carriage, wore the Cross of Nantes around her neck. The family's priceless heirloom, lost long ago, had returned home.

It was impossible. It was ominous. Xavier found himself backing up, until l'Oublié's hand on his shoulder forced him to make a conscious effort to stop.

The Cross had come through time and across the world. It was not just in France, not just in Nantes - it was home.

It simply could not be.

It had to mean something.

1788

Guillaume

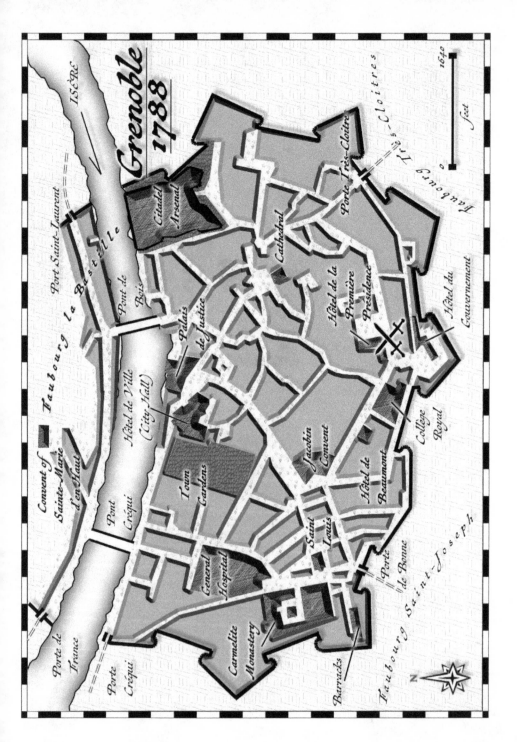

Grenoble
1788

Isère

Port Saint-Laurent

Faubourg la Bastille

Faubourg Saint-Laurent

Citadel
Arsenal

Pont de
Bois

Pont
Créqui

Convent of
Sainte-Marie
d'en Haut

Hôtel de Ville
(City Hall)

Palais
de Justice

Cathedral

Porte Très-Cloitres

Très-Cloitres

Faubourg

1640

Feet

0

Hôtel de la
Première
Présidence

Hôtel du
Gouvernement

Town
Gardens

Jacobin
Convent

Hôtel de
Beaumont

Collège
Royal

Saint
Louis

Porte
de Bonne

Faubourg Saint-Joseph

Porte de
France

Porte
Créqui

General
Hospital

Carmelite
Monastery

Barracks

N

Chapter 23

Guillaume received two letters. If he had read them out of order, he probably would not have read the second.

> *Dear Guillaume,*
>
> *I miss you desperately. Please write me more often. Write me even if it is only a few words. Your letters bring me such happiness. Remember to use my new address. If you send them to Saint-Florent-le-Vieil, sometimes they can take forever and a day to finally find their way to me in Nantes.*

Guillaume felt guilty. He loved his sister, and missed her. He should have written her more often, but he was forgetful. He couldn't understand how she could be so attentive to everything. Guillaume became bored with mundane details, and she delighted in organizing them. He wished she was not so far away.

> *I am so sorry to hear about the price of bread in Grenoble. Just remember though, we are meant to eat food, not just bread. God provides. If you walk outside of town, and plant some potatoes in the shade of the forest, no one would disturb them because no one even knows what they look like.*

The French think they are too good for potatoes, which is really quite puzzling. They are not above starvation, but they are above potatoes, rice and beans. I don't understand.

Guillaume rolled his eyes. He was far too busy to plant potatoes. In a complex society, there was division of labor and specialization. When food did not go where it is supposed to go, the system was broken and needed to be repaired or replaced. When everyone goes out and plants potatoes, who writes books? Who builds carriages and ships?

Estelle was such a girl.

There are edible greens and chestnuts virtually everywhere. In every stream and river, you will find fish. Food is in abundance. Do not feel entitled to white bread with every meal. Don't rely on anyone, and provide for yourself. It is not difficult, if you put your mind to it. Sometimes the city blunts our instincts. We become like house pets. We are like a poor cat, surrounded by mice, starving because no one puts scraps in our bowl.

Guillaume was sure the peasants had fished out the rivers and eaten the chestnuts. There were plenty of cattle, horses, goats and sheep to eat the greens. The problem was the system. But the rest of the letter was about her.

I have come to find myself in the most peculiar situation. I am, what is called, a companion. I can just now see you rolling your eyes, and asking me what I mean by that. Well, a companion is a paid friend for a rich young lady. They have fancy words for mercenaries fulfilling family positions. Paid mothers, for example, are called au pairs, nurse-maids, nannies and governesses. I am a paid friend, and I am properly called a companion. My only job is to accompany a wealthy, young lady, and keep her amused, educated, and out of trouble. I feel ridiculous. I feel utterly selfish.

I must admit that when people in my life said that I was kindly, or pleasant, that I felt pride. I have come to realize that I am none of those things. I am just a selfish, vain girl, who is skilled at looking after herself. I remember the priests of the cane slaves, who dedicated their lives to people who were beyond hope. They loved, and invested their emotions, in people who would be dead within a few years. They sacrificed themselves to help those in most need. And here is kind, noble, good Estelle - paid companion. Speaking of house pets, I truly am one. I am a cat with a jeweled collar. I am all silk dresses and hair ribbons now. I even wear makeup on occasion. I sleep on satin sheets, and a girl makes a fire in my room in the morning, and another one helps me dress – not to mention the teams of servants who create my meals. I feel utterly ridiculous.

She felt ridiculous because she was acting contrary to her nature, which was not like Estelle at all. Guillaume wondered what forced her to make such a choice. She wasn't telling him everything.

I'm afraid that my poor opinion of myself has made me a bitter critic of my surroundings, an attribute I find utterly unattractive in myself, but impossible to avoid. I will keep my employers anonymous, so that I can speak freely about them to you, and preserve at least a hypocritical semblance of Christian spirit.

Monsieur is well-mannered and pleasant, and is never at home. Madame feeds off the misery of others, and becomes despondent when she cannot produce enough suffering for a meal. My charge, whom I will call Femme, is a constant mystery to me. She is the most beautiful woman I have ever seen. I am not exaggerating. Her appearance is spell-binding. You can simply stare at her and marvel, for every inch of her is a wonder. It is good that she is beautiful, for her personality is quite aberrant. She is mostly emotionless, even unreachable. Her words do not come from her heart. They are scripted, and when not scripted, said because they are what she thinks someone else would say in the same situation. She is utterly hidden. Occasionally, one gets a glimpse into how she truly is, and, when I do, I pity her. She is the most fearful person I think I have ever met. Deep down, I think she is afraid of everything. She thinks every situation will end in its worst case, and every bad thing will continue forever. All events are simply harbingers of betrayal, or omens of worse things to come. Yet, if one did not know her well, you would think she was quite confident and brave. Her front is quite remarkable. Perhaps the acting of her front will honestly create those traits in her someday, God willing. I believe a casual observer would describe her as aloof, proud, calculating, sophisticated, metropolitan, graceful and elegant. I see her as a child, innocent on one hand, but filled with terror when she finds herself anywhere outside her understanding. She is remarkably intelligent, artistic and creative, which makes her company much less odious than it would seem. I try to be as open and honest with her as I can, but not a shred of it has been returned. I'm sure you can tell I am frustrated. My soul longs for true company.

Guillaume shook his head. He did not envy his sister, or women in general. The world of men was so much better. If there was a chap projecting as much nonsense as Femme, he would be beaten by his fellows until he snapped out of it, and quit his idiotic airs. Men cannot get away with half as much as women - and their lives are commensurately better for it.

Things would not be so bad if there was more of a Catholic community here. There are a few really strong churches, but, all in all, the ardor of faith is lukewarm at best. The religion of Nantes is money, like Le Cap, but it is much harder to get outside of town. My poor Femme has a bizarre prayer life. She hates going to church, but does so to vex her mother. They go to Protestant services, held in different places, many times in their own chapel, which is quite large but dismal. I find my way to Saint Clément, which is far, but worth the journey. Femme demands to pray in the family chapel at least two times per week for at least three hours. In the prior sentence, "at least" is no figure of speech. I tried to pray with her, but she simply kneels, prays in contemplative silence, and will not tolerate noise. I don't know if you have ever tried to kneel in silence for three hours, twice a week or more, but I nearly lost my mind. Femme was kind enough to talk to her father, and now when Femme goes to chapel, I have three hours all to myself. I usually spend them walking around town - it is so good to get out of the house. Nantes is an interesting place, every bit as busy and almost as wealthy as Le Cap. I think I even like the temperature more, but it certainly could be sunnier.

Of course, I am no fool when it comes to Femme and her machinations. Even to the most pious, a regimen of more than six hours a week of completely silent prayer is unusual. For some reason, she always has the door locked from the outside when she is within, so all know she does not sneak out on some perfidious errand. Perhaps that is exactly the reason for it: she just wants to be alone. She could have just asked, but that is not her way. I refuse to ponder on the matter further. If Femme wants to spend hours alone in the chapel, without books or music or company - much less a comfortable seat and adequate lighting - I gladly grant her wish. I enjoy my walks.

Something was very wrong with Estelle. Her letter did not sound like her at all. He wished she would confide in him, so he could give her some advice, but - as she would say - that was not her way.

I love you dearly and miss you. Please write me. And ignore everything I said about Femme, Madame and Monsieur. I think I might be the only person in the entire world who would complain of rich meals, satin sheets, new clothes, wigs and jewelry - and a gargantuan, luxury townhouse to live in. I am ridiculous. No one beats me, or even raises their voice to me. I don't have to do any sort of manual chore at all, really. I read a lot, and Femme and I try to learn things together. She plays pianoforte like Mozart, sings like an angel, and always has an interesting opinion on art, literature and world events. I should count my blessings, and pray to learn why God has sent me here. I must find my new purpose, and help fulfill my appointed destiny, whatever that might be. I am blessed, truly.

Forever bound to you, oceans of love,

Estelle

PS - Can you send me more of your used paper? I have tried to discard sheets where I have made some kind of mistake, and I can't bear to throw away such expensive stationary. Thank you ever so much! Please tell me what to send you. I have no needs, and many resources.

Guillaume smiled and shook his head. That was his Estelle. She was a lake. Try as you might to roil the surface, it simply became placid and tranquil in no time at all. She wanted the used paper so she could throw away her written thoughts when she reconsidered them. The current letter was written on such expensive stationery that she could not bring herself to do so. Her thriftiness forced her into entrusting Guillaume with her true feelings. He would never send her paper again. He thirsted for all of her opinions. Her tranquil pond letters did not tell enough of the truth.

Guillaume opened the second letter.

Dear Guillaume,

My Second Son, I mourn truly, for it is my duty to tell you that your brother in spirit, Raphaël, has passed away.

I mourn with you, Second Son Guillaume, for we loved him truly, and only we can understand each other's depth of sorrow in this moment.

His last words were of you and of Estelle, although I do not believe either of us has met her. However you described her to him must have made an impression, and she was as real to him as wood, and he loved you both with a full and pure heart, as was his way.

I realize that I was less of a father to you as Raphaël was your brother, but I want you to know that I am your family, and you are always welcome here. You and your sister, and even your father, are always welcome here. What is mine, is yours. You will always have a home, and a destiny, in Le Cap.

A Second Father's Love,

Papa Pinceau

Guillaume felt the strangest sensation. It was as if color was a liquid on the world and it suddenly evaporated, leaving everything dull and grey. He simply sat on his bed, the letter resting gently between two of his fingers, until he realized he was cold, and it was dark.

Over the next few weeks, his attitude did not change. His professors were concerned. The few friends he had were concerned. Guillaume and his class were close to graduating. There was a giddy excitement running through the school that Guillaume did not share.

Guillaume graduated in a fog. He half-expected Estelle to be there, even though he had not written her. He thought she would somehow know he was graduating, and undertake to be there on her own. He was actually surprised when she wasn't, and vaguely concerned. His father was not there, but he did not expect him to be. He graduated *cum laude*, which was quite an honor, but could have done better had he been a more diligent student. Unfortunately, due to his lack of mental discipline, he simply could not apply himself when he was bored.

After graduation, Guillaume put everything he owned on his bedsheets and tied it all together. He left school, and ambled aimlessly through the city. The smell of fresh bread stopped him. He found himself next to a bakery, open to the street. He realized he was very hungry, and had not eaten in some time. He took all the coins he possessed out of his pocket. He had half a livre - ten sous. It would be enough for a four-pound loaf, with a little left over.

"Quarter loaf, Monsieur," he said to the tall, thick, balding baker.

"Fourteen sous, six deniers," he replied. Guillaume was dumbfounded. A workman's daily salary might be twenty sous.

"Why, that is absurd, Monsieur, "said Guillaume, "How are people eating at all?"

"They aren't. Just be glad you are not sick or old," the baker said grimly.

Guillaume found himself getting angry, "So the sick and old simply have to die? Of starvation?"

"I have nothing to do with this, Monsieur."

"Then who does? Whose responsibility is this?"

"The weather was too cold for a good harvest."

"Why doesn't the King help his people in these challenging times? Is he bankrupt? Why is he not flooding the nation with Polish grain? Or better yet, good, dry American flour?"

He shrugged, "It is the war debt."

Guillaume did not realize it, but his voice carried, and a few people had gathered. "You are making too much money from this famine, Monsieur."

The Baker saw the crowd, and broke into a sweat. Men had been hung from the lampposts and murdered for such an allegation. "No, no, Monsieur. Far from it. The flour is expensive; therefore, the bread is expensive. That is all. Fetch the police if you wish. They will tell you."

"*En enfer* with the police. Is wheat expensive, as opposed to flour? Why do you not buy wheat, and grind it yourself?"

"Monsieur, come now" the Baker nervously laughed, "It is expensive to grind wheat, and one needs specialized equipment."

"I demand a loaf of *merdique* bread," said Guillaume. The baker was a big man, but Guillaume did not care. He was a *Mamelouk* from Le Cap, and he had killed someone with his bare hands. He was a hairsbreadth away from pulling the baker over the counter, and beating him against the floor.

"Now, now, Monsieur. I know that you are a good man," said the Baker.

"I am no thief, Monsieur! I do not want to rob you. But you will sell me a *foutu* loaf of bread for nine sous, or I will beat you senseless, take the loaf of bread, and place the nine sous in your *bordel de* pocket as you lay!"

There was a moment where anything could have happened.

But just then, a young man in a warm coat pushed his way through the crowd to the inside of the bakery, "Bonjour, Gabin," the man said to the baker.

"Bonjour, Victor," whispered the relieved Baker.

Guillaume turned, and saw the man, and the crowd behind him. Now he was properly incensed. If the baker believed the arrival of these people and his friend would change anything, he needed to be disavowed of the notion immediately. Guillaume turned to the new arrival, ready to take him on. But the man was looking at him with a smile, as if Guillaume was his friend and not his foe. He traded similar looks with others in the crowd, as if he had great news of import. The man spoke, "Grenoble is in need. You will never believe this."

"What?" asked Guillaume.

"Do you know of Brienne?"

"I know of Cardinal Étienne Charles de Loménie de Brienne, the Archbishop of Toulouse, and Controller-General of the King."

The attention of the crowd was on him as he replied, "The very same."

There was a female snort, "All pagan noble sons need two salaries, one from the church, and one from the Throne. How else to pay for courtesans and coffee?"

A male voice from the crowd, "We need more cardinals who have never performed mass. It saves on bread." Dark laughter erupted.

A woman spoke from the crowd, "What of Brienne?"

The coated man spoke excitedly, "Brienne is trying to achieve the goals of his predecessor Calonne, and the Assembly of Notables."

A man spoke, "What did they suggest?"

Guillaume answered quickly, "The King appointed Calonne to create an Assembly of Notables to come up with solutions for our financial troubles. Their recommendations were revolutionary, and would help everything: an equal land tax, hiring workers to perform public works, the abolition of internal tariffs, and the creation of real elected provincial assemblies. Brienne took over, and has not proven the man for the job, I will tell you."

Another woman, holding a listless, dirty baby, snarled from the back, "What does this have to do with the price of bread, and this *foutu* baker?"

Victor took off his hat, and bowed to her, "Madame, it has everything to do with him. Brienne has issued an edict. It is complicated, but it effectively dissolves the Parlements. The nobles can no longer keep their privileges, or block the King's attempts to tax them. But Grenoble has had enough."

"What do you mean?" asked Guillaume.

"I mean, the judges rejected the edicts. They said the edicts violated the terms that France made with Dauphiné when the two countries merged. But then the King's men effectively made our leaders sign them into law - at bayonet point, *Messieurs et Mesdames*, literally at the points of bayonets!"

Guillaume could hear the crowd muttering, rumblings which were gaining in magnitude. He narrowed his eyes. The King was acting against the privileges of the nobles on behalf of all of France, albeit in clumsy and tyrannical fashion. Why would the townspeople be angry? Are they for the nobles, against tyranny? Did he miss reading a pamphlet?

A woman shouted, "There is a pamphlet everyone must read. It is called *The Spirit of the Military Enforcement of the Edicts of May Tenth*!", and she began to hand them out. Guillaume took one and smiled. "Vive Dauphiné!" she shouted, and the crowd took up the cheer.

Victor continued, "This would not stand, and it did not! The nobles of the Grenoble Parlement and the city councilors have rejected the edicts. Brienne has sentenced them to exile! Brienne has exiled the Grenoble Parlement and the Grenoble city council... *from Grenoble!*"

The crowd was growing more agitated - and, looking around, Guillaume saw shops were closing and men and women armed with axes, shovels, and staves were marching down the street - excited by some prior exhortation, some prior reading. Who knew? It probably had more to do with cold Winters than politics. Anger made people into hammers. Hammers sought nails. Sometimes it was that simple.

Victor shouted over the din, "Troops are coming to take them away and enforce the exile! We cannot let this happen! With me!"

With that, the dam broke. Guillaume's small crowd of onlookers followed Victor and moved away. Guillaume saw that the baker was quickly closing his shop. "Pardon, Monsieur," said Guillaume quietly, "I'll give you half a livre now for the loaf, and the rest tomorrow. I'm sure I'll be able to loot something worth a few sous within a couple of hours, the way things are going."

"All right then," resolved the baker. He handed a loaf to Guillaume and took his coin.

"*Merci*, Monsieur," said Guillaume, "I apologize for losing my head. I was very hungry, and the last few months have been regrettable. I-I lost my brother."

"It is of nothing, *mon ami*. Go with God."

"Thank you," said Guillaume. He moved off into the street to join the crowd.

Guillaume

***

Guillaume chewed his bread and waited for the city to unhinge. He read the pamphlet, which was interesting and upheld Grenoble law against tyranny. Men and women ran everywhere, screaming and yelling, and waving staves and axes. At some point, the idiots must have taken the cathedral because the bells sounded out of time, and once they did, they rang continuously and discordantly. Guillaume thought the bells were as good a sign as any. He guessed the best place to procure his four-odd sous was the Hôtel de la Première Présidence, where the Duke of Dauphiné resided. The Duke had authority over the local troops who would be tasked to fulfill the exile orders of the Throne, and his residence would therefore be a target of the mob. He ambled toward it, since it was just down the street from the university school on the Rue Neuve. It was a high building on a square off from the narrow street, and both square and street were already crowded with the mob. Servants were yelling out the upper windows, telling the crowd to disperse. The crowd shouted retorts, and some of them threw stemless roses at the open windows. From the pamphlet, he knew the roses symbolized the three roses on the Grenoble coat of arms, which in turn symbolized the three ruling branches of the city: the bishop, the duke and the city consuls. Guillaume marveled. It was centuries since Grenoble was independent, yet here was all the patriotic fervor of Thermopylae spearmen.

Guillaume noticed wealthy townhomes set against the walls of the city, directly across the street from the Hôtel on Rue Neuve. He imagined the inhabitants of the townhomes probably were more inclined in sentiment toward the duke, rather than the mob, and were, most likely, properly terrified over the morning's events. Guillaume strode to the front door of a townhome, bold as brass, and dropped the knocker four times. There was no answer, and he dropped it four more. Finally, a pipsqueak of a voice from an old man was heard behind the door, "Go away! Leave us in peace."

"Yes Monsieur, that is precisely what I need to speak with you about. If you could but open the door."

"Are you a policeman?"

"No, Monsieur. I am only a guard."

"A guard? For whom?"

"For you, Monsieur."

"I hired no guard."

"Precisely, Monsieur. But you need to. Right now. If you do not believe me, look out your windows."

There was a long moment of silence. Guillaume did not think the man was looking out his windows because he believed the man knew exactly what was happening. The man was calculating, that was all. He was finally heard again. "We don't have any money."

"That's all well and good, Monsieur. My rate is only one livre an hour."

"That is highway robbery."

"No, it is the best money you will spend all year, Monsieur. I guarantee it."

"How do I know you will stay?"

"You will pay me at the conclusion of every hour. I am just graduated from the university school, Monsieur. I am an honest man, and a fearless one. No harm will come to you while I am here."

There was a moment of silence, then the old man spoke, "Very well."

"I will begin my post. If you have something to drink, that would be marvelous."

"All I have is well-water."

"And it is appreciated. As long as it is pure and clean." Guillaume sat down in the middle of the steps, so no one could pass without confronting him first. The water was brought out by a young maid, quivering with fear. "Thank you," Guillaume said, and she disappeared behind the locked door without a word.

But his attention was pulled to the scene across the street. The crowd was surging in and out of the Hôtel. The servants of the duke, police and soldiers were pushing them back, and were in turn pushed inside. More soldiers were showing up, but were still outnumbered. They looked like Marines from the *Régiment Royal-La-Marine*, based nearby. The Marines had their rifles slung, it was just a pushing match, not even to the level of good tavern brawl. As more Marines showed up, however, the situation seemed to get worse, not better.

Guillaume was becoming increasingly angrier. It had been over a *foutu* hour, yet the door had not been opened again, and he had not been paid. The *damné* insolence! Did they not know the danger they were in? Did they not see what was happening right outside their door?

A knot of four young men walked by. One of them grinned at Guillaume, "Having fun, Monsieur?"

"Guard duty," he replied, "But my thoughts are half-way to kicking in the door."

"As you were then, *Soldat*," the man said and saluted. The rest laughed and joined the fray.

People were coming from both directions. It wasn't just Marines and townspeople. Peasants, wet from swimming the Isère, were showing up in knots and bolts. The noise, amplified by the tall buildings, was getting ridiculously loud.

A flying, fist-sized stone nearly brained Guillaume. He stood immediately, and looked for the culprit. No one was holding rocks, no one was looking in his direction. He sat back down, one step higher, and held the stone in his right hand. Whoever was throwing stones was going to get a hard surprise.

Fifes and drums were heard as the mob was pushed southwest. Soon an organized company of Marines appeared from around the bend to the north. The second rank had bayonets on their rifles, while the first did not, and pushed the crowd back with barrel pokes. They were led by a young officer on horseback. Slowly they were making their way to the Hôtel, forcing the mob to retreat. Soon they made the square – but now there weren't enough Marines to completely clear the space. The mob clung to the south walls and moved west. A chant of "Dauphiné! Dauphiné!" shot up from the crowd. The closer to the Hôtel the soldiers came, the more violent the action. By the time they were in front of Guillaume, the violence had now escalated beyond the level of a brawl, and was gaining intensity. But every time one member of the mob took a barrel-jab to the face, had enough and stepped back, three more took his place.

Guillaume wasn't having fun anymore. He stood and watched, a bit horrified, but not sure which side he was on. He knew the mob was composed of idiots, fighting on the wrong side of everything, but somehow the sight of them being roughed up by the soldiers - who were increasingly angry and violent - was not sitting well in his stomach. Except for the push-pull at the Hôtel entrance, the citizens of Grenoble had only been throwing flowers and epithets. Now there was blood aplenty, coming from broken noses and knocked out teeth.

Space opened up between the soldiers and the mob, right in front of the Hôtel. The soldiers were screaming and the crowd was cowed – except for an old man, very old, perhaps in in seventies, who moved toward the line of soldiers. He tried to fight past the front ranks but didn't have the strength to do much. He did grab a man's musket, and would not let go. The soldiers, try as they might, could not dislodge his grip. Soon a member of the second rank came forward and helped, and finally the old man's grip was broken and he was thrown back. He made the mistake of rushing forward again, and found himself accidentally impaled on the second rank soldier's bayonet. The soldiers pushed him away. He fell to the ground, and soon after his shirt turned bright red from the wound. Men from the crowd bolted out, grabbed the wounded old man, and quickly pulled him to safety.

Guillaume moved forward on instinct.

It was now only Guillaume who confronted the Marines. The soldier from the second rank, the one with the bloody bayonet, turned to Guillaume and snarled, "Get back, *fils de salope!*"

There was something about being violently confronted by a man, blood on the ground, being yelled at - whatever mix of present factors and recent history - but Guillaume snapped. He threw the stone at the soldier. It hit him hard in the face, badly cutting him open. He went down, clutching his cheek.

Now time stood still. The mob was well-back from the soldiers. Guillaume was fifteen feet from the nearest uniform. He was alone, totally alone, as the soldiers turned to face him. They were together a tableau for the mob, who were now transfixed spectators.

Guillaume found himself without fear. He was not only fearless, he felt a surge of power through his veins as if he was utterly indestructible, as if this moment - where his life hung in the balance, completely outgunned and outnumbered - was empowering. Everything was clear and uncomplicated. There was no shame, no humiliation, no wretched mix of conflicting emotion. Everything was black and white, simple. A musket ball could kill him, but it could not make him feel ashamed. A bayonet could pierce his heart, but it could not break it. There was nothing here that could injure him in a meaningful way, only in ways he did not care about at all. Without thinking, he felt himself take two steps forward. The soldiers raised their rifles.

Guillaume was going to die in less than a second. In a heartbeat of time, the soldiers would pull their triggers, he would be riddled with lead, and he would be dead. None of this occurred to him. In fact, looking at the soldiers, and the fear in their eyes, he again felt empowered. He raised his hands - not in surrender, but in defiance. His teeth flashed in a scornful snarl.

An incredibly loud series of reports came from the muskets as they fired at Guillaume, scaring the mob into screams, then horrified silence.

But when the smoke cleared, Guillaume stood completely unhurt. He was, incredulously, still unafraid, a sneer of utter contempt on his face. He spat, then spoke, "Now what, *jean-foutre*?"

There was a moment of total silence. No one could believe what they had just seen. Guillaume had to be the son of a god, dipped in the river Styx. If an actor attempted such a scene, he would have been derided and booed, for such a thing could not happen – it was impossible. But this was real. It had just happened. Everyone had just seen this play out before their own eyes – and Guillaume's attitude of complete contempt for the soldiers, absent any fear whatsoever, was absolutely real.

Out of nowhere, a woman put her hand to her heart and shouted, "*Beau Brave!*"

Beautiful Brave One.

She said it again in the silence, "*Beau Brave!*" Her voice carried a perfect mix of love and awe, honor and reverence. The moment, and the woman's voice, tempered the crowd from iron to steel. Almost without a word, the mob began tearing up the stones of the street, bursting into homes to access the roofs of the buildings. It was as if silent orders were issued.

The young Marine officer rode up behind his men, "Who fired? Who violated my orders?" The Marines reorganized to more shouts and curses.

Guillaume thought the officer had miscalculated. If he was smart, he would have immediately charged the crowd, or removed his men completely. There had been a sea-change, a tactical epiphany. It would have been best for that particular moment to either be forgotten - or expunged. The officer performed no action to achieve either.

Suddenly the ground exploded, as the Marines were pelted with roof tiles raining down from four stories up. From deep within the ranks of the crowd now flew cobblestones as well. They were forced to move back.

The war had begun.

The door behind Guillaume opened. The young, terrified maid came out. In her shaking, outstretched hand was a one livre coin.

Guillaume took it. "I will be going now. Find a flag - preferably the three roses of Grenoble, or the dolphins of Dauphiné - and hang it on the door. You'll be fine."

And, with that, he walked away.

***

There was more looting, and more shooting. Tiles were thrown in abundance, regardless of next season's rain. A few people died in the fracas, but not many. Later that evening, the Duke withdrew his troops from the city to prevent further violence, in an attempt to deescalate the situation.

The city did not return to normal that night. It did not return to normal the next day - nor the next week. In fact, if anything, the resistance became more organized, and more cogent. The leaders of the resistance demanded that the Estates-General of Dauphiné be called, to solve the problems of the nation independent of the hated Brienne. Heroes of the people were made: Jean Joseph Mounier, Antoine Barnave - who admitted to writing the inciting pamphlet, and a mysterious man known only as *Beau Brave*, the heart of the mob.

Finally, in mid-July, over a month after the beginning of the riots, order was finally established by the King's Marshall. He found the situation so dire that he allowed the Dauphiné provincial Estates-General to convene, in an attempt to pacify the region.

The Dauphiné Estates-General passed into law three demands: first, that the national Estates-General be immediately convoked; second, they pledged not to pay any taxes unless passed by the national Estates-General; and, third, they demanded the abolition of the *lettre de cachet*, warrants allowing arbitrary imprisonment on the King's authority.

These demands were accepted by the Throne. Brienne was sacked, and his last act as minister was to convene the national Estates-General, for the first time since 1614.

The trouble in Grenoble in the Summer of 1788 was to be known as *Journée des Tuiles* - the Day of Tiles. It found itself in every history book, large or small, for it was the official start of a far larger fire.

He did not know it, nor would he ever realize it, but Guillaume had just started the French Revolution. If it wasn't him, it would have been another - but it was him. Inadvertently, he grasped the mob like a sword blade and quench-hardened it. He was perfect for the task. Not only was he as handsome as a hero from a painting, he was fearless, smart, and inspirationally calm. Unknowingly, he was the ultimate product of the devil's thousand year-plan - a plotted series of events stretching into antiquity.

The tale of the heirlooms was about to begin.

1832

Jake

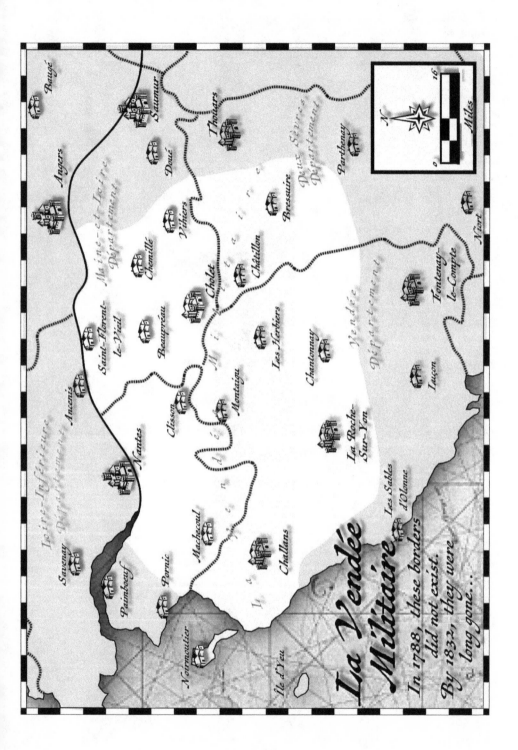

La Vendée Militaire

In 1788, these borders did not exist. By 1832, they were long gone...

Chapter 24

On the way back to Nantes, Jake tried to be more alert in regard to possible pursuers, who had plenty of time to catch up. There could be two groups – one from Tyran and one from *The Society*. He did not notice anything suspicious, and wondered if he had so easily lost his stalkers. Perhaps they did not exist at all.

In spite of this, he had plenty of time to think.

Jake was of two emotions regarding his quest. He was naturally apprehensive. A few more concerns had even cropped up, such as the possible threat of Monsieur Avenir, the return of L'Oublié, and the conflict between Tyran and *The Society*. But there was a part of him that considered himself abnormally lucky. The search had already taken him to new places - there were few people who could even dream of doing what Jake was being forced to do. It was a hollow thought, however: he could not rid himself of apprehension.

On the long ride from Liverpool to London, he journaled his experiences for Monsieur Tyran, who – he was sure – would be satisfied with nothing less than a full account. But as Jake wrote, he found it increasingly difficult to concentrate, at least on the journal. Try as he might, one fact kept playing in his mind over and over, something Monsieur Roquer had said.

For months, Tyran had been expected at the Château Meilleur.

Months.

Notices are not sent months ahead of time unless the destination is very far – and the travel has definite purpose.

It was reasonable to assume that Tyran had planned to come to France long before *The Society* knew it was going to rebel.

Such a thought begged a host of other questions.

Could Tyran have come to France specifically to find Jake? It was almost too absurd. There was no reason for Jake to be singled out for any reason, or that Tyran would know of him at all.

Except...

Jake thought of Isaäc's words. He had indeed been singled out by someone powerful – who ended up to be Monsieur Tyran.

Tyran then, more than likely, came to France for Jake.

Could that possibly follow?

Even if it didn't, it had all been planned from the beginning.

And that made absolutely no sense at all.

When Jake found himself captured, Tyran made sure he went to trial. That meant before the *avocats* spoke their first words, the judges knew he was to be found guilty and sentenced, and knew also the coffers of France would be sixty-thousand francs richer once Jake was in Tyran's service. Jake would probably have been deported, had Tyran not shown up. The trial was worth the coin for the government coffers, and – to the judges – the farce was probably not considered a particularly serious breach of ethics, considering the communal benefit.

But what if Jake had not been captured?

Perhaps Tyran would have done nothing more exotic than offer him a job and a large bonus. Perhaps the capture was completely unexpected - but may have benefitted Tyran by taking away Jake's choice from any equation.

But *why?* Why Jake at all?

Tyran had worked for the Traversier Trust, indeed he was a trusted member of the inner circle. He was recalled to Nantes during the last fateful meeting with Xavier, but was not present at the Château Meilleur.

Why? Why was he brought all the way back to Nantes – just to miss the meeting for which he was recalled?

Jake had a strong intuition that Tyran knew of the cross around his own neck, who gave it to his family - and why. The thought irritated him. The design on the cross, and its promise, was a mystery to Jake, at least when he became old enough to know how strange it all truly was. If Tyran knew, why would he not simply tell him. But Jake did not know this for a certainty – which was maddening. It was certainly possible that Tyran could have been utterly ignorant of his little cross and its designs until the trial.

But most likely not. After all, he had come a long way for Jake. He might know a lot more than he let on.

No, he *certainly* knew more than he let on.

Had he come only for Jake? Were there others? What was Tyran's network like? Were their dozens of men on his payroll – or only one?

And then there was the Second Heirloom – the insane quest for the devil's song of the Vendée. Tyran said he had heard the devil's song first hand, meaning he had presumably fought in the Vendée – and so had Xavier, according to Roquer. Is that where they met? Did something significant happen between them? Did they hate each other; were they brothers? Was it complete coincidence, and their meeting was actually later in time, and in a different place altogether?

Jake thought not. As he learned more, he believed that his cast of characters, and his theater sets of places, were all about to collide in a horrible, deadly accident, where the debris of Tyran's motivation and purpose could be pulled from the wreckage.

Tyran.

Tyran had an almost superstitious fear of the Cross of Nantes. His words describing it were worthy of a Philistine regarding the Ark of the Covenant. He was utterly convinced it was laced with some kind of power or destiny.

When Tyran discussed his motivations, it was always from a purely selfish perspective. He spoke of his own salvation, spreading light to counteract the infernal song – or some such equally dramatic nonsense. What else? Jake couldn't remember. He did recall that Tyran only discussed him as a means to an end.

And what of the devil's song?

Was Tyran mad? His words were moon-kissed, but Tyran did not comport himself like the lunatic who should have uttered them. Tyran appeared bellicose; appearance-minded; well-spoken, of hard words – but not insane.

…except for the fantastic nature of the quest itself – which was, admittedly, enough. Surprisingly, *The Society* took him and his quest quite seriously. Perhaps their hopes blinded them. Perhaps they thought he was mad – but might find the Cross anyway in spite of it.

Neither could Jake forget the Irishman's story. There was a part of him that believed the old man was planted by Monsieur Tyran, because his words were so reminiscent of the details of the Crimson Heirlooms. But such a thing was impossible. The Londonderry sheriffs had been very familiar with the old drunk.

Had Tyran come to Ireland and spoken with Aodh Dubh?

No – of course not. Jake had barely been able to speak to him. If Tyran had tracked him down and asked him the same questions, Aodh Dubh would have certainly said something to Jake, surprised at such an agonizing coincidence. That did not happen. Aodh Dubh's words were no planted evidence.

Jake was forced to acknowledge that some sort of eerie, supernatural coincidence had occurred.

Except that the supernatural did not exist.

If a carnival gypsy had been paid to tell one's future, it was a good bet to wager for an omen of toil and trouble, followed by great wealth and happiness. The charlatan priest did no better. Everything was then serendipitous for very good, common-sensical reasons. Snake oil salesmen had the same techniques, whether they wore top hats or collars. Jake, armed with this conviction, dismissed the priest's words entirely.

The supernatural did not exist, and neither then did the second heirloom.

But Tyran believed that it did, and forced the court to put it in writing. Tyran said he had already heard the song, indeed, heard it practically everywhere – some kind of ubiquitous, nightmarish sonata.

Why then was it so important that Jake learn the words to a song Tyran *already knew*?

Jake shook his head at the inanity of having to ponder over such fairy dust.

The girl in the painting, the Cross, the Vendée, Xavier, Seonaidh, Tyran, Nantes, Haïti - those were the branches upon which the spider had spun its web, and they were real. Eight carriages sped inexorably toward the same intersection, destined for a diabolical collision - as it had already happened decades ago. Now through his detective work he had to witness the accident second hand as best as he could, and shift through the ancient rubble for clues.

But there was another question that had to be asked. Could Jake possibly be connected to the actors of this play? Could he somehow be instrumental in the recovery of the Cross of Nantes – and not just in his ability to travel in Haïti, which was certainly not worth sixty-thousand francs. Was he one of the coaches headed toward the intersection as well?

As he thought of it, he realized that such a thing was impossible. His grandfather, may he rest in peace, was an American-born, very religious reformed Protestant, whom some called Puritans. His father was almost as religious, but was somehow a Catholic, a nearly impossible feat to achieve in Massachusetts. Neither his father nor grandfather had struck him as being particularly adventurous – quite the opposite. They were peaceful family men until the great tragedy of his mother's death. Jake found it hard to believe that his grandfather had been to war, had it not been for the faded scars of his wounds. There was no chance they were somehow involved in this.

His mother's death.

The thought of her brought pain, but he forced himself to remember. Her maiden name was Svajone Smilte Shaulis. She was thin as a pine, white-haired, pink-scalped and had blue eyes. She smiled a lot more than her parents, who were grimly German in outlook. They had all come from Klaipeda, a little town in Lithuania, when his mother was but a girl.

"What was it like, Mommy?" he remembered asking.

"Little, painted, wooded and flat, right on the gentle waves. The Baltic Sea was Poseidon's little princess, you see, and she slept on the sand, with her hair of reeds and grasses spread over the dunes," she replied with a smile and a twinkle in her eye. *What a beautiful way to describe a place*, Jake had thought. The only thing she had in common with his father was mutual love and Catholicism. Her parents spoke mostly Lithuanian, which Jake knew but few words, or Polish, of which he knew none. There was no chance his mother, or anyone else on her side, was the spark behind his current conflagration.

Jake's mind suddenly switched to another track altogether.

What if there was a lie, something incorrect, in the information he believed to be true? What if there was a false lead that, when removed, revealed all?

Perhaps he truly was the center of it all. Maybe, when all was revealed, his involvement made perfect sense; that there could be no search for the heirlooms without him.

Maybe the Cross belonged to him – and maybe the devil's song as well.

Jake rifled through the oilskins containing his important papers. He found his copy of the court's decision in his case. He looked over it carefully. To his surprise, there was nothing in the decision detailing who would get the Cross once it was found. Jake's responsibility started and ended with the search.

Tyran needed a better lawyer than himself. Isaäc had magnificently outmaneuvered him without his knowledge. Unbelievably, and legally-speaking, the Cross was still anyone's for the taking.

***

In London, Jake had to switch coach lines to get to Dover. Footmen took his luggage to the new coach, which was leaving in two hours. Jake decided to ask a nearby policeman where he could eat a gentleman's meal.

A middle-aged, well-dressed woman appeared in his path and moved toward him. Jake altered his direction, and she did as well. She wasn't looking at him and appeared unaware of the path of her meander. Jake altered his course again – and she did as well. Jake sighed. She was then proved well-aware of her course.

A pickpocket.

Jake put his hand over his wallet and watch, and changed course once again. The woman predictably did the same and they collided. Unpredictably, her purse upended and its contents scattered over the ground.

"Pardon me, Madame."

"It is no problem. I am so clumsy, Monsieur."

A thick French accent.

Jake checked his belongings. They were all there. He bent down to help the woman with her things. The policeman crossed to them.

"Good afternoon. What do we have here?"

The woman looked a bit nervous.

Jake spoke, "We have collided, sir. I have checked all of my belongings, and nothing has fallen to the ground. Unfortunately, Madame was not so lucky."

Madame, belongings back in her purse, stood. So did Jake. The policeman had not moved, wary of some kind of mischief.

The woman's eyes swiveled upwards and met Jake's. She held up a folded letter with his name on it. "I believe you dropped this, Monsieur."

Jake had never seen the note before. "So I did. Thank you."

"Are we sure you both have everything?" asked the policeman.

Jake and the woman spoke over each other, assuring him all was right.

The constable nodded and walked away. Jake's eyes followed the woman as she darted off.

He did not follow.

***

Jake rented a private cabin on the ferry to Calais. Only then could he afford to open and read the note.

> *Dear Jake,*
>
> *Why haven't you written me? I am in such a state. Please write me, for certain certainly! Why why why?*

It continued in that manner, inane and superficial, page after page, until the end. It was signed, "Brigitte". The name meant nothing, which meant it had to be a missive from *The Society*, which was what he suspected upon receiving it.

Jake got to work. He brought out the Ostervald Bible that *The Society* had given him. He wrote a guide that he would burn later.

$$A\ B\ C\ D\ E\ F\ G\ H\ I\ J\ K\ L\ M\ N\ O\ P\ Q\ R\ S\ T\ U\ V\ W\ X\ Y\ Z$$
$$1\ 2\ 3\ 4\ 5\ 6\ 7\ 8\ 9\ 0\ 10\ 11\ 12\ 13\ 12\ 11\ 10\ 9\ 8\ 7\ 6\ 5\ 4\ 3\ 2\ 1$$

The first word of every sentence always referenced the book. *W* equaled 4, *H* was 8, and *Y* had the value of two. Together they added up to 14. Jake, for the first sentence, was referencing the Second Book of Chronicles, the fourteenth book of the Ostervald. There was an apostrophe, which meant the code sentence only referenced one missive word. *Haven't* did not count for anything, except the apostrophe – all apostrophe words were void otherwise. Jake then went to the word *YOU*, which added up to 20 – and referenced the page of the book. He carefully counted twenty pages into Second Chronicles. Next was *WRITTEN*, which added up to 53. The fifty-third word on the page was "when." Nothing else in the first sentence then counted, and Jake moved on to the second.

Jake pressed on, carefully working out his code. Occasionally, the letter would have a sentence with a dash, indicating that Jake was referencing first letters of indicated words and not the words themselves. Slowly but surely, a message took form:

> *WHEN YOU ARRIVE IN H-A-I-T-I YOU WILL F-A-K-E YOUR OWN DEATH AND MEET US IN P-U-N-T-A-D-E-M-A-I-S-I-C-U-B-A GO TO V-I-L-L-A-D-E-B-U-E-N-O-S-S-U-E-N-O-S*

Jake pulled open the lantern on the table to expose the flame. He lit the message, the letter and the guide on fire, placing all on a brass plate to burn.

Then he sat back in his chair.

Interesting.

The Society wanted him to separate from Tyran. That meant, after the mysterious Grand Masters had put their heads together, they believed Jake had taken all he needed from Tyran, and was now ready to continue the quest alone. Who was Jake to gainsay them? They must have given this a great deal of thought.

So had Jake. And if Jake no longer needed Monsieur Tyran, he certainly did not need *The Society*. In fact, if both parties thought him dead, there would be no reason for him to continue the quest at all. If he did continue, it would also be up to Jake's family - if they decided to finance the venture, and had the funds to do so.

The Cross was most certainly in France. Jake had the paperwork to travel nearly anywhere. It was not illegal for Jake to return to France after his probable future jaunt to Haïti. If Tyran found him after he played dead, then Tyran was simply mistaken as to his circumstance, for Jake was alive and on the quest. If *The Society* found him, he would simply say Tyran had forced him to the action of subterfuge. One could be pitted against the other.

After all of the second-guessing and mostly clueless postulating, Jake did not know whether he wished to continue the quest. He did know, however, that he was faking his death in Haïti – to fool both parties. Running the risk of making powerful enemies, he was eluding them both, and returning home.

For now, his return was to Nantes, in order to receive his next orders from Monsieur Tyran. He would be shocked if his next destination wasn't Haïti. Once there he would elude both his pursuers with a good plan, hopefully inspiration would come later.

Jake

Then he was Boston bound – a place he never thought he would ever see again.

To Be Continued

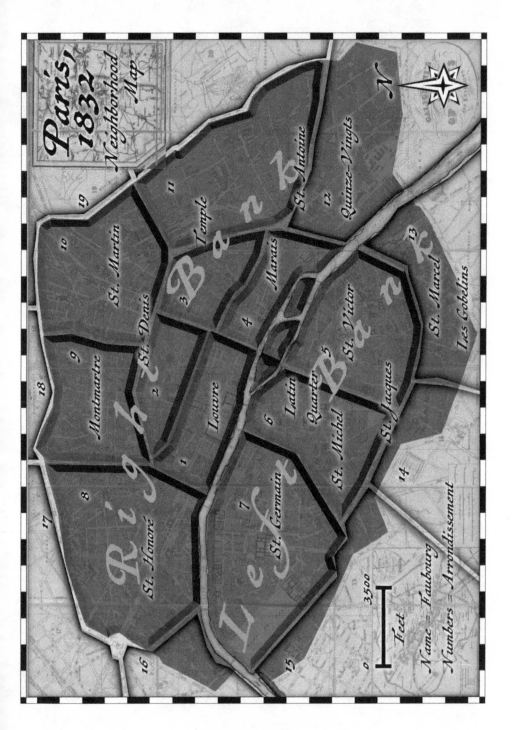

Appendix:

Pronunciation and Definition Guide

Only for the sake of easing the process of alphabetical search, *ce*, *le*, *la*, *d'* and *de* will be ignored, except for quoted passages. All words are French unless otherwise noted.

French "zh" is meant to be the "z" sound in "azure," but is actually even more pronounced and exotic. "R" is a mild trill, akin to Spanish but to a politer degree.

There are three very distinct Irish dialects. With apologies to the south, all Irish herein is in the Ulster dialect for obvious reasons. Unfortunately, Irish spelling does a drunk bee twirl through the ages, and not all words are in Modern Gaeilge.

"Historical Figure" denotes a character in the book who actually lived. This does not include historical figures only mentioned in passing.

***

"Bon sang ne saurait mentir" – (bohn sohn na-SUR-ray MON-tier) "Good blood cannot lie."

"Ego sum umbra, olim magnus. Lignum in umbra mortis - nisi illud occidit scutum lux" – (EH-go some OOHM-bra, OH-lim MAN-yus. LEEN-yum in UM-bra MOR-tis. NEESY ill-ood OCH-chid-it SCOOT-em LUKES-ah) Poor Latin.

"Être foutu tout les messieurs!" – (ET-tra FOO-two TWO lay MAZE-uhr) "F--k all gentlemen!"

"Guillaume Tell" – (GIE-yome Tehl) "William Tell."

"Le Menu du Duc Mort" – (LUH MEN-oo doo DOOK MORE) "The Menu of the Dead Duke."

"Le professeur a réussi au moment où son élève devient original" – "The teacher has succeeded the moment his pupil becomes original." This is a Lane Cooper quote. He was an American, a polyglot, a Cornell professor, and known around the world – far more than his own nation, being neither Kardashian nor Marvel.

"pour encourager les autres" – (POOR AHN-coor-ah-zher lesoht) "to encourage others," a quote from Voltaire.

"Pour les droits de l'homme, mon ami"- (POOR lay DWAH de-LOME, MOHN AH-mee)

"Robert le Diable" – (ROH-behr lay DIA-bleh) "Robert the Devil."

"Vive la France" – (VEEV leh FROHNZ) "Long live France."

"Vive le Roi" – (VEEV leh RWAH) "Long live the King!"

A Coruña – (ah CORE-OON-ya) Spanish.

abbé – (ah-BEY) "abbot," the second lowest rank of priest in France.

Abruti – (AH-broo-tee) "fool."

absagen – (AHB-sahgen) German, "cancel."

actions au porteur – (AK-zion OH POR-tair) Royal France was behind on the paper money train. *Actions au porteur* was as close as it came. They were more like bearer bonds or travelers' checks.

Adela – (AH-del-lah)

Adèle – (AH-del)

Adelgunde – (AH-DEL-gun-DEH) German, fantastical.

adieu – (AHD-dyu) "goodbye," literally "with God."

Agesilaus c. 444 – c. 360 BC (ah-JESSE-lay-os) Greek. He was a great king of Sparta, some would say the ideal king, and a brave and competent warrior. Ironically, he was lame from birth, and the Spartans were deeply prejudiced against the handicapped - even after his reign.

Agwé – (ahg-WAY)

aides – (AY-duh) "succor," "assistance," "help."

Albanach – (ah-la-bah-nah) Irish, "Scottish."

Allou, Gilles – (AHL-loo, Zheel)

Almo – (AHL-MO)

Angers – (OHN-zher)

Anjou – (OHN-zhoo)

ansagen – (on-ZAW-gen) German, "declare."

Aquinas, Thomas – (ah-KWAI-nas or ah-KEY-nahs) but he was actually Tommaso d'Aquino (toh-MAH-so dah-KEY-no), 1225 – 1274, an Italian Dominican friar, priest, and juror. He was an immensely influential philosopher, theologian, and jurist in the tradition of scholasticism. His impact, in the Catholic church at least, is still omnipresent. If one wished to pursue a moral path in any pursuit, Aquinas codified a route. It is odd to think modern man is philosophically primitive compared to man in 1274, but, I assure you, this is indeed the case. Our downward slide started in the Renaissance. Modern man is intellectually savage and primitive in many key respects - albeit relaxed, entertained and well-fed.

arachide – (ARA-sheed) "peanuts."

Aristobelus – (AH-ris-to-BEL-us) German, fantastical.

Aristobolus – (AH-ris-to-BOH -lus) German, fantastical.

Arouet, Daumard and François-Marie (AH-rooay, DOO-mar, fran-swah mah-ree) François-Marie Arouet was Voltaire's real name. Daumard was the maiden name of Voltaire's mother. These are very Republican aliases.

Arquebus – we say AR-kwib-is, most Europeans say AR-kay-boos. This is a catch-all term for a heavy, one-man firearm mounted on a forked stick, utilizing some kind of pre-flintlock firing mechanism. They were not regular in parts or caliber, and were created by a variety of craftsmen - or sometimes even the shooters themselves.

Arthaud, Éric – (AHR-too, AIR-eek)

Artus, Charles-Melchior, Marquis de Bonchamps – please see "Bonchamps."

aspirans – (as-PEE-ran) "midshipmen"

d'Aubeterre – (DOOB-tear)

d'Auray, Marquis – (MAR-key DOO-ray)

Aurélien – (AH-rel-yah)

Austerlitz – (OUSE-ter-litz) German, a small town currently in the Czech Republic, and site of one of the greatest battles of all time – Napoleon's crushing, brilliant victory over the Austrians, assorted Germans and Russians at the battle of the same name in 1805.

Autolycus- (AU-TUL-ih-cus) Greek. In Greek mythology, the son of Hermes and the grandfather of Odysseus.

Avenir, Marc Marie-Florent – (AF-neer, MAH-rkh MAH-ree FLU-rahw)

avocat – (AV-oh-cah) "lawyer."

baise la taxe – (BEES la tax) "F—k the tax."

Barnave, Antoine – (BAR-nev, ON-twon) Historical figure.

Barrière d'Enfer – (bah-REE-air DON-fair) "Hellsgate."

bâtard, ce – (SOO bah-tar) "this bastard."

Béarla – (BYUR-lah) Irish, "English."

Beau Brave – (BOO brahv) "Beautiful Brave One."

Beccaria – (BEY-cah-REE-ah) Italian.

Bedos, Thierry Alain – (BED-ohs, cherry AL-ahn)

Benyovszky, Comte de – (BEN-yov-skee, COMPT duh)

Bergères – (BEAR-zhair) – An enclosed, completely upholstered French arm-chair.

Berlière, Jacques – (BEAR-lee-air, ZHACK)

Bernier – (BEAR-nee-ay)

Bhiorog Ó Baoighill – (BEA-wok OH-BOY-ill) Irish.

Blin, Francois-Pierre – (BLAH, FRAN-swa PEE-air) Historical figure.

Bò – (BOH)

Boissière-sur-Èvre – (BWA-sair-sur-EHV)

bon soir – (bohn-swah) "good evening."

Bonchamps, Charles-Melchior Artus, Marquis de – (BOHN-shamp, SHARL-MEL-key-or AHR-tus, MAR-key duh) Historical figure. One of the greatest unsung heroes of France. George Washington meets Dietrich Bonhoeffer. He was truly a model for the ages, in every way.

bonjour – (BON-zhoor) "good day."

Bordeaux – (BOAR-doo)

bordel – (BOAR-del) "whorehouse."

Borgia – (BOAR-hee-ah) Spanish.

Botz-en-Mauges – (BOOTS-uhn-moozh)

bouche – (BOOSH) "mouth."

Bouchon – (BOO-shawn)

Boufflers, Stanislas de – (BOO-flay, STAN-is-slaws dey) Historical figure.

bougre – (BOOG-r) "buggerer."

bougre de vérolée – (BOO-grah duh VEY-roh-LAY) "sodomizer of the syphi-litic."

Boulevard du Crime – (BULL-vard du CREAM) "Boulevard of Crime," actually Boulevard du Temple, but called such because of all the theaters on the street and their salacious dramas.

Bourbon-Penthièvre, Louise Marie Adélaïde de – (BUHR-bon-PAR-tiev, LOO-ease-MARIA-de-laid-doo)

Bourdaloue – (BUHR-dah-loo) a woman's chamber pot.

bourgeois – (BOOR-zhwa)

Bouteiller, Guillaume – (BOO-tay-yay, GHEE-yohm)

Bouvillon – (BOO-vee-yohn) Jérémie D'Uts (ZHER-eh-mee DOOT), Sitis (SIT-tees), Jemima (ZHEM-mima), Ketsia (KET-zia) and Kéren (CAIR-ren)

Boyve, Abraham – (BOY-vee, AY-bra-HAM) Europeanized Hebrew

Brevet – (BREV-ae)

Brienne, Cardinal Étienne Charles de Loménie de – (BREE-en, CAR-dee-nahl ET-tee-en SHARL duh LOH-men-ee duh)

brocóg – (BRAH-COG) Irish, "smudgy-faced girl."

Bue-Bue – (BOO-BOO)

ça ira – (SAY-rah) "it'll be fine."

café – (KAHF-fay) "coffee."

Caïn le Laboureur – (KAH-ahn le LAH-boo-rare) Cain the Farmer, from the Bible. He didn't have much luck with his offerings either.

Caisteal Dhuni – (CAIS-til DOO-nie) Scottish, "Castle Dhuni", the battle cry of the Frasier clan.

Calais – (KEL-lay)

Cale, Jacques Bonhomme – (CAL, ZHACK BON-uhm)

Calonne – (CAL-uhn)

Camembert – (CAH-mohm-BARE) A cheese from Normandy.

Candes – (COND)

Cap Français – (CAP FRON-say)

Cap-Haïtien – (CAP HEY-ee-si-ohn)

Capitaine – (CAP-ee-tan)

Carême, Marie-Antoine – (CAH-rem, MAH-ree-ON-twon)

Carrara – (CAH-rar-RAH) Italian.

Cathédrale Saint-Pierre-et-Saint-Paul – (CAT-eh-drahl SAN-PEE-aire-ee-SAN-pohl)

Cavalla – (CA-vuh-lah) Portuguese. A river that meanders through Côte d'Ivoire, Guinea and Liberia. Also called the Youbou and the Diougou.

céalmhaine – (KAYL-woon) Irish, a classification of "oracle" "augury," or "omen." There are not enough words regarding magic and the supernatural in English to properly translate this. It is an omen, but one that does not deal with death or battle.

Centre-Ville – (SON-tra-VEEL) "downtown."

Chambarde, Pierre de la Ville de – (SHAM-bard, PEE-air-duh-leh-veel-duh) Historical figure.

Champ-Élevé (SHAWM-EL-vey) "High Fields."

Chapelle-Saint-Florent - (SHAW-pell-SAN-FLOR-on)

Charentais – (SHAW-ron-TAY)

Charlemagne – (SHARL-lo-MAN-yeh) The greatest king of all time, ever. The model for King Arthur.

Charles – (SHAR-leh)

Charleville - (SHAR-le-veel) A town with an important armory for the manufacture of muskets which were called by the same name. There was a bewildering variety of Charleville models and upgrades. The Charleville was the official arm of the French infantry from 1717 to 1840.

Chartres – (SHART)

Chasseurs-Volontaires de Saint-Domingue – (SHASH-air-VO-LOON-taire duh SAN-DOM-ang) "Volunteer Light Infantry." This unit existed historically and performed well.

Château de la Baronnière – (SHA-toh duh la BAR-roh-NEY-air) Historical place.

Château des Ducs de Bretagne – (SHA-toh de DOO du BRE-tain) "Castle of the Dukes of Brittany"

Château Meilleur – (SHA-toh ME-yair) "Best Manor"

châteaux – (SHA-toh) "castles" "manors"

chatte – (SHAT) "twat."

De Chauvirey, Maurice Roland – (doo SHOW-ver-eh, MOH-reese ROH-lon)

Chef de Bataillon – (CHEF duh BA-tai-yon) "Battalion Leader"

chefs de cuisine – (CHEF duh COO-zine) "cooking chiefs," "cooking heads."

chèvre – (CHEV) "goat"

chinoiserie – (SHIN-wahz-ree)

Chouette – (SCHWET)

Ciarraighe – (KIA-ray-HE) Irish, an ancient tribe who gave their name to County Kerry.

Cicero – (KEY-KAY-roh) Latin.

cinniúint – (KEN-you-went) Irish, "fate," "destiny," "chance." Another word with no true English equivalent, English being a language of muggles.

Cloître Saint-Merri – (CLOY-ahtr SAN-MARE-ree) If you have been to the obnoxious Centre Pompidou and its grounds, most likely you have walked on the footsteps of rebels and troops from 1832.

Code Noir – (KOOD NWAH) "Black Code." Kicked the Jews out of the colonies for fear of Dutch influence, made the Catholic conversion of slaves nearly mandatory, gave some rudimentary laws for the treatment of slaves... and enabled freed slaves to become almost normal citizens. Although French slavery was brutal and efficient, its end result was quite different from other nations.

Cœurfroid – (KER-fwah) Maurice Adam (MO-rees AH-dom) Jeannine (ZHA-neen) Caroline Lacroix (CAR-oh-leen la-kwah)

Colle – (CULL)

Colonne – (CO-LOAN)

comte – (COHMT) "count", the noble title.

comtesse – (KUHM-tess) "countess."

Conciergerie - (COHN-serg-zher-ree)

conversatio morum – (CON-ver-ZAH-tio MOR-um) Latin, "changing behavior." An oath to lead a good and godly life.

corail – (COR-rai-yeh) "coral."

corvée – (CO-er-vey) literally "drudgery"

Cour d'Assises Spéciale (COOR-da-ZEEZ-SPESS-al) "Special Assessment Court" would be a somewhat close translation.

Courbet, Marcel – (COOR-bey, MAR-sell)

Courgeon, Father Jonathan (COOR-zhon, ZHON-a-tohn) Historical figure.

Cousin, Jean Younger Elder – (COO-za, ZHON)

Cowan – English, actually, for a sneak or eavesdropper.

Coypel, Charles-Antoine – (KWUO-pel, CHARL-ON-twon)

Creeslough – (KREES-low) English.

Crémieux, Adolphe – (KREM-you, AH-dolf) Historical figure.

croissants au beurre – (KWAH-son-au-bear)

croix pattée – (KWA PAH-tee) Think the Iron Cross or what's on the side of the
    Red Baron's Fokker.

culotte, Sans-Culotte – (SAN-COOL-loht), "leggings," "no-leggings."

cum laude – (KOOM-loudy) Latin, "with honors."

Cyril – (SEE-reel)

Cyrille – (SEE-reel)

de Damas, Duc – (day DAH-mas, DOO)

damné – (DAM-nee) "damned."

Dauphin Royal – (DOO-fohn ROY-ahl) "royal dolphin." *Dauphin* was the nick-
    name for the heir apparent to the throne of France.

daus – (DOWS) German, "deuce."

David, Jacque-Louis - (DAH-veed, ZHACK-LOO-ee) Historical figure.

décolletage – (DEE-cohl-tazh) "a low neckline, or that area thereof."

Déguig – (DAY-geeg)

déjeuner - (DAY-zhun-ae) "lunch."

Denis – (DUN-nee)

Descartes – (DAY-cart)

Deschenes – (DUH-shen)

Desmoulin – (DAY-moo-lon)

Despres, Franck – (DES-preh, FROHNK)

Dessein, Onfroi – (DEE-sahn, ON-fwa)

détective – (DEE-take-tiv) surprisingly, "detective."

Deux Frères – (DOO FRARE)

Diarmuid and Gráinne – (DEER-mut and GRON-ya) Irish. These two created a
    love triangle with Fionn Mac Cumhaill, who was a terrific badass. This
    is never a good idea, and flight precipitated.

Diderot – (DEED-roh)

Dijonnais – (DEE-zhon-ae)

dîme – (DEEM) "dime."

dîner – (DEEN-ae) "dinner."

dis tout – (DEE-too) best translation is "crap!"

Donegal – (DONNY-gol) English.

doppelkopf – (DOP-el-KOPF) German, "double heads."

draíochta – (DREE-oc-tah) Irish, "magic."

drochthuar – (DROCK-oo-er) Irish, "bad omen, evil foreboding."

droits féodaux – (DWAH FEO-do) "feudal rights."

DuBois – (DO-bwa)

duc – (DOO) "duke".

Dumas – (DYU-mah) see *gens de couleur libre* for more information.

Dumort (DYU-more)

Durain – (DUHR-ah)

eau de Cologne – (OO doo COL-own-yeh) "Water of Cologne." Giovanni Maria Farina, an Italian, made the first mass-produced men's scent with a consistent smell in the German city of Cologne in 1709. It became such a sensation that the city's name became synonymous with men's perfume, probably to the irritation of Italians ever since.

eau de vie – (OO-doo-vee) "water of life." In France, a general term for strong fruit spirits of various types, which may be differentiated further, i.e. *eau-de-vie de vin* – "water of life of wine," which would be brandy.

Écureuil – (EE-coo-ray)

Éirinn go brách – (AYE-rin GOBROCK) Irish, "Ireland forever."

élégant – (EE-LEE-gah) "elegant."

Eliphas – (EL-lee-fah)

Emile – (EM-eel)

en enfer – (ONON-fair) "in hell," but a better translation would be "to hell."

en masse – (ON-MAHS) "in mass."

en vogue – (ON VUG-uh) "fashionable."

encule toi – (ON-cool TWA) "f—k you."

Enns – (ENCE)

entré – (ON-TRAY) "entry"

Eoin, Athair Mac Giolla – (Owen, Uh-hair MUCK Gihl-lah) Irish. Athair means "father."

Erdre – (AIR-dreh)

Ériu – (AIR-ru) Irish, ancient name for the island of Ireland.

esprit de corps – (ES-pree doo core) "spirit of the body," body used in the English sense of group or unit.

Estaing, Comte d' - (COMPT-DES-tohn)

Eugène – (OO-zhen)

D'Évreux, Pierre – (DEEV-roh, PEE-yair)

Fabre, Captain Henri-Marie Jacques, Comte l'Aigle – (ON-ree-MAR-ree ZHACK FARB, COMPT-laig-leh)

faim de plus – (FAM doo PLOOS) "hungry for more."

fais ce que voudras – (FACE-say-kay VOO-dra) "do whatever you want."

Falaise – (FAL-laze)

famille – (FAHM-ee-ya) "family."

fasces – (FASH-shehs) Latin.

fatiguer – (FAH-tee-gay) "tired"

faubourg – (FWAH-boor) "suburb." Keep in mind, a suburb for walkers is a lot different than a driver's. In the 18th Century, being less than a mile from the city center usually put you in a faubourg.

Fidèle – (FEE-del)

fils de salope – (FEES duh SAL-ohp) "son of a whore."

De Flaine, Marquis – (FLANE, MAR-key duh)

fleur-de-lis – (FLOOR-doo-lee) sometimes *fleur-de-lys*, "Lily Flower." The three petals of the stylized lily had a legion of symbolic meanings and representations. It represents the Trinity, the French monarchy, and the three classes, amongst other things. No one knows for sure, but most likely (i.e. in my opinion) the symbol was brought to France by the Umayyad Muslim invaders in 719 AD. The Umayyad used the emblem as a symbol of warrior prowess.

Fleury – (FLU-ree)

förbaskad – (fer-BAS-kad) Swedish, "damn."

foutre – (FOOT-reh) "f—k."

foutu – (FOO-chew) "f—king."

franc – (FRON) First used as the name of the one livre coin, it became the name of the entire French currency in 1795, and remained so until the adoption of the Euro which took place between 1999 and 2002.

Franche-Comté – (FRANSH-a-COMP-TAY)

frappante – (FRA-pont) "striking."

fricassée – (FREE-cah-say)

gabelle – (GAHB-el)

Gabin – (GAHB-on)

Gaeilge – (GAY-lick) Irish, "Irish." The Irish are Celts... but a celt is actually a tool, a kind of implement - archeologists named a people after something they dug up from ruins. The Celts call themselves *Gaels*. It is the origin of words such as Gaul, what the Romans called Celtic France.

Gap – (GAP)

garance – (GAH-ronce) "madder," the plant, not the emotion.

gens de couleur libre – (ZHON DAY COO-lore LEEB) "free people of color." One of my favorite authors was an aristocratic *gen de couleur libre*. His name was Alexandre Dumas, père ("father," his son of the same name was also a writer) and he lived from 1802-1870. He wrote *The Three Musketeers*, *The Man in the Iron Mask*, and *The Count of Monte Cristo*. He was also responsible for most of our modern Robin Hood stories, and our mythology regarding werewolves and vampires. Jake saw one of his plays!

Gerard – (ZHER-ahr)

Glonne – (GLUN)

Gobelins – (GOOB- lah)

gomme arabique – (GAHM AH-ra-beek) "gum arabic," acacia sap, used in makeup, paints, wine production, and food as a stabilizer and sweetener. It is also an edible glue. We use it on postage stamps.

grande cuisine – (GRAN COO-zine) "grand cooking."

Greffier, Antoine Thibault – (GREF-yay, ON-twon TEE-bolt)

Griffe – (GREEF)

Grimpeurs – (GRAN-pear)

guède – (GEHD) "wode." Remember the blue face paint in *Braveheart*? That was made from wode. I think *"Getcher wode on!"* needs to become an expression… immediately.

Guerrier – (GEH-ree-ay), Féroce (FAIR-rus), Seonaidh (SHIN-aid), Estelle (ES-tell), Guillaume (GHEE-yome).

Guigou, Solange – (GIE-goo, SO-lahnzh)

Guillere – (GILE-ray)

Gutek – (GOO-teck) Polish.

Haïti – (AE-ee-tee)

Halle – (ALL-eh) "halls."

Hamann, Johann Georg – (HAH-man, YO-hahn GAY-org) German.

Haute Grande Rue – (HUT GRAN ROO) "High Street," more or less. Now Rue Saint-Pierre.

haute société – (HUT SO-see-eh-tay) "high society."

Hervé – (AIR-vay)

De Heulee, de – (doo OO-lee)

Horatii – (ORE-ah-tee)

Horatius One-Eye – (HOR-ah-tee-us) The Romans, early in their career, were routed in battle nearly at the gates of Rome. A junior officer, Horatius Cocles (COCK-lees, One-Eye – having lost one in battle previously), waited until the Roman forces were across the Tiber, then he held the Sublicius (SOO-blee-choos) bridge himself - and ordered the Romans to destroy it… while he was still fighting on it. He fought the entire enemy army until the bridge was gone, then uttered a prayer to the Gods, jumped into the river, and managed to swim to safety. He single-handedly saved Rome. I'll hold your beer – your turn.

hors d'âge – (ORE dazh) "past age"

hôtel – (OH-tell) This word means "manor," or "great house," more than "fancy inn." Although a fancy inn can certainly be in a manor…

Hôtel de la Première Présidence – (OH-tell doo la PREM-ear PRES-ee-dahns) "Manor of the First President."

Huguenot – (OO-gen-oh)

Île de Gorée – (ILL doo GO-RAY) Historical Place.

Île de la Cité – (ILL doo la SEE-tay)

Íosa Críost – (EE-sa CHREEST) Irish. "Jesus Christ."

Isaäc – (EE-zak)

Jacmel – (ZHAC-mel)

jardinière – (ZHAR-deen-yair) "planter, vase."

je ne sais quoi – (ZHU-neh-say-kwah) "I don't know what."

Jean – (ZHON)

jean-foutre – (ZHON-FOOT-reh) "John f—ker". An American would say "motherf—ker."

Jeziorkowski, August "Gutek" – (YEZH-er-KOF-ski, AU-gust "GOO-tek") Polish.

joie de vivre – (ZHWAH doo VEEV) "joy of life." It is a philosophy of finding joy in the moment, especially through the elevation of small and routine tasks. Sitting down and enjoying your coffee, rather than getting a paper to-go cup. To an American, in regard to caffeine, this is more like torture. Bring good instant coffee to France. You are warned.

Joliefille – (ZHO-lay-fie) "Pretty Girl."

Journée des Tuiles – (ZHOR-nay day TWILE) "Day of Tiles."

Jozef – (YO-zef) Central European

keine – (KINE-ah) German, "Negative."

kontra – (CONE-tra) German, "counter," as in something that is contraindicative.

Lamarque – (LA-mark)

De Landerneau, Marquis de – (doo LON-der-no, MAR-kee)

Lefaucheux, Casimir – (LOO-foo-shoe, KAS-ee-meer)) Brilliant weapon smith, easily forty years ahead of his time. He invented the first metal cartridge. Most of his weapons were categorized by his last name and a number or date.

Lefleaur – (LEF-fluer)

Leroux, Pierre – (LOO-roe, PEE-yaire)

lettre de cachet – (LET-treh doo CASH-ae) "sealed letter." With a signature, the king could arrest anyone. Amongst the drawbacks of this arrangement was the fact that people with royal influence could get the king's signature on a *lettre de cachet*, and arrest anyone too.

levée – (LOO-vey) "raising."

livres – (LEEV-reh) French currency. Established by Charlemagne as a pound of silver, it was divided into 20 sous (or 20 sols), and each sous of 12 denier. It was the model for nearly every other European currency, including the British pound, Italian lira, Spanish dinero and the Portuguese dinheiro. In use from 781 to 1794, discontinued due to the revolutionary slogan of "if it's working, change it."

Loa – (LEW-ah)

Loire – (LOO-ar)

Louis-le-Grand – (LOO-ee-le-GRAHN)

Louis-Philippe – (LOO-ee FEE-leep)

Louvre – (LOOV-reh)

Loys – (LOO-ah)

Lundberg – (LUND-bear) German.

Lycée – (LEE-say) "high school."

Lycurgus – (LIE-kur-gus) Greek. Lived during the 9th Century BC. The founder of the Spartan way. Also called "Triple Badass Motherf---er."

Lyon – (LEE-ohn)

Mac Cumhaill, Fionn – (MA-cool, FYUN) Irish. The Hercules of Irish mythology.

Machiavelli – (MA-kia-VELL-ie) Italian. Pray for his soul.

MacInnes, Ivor – (MAC-innis, EYE-vor) Scottish. A character name from "Trinity," a nod to Leon Uris.

Madame – (MAH-dam)

Mademoiselle – (MAH-dem-wa-zell)

Maine – (MEHN)

maître d'hôtel – (MAY-treh DOH-tel) "Master of the Manor." Head servant, majordomo, butler.

Maman – (MAM-oh) "Mom."

Mamelouk – (MAM-loke) "Mamluk". Ancient Muslim warrior-slaves.

manoir – (MAN-wah) "manor."

marabou – (MAR-ah-boo) an African stork.

marais – (MAR-ae) literally "swamp."

Marat, Jean-Paul – (MAR-RAH, ZHON POHL)

Marie-Lynn – (MAH-ree LEEN)

Marillais – (MAH-ree-yay)

Marquer, Edmée– (MAR-kay, ED-me)

Marquis de Bonchamps – see "Bonchamps"

Marseillaise – (MAR-say-yehs) This genocidal Nazi rant is still the national anthem of France. Read the lyrics carefully, they are horrifying.

Marshalbes – (MAR-shalb)

marshall – (MAR-shall)

Martin – (MAR-tohn)

Massillon – (MASS-ee-yohn)

Meaux – (MOO)

merci – (MARE-see) "thank you."

merde – (MARED) "shit."

merdique nègre – (MARE-deek NEG) "shitty n----r." Americans would say (or hopefully not say) "f---ing n----r."

mes amies – (MES-ah-me) "my friends."

mesdames – (MAY-dam) "ladies."

messieurs – (MISS-yer) "gentlemen."

Méthode – (MAY-tod)

Meyerbeer – (MY-er-BEER) German.

Miette – (ME-et)

mignonette – (MIN-yahn-et)

Milot – (MEE-low)

míthuar – (ME-huar) Irish, "ill omen or foreboding."

Moliniere – (MO-leen-yair)

mon ami – (MON AH-me) "my friend."

mon dieu – (MON-dyuh) "my God."

monsieur – (MUH-schur) "gentleman, sir, lord, mister."

Montesquieu – (MON-tes-queue)

Montreuil – (MON-tray-ee)

Montserrat – (MON-ser-ah)

Morte d'Arthur, le – (lay MORT de-DAR-tour) "The Death of Arthur." Elaine (EE-lay-neh), Astolat (AZ-do-lah), Lancelot (LON-say-low), Guinevere (GUIN-vair), Arthur (AH-tur), Camelot (CAM-low).

Du Motier, Gilbert, Marquis de Lafayette – (doo MOH-tee-ae, ZHIL-bear, MAR-kee doo LAF-aye-yet) Historical figure.

Mounier, Jean Joseph – (ZHON ZHO-sef MOON-yee)

Mulâtre – (MOO-latr) "Mulatto."

De Musset – (doo MOO-say)

Nantes – (NONT)

Napoleon – (NAH-po-leon) There are only three titans of war: Alexander the Great, Hannibal, and this man – Napoleon. He was brilliant and devious in just about every way in which a person could be. His only mistake was severely underestimating the Russian will, and their absurd, nearly inhuman capacity for self-sacrifice. If not for that, the world was his oyster. In his defense, he was not the only one to ever make that mistake. Russia is God's cure for martial narcissism.

Nattier, Jean-Marc – (NAH-tyae, ZHON MARK)

ne plus ultra – (NEH ples UHL-TRA) "nothing above," the perfect example of its kind.

Nîmes – (NEEM)

Nooit Sterven – (NO-it STAIR-va) Dutch, "never die." We would say, "die hard."

Notre Dame de Paris – (NO-tr DAHM doo PAH-ree) "Our Lady of Paris."

Ó Baoighill, Bhiorog – see "Bhiorog Ó Baoighill."

Ó Brollachain – (OH BRAHL-lehk-ahn) Irish. Seonaidh (SHIN-aid), Iníongael (EE-nan-gail), Aodh Dubh (AE DO), Ingen (EHN-ghen), Eigneachan (AE-gah-nakh-an)

Ó Conchubhair – (OH CON-aghk -wer) Irish.

obers – (OO-bahs) German, in cards, the equivalent to a Queen.

octroi – (OOKED-twah) "granting, bestowal."

Olivier, Jérôme Charles – (ZHER-ome SHARL OH-liv-ee-ae)

orans – (OH-rans) Latin, "praying."

Orinoco – (OH-reen-OH-co) Spanish.

Orléanais – (OR-lay-on-ae)

Orléans – (OR-lay-on)

Oscuro – (OHS-cureh) Spanish, "dark." Alternatively, OHS-coo-ROH.

Ostervald – (OOS-ter-vad) German.

L'Oublié – (LOO-blee-ae) "the forgotten."

oui – (WEE) "yes." You should really know this.

l'Ouvrinière – (LOOV-rin-yaire)

Palais de la Cité – (PAH-lay doo la SEE-TAY)

Panthéon – (PAHNT-eon)

Panza, Sancho – (PAHN-zah, SAHN-cho) Spanish. Sancho Panza was the
    trusted side-kick of Don Quixote in the novel by Miguel Cervantes en-
    titled *El Ingenioso Hidalgo Don Quijote de la Mancha* written in 1605.
    El Don was a little Cloud Cuckoo Land, and poor Sancho had to follow
    him everywhere.

Paris – (PAH-ree)

Parisii – (PAH-ris-ee)

Passage du Saumon – (PASS-azh doo SEE-mon)

Pechegru – (PAY-shay-groo)

Le Peletier – (le PAY-LOW-tyae)

Pépin, Anne – (PAY-pohn, AHN) Historical figure. She had a bit of a reputation
    in her day, something between Mata Hari and the Queen of Sheba.

Périer – (PEHR-ee-ae)

Petit – (POO-tee)

Petite Princesse de Nantes – (PET-ee PRAN-sess doo NOHNT) "little princess
    of Nantes."

Petite Rue de Reuilly - (POO-ee ROO doo ROO-lee)

Pianoforte – (PEE-ah-no-FOR-tay) Italian, "piano."

Pierre, Jean-Baptiste Marie – (PEE-air, ZHON BAP-teest MAH-ree)

Pinceau – (PAN-so)

Pistole – (PEES-tohl)

Place d'Oratoire - (PLAHS DORA-twah)

Place de la Bastille (PLAHS doo la BAS-tee-yeh)

Place Plumereau – (PLAHS PLOOM-air-roh)

Place Royale – (PLAHS ROY-ahl)

Place Vendôme – (PLAHS VON-doom)

Pluche – (PLOOSH)

Poissard – (PWESS-arh)

Poitín – (PWAH-teen) Irish. Do not drink this shite. Ever.

Poitou – (PWA-too)

Pompadour, de – (POM-pa-durh, doo)

Le Poney Piquant – (lay PO-nay PEE-cahn) "The Prancing Pony." Hobbits, wizards and rangers are usually not seen in the Paris franchise.

Port au Vin – (PORO-vah)

Port Saint-Nicholas - (POUR-san-NEE-co-lah)

Port-Au-Prince – (PORU-PRANCE)

Pour le Mérite Militaires – (POOR lay MAY-reet MEE-lee-taire) The vaunted Blue Max, the highest Prussian, then German, military medal. The influence of French thinking and culture was such that it was named and inscribed in French, and not German.

Pourboire – (POOR-bwah) "for beer." We would call it a tip.

Presbytère – (PRES-bee-taire) "presbytery." Priest's quarters.

Président – (PRES-ee-dohn) "president."

Prévost, Augustine – (PRAY-voh, AW-gus-teen)

procureur – (PRO-kyu-aire) "prosecutor."

Prospel – (PRO-spell)

prostituée à bas prix (PROS-tit-oo-AE ah-bah PREE) "cheap whore."

Pułaski, Comte – (POO-ahs-kee, COMPT)

putain – (PYOO-tah) "whore."

Quarteron – (CARE-tour-on) "a small number."

Quartier-Morin – (CAT-ee-ae MOHR-uh)

quéquette – (KAY-ket) "pecker," as in the male member.

Quinze-Vingts – (KONZ-ah-VAH) "Fifteen Score."

Rabelais – (RAB-lay)

Rabourdin, Daniel – (RAB-or-dohn, DAN-yell) unless he's in America… then its Daniel Rabordin. But he needs to be in France, because France needs him.

Raphaël – (RAF-ah-el)

Rapide – (RAH-peed) "fast."

Le Ray, René, de Fumet - (REN-ae le RAY doo FOO-may)

Raymond – (RAY-mohn)

Régiment d'Agénois – (REYZH-ee-mon DAZH-en-wah)

Régiment Royal-La-Marine – (REZH-ee-mohn ROY-ahl la MA-reen)

Régiment Royal-Suédois – (REZH-ee-mohn ROY-ahl SWEE-dwah)

Reims – (RONCE)

République d'Haïti – (RAY-poob-leek DAY-TEE) "Republic of Haiti."

restaurant – (REES-tah-ranh) unbelievably, "restaurant."

réverbère – (RAY-ver-BAYR) "street lamp."

robe à la Français – (RO-BELLA-FROHN-say) "French dress." A formal, very beautiful, wide skirted dress of the 18th Century. Sometimes called a "sack-back dress" by the muggles.

Robespierre – (ROHB-ess-pee-yaire) one of humanity's many angels of death.

Le Roi Midas – (leh RWAH MEE-das) "The King Midas."

Roitelet, Étienne (ROIT-lay, ET-tyehn)

Roquer – (ROH-kay)

Rosalie – (ROOS-ah-lee)

Rossini – (ROH-see-nee) Italian.

Rousseau, Jean-Jacques – (RUE-so, ZHAHN ZHAHCK)

Roussel, Joseph and Casimir – (RUE-sell, JOE-zeff, KAZ-eh-meer)

Roux, Marie-Pierre Alphonse – (ROH, MA-ree PEE-yair AL-fohns)

rúad – (RA-uht) Irish, "red."

Rubens, Peter Paul – (ROO-bahns, PEE-tear POL)

Rue Cambon – (ROO CAM-bohn)

Rue de Castiglione – (ROO de CAS-tee-lyon-ae)

Rue de Charenton – (ROO de CHAR-ohn-tohn)

Rue de Goyon – (ROO de GWEE-yon)

Rue de Rivoli – (ROO de REE-voh-lee)

Rue du Fer - (ROO doo FAIR)

Rue Neuve – (ROO-nuhv)

Rue Saint-Honoré – (ROO SANT-OHN-or-REE)

Rue Saint-Jacques – (ROO-SAN-ZHACK)

Rue Saint-Nicolas – (ROO-SAN-NEE-coh-lah)

Sacatra – (SAH-CAH-tra) Hindi? Taken from an Indian word for those of mixed
    race in India.

Saint Florent le Jeune, le Vieil – (SAN FLOR-en lay ZHUN, lay VEE-ae)

Saint Martin – (SAN-MAR-tuh)

Saint-Antoine – (SANT-ON-twon)

Saint-Bernard – (SAN-BER-nar)

Saint-Clément – (SAN-CLAY-moh)

Saint-Denis – (SAN-DON-ee)

Saint-Domingue – (SAN-DO-mang)

Sainte Geneviève – (SAN-JUHN-viev)

Saint-Gatien – (SAN-GAS-tyah)

Saint-Germain-des-Prés – (SAN-GER-man-DE-PRAY)

Saint-Just – (SAN-YOOST)

Saint-Laurent-du-Mottay – (SAN-LOO-rahn-DOO-MOH-tay)

Saint-Malo – (SAN-MAL-oh)

Saint-Recipas – (SAN-RESS-ee-pah)

De Saint-Vincent, Gabriel de Bory – (doo SAHN-vahn-sant, GAB-riel doo
    BORY) Historical figure.

salon – (SAL-ohn) "living room."

salope – (SAL-up) "slut."

salpêtrière – (SAL-petrie-aire) "saltpeter."

Samana Cays – (SAH-MAH-NA) Lucayan, "Little Forest."

Sanaga – (SAN-AH-GAH) Bastardized German, a river meandering through Cameroon.

Sang du Christ – (SOHN doo CHREEST) Christ's blood.

Sangréal – (SOHN-grey-ahl) "real blood." Anything pertaining to the Holy Grail.

Sans-Culotte – (SAN-COOL-oht) "without leggings."

Santa Cruz de Tenerife – (SAN-TAH KROOZ day TEN-air-EE-fay) Spanish.

De Sarra, Jean-Augustin Frétat de – (doo SERA, ZHON-au-GOOSE-than FREY-tah) Historical figure.

Saumur – (SOO-muir)

savoir-faire – (SAV-wa fare) "expertise."

De Scépeaux, Marie Renée Marguerite Françoise – (DES-ee-poh, MAH-ree REN-ay MAR-gah-reet FRAN-swaz-eh) Historical figure.

schwars – (SHWARZ) "black suit."

Seigneurs, Les – (les SEN-yehr) "the lords."

Sené bergère – (SOO-yay BAIR-zhair) a type of comfortable upholstered chair.

Senegal – (SOO-nee-gahl)

sensuelle - (SAHN-shoo-el) "sensual."

Sèvre – (SEV-reh)

Shaulis, Svajone Smilte – (SHAO-lis, SVI-oh-nee SMILE-tah) Lithuanian… with a Polish accent…

Sherbro – (SHER-BRO) Sherbro. An island and river in Sierra Leone named after the Sherbro people.

soirée – (SWA-ray) "evening," "a party in the evening."

soldat – (SOL-dah) "soldier."

sorcière d'eau – (SO-see-air doe) "water witch."

sous – (SOO) see *livre* for definition.

Spiorad Naomh – (SPEE-rad NOY-am) Irish, "Holy Spirit."

Studium Generale – (STOO-dee-uhm GEN-ai-RAHL-ae) Latin, "general studies."

sud-est – (SOO-dest) "south-east."

Sylphide – (SILL-feed-uh)

Taig – (TAYG) Irish, masculine name meaning "Poet." It is alternatively spelled *Tadhg*. It was such a common name that it became a nickname or slur for Irishmen, i.e. Johnny as a term for American Confederates or Fritz as a term for Germans.

taille – (TIE) "cut."

Taillon – (TIE-yohn) "talion," the law of equal vengeance, an eye for an eye.

téméraire – (TEM-EHR-rair) "reckless."

Thermopylae – (TER-moh-PIE-lay) Greek.

Tír Chonaill – (TIER-hahn-ahl)

Tonnelier, Quennel – (TOHN-el-yay, KEN-el)

touché – (TOO-shay) "touch." This is what a fencing gentleman says when an opponent's sword touches him – an acknowledgement that a point has been scored against him in a match.

Toulouse – (TOO-loose)

De la Tour d'Auvergne, Comtesse – (doo la TOO-da-vern, KUHM-tess)

Tours – (TOOHR)

tout court – (TOO-COOR) Best translation is "And nothing more." This is the "QED" expression of philosophy.

traite – (TRAIT) "treaty."

Traversier – (TRA-ver-syae) "ferry." The family started out as ferrymen before their own recorded history, only the name remains as a hint to their origin. Xavier Érinyes (ZAV-ee-yay EAR-en-yee) Philippine (FILLY-peen), Priam Paul (PREE-am POLE), Jules César (ZHULE SAY-zare), Sevan Gédéon (SAY-von ZHEY-dion) Gwenaëlle (GWEN-aile), Athénaïs (AH-ten-ais). Genèse de Gaul (ZHEN-ess day GAOL)

Tribus Coloribus – (TREE-buhs COH-LOHR-ih-buhs) Latin, "tri-color," "three colors."

tuar – (TOOR) Irish, "omen." Again, a hard one for the muggles. *Tuar* is more like a seer's vague outline of the future, if the future vision is forbidding and dark.

Tuffeau – (TOO-foh)

Tuileries – (TWEEL-ree)

Turgot – (TOOR-goh)

Tyle (v), Tyler (n) – a guard for a Freemason lodge. More like a bailiff or castellan than a security guard.

tyran - (TYR-ah) "tyrant."

Uí Ceinnsealaigh – (EE KEN-sha-lie) an ancient area of Ireland near present day Leister.

unters – (OON-tahs) "under," or "between."

Valiere – (VAL-ee-yair)

Valiere – (VAL-ee-yair)

Vanier, Jean – (VAN-yay, ZHON)

Varades - (VAH-rahd)

Vaucanson – (VOO-cow-sohn) They say that these programmable looms were the first true progenitors of modern computers.

Vaux – (VOO)

Vendeans – (VON-day-ahns) Anglicized French. In French proper the word is *Vendéens* (VON-day-ohn).

Vendée Militaire – (VON-day MEEL-ee-taire)

Verne, Robert Alain – (VERN, ROH-behr ALAHN)

vérolée – (VEY-roh-LAY) "syphilitic."

Versailles – (VER-sigh)

Vico – (VEE-co) Italian.

Victor – (VEEK-tohr)

Videment, Julien – (VEED-mohn, ZHU-lee-ahn) Historical figure.

Vienne – (VEE-en)

village – (VEE-lazh) "town."

vingtième – (VON-tee-em) "twentieth."

voilà – (VWAH-la) "here." Frequently used in our context of "bingo," or "there we go." *Et voilà!*

Voltaire – (VOLE-taire)

Von Stedingk, Colonel Comte Curt – (COMPT KURT VOHN STED-ink) German-Swedish

Voudon, Vodon – (VOO-dohn) Not quite Voodoo. Voodoo is Voudon plus a mixed bag of other stuff, including Catholicism and Bò.

Xavier – see Traversier.

Yoruba – (YOUR-oo-bah) Yoruba, a tribe in Nigeria and Benin.

Zacharie – (ZAH-cah-ree)

Zara – (ZER-ah)

Zut – (ZOOT) "heck," "crap."

Alexandre Dumas, père

Hunter Dennis

has lived in several places in the United States and also in Europe. Since his first script sale to the studios in 1998, he has alternated between writing full time and working feverishly to sell something written. He has been sane for over a decade, has found himself in Southern California in spite of it, and is the least dangerous member of his family.

Illustration Credits

La Baronnière

Photograph by Hunter Dennis

La Conciergerie

Photograph by Ankor Light

Ship Silhouette

Design by Bioraven

Courtroom Silhouettes

Illustrated by E K Duncan

Conciergerie Guardroom Engraving

brought to life by Morphart

Freemason Watercolor

Painting by Vera Petruk

Flags, Coats of Arms and Compass Line Back-ground

> *courtesy of Wikipedia*

Alexandre Dumas, père

> *courtesy of Wikipedia*